PRAISE FOR MICHAEL KORYTA'S

LAST WORDS

"You can't put this baby down."   —Stephen King

"Outstanding.... Koryta punctuates the intense underground scenes of *Last Words* with claustrophobia so realistic that it's palpable. He wrings every moment of excitement possible."
           —Oline Cogdill, Associated Press

"The versatile Michael Koryta's new thriller is an exercise in sustained creepy atmospherics that takes place in large part underground. It's a kind of *Twin Peaks* with stalactites. It's also a good guilt-ridden-survivor yarn.... Koryta has done his speleological homework, and when he's got his characters inching through claustrophobic crawlways and wormways in the cold and dark, he knows what he's talking about.... Satisfying.... The last page of *Last Words* hints at the plot of Koryta's next novel, and I say bring it on."
           —Richard Lipez, *Washington Post*

"Michael Koryta's remarkable ability to imbue nature with supernatural hostilities is unnervingly visible in this well-plotted cold-case thriller featuring a cast of aptly bizarre, inscrutable characters.... Another tense thriller from the consistently entertaining Koryta."
           —Christine Tran, *Booklist*

"Koryta is an inventive storyteller who's also a skilled stylist....His descriptions of that unknown realm beneath the one we know—with places like the Chapel Room and Maiden Creek and Greenglass River—possess an unearthly beauty."　—Marilyn Stasio, *New York Times Book Review*

"Koryta evokes the pitch-dark, damp, bone-cold setting so well, it's easy to share the claustrophobia and eerie visions the character experiences....Koryta's latest thriller is ingenious and gripping."　　　　　　　　　　　—*Kirkus Reviews*

"If Koryta wasn't such a good writer, these scenes would not be as intense, but he knows how to provide the words that make the experiences more and more horrible. The author places his story in a unique landscape and creates a tale of drama, passion, and darkness. Each and every character he creates is a fascinating one and each reveals his or her own special relationship that is key to the solving of the mystery. Leading it all is Novak, a man interesting enough to be the subject of many books to follow."　　　—Jackie K. Cooper, *Huffington Post*

"With each book, the talents of *New York Times* bestselling author Koryta just get better. His latest is sure to please his readers and fans of John Connolly."
　　　　　　　　　—Jason L. Steagall, *Library Journal*

"Koryta is a master of plot and pacing."
　　　　　　　　　　—Bob Cunningham, *Toledo Blade*

"*Last Words* might not make you eager to go underground yourself, but it will make you avid to keep turning the pages....A promising series kickoff; just be sure to read it in daylight."　　　　—Colette Bancroft, *Tampa Bay Times*

"This moving series launch from bestseller Koryta (*Those Who Wish Me Dead*) illustrates why he's among today's top thriller writers. Koryta sensitively portrays regret and grief while plunging the reader into exciting, claustrophobic scenes deep inside the massive cave."

—*Publishers Weekly*

LAST
WORDS

ALSO BY MICHAEL KORYTA

LAST WORDS

MICHAEL KORYTA

LITTLE, BROWN AND COMPANY
NEW YORK BOSTON LONDON

Copyright © 2015 by Michael Koryta
Excerpt from *Rise the Dark* copyright © 2016 by Michael Koryta

Little, Brown and Company
Hachette Book Group
1290 Avenue of the Americas, New York, NY 10104
littlebrown.com

The publisher is not responsible for websites (or their content) that are not owned by the publisher.

Text on page 20 is from *Blind Descent* by James M. Tabor © 2011 (Random House, February 2011).

Printed in the United States of America

Originally published in hardcover by Little, Brown and Company, August 2015
First Back Bay trade paperback edition, July 2016
First Little, Brown and Company mass market edition, March 2017

10 9 8 7 6 5 4 3 2 1

For Jayd Grossman—
Many thanks to a great friend. Hard to say
which conversations helped which pages here,
but I absolutely know that they did.

History has many cunning passages,
contrived corridors.

—T. S. ELIOT

LAST
WORDS

The last words he said to her: "Don't embarrass me with this shit."

In later days, months, and years, he will tell everyone who asks, and some who do not, that the last words from his lips to her ears were "I love you." Sometimes, during sleepless nights, he can almost convince himself that it is true.

But as they walked out of their building and into the harsh Florida sun that September day, Mark Novak didn't even look his wife in the eye. They were moving fast even though neither of them was running late. It was the way you walked when you were eager to get away from someone.

"It's a leaked photograph," he said as they reached the sidewalk. "She knows two things that would both be available through a single leaked photograph."

"Maybe. If it is, wouldn't it be good to know how she got it?"

"She's not going to admit that. She's going to claim this psychic bullshit."

"You need to open your mind," Lauren said. "You need to consider accepting that it's a complex world."

"*You* need to be able to have the common sense to identify a fraud when you see one."

"Maybe she *is* a fraud. I won't know until I look into it."

"Nobody's stopping you from wasting your time."

She looked up at him then, the last time they ever looked at each other, but any chance of eye contact was prevented by her sunglasses.

"Mark." She sighed, still patient. "Your personal understanding of the world doesn't invalidate another's." Her last words to him. She'd stopped walking because they'd reached her car, an Infiniti coupe that was parked a block closer to the building than his Jeep. Here he had the chance for the customary kiss, or at least a hand on the shoulder, a quick squeeze, some eye contact. Here he had the chance to say *I love you.*

"Don't embarrass me with this shit," Mark said. He had a hand over his eyes, rubbing his face, and his voice was weary and resigned and the words were soft, and though now he likes to allow a few beers to convince him that she didn't hear them, she did.

By the time he was behind the wheel of the Jeep, she was already at the end of the street, waiting to turn left onto Fifth Avenue and head for the interstate. The hole in traffic held, and he made it through just behind her. For two blocks they were together, and then they pulled onto I-275. The added height of the Jeep allowed him to see down into her smaller car, catch a glimpse of tan skin and blond hair that made her look like she belonged to the beach, which was true enough, as she'd grown up on it. Her eyes were hidden behind her sunglasses, so he never knew if she glanced in the mirror to look back at him. He likes to believe that she did, and that his face was kind.

For a few hundred yards he was tucked in just behind her,

and then the interstate split. One ramp peeled right, north toward Tampa, and the other peeled left, south toward Sarasota. The Infiniti glided north. Mark turned south.

He wasn't angry. He was annoyed. They'd known that there would be conflicts when they began working together, but so far those had been minor, and they were both happy to be part of the dream team—Innocence Inc. was doing the best pro bono legal work in the country, challenging death row, freeing the wrongfully convicted. Seventeen successful exonerations in just three years. Mark and Lauren knew that it was going to be their life's work. Lauren would be playing at a higher level—what lay ahead for her was the actual courtroom, while Mark was part of the investigative team—but that separation was never a discord. If anything, the interview she was heading off to now stepped on his toes because it was lower-level work, and that would infuriate Jeff London, their boss. Lauren was driving to Cassadaga to talk to a self-proclaimed psychic about a vision the woman believed relevant to a death penalty–defense case. The woman had known two things she couldn't have learned from media reports: the color of a victim's socks on the night of her death and the fact that the victim hadn't shaved her legs in several days.

Mark had told Lauren not to make the trip, and though the last words he'd said—*Don't embarrass me with this shit*—were surely selfish, he didn't think his argument was. Jeff London, who ran the show, did *not* have tolerance for bullshit. Psychics were high on the bullshit meter for most people, Mark had explained, but to Jeff, they were going to be off the charts.

He didn't know that for sure, actually. They were off the charts for him but perhaps not for Jeff, and that was where the disingenuous, if not outright dishonest, portion of the argument existed. Making the debate personal seemed to weaken it, though, coming from his own experiences with cons and scam artists who preyed on the most desperate of people—the grieving—and Lauren would be quick to point out that bias, so he put it on London instead.

He was driving south on the Sunshine Skyway, and the bridge was living up to its name, the sun angling through the windshield and reflecting harshly off the Gulf of Mexico. He fumbled for sunglasses, couldn't reach them, and almost lost his lane. A horn blew, and he corrected fast and didn't blame the other driver for the middle finger that flashed. It had been close to a wreck, and it had been Mark's fault. A car accident was not going to help the celebration he planned for tonight, and that was already staggering.

At the tollbooth, he finally had a chance to grab the sunglasses, and he also plugged his phone into the charger and, for an instant, thought about calling Lauren. Thought about imploring one more time: *Let's just enjoy the weekend and you can think about it. We can talk about it. And if you still want to do it, then go on Monday.*

He didn't make the call, though. He knew they'd work it out later. They had the whole weekend, and they had rented a beach house on Siesta Key, a getaway they couldn't afford but had still decided to splurge on. A diving trip loomed, the activity that had brought them together. The first time he'd seen his future wife, in fact, she'd been underwater.

"The hell with it," Mark said, accelerating south. Let her learn her lesson on the wild-goose chase, and let him learn to keep his mouth shut. Working with your spouse wasn't easy, but it was easier when the work was a passion project. There were far more good days than bad, and most of the time they were able to leave it at the office. This weekend, he would make sure that they did.

* * *

He had the beach house ready for her by late afternoon. It was a gorgeous place, the crushed-shell drive shaded by thick palms, the back deck looking out on white sand and the sparkling waters of the Gulf beyond, private in a way few areas on the Florida coast were. He eyed the chaise longue on the deck and thought that it would be a fine place for some starlit sex. The deck would cool down by evening, particularly with that breeze off the water, the palms kept things private, and the sound of the waves would be just right.

Shouldn't have said it, he thought then. *Shouldn't have risked ruining a good night with a prick comment like that.*

He'd make it right, though. He'd keep his mouth shut while she talked about the crazy woman in Cassadaga, and he would apologize for his parting shot. In this place, it would be hard to hold on to anger for long, and Lauren was never one for that anyhow.

He read on the deck for a while, fell asleep, and woke at five with the sun in his eyes. Time to get to work on dinner. He'd stopped in Sarasota to buy food and a few bottles of wine, and Lauren had promised to be there no later than six. He made a Caprese salad—her favorite; this was sure to help take the edge off—and opened the wine, and at ten to six he preheated the grill. He even set a pack of her cigarettes and an ashtray on the deck, a clear gesture of apology because he was always bitching at her to give up the habit. Beside them he set a small plastic disk—her diving permit from the first trip they'd taken together, an outing to the Saba National Marine Park in the Caribbean, where she'd given him his first lessons. She'd talked her father into bringing him, insisting that Mark would make a great instructor one of these days. That had been the weekend of their first kiss, and he'd retrieved the permit from her bag at the end of the trip and saved it. Overly sentimental? Sure. But she'd brought that out in him when he'd thought nobody ever would. He carried no artifacts with him from the West, and most of his life had been spent there.

Beside the old tag, and weighed down against the wind by her ashtray, were two tickets for a return trip to Saba. He'd pushed the AmEx card toward its limit with that one, but you passed the bar only once (ideally) and Mark—who'd grown up in a family where six months of steady work was considered a rarity—was determined to recognize Lauren's achievement. Still, he was certain the old permit tag and not the pending trip would mean the most. He'd taken the tag because he couldn't believe he'd be able to hang on to her— there was no chance of such a blessing for him—and he'd wanted something tangible to remind him that he'd been granted at least that one weekend.

That had been five years ago.

At six she wasn't there, and he didn't want to put the steaks on the grill if she'd been held up, so he called to check on her ETA. The call went straight to voice mail, and he left a message: *Our place is beautiful and so are you. When will you be here?*

He called again at six thirty, and then at seven. Voice mail, voice mail. By the third message, he couldn't keep the irritation out of his tone.

At a quarter to eight, he put a steak on the grill, cooked it, and ate it alone on the deck, tasting nothing but anger. It was one thing for her to ignore his advice; it was another entirely to allow it to ruin a night that was supposed to be special.

It was eight thirty and the sun was easing down behind the water when the anger began to ebb toward concern.

Lauren wasn't a grudge holder. She always wanted to talk emotions out, a habit that ran so contrary to Mark's style that it felt like listening to a foreign language. Even if the lunatic in Cassadaga had delayed her, she would have called by now to issue a mea culpa and tell Mark when she'd make it to the beach.

Something was wrong.

He thought of the near miss on the Sunshine Skyway then, the way he'd almost lost control of the car as he reached for his sunglasses, and for the first time he felt true fear.

He called every five minutes until ten o'clock. Voice mail, voice mail, voice mail. Sometimes he left a message, sometimes he didn't. The call trail would later be used to clear him as a perpetrator of the horrors that had already happened in Volusia County, but he didn't know it then. All he knew was that he'd gone from annoyed to worried to terrified.

He found the name of the psychic in Cassadaga, but she had no phone and so, short of his driving out there, her name wasn't going to do him much good. He sent a text message to Jeff London, trying to remain low-key: *Hey, Jeff, any chance you've heard a report from Lauren this evening?*

Jeff answered immediately: *No. Thought you guys were supposed to be doing the romantic weekend. She find a better offer?*

Could be. I live in fear of it.

As well you should, Markus, Jeff responded.

Mark sat on the same chaise longue that he'd imagined he would be sharing with Lauren by now. Everything was as he'd pictured—the stars were out, the breeze was fresh and warm, the palm fronds rustled, and the waves splashed gently onto the sand. Everything was in place but his wife.

"Please call," he whispered in a voice that belonged more to a prayer than anything else. He was draining the battery on his phone, checking the display over and over as if it might refute the silence and show a missed call. "Please, Lauren."

She didn't call. He did, yet again, and he said "I love you" to her voice mail, and so this much is true about the last words: he said them. He just didn't realize he was saying them to a cell phone that lay in the bottom of a water-filled ditch and that the first bullet had entered his wife's brain more than three hours earlier.

His mouth was dry and his legs felt unsteady when he stood and walked down to the beach. He took deep breaths, tasting the salty breeze, telling himself that it would be fine. There would be a story to it, sure—a flat tire in the back-woods, something like that—but it would be fine. They were young and they were healthy and so of course things would be fine, because this was promised to them, wasn't it? They had more time. They had more days.

A beam of light passed over the dark sand then and tires crunched on the crushed-shell drive and he was so relieved he could have fallen to his knees. *Thank you, thank you, thank you.*

He hurried up the deck steps and through the house, thinking that none of it mattered, not the argument or the missed dinner or any of it, nothing mattered except that he was going to pull her into his arms. Then he opened the front door and saw that the car waiting there wasn't his wife's.

It was the Sarasota County sheriff's.

Part One

GARRISON

I

January 24, 2014

It was snowing in Indiana.

Mark had boarded the plane in sunshine and seventy degrees, and two hours later it touched down in swirling winds that whipped snow around the tarmac. It was just beginning to accumulate, a dusting in the distant fields. The ground crew wore face masks and gloves. Passengers were pulling heavy jackets down from the overhead bins. When the flight attendant handed Mark his thin cashmere blazer, he realized that it might have been prudent to check the forecast. The truth was he didn't even own anything like what the others were putting on. He hadn't been north of Atlanta in five years now and hadn't intended to be again. He'd seen enough blizzards in his youth. When he'd left Montana at seventeen, he'd hoped never to see snow again. Never to see a lot of things again.

The car waiting for him was a Ford Escape, and he was grateful to see it had all-wheel drive.

"How bad is it supposed to get?" he asked the rental attendant at the exit booth as he pulled out his driver's license. The attendant was also wearing a wool mask and gloves. Everyone here was dressed like they were prepared to rob a bank.

"This? Just flurries, my man. Not bad at all. You'll be fine."

"All right." Mark put up the window fast because the snow was landing on his lap and he was freezing already. Brought back memories: an April blizzard howling out of the mountains and across the plains, Mark searching for his mother in the snow, finding her half frozen and fully drunk. He'd left her three weeks later, taking only a backpack and a small wad of cash secured with a rubber band.

He pulled away from the airport and got on the highway, bound for Garrison, Indiana, on a fool's errand while back in Florida, the board of directors for Innocence Incorporated gathered to discuss whether they had to terminate him or if a suspension and pay cut would suffice.

"Get the lay of the land and a sense of the players," London had told him, shoving a small case file across the desk, "but mostly, just get the hell out of my sight. I'll be in touch once the board has met."

The truth of it was that his boss didn't want to risk Mark's speaking personally to the board. The questions they would ask—*How can you reconcile your actions with the mission of this organization?*—were not questions London could afford to have Mark answer.

Thus Indiana. You wanted to keep the live grenades out of the room when you could.

He had to leave the interstate almost immediately, and then it was onto state highways blasted by strong gusts of wind as he drove first across flat farm country and then into unbroken, old-growth forest, heading southeast. He was surprised by how wooded and steep southern Indiana was. The flat fields around Indianapolis had fit with his vision of the state, but these forested hills did not. He'd been on the road for two hours before he reached Garrison and rolled into the downtown square—which was literally a square, with a courthouse at the center and storefronts on the sides facing it, like a Hollywood set for a middle-American small town. Cue up the John Mellencamp. The square had buildings on only three sides, though. The fourth was an empty expanse, leaving the downtown feeling unfinished, as if somewhere along the line, the people who'd settled here had decided they'd made a mistake. Street signs promised him that the sheriff's department was just a block beyond the courthouse. Step one. The case started wherever the file ended.

This was what he knew from the case abstract that Innocence Incorporated had provided: In September of 2004, a seventeen-year-old girl named Sarah Martin had entered a recently opened tourist cave called Trapdoor Caverns with her boyfriend with the intention of teenage romance. Noises spooked them, the boyfriend went to check things out, and the girl hid, but she did too good a job of it. When the boyfriend returned, she was missing, and he ran out of the cave and reported that she was lost. Security cameras validated his story and his timeline. There was no indication of criminal activity. Searchers had no luck finding her. Then a man named Ridley Barnes, whose reputation underground was without peer but whose reputation above the shoulders was not as impressive, pulled away from the search party. For days, he was considered as lost as Sarah. Then he returned, hypothermic and raving, carrying the girl in his arms. She was dead, handcuffed and beaten. Barnes initially claimed that he'd spoken with her, but when the coroner's time-of-death assessment called that into question, he said that he must have been mistaken. When asked to take police to the place where he'd found her, he said he couldn't remember where it was or even come close to locating it again. He then explained that he had no memory of finding the body. After that, he decided to stop talking to the police entirely. Ridley Barnes had not given an interview in the past decade.

This was what Mark knew of it. What he cared about it: nothing. There was no point in investing emotionally in this one because he'd be called off it within days. He knew it, and Jeff London knew it. Still, he had to go through the motions.

He hugged the blazer around himself and blew on his palms as he walked down the street to the sheriff's office. It was adjacent to the Garrison County jail, which was the largest building in town. That suggested promising things about the community. Inside, three empty chairs stood beside a soda machine and a bulletin board filled with pictures of local people with active warrants. They were all white faces. Across from this was a pane of tinted bulletproof glass, and a uniformed woman stood behind it.

"Can I help you?"

"I'm hoping to speak to whoever handles your homicide cases."

"You're reporting a homicide?"

"No. I'm inquiring about one."

"Which one?"

"Sarah Jean Martin. From 2004."

Her face froze. When she spoke again, it seemed to take effort. "Is this a media inquiry?"

"No." Mark took out his wallet, found a business card, and slid it to her through a slot in the glass along with his investigator's license, which was still active, though in jeopardy. She studied both and said, "Florida, eh?"

"That's right."

"Explains the coat," she said, and then she hit a button and the door unlocked with an electronic buzz. Mark pulled the handle and stepped through and she met him on the other side. "Follow me. You can speak with the sheriff."

"His name?"

"Dan Blankenship. Don't know much about what you're getting into here, do you?"

Her age and her lack of interest upon his arrival had suggested that she was waiting to get her pension and walk out the door, but now there was a little spark, and it had come from Sarah Martin's name.

"I'm here to learn," Mark said. When they reached the sheriff's office, the door was open, and she entered without knocking, the way you did only after you'd worked with someone for a long time.

"Dan? This gentleman wants to talk with you. Markus Novak. He's from Florida."

"It explains my coat," Mark offered, to save her the trouble.

The sheriff was a tall man of about sixty who looked like he should be advertising pickup trucks. His hand completely enveloped Mark's when they shook. When they were alone, the sheriff sat down and leaned back in his chair as ice blew against the window behind him, a sound like tiny claws working to get through the glass.

"Florida. Bet you wish you'd picked another day to visit us, eh? Another month, even."

"It's a little brisk out there."

The sheriff smiled. His eyes didn't. Mark thought that he probably politicked just fine, as evidenced by his elected position, but probably was pretty good police too. He looked at Mark's business card and said, "The death-row outfit. I've heard of you. Only case we've had in thirty years that landed anyone on death row has already ended in an execution. I'm afraid you're a bit late."

"Actually, our case doesn't have a conviction yet, or even charges. The victim's name was Sarah Jean Martin."

Without even moving, the sheriff seemed to contract, as

if something inside him had opened up and pulled in his exterior strength to fill the void.

"Sarah," he said.

"Yes. She went missing in a cave ten years ago and it was assumed she'd gotten lost until a man named Ridley Barnes brought her to the surface in handcuffs, is my understanding."

Blankenship blinked at him as if to refocus. He had the look of someone who was pretending to be interested in a conversation at a party while really eavesdropping on a discussion carrying on behind him.

"That's your understanding," he said.

"Is it incorrect?"

"Who brought you into this?"

"We received a proposal from Ridley Barnes. I'm just vetting it."

Blankenship's professional demeanor vanished and his eyes went from unsmiling to unfriendly.

"Ridley himself." His voice was tight. "That makes sense. Been too long since people hurt over Sarah, at least visibly, at least so he could enjoy it."

"You think he killed her."

"He killed her, yes."

Mark withdrew the original letter from his folder and passed it across the desk. "Tell me what you think of this."

"I just did." Blankenship made no move to take the letter.

"Read it," Mark said. "Please."

Blankenship accepted it with distaste and then began to read it aloud, in a voice filled with contempt.

I am writing first of all to say how much I appreciate the goals of your organization. I think that it fills a hole, as there are not, as you say, sufficient funds or resources to properly pursue cases in rural locations. There are people all around this town who would tell you that I have benefited from just such a situation. I don't think they are correct, though. We're all the same in this town when you get right down to it, me and the ones who hate me and all the other people who have simply cared about that girl and what happened to her. We are all the same because we live with the not-knowing.

The sheriff looked up. "Now, ain't that touching? Ridley, he's feeling all of our pain. Carrying it, apparently. This story come from his pen or from the Gospels themselves?"

Mark didn't answer, and the sheriff cleared his throat theatrically and returned to reading.

We live with that every day and we think about it every day or at least some of us do. And while some people think that if things were known then I would be in prison or maybe in the electric chair, I would just like to know what happened, the same as them. That's all that I want to know. My question is the same as theirs—did I do it?

I expect that you will take the opinion of most people who read anything about this case, which is that I'm a liar or a crazy person because I would know if I did it. I had given up on ever explaining that but then I came across some things in a book and I thought maybe this would explain my situation better than my own words ever could. So I hope you read it and consider it and then maybe consider talking to me. Here is what was in the book, which is called Blind Descent, *by a man named James Tabor.*

Supercaves create innate dangers as well, warping the mind with claustrophobia, anxiety, insomnia, hallucinations, personality disorders. There is also a particularly insidious derangement unique to caves called The Rapture, which is like a panic attack on meth. It can strike anywhere in a cave, at any time, but usually assaults a caver deep underground.

And, of course, there is one more that, like getting lost, tends to be overlooked because it's omnipresent: absolute, eternal darkness. Darkness so dark, without a single photon of light, that it is the luminal equivalent of absolute zero.

I can't tell you anything I experienced better than those words do it. That bit about The Rapture. You'd have to have a jury of twelve people who'd lived through it to believe me. There might not be twelve people alive who have been through such a thing as what I endured down there. But here's the deal— it's never going to get to a jury until we know what happened. And whether it helps me or hurts me, I can't take that anymore. The not-knowing. I just can't take it, and I'd rather go to prison and know that I belonged there than live another day in my own skin wondering what happened. So that's what I'm asking you for. I don't have money. You say you don't need money. That you only need cases that deserve attention. Well, this one always did. Still does.

I'm hoping you can tell me if I did it.

Best regards,
Ridley Barnes

The sheriff said the name with a disgusted drawl, then spun the letter back across the desk to Mark the way you'd flick a greasy fast-food wrapper into a trash can.

"You guys must have more money than brains if that letter from that loon was enough to bring you up here."

Mark couldn't very well tell him that nobody would have considered sending someone up here if Jeff London hadn't wanted to get Mark out of sight, so he just said, "Why so convinced that he killed her?"

Blankenship began to tick off the points on his fingers but never made it beyond the first one; as his anger grew, his counting stopped. "Because he's the only one who knew that cave well enough to hide her in it. Then he decided to bring her back because it covered his ass. We had other experts searching in there, and they worked in a team. Ridley Barnes decided to go it alone and vanished in the cave. For a few days there, we figured he was as lost as she was. Then..." Blankenship's jaw tightened. "Then he returned, with her body. She was wearing handcuffs and had been for a while."

"Cause of death?"

"Hypothermia. Classified as a homicide investigation because Sarah died after being abducted. She didn't die of the cold in that cave because she'd gotten lost. She had some help."

"Had she been sexually assaulted?"

Blankenship swallowed and looked away. Mark thought the display of discomfort was odd in a man who'd spent a lifetime in policing.

"Not yet."

"Yet?"

"My point is, somebody had kept her alive for a time. Maybe wanted to keep her alive much longer. You know the kind, like that guy in Cleveland, the one who had the girls in his basement for, what, ten years? Hell, maybe Ridley couldn't get it up and took out his anger on her. That happens. Guys blame their own victims."

"Why would he produce the body if he'd succeeded in hiding her so well?"

Blankenship looked down at his right hand as he curled it into a fist and then loosened it, as if it were a required exercise, some sort of stress release that allowed him to exhibit the demeanor he wanted instead of the one that threatened.

"Because Ridley's a game player. Because he's a sick son of a bitch who got a kick out of the idea that by rescuing his own victim, he'd give the prosecutor a hell of a hard time using the physical evidence against him. And that is precisely why we never got a conviction. Never even got it to court. The DNA results, her blood on him, all of that? Well, he did carry her body through a cave, didn't he? Reasonable doubt."

"It is reasonable," Mark said. "But you don't buy it."

"No, I certainly don't."

"Why not?"

"Because he claimed not to remember where he'd found her, or how. Because later he refused to speak to us. And because when he first emerged from the cave, he told us that he'd heard her voice and followed the sound to locate her."

"Seems plausible."

"It sure does. Right up until the coroner gave us a time of death that completely contradicted Ridley's story. She would have been dead before he found her, but somehow he still heard her last words?"

Mark thought, *Don't embarrass me with this shit.* He said, "What were the words? What did he hear her say?"

"'Please, stop.'"

Mark was confused. "That's what Barnes heard the victim say, or that's what I should do?"

"Both," Blankenship told him.

"Any motive?"

"He's a deeply disturbed man. He'd told other people things about the cave that summer, including the following highlights: The cave had a soul; the cave did not like intruders; the cave required that anyone who entered it demonstrate respect. Unwelcome visitors, he said, would be treated harshly. Here's another gem: If you spent enough time in the cave, if you listened to it carefully enough, you'd learn what it required of you. If you performed those tasks, you'd be granted powers that would travel with you back to the surface. You liking the way his mind works so far?"

"Not especially. But when I ask about motive, I mean a direct connection to the victim."

"I'm well aware of what a motive is, Mr. Novak. Ridley had no direct connection to Sarah Martin beyond the fact that she worked at the cave as a tour guide all summer when he was working there exploring new tunnels and holes and pits. She was a beautiful young girl and he was a disturbed and lonely man."

"So no motive."

Blankenship looked at Mark as if he were wondering whether he could justify arresting him on charges of aggravated annoyance.

"I'll tell you what you ought to do right now, Mr. Novak," the sheriff said, getting out of his chair and unfolding to his full, impressive height. Mark was six foot, and Blankenship towered over him. "Don't waste my time questioning me about motive before you've even met the man. Go visit Ridley Barnes. Talk to the wrongfully accused old boy in person. Then you give me a call. You tell me after meeting him if you really think this one is worth your time and dollars. You tell me what you think about motive."

"Fair enough," Mark said, knowing that Jeff London would be furious with him for letting the interview end so abruptly but not caring because Jeff didn't want this one anyhow. As the sheriff had aptly observed, the case didn't even meet the standards for Innocence Incorporated. Jeff had exiled Mark up here, and all Mark had to do was play out the string and wait to be summoned home.

"Let me show you out," the sheriff said. They left the office and walked back down the hall and to the main door.

"Where are you staying?" the sheriff asked.

"Haven't decided yet."

"Really? All the way up from Florida without a hotel reservation?"

"Didn't realize it was peak season in Garrison."

The sheriff gave a wan smile as he opened the door. "I suspect you'll find a room still available. And you let me know what you think of Ridley. Be mighty curious to see how he tugs on your heartstrings."

"I'll let you know. Say, whatever happened to the kid she went in there with? The boyfriend. He still around?"

That provoked a thoughtful nod. "Evan Borders. He's a treat. There were plenty of police who had a hard-on for him ahead of Barnes in that case. Not because of the evidence. More because of the...character, I suppose you'd say."

"He's trouble."

"His daddy was trouble, and Evan and the Leonards, his cousins, they carry on the legacy. The three of them run round here like a pack of feral dogs looking for things to snap at. But they pale in comparison with Ridley. He may be a true sociopath."

"Right."

Blankenship scrutinized Mark and said, "Mind if I ask you a question?"

"Feel free."

"You're in the pro bono investigation business, am I right?"

"Yes."

"I would think a man finds himself in that line of work because he cares. No offense, Mr. Novak, but I don't get the feeling that you give a damn about this."

"Until I know whether we're taking a case, I try to keep my emotional distance," Mark said. "It's tough to get invested in one when you might be pulled off it. Make sense?"

"I suppose," the sheriff said, but he didn't seem satisfied with the answer. "Something you need to consider, whether you want to preserve your, um, emotional distance or not: Sarah matters to people here. The people you'll be talking to? They don't have that distance, son."

"I'll keep that in mind when I see them," Mark said.

"You be careful what doors you knock on around here, Novak."

"That a threat?"

"Not in the least. You're just...not acquainted with the place yet."

"That doesn't sound like a real warm endorsement of your hometown, Sheriff."

Blankenship looked off to the darkening sky above the old limestone courthouse.

"Real storm's coming tomorrow, you know. If you *were* to want to go back to the Sunshine State, tonight would be the time to fly out."

"Going to get that bad, eh?"

"I don't put much stock in forecasts, personally. There's some calling for ten inches of snow here, others are saying it'll be warm enough to keep it mostly rain. Like I said, I've learned not to trust them. Just to be ready. You learn the same in Florida, with the hurricanes and whatnot? Or do you trust the forecasts down there?"

"We still talking about the weather?"

The sheriff gave a humorless smile. "You're a symbolic man, are you?"

"Actually, no."

"Good, because I like straight talk. And I've given it. The weather is the weather. The warnings are the warnings. If I were you, I'd pay attention to both."

2

He'd have to speak with Sarah Martin's family at some point, and part of him wanted to have that done before he met with Ridley Barnes. It wasn't a large enough part to win the day, though. He knew the family already in ways that they wouldn't understand, and he wanted to protect them until the last possible moment.

Instead, he drove out of town, following the GPS directions to the address Ridley Barnes had provided. He called Jeff London while he drove and got his voice mail.

"Jeff, it's Mark. Local law wasn't real happy to see me, and they're curious why in the hell we're up here when nobody was charged, let alone convicted. I've got no answer for that. I don't like being put in a position where I've got no answers. I know you'll say I earned my ticket here, but these people don't understand that, and it's not fair to them. I don't want to sit down with that girl's family and lead them on. Consider that and give me a call, please."

Ridley Barnes lived about nine winding miles outside Garrison in a single-story house with faded stone walls and a slouching roof. Undulating fields spread out in every direction, broken stalks of wheat protruding from the snow. Smoke rose from the chimney of the house and blended into the gray sky. By the time Mark was out of the car, the front door was open and a man in jeans and a hooded Carhartt work coat peered out at him.

"You lost?"

"You Ridley Barnes?"

"Yes."

"Then I'm not lost." Mark went up to the porch. Ridley Barnes watched him suspiciously. He had long, unkempt gray hair and a matching beard. His blue eyes seemed bright against it.

"You know my name, then I ought to hear yours."

"Markus Novak."

No reaction.

"I'm with Innocence Incorporated."

The bright eyes widened and Barnes said, "No shit! Didn't figure to hear from you, but I *did* figure I'd hear by phone, if anything, not have you just show up like this."

"It's not our standard procedure," Mark acknowledged. He was looking at the heavy canvas jacket. You didn't encounter them in Florida, but there had been other places in his life where they'd been common. His mother had given him one for Christmas, paid for with money she'd conned off tourists by telling them she was a Native American spirit guide even though she wasn't even Native American, and told him, *It's rugged and durable, kiddo. Just like you.* The first real fight he ever got into was with an older kid who'd tried to steal that coat. You weren't supposed to win your first fight, but if you did, as Mark happened to, it was awfully easy to get a taste for it.

"I wasn't even sure you'd talk to me," Barnes said. "Seeing as how I'm not on death row."

"The good news, Mr. Barnes, is that I *am.*" Ridley gave him a confused look, and Mark said, "I'm a little out of favor with my boss at the moment. I think he liked the idea of sending me into the snow. You know how it goes."

"Sure, sure," Barnes said, and he offered an uncertain smile. "Come in out of the cold."

Mark followed him inside. A fire was going in an old cast-iron woodstove in one corner of the living room, and ropes were draped all around it. Ridley stepped through them nimbly without appearing to even watch his feet.

"Caught me tying," Ridley said.

"Tying what?"

"I'm going vertical this weekend. Getting everything ready now. Shitty day, why not, right?" He lifted a neat loop of black rope off an old recliner and set it on the floor, then indicated that Mark should take the chair.

"Going vertical?"

"In a cave, man."

"I don't follow."

"People who haven't been underground, they always think a cave is like a bunch of tunnels. You just walk or crawl or whatever. But they develop in layers, right? Layers of time and stone. That means you're not just moving horizontally, you're moving vertically."

"Got you." Mark sat down and looked at all the rope and tried to estimate how many feet were laid out. At least two hundred. Maybe more. Ropes of different sizes, from thick static lines to paracord, hung nearby. Along the far wall was a row of shelves covered with what looked like more climbing gear: Harnesses and carabiners and bolts. Several battered helmets with lamps mounted on them. On a low shelf, there were also face masks and oxygen tanks.

"You're a diver," Mark said.

"Not a diver. Still a caver."

"You use that gear inside of caves?"

"Sure. Water carves the caves. It's still carving them. Got to be willing to go through the water to find out what's there."

"I suppose so," Mark said. "But I'm not here to talk about caving. I've got to make a decision about this case. Whether it's the right fit for us. To know if—"

"Novak!" Ridley barked the name the way a furious coach might call out a player who'd just screwed up. Mark raised his eyebrows but didn't say anything.

"You're the one!" Ridley said. "I read about you. The investigator biographies, I read each of them, and you... with you, I *knew.* You had to be the one."

"Why's that?" Mark said. He'd gotten his first uneasy chill from Ridley, the first indication that this man's cylinders didn't fire in the standard patterns.

"You noticed the date, didn't you?" Ridley's eyes sparkled.

"What date?"

"I knew you would. Right there on your website it says that your work is dedicated to the memory of that girl, you know, and—"

"That girl," Mark said, "was my wife."

"Of course. But did you notice the dates? She was killed the *same day* that Sarah Martin went missing. Different years, of course, but the same day."

Mark had not noticed the dates. He hadn't had a chance to look at much more than Ridley's letter, in fact, because he'd been shuffled out of town in such a hurry. Time had been short, and Mark's information about Sarah Martin was so minimal, it would have been embarrassing if he'd actually cared about the case. He'd done no preliminary research, just proceeded with the one-page abstract and Ridley's proposal letter. That why-bother approach was based on the knowledge that he was only marking time here until Jeff called him back, but now the lack of preparation was catching up with him.

"Is that so," he said, his voice hollow.

"Absolutely. I noted it in my letter when I requested you, but maybe they didn't show you that one?"

Frost spread through Mark's veins. "You *requested* me?"

"Sure did. There were two letters. I guess they only showed you the one? But somebody must have agreed with me when I said that you were the right person for this."

Mark felt an old tug, an instinct he'd thought was gone, one he'd tried so, so hard to put away: the urge to punch and keep on punching, swing until he could see the bones of his own hand through torn skin. He wasn't thinking of punching Ridley Barnes, though; it was Jeff London's face that he saw.

There are unsolved cases beyond Lauren's, London had said. *You're going to need to prove you can continue to work them. Show me that you can still care about another case, Markus. If you can't, then tell me.*

Mark had insisted that he could and said that he understood Jeff's point—Lauren's case belonged to police investigators and not to him and if he didn't accept that, he'd drown in it. All understood, check, check, check. But still Jeff sent him to Indiana to deal with this lunatic and, what, have some moment of clarity? It was a pathetic ploy, and an infuriating one.

"The date is irrelevant," Mark said. "My only interest here is Sarah Martin. I've had a preliminary visit with the police, and that's what I'm hoping to have with you. Explain what it is that I do, and what I don't do, and—"

"Do you know what your name means?"

Mark tilted his head and stared at Ridley. "Excuse me?"

"The origin of your own name. Are you familiar with it?"

Mark took a deep breath and decided to indulge him. "My full first name is Markus. *Markus* means different things in different cultures. 'Warring' in one. 'Hammer' in another."

"Mars was the god of war, you're correct, but I mean your surname."

"No idea. It's Czech."

"Excellent! Then you're the new man, the stranger." Ridley smiled. "*Novak* is the term for a newcomer in town. A stranger arriving."

"Then it suits my family well," Mark said. "But if we could get back to *your* story, I'd—"

"You want my notes? Hang on." Barnes left the room, stepping through the ropes with an athlete's grace that his weathered appearance didn't hint at, disappeared down a short hallway, then returned with a stack of overflowing accordion folders. "Just take the files. I know it all inside out. Read it many, many times." He pushed his shaggy hair back and said, "Trying to remember, you know. Trying to remember."

"You do understand that if we undertake any investigation, the results could be damaging to you?"

"Obviously. But *somebody* needs to undertake it." If Ridley Barnes was nervous about the idea, he didn't show it. All that came off him was enthusiasm. There was something alarming about that.

"There's a surveillance video in there," Ridley said. "That one is a head-scratcher. Shows the cave entrance. Shows them go in and him come out. Shows the police going in and police coming out. And then...then me." He ran a hand through his hair and shook his head violently. "Ah, damn." A deep breath. "Someone needs to speak for her, you know. That's why I went looking for people like you guys."

"Yes," Mark said. "Someone does need to speak for her." He was looking at Barnes and wondering if this was a game to him, as Blankenship had suggested, if he'd killed the girl and gotten bored after the detectives went away and the years passed. If he wanted them back to play some more.

"Did you retain anyone to investigate on your behalf previously?"

"No."

"Why now?"

Ridley shook his head, and he looked distressed, a patient who wanted a cure but didn't want to have to describe his embarrassing symptoms.

"Ah, man, you know…patience was the thing. I'm struggling with that now. I'll be honest with you. I'm struggling with it."

"Clarify that."

"Hard thing to clarify. What she wanted from me was patience. Maybe what she *still* wants from me. I have the promise, you know? She'll tell me in time. I've tried to accept that, but, brother, it gets *hard*. The not-knowing? It gets hard."

Mark had interviewed countless people with disturbed minds, including four in mental institutions, but he'd never felt as uncomfortable with any of them as he did with Ridley Barnes.

"By *she*, you mean Sarah Martin?"

"And Trapdoor. Either/or."

"Either/or? One's a dead child, Mr. Barnes. The other is a cave."

Ridley frowned as if offended. "You're going to need to start considering that from a different perspective if this is going to work."

Mark held up a hand to silence him.

"I'm not going to get caught up in that before I understand the backstory. One question I have no answer to yet: Was there *any* reason police would have looked at you before you found her body? Did you have any prior knowledge of her?"

"Tangentially."

Mark raised an eyebrow. "Tangentially?"

Barnes shrugged. "She worked at Trapdoor. I was mapping Trapdoor that same summer. So I'd encountered her a few times. I mean, you know, I'd watched her. Sure, I'd watched her."

Mark felt a spike of distaste. "What do you mean by *watched* her, exactly?"

Another shrug. "I paid attention to everyone who was going to be around the cave. She was just a girl, you know, but she caught your eye. Good-looking girl, big smile, big laugh. Lot of joy. She caught your eye."

One of the interviewing techniques that Mark brought naturally to the table and that impressed Jeff London was a comfort with silence. You developed that sort of comfort when you grew up listening to drunks and blowhards in places where the weather could lock you down for days at a time, nowhere to go even if you wanted to. It had taken him a while to realize just how effective a tactic silence was. Most people viewed an interviewer's lack of response as judgment at best and a threat at worst, so when faced with calm silence, they tended to start talking again, to volunteer more than they'd intended. Ridley Barnes was not of that breed. When Mark went silent, Ridley matched it with equal stillness.

"Anything else you recall of Sarah?" Mark said at last. "Or her family?"

"Not a bit. And I don't mean to tell you your business,

you're the expert, but I'd say you ought to talk to people who did know her. Get their viewpoints on it."

For a moment it was silent again, and then Ridley smiled. "You're wondering, aren't you? Wondering if I'm bat-shit crazy."

Mark nodded.

The smile vanished and those bright eyes darkened. "Me too. You know what you ought to do? You ought to get into the cave. Before you make a decision, you ought to spend some time down there. In the dark. Think about her, think about me."

"I don't believe that will be necessary."

Ridley Barnes showed anger for the first time. He wore it well. Like a natural color.

"Oh, I think it is. I think that anybody who even *considers* that girl's story should sit down there in the dark for a time."

"Let's agree to put a pin in that particular idea, how about that?"

"Are you familiar with the term *false necessity*, Mr. Novak?"

"No."

"I'm not surprised. You're going to need to be. I had much higher hopes."

"I'm often disappointing."

Several seconds passed while the wind moaned around the old house, and then Ridley Barnes nodded as if Mark had said something that pleased him.

"Got yourself some spark, don't you?"

"Pardon?" Mark said.

"More fuses than you'd like people to know you have. Oh, I understand. Don't you worry, I'm not judging you. I understand it fine."

"I'm not worried about you judging me," Mark said. "But

I'm not interested in wasting time either. If you insist on that, then—"

"Not insisting on anything. What would you like to discuss? I'm an open book. Just one with missing pages."

His laugh was low and delighted. Mark felt a prickle ride along his spine.

"If you're so curious about your possible involvement in the crime, then why not talk to the police? They say you shut down on interviews. Yet you're talking to me."

"The police don't have *distance,* Mr. Novak. It's too small of a town. They have pressure from all sides to get a conviction, sure. But not to get the *truth.* In your line of work, the difference between those things must be clear."

"We pursue the truth, yes. But the truth could really hurt you, Ridley."

He waved an uninterested hand. "So long as it's told. Everything is connected. That's why you're here. The date *does* matter. It connects us, you see? You *know* that. This is what I mean when I say that everything is of consequence. The date connects you and me and Sarah and Lauren and—"

"Do not say her fucking name." Mark was on his feet, and for the first time, Barnes looked nonplussed.

"You're not understanding me," he said. "What I mean is—"

"I don't give a shit," Mark said, stepping closer. "You were told, damn it, and you went back for it again, and I will not—"

He stopped talking when he saw Ridley move back. A subtle shift, but still visible. He was bracing, readying for a fight, or at least considering the possibility of a punch.

Now it was Mark's turn to step back. He was holding tight to the file. Too tight. He looked down at it, at his knuckles pressed hard against his skin, and said, "I'll review the file. I'll review it and let you know what I think. Good-bye, Mr. Barnes."

"Don't go like that. You came all this way and you're willing to go like that?"

"I'll let you know what I think," Mark repeated, and then he walked out of the house and back into the cold. It had started to snow again while he was inside, more of a sleet, really, and his windshield was already iced over. He cranked the heat up and turned on the defroster. While he waited for it to work, he opened the first of the folders.

Sarah Martin's dead face looked up at him.

Morgue photos. About twenty of them. He went through them one at a time, handling them gingerly, as if he might disturb her. Lord, what someone had done to her. Dear Lord. Bruises showed around her eyes and throat, and scrapes and abrasions lined her entire body; it looked like someone had dragged her over concrete as if she were as inconsequential as a bag of garbage.

Good-looking girl, big smile, big laugh, Ridley had said. *Lot of joy. She caught your eye.*

Her eyes looked black in every picture. Dulled to something beyond death. Mark was holding his breath by the time he turned the last picture over, and then he found a sheet of yellow legal paper covered in scrawled notations with a heading: "Photographic Evidence—Ridley's Notes."

The first three notes, labeled with Roman numerals, were questions about the physical evidence, what had been considered and what might have been neglected. Other than some awkward grammar, they could have been an attorney's notes, or a detective's. Then the precision vanished, and the rest of the page was filled with scribbled questions.

Did I do it?

Did I do it?

Could I have done it?

Could I have done it? Could I?

The ink was darker with each new word, the scrawls becoming frantic by the end.

Mark looked up at the windshield. The ice had melted and was now dripping water down the glass, and beyond it, leaning on his porch railing, Ridley Barnes lifted one hand and waved at him.

3

Don't scare him off. Ridley, do not scare the man off.

Those had been his only instructions, and now as Ridley stood alone on his porch, the Ford out of sight, exhaust steam all that remained in the air, he knew that he had failed. He went back inside, gathered the coil of rope, and put it back on the chair where Mark Novak had sat. Then he took the free end of the coil in one hand and began to tie hitches, never looking at the rope, trusting his fingers as they looped and twisted and tightened, looped and twisted and tightened. A man who had to look at his hands to tie a knot was a man who was likely to die in the dark.

"He's here," Ridley muttered. "He came."

Somehow, he'd known all along that it would happen. He'd been expecting a call first, but this was better. So much better.

But now...now it needed to be handled gently, and Ridley hadn't done that. He'd seen the spark that Novak had wanted to keep hidden, and he'd returned to it, and that was a mistake. At least for so early in the game.

"Have to keep you in town, Mark Novak," Ridley whispered. "Can't let you get back on a plane. Can't have that." His hands were moving faster and faster, and he closed his eyes. He could feel sweat on his forehead, dripping down his cheeks, but his breathing was steady. Ascender hitch, taut-line hitch, clove, Munter. A Prusik with two wraps, then one with three. He began to work backward now, the sweat flowing freely—too much wood in the woodstove; it had to be sixty-five degrees in the house, too warm, Ridley liked it cool, cooler, cold. His hands moved even faster, always you could be faster, reverse order on the hitches, three-wrap, two-wrap, done, on to the Munter, done, then the clove, the taut-line, the ascender, *done!*

His breathing hadn't changed. His heart rate hadn't changed. If the temperature had been right, he wouldn't even be sweating. He'd worked fast and he'd worked hard but his hands were steady and smooth and his adrenaline had never spiked.

Control.

It was a good feeling. One that didn't come easily. One that had to be earned; one that could be lost.

It wouldn't be lost again. Never again.

You lost control.

No. No, he hadn't, and he wouldn't. *Novak* had lost control, and that was why he'd left the house. He wasn't as strong as Ridley had hoped. Not as composed. But it was hard for Ridley to see those things, because Ridley couldn't relate to fear; he was a man who toyed with panic, teased panic, tormented panic. He didn't lose to it.

You did. You do.

Damn it, *no.* He opened his eyes, dropped the rope, and rushed back out onto the porch, welcoming the cold air. The wind pushed right into his face.

Don't lose Novak.

He wouldn't lose him. Novak was here because he'd already taken the bait. He wanted Ridley to believe that he was merely nibbling. Bullshit. You didn't fly from Florida to Garrison for a nibble.

Things were in motion, and Ridley was in control. He let himself feel some satisfaction with that as he packed his bag. It was a small, battered backpack that contained carabiners, two helmets with headlamps, a flashlight, protein bars and almonds, a first-aid kit, and two Benchmade pocketknives. Assisted-opening, one-handed operation, the spring assist making it nearly a legal switchblade. Actually, switchblades were legal again in Indiana. The legislature had taken the time to consider that law and pass it. There was something about this that entertained Ridley to no end. Elected officials often did.

Mr. Barnes, something you need to understand—the people of this county have elected me to preserve law and order and punish all those who do not follow the law. I intend to do the job that I promised to.

Ridley's smile was wider now, memories flooding back, and he knew that it was time to get underground, and fast. It was earlier than he'd intended to go, but Novak's visit had him excited—not nervous, just *enthused*—and he wanted to be in motion, wanted to be alone in the cool dark where his mind could clear and his thoughts crystallize. There was much to think about, and Ridley always thought better when he was alone in the dark.

He changed out of his jeans and into heavy canvas pants, slipped knee pads on, then added a few loose layers of shirts and grabbed a backpack. When he left the house, he simply crossed the road on foot and started across the fields. There were three accessible caves within walking distance from his house, the reason he made his home there. Drive ten miles and there were five more. Burn the whole truck tank of petrol and he could reach fifty, maybe sixty. Hell, he had no true idea, didn't keep count. Most cavers did, loved to talk about it, got a hard-on boasting about how many caves pocketed this part of the world, but they were missing the point.

There was only one.

Ridley had known that for years now. Most people counted entrances as separate caves because they reached walls and they said, *Here's the end of it.* It was a poor understanding of both caves and walls. There were ways through walls, and once you were past them, were you really in a new place? No. You were in a different room of the same house.

The snow had stopped but the wind was still blowing as he walked across the field, his lug-soled boots crunching on frozen shafts of broken wheat. Ahead of him the land fell gently to the left and at the base was a small brook. Dry in the summer months, it was flowing now, or at least it was flowing just below the skim of ice. Along its banks, slabs of limestone showed, and then, just far enough away that all you could see of Ridley's house was one edge of the roof, a small hole yawned in the rock. Ninety-nine out of a hundred people would walk past it and dismiss it the way they would a storm drain. To them, it was just a place where the inconsequential was swept away from the world that mattered.

Oh, what sorry lives most people lived.

Ridley dropped to his knees and slipped off the backpack. He removed the helmet from it, this one outfitted with a new headlamp, slid the helmet on, and fastened the chinstrap. Then, without bothering to turn on the light, he put his head into the hole in the rocks. His shoulders stuck immediately. He made one quick squirm, a side-to-side shimmy, and then he was through. If he could clear his shoulders, he would always be fine in a passage, because Ridley took care to keep himself in shape. It occurred to him that Novak was built for caving, with a clear V taper to his torso that would allow his shoulders to tell the tale of the tunnels just as Ridley's did. Very fit but not overly tall. Probably a shade over six feet, which was still a few inches taller than Ridley. The tall men Ridley had seen in caves tended to be uncomfortable men. Novak's musculature was right, though, lean and ropy, his physical strength evident but not overdeveloped bulk. Too much bulk turned a belly crawl into a challenge. Yes, Novak would do just fine underground if he would only show the initiative to go there. Perhaps some encouragement was needed.

Although the entrance Ridley had taken looked tight from the surface, it opened up into a chamber the size of a bus, walled in by cool damp stone. Once he'd cleared his feet and was completely underground, he pivoted and reached back, grabbed his bag, and pulled it in with him. Then, for the first time, he turned on the light. The world was lit in all directions, and he frowned and clicked the lamp again, dimming it to a tolerable level. There was no sign that any creature had been here since his last visit. Once, he'd encountered a coyote who'd taken the place as a den. That had been an adventure, and one that ended badly for the coyote. Ridley's hand drifted toward his knife as he remembered.

The large room faded to an angled shelf of rock about twenty feet from him, and below the shelf was a shadowed passage. He braced himself on his forearms, so the elbow and knee pads would take the brunt of the bruising, and crawled. Soon he had to drop all the way down to his belly and wriggle forward again. If he'd attempted to lift his head to see what was coming, he would have cracked it against the stone ceiling, and on either side of him, the walls were close enough to squeeze the shoulders. A classic panic passage for rookies, but a short test, thirty feet. The passage bent to the right and led down and then the cave opened again, this room larger than the last, stone formations showing, including a wall so pocked that it looked as if it had been riddled by cannon fire.

Though he'd hardly worked, he was surprised to feel a bead of sweat on his forehead. When he lifted his gloved hand to wipe it away, he froze.

His hand was shaking.

He looked at it with disgust, as if the appendage didn't belong to him, then wiped the sweat away and laid his fingers against his throat. Even through the gloves he could feel that his pulse was too fast. This angered him. There was no excuse for these reactions. He should be in control. He always was.

Novak. He was the reason for the trouble, the reason Ridley didn't have the control he should have. Ridley turned off the headlamp, plunging himself into a world of blackness, and waited for the silent dark to soothe him.

It always did.

4

There were four hotels in Garrison—two were locally owned, shotgun-style buildings with about a dozen units that looked like they were competing for the next remake of *Psycho,* and two were chain hotels on the outskirts of town where things had grown up a bit and turned into a sort of minor interstate exit. There were a few chain restaurants near the chain hotels, and a couple of gas stations. Mark chose the only hotel that didn't have rooms opening directly to the outdoors. He'd never liked those. When you thought of crime scene tape over a hotel-room door, the image that sprang to mind was inevitably of a door that opened to the outside.

The clerk, a pretty brunette, smiled when Mark asked if there were rooms available.

"A few. How many nights?"

Mark hesitated. "One. I'll just stay the night."

Once inside the room, he cranked up the heat by ten degrees, dropped his suitcase, and set Ridley's case file on the little desk by the window. He'd asked for a smoking room, and it stank like one. He always hated that. He'd never been able to get used to the smell. The taste he'd acquired with time. Some people lit candles for the dead, but that showed more than Mark liked to reveal. So he smoked Lauren's cigarettes, filling his lungs daily with the thing he'd once feared would kill her.

He slid the ashtray over beside the case file, took out an American Spirit, and lit it. He smoked while he watched the wind push the snow around the pool cover, and when the cigarette was done and his mouth was full of the taste, he reached for the phone, ready to call Jeff and confront him. Jeff would have an answer, of course, a bit of sage wisdom, but Jeff should have realized that there were some buttons you didn't push, no matter how good your intentions.

He had his cell phone in hand when the hotel-room phone rang, and for a moment he was confused and almost answered the cell. Then he picked up the room line, expecting the front-desk clerk because nobody else knew he was here, and a female voice said, "Who in the hell are you, and what do you want out of this?"

After a beat, he said: "My name is Markus Novak. Who in the hell are *you?*"

"What are you doing asking about my baby?"

The mother. Shit. *Should have gone to her first,* Mark thought. *Not to the police, not to Ridley. Damn it, you knew better.*

"I was going to call you, Mrs. Martin. You were next on my list. I was—"

"I was *next* on your list? You think that's proper?"

My baby. Mark had a flash of memory: Lauren's father down on his knees on the afternoon of the funeral, robbed of his ability even to stand.

Sarah Martin's mother said, "What, you have no answer for that?"

Mark blinked, refocused. "I'd like to explain my role."

"You don't have a role. But I'd like to see you."

"Tell me where to meet you, then. I can head out right—"

"I'm in the lobby of your hotel. And I won't be leaving until I see you."

"Be right down," Mark said, but the line was dead.

She was supposed to look weary. Beaten. He'd met a lot of her kind over the years, enough that he'd begun to believe he could spot them in crowds. Grief took its toll, but grief without answers? That was acid. That ate you slowly but relentlessly.

Sarah Martin's mother didn't fit the profile, though. She was lithe and blond and, right now, equipped with a hunter's stare. She radiated energy, the focus of a master at work on a task, and that was worse, because Mark was the task.

She had her hand extended as he crossed the lobby toward her, which seemed an odd formality, not in keeping with her anger on the phone, but when he reached out to shake it, her fingers moved quickly from his palm and gripped his wrist instead. He looked down, surprised by the strength of her grasp, and when she spoke, her words were hissed.

"*Next on your list?* You really said that to me? Come into this town asking around about Sarah, and I'm *next on your list?*"

"I gather the sheriff called you," Mark said. She moved her fingers higher on his wrist, and his blood pulsed against them. He glanced down again, struggling for words. "I wish I'd been able to introduce myself first. That would have helped. I'm sorry."

"You're not a police officer, correct? So who are you? Who sent you here?"

She had the interest of the desk clerk now, and someone else poked a head out of an office. Sarah's mother, still holding on to his wrist, her eyes scorching, said, "What, would you like to be somewhere else? Don't want to be embarrassed here, with an audience? You'd rather sneak around the town?"

"Let's walk and talk, Mrs. Martin. Please."

"We can stay right here."

"We can, but we won't." Mark went to the doors, and when they slid open, he looked back at her, waiting. He was struck by how unbothered she looked there in the middle of the lobby with everyone staring at her.

Used to that now, he realized. *It's been a long time, and in a town like this, so small? She knows her role now. She's the dead girl's mother. Stares don't bother her. Not anymore. They're just part of the landscape.*

He turned from her and walked through the doors and knew without looking back that she would follow. She was, after all, there for him.

It was getting on toward dark and the wind was blowing harder, and in his hurry, Mark had left even the blazer upstairs. He'd have pneumonia by the time he boarded the plane for Florida. He didn't know where he was going; he just wanted out of the hotel. There was a steak house across the parking lot, the only target in sight, so he angled toward it. It was some sort of Western-themed thing with wagon wheels on the sign, the type of place that disgusted people who were actually from the West because it reminded them of the moron tourists. Or the *tourons,* as Mark's uncles had called them, usually when aggravated by the driving of some *fucking flatlander* who was uneasy on the mountain roads.

"Don't you run away from me," Sarah Martin's mother called, hurrying in pursuit.

He turned back to her.

"I'm not running. I'd like to sit down and talk. I always intended to."

"You always *intended* to. Well, that's sweet of you to say."

"I'm not going to cause you any trouble. I'm not going to be in this town for one damn minute longer than I can help it. I'm doing what I was told to by my boss, but the truth is, I'm biding my time up here because my boss is worried about me. You want to know why?"

"Not particularly."

"Because he thinks I'm doing a poor job of coping with my wife's unsolved murder."

Several seconds of silence passed. The wind was howling in, and it was hard not to turn away from it, but Mark stayed in place, facing the wind and Mrs. Martin. Her hunter's eyes had softened. Almost too much. They were harder to face now than the wind. He was so much better with anger than grief.

"Would you be willing to at least hear from Sarah Martin's mother? While you're busy talking to other people, perhaps you should pause to hear from Diane Martin. Are you willing to do that?"

"I never wanted to ignore—"

"It's your choice. I just need to know if you are willing." Silence again. He tried to avoid her stare but couldn't.

"Buy me a beer?" she said. It was a strange question, like she was asking for a date, but he nodded.

"Buy you plenty of them."

They were nearly alone at the restaurant bar, drinking a local beer called Upland that was actually damn good, when Mark finished explaining Innocence Incorporated and why he'd come to Garrison. Diane Martin didn't speak at all, just sipped her beer and watched him. He found himself avoiding her gaze, the reverse of his typical habit. He favored direct eye contact at all times because he'd learned that it often told you more about someone than words did, but her eyes unsettled him. She was so balanced, so composed, as if she understood him well from his one disclosure.

Maybe his biggest concern was that she did.

"I can't tell you with certainty that we won't take this case," he said, "but I can tell you that it would be a first if we did. The whole point of the organization is death-row defense."

"So why are you here? You said your boss—"

"I'm in exile," Mark said, and gave a weary smile. "And maybe I'm fired. It hasn't been decided yet. My boss wanted me out of the way of the board of directors. He's fighting for me, and he shouldn't be."

"What's your great transgression?"

He wasn't going to tell her that. He hadn't told anyone that, had admitted the truth to only London, who was now busy trying to convince everyone that it was a bullshit story concocted by a desperate inmate seeking attention.

"I can't disclose that," he said, but her damn eyes were fixed on his and he couldn't look away from them. They were magnetic, but not in an attractive sense. Just a powerful one.

"Yes, you can. If you would like to tell me, you should tell me. Would you like to?"

Her voice was almost intimate. He tried to separate himself from her gaze by turning back to his beer, but she said it again: "Would you like to, Mark?"

She hadn't used his first name before. He looked back up, back into that stare, and said, "I had a snitch in Coleman prison down in Florida. He told me that he'd heard a rumor that someone in there had killed Lauren. And so I offered him ten thousand dollars and free legal assistance for his appeal if he . . . if he *confirmed* the rumor."

"And how was he going to do that?"

"By any means necessary," Mark said, and his voice was steady. "And if it was confirmed, he had another hundred grand coming his way, though even he didn't know that, because we didn't get far enough along."

"What was the other hundred grand for?"

"Killing him." He had never told anyone this, not even Jeff. All that was understood of his negotiations in Coleman were that they'd been conducted in pursuit of information.

Diane Martin didn't move or blink or even seem to breathe.

"You would have arranged a man's murder?" she said at length. "You would have been comfortable with it?"

"If I could prove that he was the one who'd killed my wife? Absolutely. Without hesitation. My only regret would be that I couldn't do it myself."

"Are you at risk for criminal charges?" She held up a hand and said, "If you don't want to talk about that, you don't have to. Only tell me if you want to."

"Nobody knows what I just told you. I don't know why I chose to." But he did. He'd told her because she was the only person he'd met who would understand. Not logically, not in the way a shrink or a counselor would claim to understand, but down in her bones, down in the place that had been hollowed out of her and could never be filled again. "Even with the other issues, though, things could have gone badly for me. My boss made sure that they didn't. The snitch I talked to has a credibility problem. My boss built on that. He sent me up here so I wouldn't have to answer questions myself. I think he knew that if I did, I'd tell the truth."

It was an odd answer, and he wasn't sure why he'd offered it. He was fine telling her that he'd plotted to kill a man, but he also wanted her to know that he hadn't lied?

Maybe it was because he thought she'd respect the former but not the latter.

"I would imagine it is also a problem for your boss because the approach does not fit well with an organization that abhors capital punishment."

"No," Mark said. "It does not. And that's what brings me here, Mrs. Martin. I am just supposed to be out of the way, and I was happy to agree to it, because I need that job for reasons I can't explain. It is all that I am now. I'm here so my boss can go about protecting me, and your daughter's death, truth be told, is simply not a case we will take. I'm sorry for any trouble or grief it causes you."

"What causes grief is Sarah's absence, and the absence of any resolution."

"I understand."

"So perhaps you can convince your organization that this is worth their time."

Mark frowned. "I thought you didn't want me doing anything with it. I thought you wanted me gone."

"Now I'm not so sure. I'm beginning to think you're supposed to be here."

He was *supposed* to be in Florida. He wanted to tell her that, but he couldn't, not while he was looking into her eyes. So he glanced away again, a coward's move but a necessary one, and he was ready to explain that this was not the right situation when she said, "What do you think Lauren would say? If she had the chance."

His first instinct was anger. The question was unfair, and he didn't like the sound of his wife's name said in such a familiar fashion from a stranger. But when he turned back, Diane Martin's eyes were gentle, that unique stare of hers, penetrating curiosity but soft-edged, and he found himself saying, "She'd be a poor judge."

"Why?"

"Because she wanted to take them all," he said. "Because she could not hear a story like yours and tell you no. Ever."

"Can you?"

"Sure."

"How about I tell you what I think," she said. "How about I give you what you came for, and then . . . then you do what you want. But at least you'll understand the full story. Or as much of it as I can tell."

Mark took a breath, nodded, and then turned to the bartender and held up two fingers. "We'll do another round," he said. His fingers were trembling.

5

Two hours later, they were still talking.

"Do I think Ridley Barnes did it?" Diane said. "Probably. But I can't say for sure. It's that element that haunts me, haunts this town, haunts everyone. From friends to strangers, no one can look me in the eye when Sarah is mentioned because no one really knows. If the man who killed her is just walking around free, enjoying his days, and knowing all the while that he…" Her voice broke. It was a musical voice most of the time, one that didn't betray her own pain so much as offer to take yours away. Mark wondered who or what had given her the deep wells of composure.

"I understand the basics of the prosecutor's decision not to pursue charges," Mark said, "but what did they tell you? Anything different?"

She shook her head. "I can't think of anything substantially different. It would have been what you heard—lack of usable physical evidence, right?"

"Yes."

"That's my understanding." She paused, swallowed, and said, "But then Ridley brought Sarah up and said he couldn't remember where he'd found her. Then he stopped giving interviews to the police entirely. Offered no cooperation. The prosecutor was worried about getting the physical evidence into court, because Ridley had an explanation for it, since he'd carried her out. They also couldn't ascribe a motive. Unless he's just a sociopath, which is my vote."

"When we talk about motive, we have to talk about your family," Mark said. "I'm sure you understand that. Are there people you and your husband might have had problems with who—"

"No. No one who came to mind. And my husband died when Sarah was fourteen. I don't think he left enemies behind. I think he just left a lot of emptiness and sorrow."

"You said you think Ridley did it," Mark said. "But who else do you wonder about? Who keeps you awake?"

Diane swirled her beer—it was still her first, the second one was warming beside it, untouched—and considered the question. "Who keeps me awake," she said. "I like that. Yes. Excellent. That's just the right question."

Mark waited.

"Evan Borders," Diane said. "He was the flavor of the week before Barnes."

"What was your take on Borders? Obvious suspect, being the one who took her down to the cave, but is there more to it?"

"He was a troubled kid. Or at least from a troubled family. The family was just a wreck. Dad got arrested as often as most of us go to the movies. Mom went through jobs faster than that until she left, when Evan was maybe eight, nine years old. Then Dad, he'd take off, only he'd wander back, time to time. You ever read *Huckleberry Finn*?"

"Yes."

"Picture that father, and you've got a sense of Carson Borders. Evan was pretty well on his own as a kid. Had an uncle who as good as raised him, a man named Lou Leonard. When Sarah started dating Evan, I thought that

by showing him trust, I was helping him overcome that up-
bringing. But then…then it happened, and I wondered…"

"Right," Mark said. There was no need to make her
finish.

"It was probably for the best that Carson was out of
Evan's life, honestly," Diane said. "Evan worked, he showed
some initiative, and I think he carried a lot of shame, which
I always felt bad about. It's hard for a child to have to deal
with that sort of family reputation, particularly in a small
town."

Mark nodded. It certainly was hard. He'd never known
his own father, but he knew small towns and family reputa-
tions. He'd been raised by uncles who were on a first-name
basis with every jailer in western Montana and northern Wyoming and a mother who changed her name almost annually
to try to keep her scams from catching up with her. The
worst part of the family burden was the lack of surprise people showed. The way they just nodded over the news, as if
they'd been expecting it, and then they looked at Mark with
eyes that said, *Wonder when your time will come.*

"Was Carson Borders ever considered a suspect himself?"

"Briefly." Her eyes flickered away. "Then he
was…cleared, I guess you'd say."

"What cleared him?"

"His teeth."

Mark cocked his head and raised an eyebrow. Diane
Martin took a drink of her beer and said, "Someone mailed
a bag to Evan with Carson's teeth in it."

"Good Lord."

She nodded. "The package was sent from Detroit. Evidently Carson had tried to negotiate his way out of prison by
giving up some information on cell mates from Detroit."

"Evan must have understood something about them too.

You get *that* package in the mail, you know why. It was a message to him."

"If it was, he never explained it."

"Which means the message was received." Mark thought about that for a minute and then said, "Did Ridley have a similar reputation? Any history of violence, of crime?"

"He had a reputation, but not for being a criminal. He was viewed as an eccentric, that was all. But he was never *right*. He was always saying strange things, giving you strange looks. Ever met someone who doesn't seem to fit into the world the rest of us share? People who seem to belong to another one, up in their own heads? He had that sort of reputation. He used to go caving with some of the groups around here, but he made them uncomfortable. He'd talk to the cave, he'd say odd things, and most people who went out with him once never went back to him again, even though he was apparently very skilled at what he did. He was as comfortable underground as any snake."

You ought to spend some time down there. In the dark. Think about her, think about me.

"Anyone else?"

"Brett and Jeremy Leonard. They're Evan's cousins. Bad kids. He felt some loyalty to them, I think, but they were always trouble and he wasn't, at least not back then. One of my rules for Sarah was that she was not to be around those two."

"But you'd put money on Ridley?"

"Yes. If he had just stayed with the group and not broken off on his own, well, then his story would either hold up or it wouldn't, right? Then we would know the truth. But instead, he went off alone and conveniently forgot the path he'd taken, so whatever happened down there became harder to prove."

"He says he doesn't remember anything. What do you think of that?"

She fixed that penetrating stare on him again but this time added are-you-kidding-me raised eyebrows.

"Yeah," Mark said. "I know."

"Total memory loss? Please. *Something* happened down there. He has to remember *something*."

"I agree. Now, what happened once he was inside, we don't know. But what about before he was called out?"

"He was already underground."

Mark frowned. "He was *inside* the cave when this happened?"

"Another cave. Or so he says. The surveillance videos say he didn't go into Trapdoor. But Ridley was the one person on earth who might have known another way in."

"My understanding," Mark said, "is that the police were never able to locate the spot where…where Sarah was found." He was careful to say *Sarah,* not *the body* or *the corpse* or *the remains.*

"That's right. And that's another reason that Ridley Barnes becomes so hard to believe, because he's an expert, right? He supposedly knows the place better than anyone alive, but he claims he can't even *begin* to remember where he was when he found her?"

"Okay," he said. "So it's Ridley, Evan, and these cousins of his. Nobody else stands out to you?"

Diane went quiet. When she spoke again, her voice was lower.

"I lied to you," she said.

"When?"

She turned to face him, and her eyes were bright with unspilled tears. "You asked who keeps me awake at night. I gave you three names. But I didn't give you the one that matters most. *I* keep myself awake at night. I'm the one. Because isn't it my job to see that someone finds out the truth, finds out who did it? Isn't that my job?"

Mark shook his head and said, "No, it's not yours," but he'd never convinced himself to believe that either.

"Then whose is it?" Diane Martin asked.

"The police."

"And when they can't do anything? When they *don't* do anything?"

"Then you need help," Mark said. "Then you need..."

"Someone like you," she said when he didn't finish.

He drained his beer and put some cash on the bar. "I appreciate your time, Mrs. Martin. I truly do. You had every right to be angry with me, and yet you heard me out."

"So you'll help?"

"I'll do what I promised. I'll evaluate things, and the rest is up to my boss."

"You should go there."

"Pardon?"

Her face was intense; she was leaning close to him now, one hand on his arm. "To Trapdoor. To the place where she died. I think you should see it for yourself."

"People keep telling me that," he said, and he was afraid she'd ask who else had said it, but she didn't.

"People are right. You should go down there and think about your wife, and then make up your mind."

"My wife has absolutely nothing to do with this. That has to be understood."

The silent smile she offered in response was impossibly kind.

6

He didn't feel that he'd had that much to drink, but by the time they left the bar and walked into the wind-whipped cold, Mark had a shakiness and disorientation that suggested he'd had a few more than he remembered. Diane Martin was rock steady, though, walking briskly through the parking lot and toward the hotel. She stopped in front of a row of cars and turned back to him and offered her hand. The parking lot was poorly lit and he couldn't make out her eyes in the shadows and was grateful for that.

"Consideration," she said. "That's all I'm asking for. If you believe you can help, and you wish to, then you should allow yourself to. It's all up to you."

Her hand lingered on his in a strange grasp, as if she was trying to communicate a sense of need that she wasn't willing to voice.

"It's not my call," Mark said. "I've got bosses to answer to."

"Consideration," she repeated, and then she released his hand and said, "Get out of the cold, and get some sleep."

He followed the instruction, because it was damn cold, and suddenly he felt damn tired. When the sliding doors parted, they revealed an empty and silent lobby, the hotel so quiet it felt like a funeral home. The girl at the front desk glanced up at him, and her eyes were hard, almost hostile.

Do I look drunk? he wondered. He hadn't had that many. Two, right? Maybe three. No more than three. He'd paid the bill; why hadn't he noticed how many beers were on it?

"Mr. Novak, I want to let you know that your room will be unavailable tomorrow."

He'd been almost to the elevator when she spoke, and he turned back in confusion.

"I booked just the one night."

"I know. I'm only informing you that if you decide to stay in this town any longer, it won't be here."

Mark stared at her. She was standing tall, shoulders back and arms folded over her chest, a just-try-and-argue-with-me look.

"There are maybe nine cars in your parking lot," he said. "Not real crowded."

"Not tonight."

"Tomorrow you're filled up? What battalion is coming to town?"

"We won't have any rooms available for you," she said. "That's all."

"For *me?* Or for anyone?"

"There are other hotels in town," she said, and then she turned on her heel, walked into the office, and shut the door behind her, leaving him alone in the silent lobby.

There was a mirror a few steps away, and he moved to it and looked at himself. Clear-eyed, if a little tired. Well dressed, if not for this weather. There was nothing about his appearance that made him an undesirable in a hotel that was probably desperate for cash this time of year.

So it's Ridley. She overheard that conversation with

Diane, thinks that I'm working for Ridley, and now I'm an unwelcome guest.

He was tired and wanted to sleep and shouldn't give a shit about a girl who was throwing him out of her hotel for whatever small-town reasons she had. All the same, it chafed. It had been a long time since he'd been told he wasn't welcome somewhere, and those days were supposed to be behind him. No matter the reason, the eviction stirred unpleasant memories and dark urges. He looked at the closed office door and considered it for a moment and then shook his head.

"Get some sleep, Markus," he said. "And then get the hell out of here."

He heard the phones ring the next morning while he was in the shower—first his cell, then the room phone. When the room phone stopped and then started up again, he shut off the water, wrapped a towel around his waist, and hurried out of the bathroom. He was expecting it to be Jeff or possibly Diane Martin. But the caller introduced himself as Gary Clay, a reporter with a newspaper in Evansville, just an hour south of Garrison.

"I understand that you're opening an investigation into the Sarah Martin case, and I was hoping to learn a little bit about that," Clay said.

"I really can't comment. I don't know who told you about this, but it's a nonstory."

"All due respect, but I've got plenty of readers who would disagree. The Martin case still has a hold around here, as I'm sure you know."

"If we move forward with it, I'll talk with you at some point."

"My editor isn't going to let me make that bargain. I've been told to write *something,* and all I know right now is that you've been hired by the only suspect—"

"No, that is not correct. In no way, shape, or form is that correct. Who told you that?"

"I can't reveal that."

"Of course not. But I'm supposed to reveal things to *you*, right?"

"I called to make sure I had accurate information," Clay said. "See, it's already helping."

"Whatever you write, you'd better make it damn clear that we are not working for Ridley Barnes. Not working for *anyone*. And if you're going to refuse to hold this story until you learn whether it even *is* a story, you'd better get your facts straight."

"My apologies. I just knew that he was the only person you'd spoken with, which led me to believe—"

"Then you don't know anything," Mark snapped. "If you write that I'm working for Barnes, you're going to need to have an attorney onboard real fast. Because that's a flagrant lie. As is the statement that he's the only person I've spoken with. As is, for that matter, the statement that he's the only suspect."

"Who else is a suspect?"

"Go read your own damn archives," Mark said. "You'll find some names. Then go call all of them and let them speak for themselves. Barnes, Borders, whoever you'd like. But do *not* put words in my mouth."

"Is it correct that you haven't attempted to locate any surviving family members but have already spoken with Ridley Barnes?"

"No, that is not correct," Mark said. "I've met with Diane Martin, and she's aware of the possibility of the investigation and supportive of it *if* we choose to move forward, and right now that's unlikely. So you don't need to waste your ink on me."

There was a pause, and when the reporter spoke again, his words were slow and careful. "You met with Diane Martin?"

"I certainly did. And she's—" Mark caught himself, grimaced, and shook his head. Gary Clay was pretty good. He'd turned Mark's refusal to speak into a back-and-forth session in a few smooth moves by making bold statements that were designed to provoke an emotional response and, thus, a quotable response. Mark should have been smarter.

"That's it," he said. "That's all I've got for you."

"I understand that perspective," Clay said, "but I actually think I might be able to help your reputation, not harm it. If you could—"

"I'm not going to let this go on any longer. If you write anything that says I'm working to clear Ridley Barnes, you'll have some trouble over it. That's not a threat. Just the truth of the matter."

"In all honesty, I don't think you can afford—"

"To continue this conversation," Mark said. "You're right. Good-bye."

He hung up and closed his eyes for a minute. It would be better to fly back, sit before the board of directors, and tell them what had happened inside the prison than to linger here.

"Time to go," he said aloud. "I'm sorry, Sarah. But this isn't the right place for me."

7

He'd meant it when he'd said it. He really had. He'd packed his bags and checked out of the hotel and was in the rental car headed out of town when he pulled over and used his phone to find the address of Trapdoor Caverns. The old web page was still active, boasting of boat and walking tours, of *unmatched underground grandeur, fun for the whole family!*

He thought then of the request, not Ridley's but Diane Martin's—*You should go there. To Trapdoor. To the place where she died. I think you should see it for yourself*—and he told himself that it was a bad idea and he needed to just keep driving. Then he thought, *You've got the time, and if Diane Martin calls, you can tell her you did that much. You can tell her that you did what she asked.* He turned off the highway and headed to Trapdoor Caverns.

Just for a look.

The place deserved a look, at least. It was the crime scene, after all, and even if he was just checking off boxes on his way to turning this one down, he needed to—

Sit down there in the dark

—visit the crime scene. That was obvious; it was fundamental.

There was a locked gate blocking the entrance to the

property, and he left the rental car parked outside and walked around the gate and down the drive, his feet crunching on the snow. Not much of it covered the ground, only a couple of inches, and today the sun was brilliant and the snow crystals sparkled like white sand.

When he was about a tenth of a mile past the gate, two buildings came into view: a log home with wide windows and multiple decks and, about fifty yards from that, a large garage. Just below was a creek, the water iced over and shining. An ornate iron footbridge crossed the water, going from the house and the garage to a wall of stone that wouldn't have drawn Mark's eye if not for the part of it that didn't belong—a set of iron bars like an ancient prison door. When he got closer, he saw that it actually was a door. Padlocked.

That would be the cave entrance.

He walked as far as the footbridge but didn't cross it. Just stood there and looked at the cave waiting beyond it.

You should go down there and think about your wife, and then make up your mind.

As he looked at the creek he found himself wincing. The glare of the sun on the snow-covered ice was too bright. Across from it and beyond those iron bars, the darkness looked welcoming. Above, the stone faded into a steep slope lined with saplings, and up on top, the ground flattened out and ran off into open fields. He could see horses, their heads surrounded by fogs of warm breath that sat in the still air. One of them whinnied, a soft sound across the distance, but it still made Mark's eyes close involuntarily.

He'd grown up around that sound. Different towns, different states, but always horses. Traveling with his uncles and his mother, staying in a place until one or the other of them got into enough trouble that they had to move on. There were always jobs to be found if you were good with horses, though, and his uncles had been good. There was a time, long ago, that he had been too.

People thought that his uncles were plagued by alcoholism and anger, but Mark believed they were really plagued by family. Their sister, his mother, in particular. They kept looking out for her when they shouldn't have, refusing to give up on her. While his uncles had their faults, his mother was the only real con in the family. She had not a trace of Native American blood, but she'd tan her already dark complexion, dye her hair raven black, and braid it, weaving feathers into the braids. Then she'd announce herself as a great-great-granddaughter of either Looking Glass or White Bird, Nez Perce chiefs who had participated in the epic flight through the Rockies, struggling to reach Canada, only to be stopped, exhausted and starving, twenty miles from the border. She'd learned early on that Chief Joseph was a touch *too* famous, and there was the chance that a tourist might know more about him than she did, so she'd given up being his imaginary relation and chosen the lesser known chiefs. Broadcasting her heritage as a spiritualist with great medicine powers, she would sell dream catchers and offer psychic readings and faith healings.

What money she made—and some summers she did quite well—went to bottles or, in the worst of times, needles. Mark and his uncles would have to track her down and bring her back to whatever was currently home. As Mark grew older, he began to dream of running away. Running south, to the land of palm trees and blue water.

He'd been seventeen when he finally left, even though one uncle was dead and one was in jail and there was nobody else to watch over Snow Creek Maiden, but it was a while before he made it to the palms and beaches of his dreams. For some years, he kicked around the West in the same tired circles he'd always known, taking jobs as a rafting guide, a stable hand, doing grunt labor for a hunting outfitter, tending bar for snowmobilers, whatever paid. Eventually he saved enough to head south with a small cushion. He'd been working night shifts at gas stations around Sarasota for a year before he got a job as a deckhand on a diving boat. He was fascinated by the idea of diving but couldn't afford the lessons and was hesitant to ask his boss for a discounted rate. It was his boss's daughter, Lauren, who offered him that first lesson. She had a small build and looked overmatched by the scuba gear but moved in the water as if she belonged to it. The first time he'd seen her, she'd been working her way up to the surface, graceful and gorgeous, her blond hair fanned out in the turquoise depths.

He put his hand in his pocket now and found the plastic disk that had been Lauren's permit on that first trip together, the sentimental touch he'd never been able to show her on that deck on Siesta Key. There were moments when he could close his eyes and see the stern of the boat from Saba National Marine Park at sunset, the two of them sitting close but not quite touching, not yet. But soon. And by the end of that year, he'd gotten into what was then St. Petersburg Junior College, just a few hours away from where she was studying in Gainesville. Two years later he was in Gainesville too. Lauren had an internship with Jeff London. Mark had never heard anyone talk about his work with the passion Jeff demonstrated, and the idea of it, of cell doors opening for people who'd never belonged behind bars, was compelling. Truth be told, though, Mark hadn't joined up because of Jeff's passion. He'd joined because of Lauren's. Because he wanted to catch some of the glow that radiated from her when she talked about Innocence Incorporated.

He was good at it too. Better than anyone had expected,

certainly better than he'd expected. The investigative work came naturally. He could be both patient and instinctive, Jeff said, a magical blend. Mark didn't know about that, but he knew he enjoyed the work. The idea that someone was waiting to die for the sins of another and that one piece of undiscovered evidence might free him was not a job you could tire of. It had seemed righteous to him. Back then.

The land of palm trees and blue water had treated him well indeed. It had been the paradise he'd known it would be, full of warm welcomes and soft edges, a place where cold pain and shame would never find him. He'd almost come to believe that before Lauren made the drive to Cassadaga.

"*Hey!* Closed property, pal! Can you not read the signs or do you just not give a shit what they say?"

The Florida memories were gone then and ice-covered Indiana was back and Mark turned and saw a tall black man in a knit hat and an untucked, half-buttoned shirt rushing toward him from the garage.

"Signs hang on that gate for a reason, you know. Hell, the *gate* is there for a reason! But you folks don't care, the world's your damned oyster, you just do as you please…"

He was walking nearly as fast as he was bitching, but it was a tight race. Mark waited until the man pulled up close and then he said, "I walked down for a look. I'm sorry."

"That's just the thing! That is *just* the thing that I mean. The signs and the gate are supposed to tell you that you *can't have a look!* But people just do whatever the hell it is they please anymore. I don't know when it became that way, I honest to God don't. But there was a shift. There was a change."

"Manners are lacking," Mark said. "Common courtesy is a thing of the past."

"You are f'ing-A right about that," the man said. He seemed to be softening now that Mark had agreed with him that the world was in social decline, and he paused to finish buttoning his shirt. He was knotted with muscle and had thick wrists and a mechanic's forearms. His face was hawkish and angular, like it had been built for cutting through the wind, and a perpetual squint added to the effect.

"F'ing A," Mark echoed. "I apologize. I shouldn't have trespassed. You the owner?"

"One worse or one better, depending on your perspective. I'm the caretaker. Cecil Buckner."

"Were you around when the cave was in operation?"

"I'm the only caretaker she's ever had. Was here then, and I'm here now."

Mark nodded. "You've always lived in the castle."

"Huh?"

"Never mind. My name's Mark Novak. I came up from Florida."

He held his hand out and Buckner looked at it suspiciously and then chose to ignore it. "Came up for what?"

"To have a look around."

"Well, that was ignorant. Cave's closed."

"How long?"

"Indefinitely. A damn shame, you ask me. If you aren't going to use it, then why in the hell not *sell* it, right? I can tell you for a fact there was two million dollars on the table from the state for this place. Had eyes on turning it into a park. That's from the *government*, mister, and you'd have to be a damn fool if you didn't realize they don't tend to pay top dollar. But instead, it sits empty, with those bars over the entrance and more locks than a prison ward. If you're hoping to make an offer, good luck and good-bye. Because Pershing ain't selling."

"He has no plans for it at all?"

"If he does, he hasn't shared them with me." Cecil Buckner pointed at the big log home above the creek. "That house was built in 2002 as a summer home for Pershing when the cave was about to open for tours. You ought to see the place; it's a gem. Now it just sits empty. Am I allowed to stay in it? Hell, no. I get the apartment above the garage. 'Course, I'm allowed to go in there and clean now and then. That's it." He shook his head. "Waste. All this place is now is a waste."

Mark looked at the huge house that Cecil was allowed to enter only to clean or repair, and he felt a surge of distaste for the owners. Cecil's was the first black face Mark had seen in town, and Cecil felt too much like a servant for comfort.

"How big is the cave?" Mark said, just to move the conversation away from Cecil's living quarters.

"Ask Ridley Barnes."

"What do you mean?"

"He's the only one who knows for sure. Most new caves, they have exploration teams. Trapdoor had Ridley Barnes."

"Why just him?"

"Because Pershing MacAlister, bless his kindly soul for my employment, did not and does not understand caves. In his business world, the fewer partners you had, the better. So he said the hell with safety, the hell with experience, the hell with everyone, and he brought in Ridley to map what wasn't obvious. That didn't go so well. Cave was discovered in 2000, opened for tours in 2003, and closed for good by the end of 2004. Ridley Barnes was hired in the spring of 2004. No, that didn't go so well at all." Cecil's face wrinkled with distaste. "What's your interest in the cave anyhow?"

"I have no interest in the cave. I'm an investigator. Here for the Sarah Martin case."

Buckner looked away from Mark and out over the fields as if in search of an oasis in a vast desert. "You have got to be shittin' me."

"Afraid not."

Buckner shook his head, overcome by disgust. "Don't go botherin' folks with that. What's the gain? If they could have convicted him back then, they would have."

"There are some people who disagree."

"Those people can go to hell. They have no stake in what happened here or what will happen here. They just like to gossip."

"I'd argue that Sarah Martin's mother does have some stake in what happened here. An emotional one but still worthy of respect."

For the first time, Cecil Buckner seemed knocked off his stride. He blinked at Mark as if trying to clear clouded vision. *"What?"*

"Her mother thinks it's worthwhile. Her mother is the one who told me to come down here and look around."

"When was that?"

"Yesterday."

Buckner looked at him in disbelief.

"Does that surprise you for some reason?" Mark said. "You think she'd have lost interest in finding her daughter's killer just because so much time has passed?"

"I thought she'd lost interest in most earthly pursuits."

"What in the hell does that mean?"

"Let me be real clear here: You say you spoke to Diane *yesterday?*"

"Last night."

"Then you're a very special man."

"I don't think so."

"I certainly do, and I'm not going to be alone in that

assessment, trust me. Not if you believe that you coaxed any thoughts or feelings out of Diane Martin."

"She's usually that tight-lipped?"

"To most of us," Cecil Buckner said, "the dead are mighty tight-lipped, yes."

8

Mark stared at him, waiting on a punch line that he was sure would be delivered, just had to be. Cecil Buckner took a shuffling step back. You never wanted to be too close to a lunatic.

"You believe Diane Martin is dead?" Mark said.

"It ain't a matter of opinion!"

Mark parted his lips but then closed them. His mind was swirling with images of the previous night: the woman's relentless stare, the way she'd put her hand on his arm and told him that he needed to go to Trapdoor Caverns.

"Someone played quite a trick on you, brother," Cecil said.

Quite a trick. Sure. It was one hell of a trick. Mark could see the intensity of those eyes, could hear her near-musical voice answering questions with such deep emotion.

"Sarah Martin's mother is dead," Mark repeated. His voice was numb. "The only mother she had? I mean, there were no stepparents, nobody who might have—"

"I'm quite sure of it. Can you hang tight for a minute? Ah, what the hell, follow me."

Cecil Buckner led Mark back up the drive and to the garage. As soon as Cecil opened the door, smells of gasoline and diesel fuel and sawdust filled the air. They went up a narrow flight of unfinished wooden steps and entered a small apartment with a galley kitchen, a living room, a bathroom, and a bedroom. A gun cabinet was squeezed in a tight space between a television and the wall, two shotguns and a small-caliber rifle inside. There was soft blues music coming from the bedroom, something with mournful horns and subtle drums.

Cecil stepped away from him, said, "Hang on a minute," and then walked down the hall. The music was silenced and replaced by the sound of drawers opening and closing. When Cecil returned, he held a folder that he was twisting in his hands as if he couldn't decide what to do with it. "Would you like to make sure?"

"Make sure? Either she's dead or she isn't. You told me there's no doubt."

"Yes, but ... well, I don't know what you saw."

"I don't *see* things. I'm not having visions, all right? I'm not a crazy man with hallucinations. Someone impersonated her, and—"

Cecil opened the folder and shoved it at him and said, "Just tell me it didn't look like her."

Inside the folder was a copy of a newspaper story: "Diane Martin Dies with Questions About Her Daughter Still Unanswered." Tucked below the headline was a picture of the woman. She was tall and broad-shouldered with brown hair and dark eyes. She was nothing like the woman who'd put her hand on Mark's arm and told him that maybe this was the right case for him.

"Not her?" Cecil said.

"Of course not," Mark said.

Cecil shrugged. "Hell, I don't know. There's some folks see ghosts, some folks see—"

"Stop that bullshit. The woman was real, she was a fraud,

and she set me up. I wish I'd taken her picture so I could ask you who she was."

"Too bad," Cecil said, but he didn't sound particularly dismayed. "If Sarah's daddy comes at you next, ignore that one too. He was killed in a car accident. So, how long were you in town before she appeared?"

"Arrived," Mark snapped.

"What?"

"Nothing." Mark didn't like Cecil's word choice. The woman didn't *appear,* the way a ghost or a phantom might. She'd arrived at his hotel and called his room, the way a real person did. "It was maybe seven hours after I got here."

"How many people in Garrison knew you were coming to town?"

"Zero," he said, not liking it any more than Cecil did, the way this had been waiting on him like a snare.

"So someone at your hotel must have—"

"No." Mark shook his head. It was the right idea, but the wrong sequence. Someone had sent her to him, yes, but not someone from the hotel. "How many places are there to stay in this town, do you think?"

"Maybe a half dozen."

"Exactly. I wouldn't have been hard to find. Not if you knew what I was driving."

"Who knew that?"

"Ridley Barnes, Sheriff Blankenship, and that's it. By the time she came to my hotel, it was just the two of them who knew I was here. I spoke to only three people yesterday. Barnes, the sheriff, and that woman. She came on fast, and she came on ready."

That part bothered him the most. She'd been prepped. You didn't just rush out of the house and pull off a pitch-perfect performance as a victim's mother. Mark had met with too many of the real deal. He'd have spotted the falseness.

"Can't believe I bought it," he said. "I mean, damn, some detective, right?"

"She was that good?" Cecil seemed intrigued by the tale now, like he wanted to sit down and put up his feet and listen to it all. It was probably the best theater to arrive at his closed-for-business cave in a long time.

"She was that good." Mark paused and then added, "And I let go of my own rule."

"What's that?"

"Question everything; trust nothing. I let it go, because she didn't seem worth questioning, you know? She had to be who she said she was. But if I'd questioned it..." He gave a bitter smile. "There were some tells. Yes, there were. She was too composed. The act was good, and all of the words were right, but the eyes? Those didn't fit. The way she looked when she told it...no, that didn't fit. I kept thinking that her calm was impressive."

He was cut off by the ring of his cell phone. Jeff London calling. Bringing him home, hopefully. That would be a gift. He couldn't wait to get out of this town.

"Sorry, I've got to take this." He answered the phone and said, "Hey, Jeff, I'm right in the middle of—"

"A disaster," London said.

"What?"

"I just got a call from a newspaper reporter in Indiana."

"*Shit.* Don't talk to him. This thing is—"

"Oh, I'm going to have to talk to him, because his article is already up online. He won't be the last reporter to call. It's a hell of an interesting piece after all. Not every day that an investigator blows into town and claims to have interviewed a dead woman."

"I'll get him to kill it. I'll get that pulled down."

"Sure, Mark, you can stop the Internet. Before you do that, would you mind reversing the Earth's orbit?"

"Jeff, you have to understand that—"

"I'm going to read this to you," London said, talking right over him, his voice tight with anger. "I want you to hear what's circulating about an organization that relies entirely on its reputation and credibility. 'Mark Novak's Florida-based Innocence Incorporated purports to have unique abilities on death-row defense cases. Based on his early work on the unsolved murder of Sarah Martin, the company's abilities certainly are unique. This morning Novak claimed he opened his assessment of the case with an interview of Diane Martin, the victim's mother. It's an unsurprising place to start, but there's one problem—Diane Martin died in 2008, after an apparent prescription-pill overdose. "I've met with Diane Martin, and she's aware of the possibility of the investigation and supportive of it if we choose to move forward," Novak said. "Right now that's unlikely." *Unlikely* seems to be the ideal word for all of Novak's investigations in Garrison.'"

Mark had his eyes closed by the time Jeff finished.

"What *happened?*" Jeff said. *"What in the hell happened?"*

"Somebody set me up. It had to be Ridley Barnes. But this woman came to my hotel and told me she was the mother. I just found out the truth. I'll call Clay and straighten him out."

"Good luck with that. The Associated Press has already grabbed it. Every time I refresh the news page, I see more hits. I've got calls from numbers in five different states so far. I can't wait to play all the messages. And I *have* to answer them, because I *have* to answer for your conduct." His voice was bristling. "Yesterday I spent *five hours* convincing my board of directors that you didn't deserve to be fired, that you had your head together. I used those words, Markus. I told them, 'Oh, yes, he has his head together.' Then I find out you're talking to dead people? Boy, do I look like one fine judge of mental health!"

"I'm not *talking to dead people,* Jeff. I talked to a fraud. What she was after, I don't know. But if you hadn't sent me to this place to begin with to look at a case that we wouldn't even consider taking, then—"

"No," Jeff said. "Do not question that. Do not even mention it. I cleared you off the decks so I could *protect* you and make you think a little, maybe get some perspective back. Don't you dare question that when I'm down here taking bullets for you. How in God's name did a professional investigator, a *detective with a license and training,* not do enough research to learn that the girl's mother was dead! It's one Google search!"

"You know damn well why I didn't do any research, Jeff. Because we weren't going to take the case! You sent me up here with a one-page abstract and Ridley's letter, that was it."

"You want to debate the blame, knock yourself out, but now I've got to do damage control, round two," Jeff said. "Because when the board sees this, I promise you, you're done. Unless we can explain it. And we are going to need to explain it with something better than what I've heard so far."

You're done. Jeff might have thought he was talking about Mark's job, but he was wrong. Without the job, Mark himself was done. The job was all that Mark had, all that got him through his days. But more important—*most* important, the only thing that mattered, now—the job gave him a way to complete the sole task that remained for him in this life.

Lauren's killer was still out there. Mark had leads that he'd gotten through his work, abuse of his position be damned, and he couldn't afford to lose them this early. After he settled the score for Lauren, fine, let them take what they wanted, let them take everything, because everything wasn't much anymore. But until then, the access Innocence Incorporated gave him was crucial. It had gotten him close already, and if he just weathered this storm, it would get him home. It had to.

"I'll find this woman," Mark said. "I'll find her, and I'll make her own up to this, and the board won't have to decide anything because it will be obvious what happened up here."

Jeff was silent.

"You got a better idea?" Mark said. "If so, I'll take it. But I think we're going to have to produce her."

"All right, go ahead, but first make *damn* sure that you're looped in with the local police. We need to have allies up there, not enemies."

Mark had a feeling that Blankenship was not going to relish the role of ally, but he told Jeff that he'd do his best.

"I'll get this cleaned up by tonight," he said, and Cecil Buckner looked at Mark as if he'd just placed a high-dollar bet on a horse with three legs.

"You'd better," Jeff said. "Or it's back to the board I go, and the fresh questions aren't going to be fun ones, for you or for me."

He hung up then, and Mark pocketed the phone and looked at Cecil Buckner, who was watching with interest.

"That didn't sound real positive, at least from this end of the call," he said.

Mark ignored that and said, "Listen, I'm going to go talk to the police and get this shit handled. I may need to call you at some point."

"Sure. And you do realize that I'm going to have to call the MacAlisters? Pershing, he's in bad shape these days. Had himself a stroke on the golf course. Never been right since. But his daughter is looking after their affairs, and that's kind of lucky, because she's a lawyer."

Lucky, indeed. The last thing Mark needed right now was a lawyer showing up.

"Can you give me a few hours before you make that call?"

"I'm sorry, but I have to do my job," Cecil said. He didn't look sorry at all.

9

Mark wasn't surprised that Blankenship had been expecting to hear from him, but he was surprised at the man's energy and anger. In their first meeting, the sheriff had been low-voiced and skeptical, more of a watcher than an aggressor. Today, that approach was gone.

"I've dealt with some stupid sons of bitches before, but you're setting a new standard," Blankenship said, boiling up to the front desk as soon as Mark's presence was announced. "What in the hell about this entertains you, son? People *hurt* over this shit, you understand that? They *hurt!*"

He glanced at the listeners around him, straightened up to his full, impressive height, and said, "We'll walk and talk. I don't need you wasting anyone else's time."

He banged the door open and Mark followed him out onto the sidewalk. Blankenship's large hands were clenching and unclenching as if he were willing down a desire to take a swing.

"I understand you don't like it," Mark said. "But can you pause to consider how *I* feel about being set up by some idiot like that?"

"I don't give a damn how you feel. I told you this thing could cause pain. *Would* cause pain. You ignored me. But this? This with Diane? I've never heard anything like it. Never."

Blankenship was walking toward the town square, his long legs moving so fast that Mark had to struggle to keep pace. Snowflakes were falling, and a plow went by and splashed slush onto Blankenship's shoes and pants but he didn't seem to notice.

"You know how that poor woman died?" Blankenship said. "She went into Sarah's bedroom, lay down on the bed where her baby had slept, and read a children's Bible she'd given Sarah when she was a little girl. While she read it, she took sleeping pills. One after another. Just trying to find some peace. People said suicide, but they were wrong. She was just looking for some rest. For just a few moments of peace."

His voice broke on the last sentence. He cleared his throat and shook his head.

"Now you've even got that damned family coming back into town. Icing on the cake, right there. I never needed to see them again. *Any* of them."

"Who in the hell are you talking about?"

"Got a call from Danielle MacAlister not ten minutes ago. I thought that whole clan was done with Garrison. But you pass through town and they decide it's worth a return trip. Next they'll probably decide it's time to open the cave again. Of course, I'm the only man in Garrison who actually thinks that it *shouldn't* be open—to everyone else, it's lost money in a town that doesn't have money to lose. Only thing Pershing and I ever agreed on was closing that cave. Him shutting that damned place down and then getting the hell out of this county, those were the only moves he ever made that had my blessing." He shook his head, and by now his hands were no longer clenching and unclenching; they were held in tight fists. "I'll see you charged for this, Novak."

"You got nothing to charge me *with*, Blankenship. And

I'd think you'd want to find out who set me up like that, and why. No interest?"

The sheriff studied him with disgust but didn't say anything.

"The reporter alone is worth your time," Mark said. "He wouldn't tell me who called him with the tip. He might tell you."

"Doesn't need to. I know who tipped him." Blankenship raised his hand. "And I'm not the least bit sorry about that either. I wanted to know what you'd say to the media that you wouldn't say to me. You sure came through, didn't you?"

"That's a bullshit small-town move, Blankenship."

Blankenship shrugged.

"It doesn't matter," Mark said. "I don't need the damn reporter. I've got witnesses. In the hotel, and in the restaurant just across the parking lot. Hotels have security cameras. I suspect the restaurant does as well. We can get video of this woman. So before you start spouting off about charges again, why don't you do a little police work? Give me fifteen minutes of police work."

Blankenship didn't like that, but he didn't answer right away either. Mark said, "You want her worse than I do, Sheriff. Let's go find her."

Blankenship followed him to the hotel. Mark had expected they'd ride together, but the sheriff said, "I don't want you in my damn car until I can put you in the backseat in handcuffs," and he'd slammed the driver's door, leaving Mark standing alone in the snow on the sidewalk, marveling at the amount of rage Blankenship showed. It wasn't *his* reputation that had taken the hit; it was Mark's.

When they entered the hotel, the same young brunette who had checked Mark in the previous day was working, a sight he took in with relief. She'd been all ears for the discussion, enjoying the theater playing out in her lobby. She would remember enough to help.

"I thought I told you that we were—" Then she caught a glimpse of Blankenship's uniform and stiffened.

"Don't worry," Mark said. "I don't intend to ask for another room. Just tell the sheriff here what happened in the lobby not long after I checked in."

"When the woman came by to get you?"

"Exactly," he said, feeling better already.

"You were here for this?" Blankenship asked.

She nodded. "Yes. He'd checked in, and then she came in and asked me to call his room. She did the talking, though. I just handed over the phone. I didn't think there was anything wrong with that."

"You didn't do anything wrong," Blankenship assured her. "I just need to understand what was said."

"Well, she didn't say a lot to *me*. But, you know, I overheard enough to get the gist. I could hear only her. Whatever he said on the phone, that was too quiet. But she said that she was a friend of Ridley Barnes and—"

"Wait," Mark said. "No, no, no. She might have mentioned his name, but she didn't say she was a friend, she said—"

"Let her talk," Blankenship said, his voice weighted with warning. Mark lifted his hands in frustration and nodded.

"So she said she was a friend of Ridley Barnes, and, well, that kind of stood out to me," the clerk continued. Her name tag identified her only as Lily, no last name.

"Why?" Blankenship said.

"Um...you know how Ridley was...well, what people thought about him when Sarah Martin was killed."

"Yes," Blankenship said coolly. "I know what people thought."

"Okay. So I knew Sarah. We went to school together. Ran track and cross-country together. We weren't, like, *super*-close, but we were teammates, so I knew her, and I followed the story, everybody did."

Mark was already concerned about his eyewitness. Not only had she misunderstood the context, but he was certain that Ridley hadn't been mentioned at all on the phone.

"Tell him who the woman said she was when I got down here," Mark said. "You were taking that whole conversation in and didn't pretend not to be. Tell him what she said then."

"The same thing." Lily didn't hesitate, didn't so much as blink. "You came out of the elevator and she thanked you for making time for her—"

"*Thanked* me? What are you talking about? She was *furious* with me!"

"Novak, you say another word and I *will* put you in the back of my car," Blankenship said. "Let her finish."

The clerk was rattled now, looking at Mark uneasily, and he knew he needed to dial down the anger—witness accounts were always varied and rarely accurate, but she was so far off base that it was hard. Her hostility from the previous night had bled over into lies, plain and simple. He exhaled and stepped back, trying to cool off.

"What did *you* hear her say?" Blankenship asked her.

"She told him that she appreciated him making time for her, and then she said that it was important for him to hear a different perspective on Ridley Barnes from what everyone else around here would tell him. I remember that, because I thought, *Well, she must be willing to say something nice about him.* Nobody else does."

"You've got to be kidding me," Mark said. "If you didn't actually *hear* what was said, then don't make shit up! What she told me was—"

Blankenship put a hand on his arm, and the grip was not gentle. The sheriff's eyes were locked on the clerk, and they were intense.

"Ignore him. Just talk to me. Did you happen to hear any reference to Diane?"

"Diane?"

"Sorry. To Sarah's mother."

"No."

"You say you were teammates with Sarah in high school," Blankenship said. "Did you know her mother?"

"Of course. Sarah's mom was always around. Mrs. Martin drove our coach nuts because she loved to bake for us and he didn't want us eating stuff like that."

"So if this woman yesterday had identified herself at any point as Sarah's mother, that would have stood out to you?"

"Are you kidding? Sarah's mother is dead! Yes, that would have stood out to me."

"She called Sarah her *baby*," Mark said. "On the phone. She said, 'What are you doing asking about my baby?'"

"I didn't hear that."

"Bullshit! You must have been standing right there! You handed her the phone! Why in the hell are you lying about this?"

"Novak—" Blankenship barked, but this time Mark cut him off.

"No, that deserves an answer! You tell me that Ridley is some sort of town pariah, but I've been here for twenty-four hours and it seems that plenty of people are willing to tell elaborate lies on his behalf. Aren't you interested in *why*? Or do you already know?"

"Novak, get out. Now." Blankenship's grip tightened and he guided Mark to the front door and then pushed him through it, out into the blowing snow. "Wait here. If you so much as open this door, you'll spend the night in jail."

He went back inside and Mark stood in the parking lot and watched through the glass as the sheriff continued talking to the girl, who cast frequent, nervous glances at Mark. He stared at them, bristling with anger and fear and trying to fathom why she was lying. Had she been paid, threatened, what? Regardless, she'd been prepped. She had been as ready for this performance as the woman who'd impersonated Diane had been for hers. How in the hell had they put it together so fast? He'd chosen the hotel at random. Nobody had known where he was.

There were answers, but the sheriff wasn't going to get them. Not from a girl who'd been either bribed or threatened. The answers would come from the people who'd started the game.

Mark left the hotel entrance and walked to his car. He was behind the wheel of the Ford and driving through the parking lot when the sheriff burst out of the hotel doors, shouting for him to stop. Mark ignored him and drove on, heading for Ridley Barnes and truth through any means necessary.

I O

Ridley's father had been a carpenter when he wasn't being a drunk, and in those rare hours, he was both gifted and willing to teach. He had no interest in power tools; a true craftsman never used them and that, he claimed, was what separated a master from a journeyman when it came to woodworking. As far as Ridley and his mother and sister could tell, though, all it separated was men who didn't have jobs from men who did.

But he'd been skilled, there was no denying that, and he'd enjoyed passing the lessons along. Between his first beer and his sixth, he was a marvelous teacher. When he edged toward the seventh, though, the steady hands vanished, and then the patience, and then the temper control. Some kids learned to count on their fingers; Ridley learned to count by his father's empty beer bottles. *Ten down, go underground,* he'd rhymed to his sister, but he'd taken that mantra literally. There was an old strip pit on the family land in Stinesville— you couldn't really call it a cave, because it went nowhere; it was just a hole in the ground, but it went deep and it went dark and it was tight. If you were committed, you could squirm far enough down that you'd never be found by a searching light or, worse, a reaching hand.

His father had been in a pine box for years—actually,

there couldn't be much of the box left by now—and what memories Ridley had of him were far from fond, with one exception: when he worked on wood with hand tools. They were the old tools, too, the ones Ridley had been taught with. And, more than occasionally, the ones he'd been hit with.

One thing his father could do better than any other carpenter Ridley ever saw was join boards so that they appeared to be one piece. He could work them in such a fashion that he seemed to convince the boards themselves that they belonged together. Even a trained eye had trouble finding the seams in Joel Barnes's work.

But Ridley didn't think his father had ever hidden a seam better than Ridley himself had with the knee wall in his attic. Under the dim light of the lone forty-watt bulb that lit the room, the wall looked flawless—one straight stretch, surely nothing but insulation and ductwork behind it. The old man would have been impressed. Between beers one and six, he might even have been proud.

As the morning wind rose to a steady moan, Ridley pressed on one corner of the attic knee wall and watched as it moved inward and another panel opened outward like a revolving door, all of it done without a sound. There wasn't a screw or a nail in the whole thing. It was all built with wood, the door turning on a dowel. The area behind it wasn't large—eight feet long by four feet deep and only four feet high. While that low ceiling would have driven many people mad, Ridley was used to tight spaces. Once he was inside and the wall was sealed behind him again, he had to use a headlamp or lantern.

There in the hidden room, surrounded by some items it was legal to have and others that would get him arrested, Ridley swung around so he was facing the wall that he'd sealed shut behind him. It was lined with maps—some topographic versions produced by the U.S. Geological Survey and others hand-drawn, produced by Ridley. The topos showed the surface world. Ridley's showed what went on down below.

Today, he was interested in the topographic maps, all of which were covered with pushpins and notations in red, blue, or black ink. Each red circle had an *X* in the center, meaning Ridley had explored the cave, or potential cave, and found that it didn't suit his memory or his needs. Each black circle had a check, which meant that he'd been in the cave and thought it held possibilities. Each blue circle had a question mark, meaning that he wasn't certain there was a cave there but the topography suggested it was likely.

Southern Indiana was a karst landscape, which meant that part of the state existed above a world honeycombed with caves, caverns, and crevices. The land was home to springs where water bubbled up from below, sinkholes where the surface was pulled underground, a river that vanished for miles at a time—countless collisions between worlds above and worlds below.

Because of this, southern Indiana, like Kentucky, was heaven for cavers. Unless you were looking for one particular place in a cave and you weren't certain that it even existed. Then it felt a lot less like heaven and a lot more like hell.

Trapdoor itself had been viewed as nothing but a sinkhole, a pocket of stone that caught excess runoff when Maiden Creek spilled its banks. Then came a week of relentless rain, and the ground opened up and revealed the entrance to an extensive cave system, but exploration efforts had stopped once the cave was closed, leaving Ridley to peck away from the outside and forcing him to remind himself, time and again, that the locked gate put in place by the MacAlister family concealed only *an* entrance, not *the* entrance.

There were others.

There had to be.

The issue was patience. That thing his father had never been able to hold, Ridley must keep firmly in hand. He put his finger on one of the maps and traced from one push-pin to the next, crossing over two blue circles with question marks. It was a swale maybe a quarter of a mile long, a small depression, and it seemed to offer little hope. But he'd searched so many better options for so long. He had to keep at it.

But not today. Today he would cut boards in his tiny sawmill operation, the only thing that still brought him any money. People had stopped hiring Ridley for carpentry ten years ago. There were rules in Garrison, and one of them was that you didn't let Ridley Barnes in your house. Particularly if you had daughters.

Still, the men who *were* hired remembered the way that Ridley could work wood. Cabinets built by his hands were in plenty of homes around the area, though the owners didn't know it. The contractors waited warily outside while he loaded their trucks, and they passed him cash quickly, and they left in a hurry.

Probably some of them had daughters.

Before he left the hidden room, he turned and took Sarah Martin's necklace down from the peg on which it hung. A simple silver chain with a blue stone—it was a sapphire, her mother's birthstone—in a setting rimmed with diamond chips. The clasp was still solid, but the chain was broken. It had been snapped, torn off her neck. The way things tore when reaching hands grabbed at them in tight, dark places. Trapped places.

He handled it delicately, running his thumb over the sapphire, remembering the time the police had come in with a list of things missing from Sarah's body, things remembered by her mother and her friends and her boyfriend, and searched his house. Both her mother and Evan Borders recalled the necklace. Her mother said she never took it off and Evan confirmed she was wearing it the last time he'd seen her.

The police had been thorough with their search, but they didn't quite understand Ridley. If they had, they would have looked at the place with different eyes. Maybe they would search again. Because they were coming back, make no mistake. Novak would see to that.

Everything old was about to be new again.

As if in confirmation, a knock thundered at his door. It wasn't the knock of a casual visitor; it was a pounding of anger and authority. Ridley let out a breath of relief at the sound, understanding that things were, finally, back in motion.

1 1

Mark had given up knocking—either Ridley wasn't home or he was pretending not to be—and was considering the pros and cons of kicking the door open when he finally heard footsteps inside.

"Now, Markus," Mark whispered to himself, "you've got to think about that temper. Got to *anticipate* it." He was speaking in an affected Southern drawl, handling each word as if he were testing the flavor. "A question of willpower, that's what you've got to figure out. That's what defines you, Markus. Willpower."

Not bad at all. He could do a pretty decent impression of Jeff London when he wanted to.

"Greetings," Ridley Barnes called as he opened the door, and Mark kept the London impression in his voice when he responded.

"How y'all doing, Mr. Barnes?"

Sweet as syrup. Ridley cocked his head, aware that it was an act and not aware of the reason for it. On a porch chair beside the door was a coiled rope, dusted with frost; it looked like it had been left out to dry in the cold air and had frozen. Mark slipped it off the chair and ran it through his hands. Stiff, but not frozen. A fine rope, expensive. It was a static line, designed not to stretch. Ridley probably used it for rappelling. You wouldn't want much stretch in a cave. Mark kept it in his hands as he walked away from the door and out into the yard. Ridley followed.

"What is this, seven-sixteenths?" Mark said.

"Good guess. You've done some climbing, I take it?"

"Not much. Spent some time with ropes, though. Trick stuff." He slid the rope out of the coil with hands that were long out of practice but still far from forgetting, then looped and twisted a quick noose. "Poor man's lariat," he said. "With trick ropes, you use a metal piece called a honda. Brass, usually. But if all you have is the rope, you make do."

Mark held the rope in his left hand, and with his right hand he flipped over the noose he'd created and gave it a clockwise spin, keeping it parallel to the ground. The rope wasn't right for the task, and the absence of the honda was noticeable, but he could spin it well enough for the noose to stay open. He dropped his left hand from the rope and kept his right hand spinning it, mostly wrist action, almost like twirling a bicycle wheel. The noose spun in a circle about one foot above the ground. Mark walked with it, testing the feel.

"Impressive," Ridley said.

"Not really. See that wobble? No good. It's supposed to be flat." Mark still hadn't looked up at him. His eyes remained on the spinning rope.

"Not the sort of trick I'd expect a Florida boy to know," Ridley said.

"Now, see, there's your problem. You know that I came up from Florida, that I've got a suntan and don't have a good winter coat, so you assume I'm a Florida boy. But that's not the truth."

"So where are you from?"

"Bozeman, Cooke City, Emigrant, Laurel, and Livingston,

Montana. Cody, Casper, Bridger, and Sheridan, Wyoming. Ashton, Idaho."

"Rodeo family or something?"

"Or something." Mark lifted his gaze from the rope up to Ridley. "My uncle Larry, he was the trick-roper. Damn good at it. Let's see if I still have any of his touch."

He kept the rope spinning, the noose flatter now, but his eyes were on Ridley, assessing the distance. He twirled the rope in front of him, bringing it right to left across his body, and then brought it overhead, spinning it faster and a little wider.

Ridley smiled. "Nice. You look like a real cowboy. Question is, can you do that and ride a horse at the same time?"

"Oh, sure," Mark said, and then he stepped straight toward Ridley and threw the rope, making sure to hold his follow-through, because it had been a long time since he'd done this. Ridley was only ten feet away, though, and he was standing still. Mark had been able to rope a post at that distance when he was eight years old. The toss wasn't as pretty as it should have been, but it was effective—the noose settled over Ridley's head and around his shoulders, and Mark gave a quick, snapping tug and cinched it. His timing was a touch off—he'd wanted to catch Ridley around the chest but got him at the waist instead—but it still served the purpose, binding Ridley's arms against his body. Ridley stumbled forward, caught himself, and then gave another smile, this one less certain.

"Not bad at all. Uncle Larry would be proud."

"Hell, no, he wouldn't. He'd have spit tobacco juice at my feet, shaken his head, and told me to do it again. He was a stickler for form." Mark was pulling the rope forward hand over hand, and Ridley walked toward him rather than resist it, still smiling. "Nobody tips a trick-roper if it doesn't look good." Mark stopped drawing the rope in when Ridley was two feet from him, studying the smaller man and his false smile.

"You're not fond of being caught in a noose, are you?"

"I thought that was a universal trait."

Mark nodded. "Well, good old Uncle Larry, he was a character, I'll tell you. And my uncle Ronny? He had some tricks too."

"Is that so?"

"It is. His were a little different, though. Let me show you one of Uncle Ronny's tricks."

Before Ridley could say a word, Mark jerked hard on the rope and brought him stumbling forward, then dipped down and snapped his forehead off the bridge of Ridley's nose.

"Wh-what the *fuck...*" Ridley stammered, trying to reel away, the blood already spilling, but then he got caught in the rope and went down. Mark moved in above him, pulled up on the rope enough to get Ridley off the ground, then grabbed him by his belt, spun him, and drove him back until he slammed into the hood of the Ford. Ridley's ribs connected with the metal, and his breath went out with a grunt. His hands were fumbling for something, had been the whole time, but Mark didn't care much about his hands because his arms were pinned to his sides, useless. When he saw that Ridley had managed to get a knife out of his pocket and open the blade, he was almost impressed. Now that mistake with the rope, getting him at the waist instead of the torso, was actually working in Mark's favor. Ridley couldn't get the knife high enough to do anything with it from a distance, but if Mark hadn't been paying attention, Ridley might have been able to stick him.

"Now, Ridley," he said. "A knife at a rope fight? Do you think that is fair?" He shook his head like a displeased teacher and then banged Ridley's wrist on the fender until the knife fell to the ground. Ridley stopped resisting and rested on the hood, gasping. The blood bubbled in his nose as he tried to get his breath back.

Mark leaned close.

"You understand that I'm going to require her name," he said. "Not the one she gave me either, no more bullshit and lies. I'm going to need to find the real woman, Mr. Barnes. You understand that, don't you?"

Ridley began with "I don't know—" but whatever he was trying to say ended in a sharp gasp of pain as Mark hit him twice under the sternum with a flashing left hand.

"You can't afford to go that way, Ridley. You really can't."

Ridley didn't speak this time. Just leaned back on the car, submissive, breathing hard and bleeding hard. Mark gave him a minute. After those gut punches, it would take Ridley a while to get any words out. Mark loosened the noose and let the rope drop to Ridley's feet, freeing him.

"How'd you get the hotel clerk to lie?"

"I don't know what you're talking about."

"It's a hell of a good trick," Mark said. "I'll give you credit there. First the bit with the woman pretending to be Sarah's mother? That was inspired, sure. But how you got the girl at the hotel in the mix, I don't know."

Ridley just stared at him. He had his sleeve pressed against his nose to soak up the blood. His gray hair fanned out in all directions. Mark cupped his hands and blew into them to warm them and said, "I'm going to need her name, Ridley."

"I don't kn—"

"Shut up. Do not speak to me unless you're going to speak the truth. Understand?"

Ridley nodded, which shook some drops of blood loose.

"I'll tell you what *I* know," Mark said. "She had to come from you. Because here's the scenario: I got into town, and I spoke to two people. You and the sheriff. That's it. The sheriff wasn't going to roll out somebody pretending to be the victim's mother, I just don't see that being an option. Sheriff also never saw my car yesterday. He didn't know what I was driving, wouldn't have been able to find me that fast even if he'd wanted to. Nobody knew I was coming to this town, Ridley. So she came from one of two sources, you or the sheriff, and I don't think it was the sheriff. You going to try and convince me that it was?"

Ridley Barnes didn't say a word, but he reached down to pick his knife up out of the snow. Mark let him do it, watching and feeling the old pulse, the sight of the knife exciting him rather than scaring him, a near-pleasant sensation of *Oh, so that's the way this is going to go.*

Ridley snapped the blade shut and slipped the knife back into his pocket.

"It won't be hard," Mark said. "Finding her? It won't be hard at all. Because she came from you, and my guess, Ridley, is that you don't have too many friends."

When Ridley took his sleeve away from his nose, his face was masked with blood. He spit into the snow, then touched his nose gingerly with two fingers of his left hand.

"What did you think of the file?" he said. The words were muffled and distorted by the blood leaking into his sinuses.

Mark stared at him. "You are truly insane."

"That's what you took from the file?"

"No. That's what I take from *you.*"

Ridley breathed deep, blinked hard, and said, "I asked about the *file.*"

Mark thought about smashing his fist into that blood

mask of a face, finding the nose again, adding pain to pain. He kept his hands flat at his sides with an effort and breathed, four-count in, four-count out.

"I don't know the point of your game," he said. "Maybe you got bored once the cops stopped coming by, I don't know. I also don't know how or why you selected me for your continued entertainment. But it was a mistake, Ridley. Sending that woman to me, asking her to impersonate the girl's *mother?* In a lifetime of bad choices, that might have been your worst."

Ridley stood and listened, blood working out of his nose and down his face.

"What I'd like to do," Mark said, "is bounce you off that car a few more times, long enough for me to get tired of the effort, and then drop your ass on the ground and drive away and be done with it. I can't do that, though, do you see? You took that option from me when you sent her. Now I'm going to find her and deal with her, and maybe you'll be a part of that, maybe you won't. I don't give a shit. Not when it comes to you, Ridley. But tell her that I'm on my way."

Ridley Barnes said, "What about Sarah Martin?"

Mark felt his hands curl into fists again and knew from experience that things wouldn't go well from here if he stayed. He couldn't afford to stay. Instead, he shook his head in disgust and got in the car. Ridley kept talking.

"You're going to need to think about her at some point, Novak! You're not going to be able to keep walking away from her. Too many people have for too many years!"

It was a relief to slam the door on the sound of that voice. Ridley was visible in the side-view mirror, standing there in the bloody snow, still babbling about Sarah Martin. Mark started the engine and pulled out of the yard.

* * *

He made it three miles before his hands started to tremble on the wheel. A mile beyond that and there was a shudder in his vision, and his head felt high and spacey. There was no shoulder to the road, just the fields, and he pulled off into one and put the car in park and got the door open and placed one hand on the snow-covered ground and gasped in air and waited for the rise of vomit in his throat.

It never came. The frigid air filled his lungs and cleared his head, and the feel of the earth brought the high dizziness swirling back down.

When it was done, he hung on the door frame and breathed in the cold air. There was blood on his shirtsleeve and the back of his hand. He wiped at his face, soaked in sweat despite the temperature, and then fell back into the seat, leaving the door open, and looked at himself in the mirror. His usually tan skin looked gray, waxen, the dark circles below his eyes standing out starkly.

Can't have that, he thought, staring at his own face. *Can't go there again.*

If Ridley wanted to make a call to the police right now, Mark would be in jail by the end of the night, and an already bad story would spiral into something far worse. He hadn't wanted it to go that way. He'd wanted to confront him, yes, get something from him, and Ridley was the type who called for intimidation, but the rope had been enough, and things should have stopped there. It was that smile, the way Ridley Barnes had looked at him, like he was enjoying the game.

So much time had passed since he'd allowed a lapse like that. But then the old feeling had knocked, and he'd known what waited on the other side of the door and still he'd opened it and welcomed the familiar visitor in.

The first time he'd gone looking for blood—his own or someone else's, it didn't matter—was nine months after Lauren was killed, and Mark had just gotten off the phone with her father, just finished summarizing another week of no answers and no leads. He'd gone directly to the worst bar he could think of, the one where he could count on a chance. He hadn't needed to wait long. All it took was the right kind of stare to the right kind of man, and things got started fast. The guy needed to be *right,* though; he couldn't be just any guy. He had to look the part, had to come straight out of central casting.

He had to look like he might have killed a woman.

Jeff London had bailed Mark out of jail after talking with a prosecutor who'd said that he understood, who'd said that Mark was damn lucky the other guy had been a piece of shit with a bench warrant out for him or things would have gone different.

You're shaming her, London had told Mark. His eyes held a sheen under the streetlights. *Forget about yourself. Forget about me. You're shaming* her, *Mark.*

It was so close to those last words Mark had offered Lauren: *Don't embarrass me with this shit.* Then came London: *You're shaming* her, *Mark.*

People had their pride. Even the dead.

Or they should have it.

He used handfuls of snow to scrub the blood from his skin and shirt as best he could, and then, as the Midwestern wind picked up and whistled over the fields, he closed the door and got back on the road.

I 2

The snow had begun to fall again, fat, wet flakes, and Mark remembered the sheriff's assertion that some forecasts were calling for as much as ten inches. He hadn't seen a plow or a salt truck yet, but that wasn't saying much, because he hadn't seen *any* vehicle until a white Chevy Silverado rattled up behind him. The truck would have stood out even on an interstate, though—the muffler had been modified to enhance the growl of the engine. The driver was pushing it hard, rode right up on Mark's ass, and Mark considered tapping the brakes to screw with him, but the last thing he needed right now was a fender bender that would roll out a deputy. He put the window down, letting snow blow into the car, and waved his hand, calling for the truck to pass him.

It didn't pass. Just stayed planted. Mark could see that there was only one occupant and that he was wearing sunglasses, which was logical, of course, because the sky was the color of an old nickel.

They went another half a mile and the truck stayed on his ass, and Mark began to understand the situation. He'd been right in his assessment that Ridley wasn't going to call the police to deal with Mark. That didn't mean he hadn't picked up the phone, though.

The snow was blowing harder, and the powder was coating the road quickly. Every now and then, a gust of wind strong enough to buffet the car came across the fields. Up ahead, where the fields ended, trees loomed, rows of tall hardwoods with bare canopies shifting in the wind.

A stop sign came up, surprising him, not just because he'd been distracted by the truck but because visibility was so poor. When he hit the brakes, the Ford fishtailed. The stop was a four-way intersection, but Mark saw no reason to divert from his plan to return to town, so he drove on. Within a few seconds, something felt wrong. There'd been a change in sound. The growl of the Silverado had faded. For an instant he thought perhaps he'd been mistaken, that maybe the truck's driver had no interest in him at all and had turned in another direction. Then he looked in the mirror again and what he saw almost made him press the brake. The truck was in the middle of the intersection, the driver executing an awkward three-point turn.

Called off? Satisfied that I'm headed back to town?

The truck didn't finish the turn, though. Once it was broadside in the middle of the road, blocking both lanes, motion stopped, the brake lights went off, and the hazard lights went on.

What in the hell was this about?

Mark kept driving, but the mirror had his attention. The truck remained in place, hazards blinking, as if there had been an accident that forced it to stop there in the road. There'd been nothing of the sort, though. The driver had come to a stop and then carefully turned the truck into that position, which achieved nothing except to...

Block the road.

You didn't block the road behind someone because you wanted to see where he was going. You blocked the road behind him so somebody else ahead of him would have time with him.

Through the blowing snow, another vehicle appeared. This one was headed east, toward Mark, driving with the wind, seeming to be pushed by the snow. A white panel van. The van slowed and pulled sideways, cutting off the road in front of Mark in an identical fashion to the truck behind him, which was no longer visible in the mirror. The road was completely blocked now, eastbound and westbound, and Mark was alone in the middle.

Mark brought the Ford to a stop. The van doors opened on both sides and two men climbed out. Both wore jeans and hooded sweatshirts and black masks. Both carried shotguns. Behind Mark there was the sound of another door. The truck's driver was out. He also wore a mask and carried a shotgun.

My guess is that you don't have too many friends, Mark had told Ridley Barnes.

He had at least three.

The men walked toward Mark, shotguns pointed down, closing the gap fast. Then they fanned out, leaving the road so they were protected by the trees, their guns raised in shooter's stances.

Mark had nothing approaching a weapon in the rental car. There was an empty Styrofoam cup that had once held coffee; a file folder of old case notes. He wasn't going to take these three down with paper cuts. The only weapon was the car itself, and given the way they were flanking him, even the car wouldn't be much use. He'd force them to open fire if he drove at them, and right now there remained at least a chance that they didn't intend to shoot.

Lauren was found outside of her vehicle on a rural road, Mr. Novak. She'd been shot.

He wanted to reach into his pocket, wanted suddenly—desperately—to feel that worn diving-permit tag that had traveled all these years with him, but reaching for anything was potentially deadly. Instead, he put both hands on the wheel and waited. It wasn't long—the men on the flanking sides closed quickly and simultaneously through the snow, like wolves. The one from the truck walked past them and then turned to face the car.

Nobody spoke. The guy on the passenger's side was small, maybe five six, and he seemed to like holding the shotgun, had a more aggressive posture than the others. A bantam, a little guy eager for a fight. On the driver's side was a bigger guy, over six feet, forced to stoop to have a clear visual on Mark. Wide through the shoulders, hands so big they curled around the stock of the shotgun as if it were a handgun grip. As long as he didn't have to catch someone, the advantage would usually be his, and he didn't have to catch Mark. Their gray sweatshirts were identical, no brand name apparent. Just generic hooded sweatshirts. Generic black knit masks. No telling features. The black pump shotguns were probably twelve-gauges, nothing fancy or expensive. Like the sweatshirts and the masks, the shotguns matched. Nobody was allowed to be an individual in this group, and that was troubling, because it was smart.

The man from the Silverado stood directly in front of the Ford, feet spread wide to give him a good base, his shotgun held at belt level, pointed at the windshield. His finger on the trigger. The wind raised the snow from the road and swirled it around him like a protective force.

It's his show, Mark thought. *Whatever happens from here, it's his decision.*

"Get him out."

When the command came, the big man on the driver's

side cradled the shotgun against his shoulder and held it in one hand so he could free up the other to grab the door handle. That would have been Mark's best chance, nine out of ten times—when the attacker had one hand off the gun and was opening a door toward himself. Mark could help the door along, kick it into his face and knock him off balance, or at least knock the gun out of his control long enough for Mark to get his hands on him, but this wasn't nine out of ten times. This was the tenth, when you had shooters on every side.

The big one pulled the door open only to have the wind try to push it shut again. He wrestled it back and got one leg inside, trapping it open.

"Step out." He had a voice that suited his frame. Loud and deep and commanding.

"I'm unarmed," Mark said. "And you can see my hands on the wheel, can't you?"

"Don't care."

"I'm just saying that if we're talking, we can do that here."

"We're not talking."

Mark nodded. "You mind if I turn the engine off? This is hell on my fuel economy."

The big man shoved the shotgun muzzle into the car and smacked it against Mark's forehead.

"You know what," Mark said, "I think I'll just get out and worry about the gas later."

Mark released the seat belt and stepped out of the car and into the snow.

"Hands in air or hands on the back of my head?" Mark said. "What's your preference?"

The big guy regarded Mark as if he distrusted the questions. "Back of the head. Then walk toward the van."

Mark laced his fingers together behind his head. The gesture pulled his coat open, and the big guy took advantage of that to frisk him. The wind rose to a scream, and Mark shivered involuntarily.

"Cold," he said. "Wouldn't mind having one of those masks myself. Maybe you could take yours off and let me borrow it? Would be thoughtful, considering you'd still have your hood."

A shotgun-muzzle jab to the forehead again. He heard his teeth click together as he fell back against the car, and he bit his tongue and tasted blood. He sucked the blood to the front of his mouth and then spit it into the snow. Looked like a small thing, but it wasn't. That copper-flavored spit held his DNA signature, and there was a chance some detective might appreciate his leaving it behind. Dark thoughts, yes, but this was how it ended for some people. Places like this, moments like this. Men with guns on lonely roads. Sometimes this was exactly where it ended.

"Walk to the van." That deep voice suggested there wasn't going to be any further discussion. Mark walked away from his car and toward the van. The path took him directly into the wind, and the snow stung his eyes.

"We leaving my car behind?" he said. "Sitting there with the engine running? Seems like a good way to attract some attention. And you probably don't want attention."

He just wanted to talk, because talking gave him a chance to see reactions and learn more about these men behind the masks, and hopefully talking would also distract them from the way he kept spitting blood, trying to leave a trail of it as he walked. Leave a clue. Lord, what he would have given for a clue on another day and another road, one where wind-blown cypress leaves cast rippling shadows.

"Don't worry about your car," the big man said. He was

walking with Mark; the bantam had stayed behind, and the headman was motionless, waiting.

"It's just that, you know, I never spring for the full coverage," Mark said. "Saves a few dollars, but it does make me worry."

They reached the point man. He was about Mark's size, maybe an inch taller, and thinner, but in a rangy way. The sweatshirt was too big for him, hanging loose.

"We could have this talk," Mark said to him, "without me getting in the van."

The other man didn't respond. The bigger one jabbed Mark with the shotgun again, a hard shot to the kidney, and while it made him wince and stole his breath, he took a sad pride in the fact that he stayed upright and didn't lower his hands.

A crunching sound came from behind them, and Mark turned to see that the third man, the smaller guy with the tense nerves, had climbed behind the wheel of the Ford.

"I'm afraid I can't allow that," Mark said. "It's nothing personal. It's not even my rule. The problem is with Hertz. They want you to identify everyone who is going to drive the car. So maybe if I could just get a real quick look at his driver's license, that would be enough to—"

This time the blow knocked him down. Mark fell onto his knees in the road. He still had his hands clasped behind his head.

"There might be some confusion," he said, "about what I'm doing in your town. I'm sure we can straighten it out. I don't intend to stay here. I never did."

When the thinner man without gloves nodded, the next blow came almost immediately, and the world wavered away. There was pain and there was darkness and there was cold, but not much else. Mark had a vague awareness of being lifted. They dragged him around the back of the van, and he thought, *License plate,* but his vision couldn't anchor on anything, and then there were two metallic snaps and he thought, *Kill shot coming.*

No gunfire followed, though. He was lifted higher and then shoved into darkness and he realized the metallic noises had been the doors on the back of the van, and now he was inside of it. He tried to bite down on his tongue again and missed it somehow—how could you fail at an attempt to bite your own tongue?—but found his lip instead. He was satisfied with that, and he ground his teeth until he tasted blood again. That was the only thought he could hold in a mind that was swimming in and out of consciousness: he wanted to leave blood in their van. A strange hope, the polar opposite of what he should want to happen, yet he knew what it could mean to someone later. Without forensic evidence, good luck. Without forensic evidence, cases stayed open. Murderers stayed on the streets. Questions added layers of grief. He was determined that a lack of forensic evidence would not be a problem for anyone working his case.

So bleed, then, and keep bleeding. Leave a mark on this world.

13

The first thing he was aware of was pain in his shoulders. The headache came second, and then a sense of motion. Mark opened his eyes and saw corrugated metal covered with a thin layer of crimson-tinted water. Snowmelt and blood.

The motion was the van's—he could feel it swaying as it took curves—and the source of the headache was obvious, but the shoulder pain seemed fixable, the product of awkward positioning. It was only when he tried to shift that position that he felt the rope binding his wrists.

Someone reached out, put a gloved hand against the back of his neck, and said, "Stay down."

He didn't need that advice; he wasn't going anywhere. The van bumped over something, then slowed, and a voice said, "Hood," and Mark was lifted and a bag was jerked over his head. The fabric was coarse. Something was looped around his throat and pulled tight enough to cinch the bag in place.

Returning the favor, he thought, remembering the look in Ridley's eyes when Mark had dropped that noose over him.

The bag smelled of something vaguely familiar, but Mark couldn't place it. An earthy, pungent smell. So familiar, and yet he couldn't locate the source in a mind that was swimming with pain and disorientation.

The van came to a stop and he heard the back doors open, and a rush of frigid air hit him. He was grabbed by his feet and pulled and then hands caught him under his armpits and lifted him easily, as if he were a child. His feet landed on uneven ground and he slipped and would have fallen if the hands hadn't kept him upright. Nobody said a word. The only sounds were men breathing and a keening wind. It was unbelievably cold.

"Move those feet, bud. We're walking."

He did as instructed, moving his feet, although they weren't particularly cooperative. He was being held by the back now; someone had a fistful of his shirt. They were walking into the wind, and he began to shiver. He wasn't sure how far they'd gone—it felt like a long walk but probably wasn't— when the same voice that had ordered the hood spoke again.

"That's good. You're all done. I've got it."

Mark's shirt was released then, and he stood alone, shivering, hands bound and the bag—*What was that damn smell?*—over his head.

"Let's get to it," Mark said.

"You in a hurry?"

Mark tried to identify some distinct quality in the voice. There wasn't much of one, though. A man's voice, not particularly high or deep, with just a trace of the South to it. Not the real South, not a drawl like Jeff London's, but a hint of hill country.

"I'm cold," Mark said.

"Not dressed for the weather. Should be glad you have that hood on. Cuts the wind."

"Let's get to it," Mark said again.

"You in a rush to die, boy?"

"That's what's going to happen?"

The answer didn't come in words. Something cold and

sharp touched the base of his neck, just below the hood. The point of a knife, applied with just enough pressure to break the skin. A trickle of blood began to work its way down Mark's collarbone.

"Still in a hurry?"

Mark didn't answer. The point of the knife moved from Mark's collarbone and sliced down. He could hear his shirt ripping. With his shirt cut, the wind found bare flesh. The blood felt very warm.

He was pulled forward, and his feet struck something unexpected. The snow was still there but the surface beneath was no longer frozen earth. Whatever it was flexed and bowed as if it was not designed to hold human weight. He shuffled forward, trying not to lift his feet, overwhelmed by the odd sensation that he was walking up and into thin air and that ahead of him the surface would vanish and he would plummet down. Like walking a plank.

"Stop there."

Mark was happy to listen to that, because whatever he was standing on seemed progressively weaker, each step producing more give. There were metallic sounds that he couldn't identify and then the hand was back on him and the voice said, "Big step now."

Mark tried to take a big step but his foot found nothing but air and he started to fall and the other man caught him and pulled him forward with an effort and Mark fell to his knees on a floor. Out of the snow now but still very cold.

"Who brought you here?" the voice said.

"I'm going to tell you the truth," Mark said.

That provoked a low, dark laugh. "I think that's the way for you to do it, yeah."

"But you're not going to like it much, I'll tell you that now."

"Why don't you tell me who brought you to town instead?"

"The same son of a bitch who sent you after me. So let's not waste our time pretending we're confused about that. Ridley called me, and Ridley called you, but only one of us is actually working for him."

"Thought you were here for Sarah Martin, not Ridley Barnes."

"I don't care about Sarah Martin."

"That's disappointing to hear from a detective. You're supposed to care. You're supposed to solve the thing. Think you'll be able to do that?"

"It's not going real well to this point."

"Don't care about Sarah, huh? Don't like Ridley and don't care about Sarah. What in the hell do you want in this town, then?"

"Not a damn thing. I just want to go home."

"Little late for that."

There was a pause, a rustling sound, and then another stab of the knife, this time high on his arm, in the flesh of his biceps. Wait. No, that wasn't the knife. It was thinner and sharper and went too deep with too little pain.

Mark got it then, understood from touch what he could not see, and said, "What did you just put in me?"

There was no answer. The needle found him again, the other arm this time, and though he tried to twist away from it, he succeeded only in falling backward as an unknown chemical joined his bloodstream, slipping through his body and carrying a black fog with it.

14

The black fog never lifted, but it had shades. For a time Mark thought he was underwater, in the dim depths. He was certain he could see a familiar reef below, and he knew exactly where he was: Saba National Marine Park. Lauren had reached the reef first—she always did, she moved like an eel. She had beaten him there, and that meant she was just to his left. He turned to his left then, eager to see her, and the water rippled like a curtain, and her face was there but hard to see. There was snow in the water now, falling fast and hard between them. He'd never seen snow underwater before. It was beautiful. Lauren was smiling at it, reaching out to catch one of the flakes in her palm, and suddenly Mark felt panic rising, because Lauren didn't know anything about snow, she'd always lived among palm trees and warm sunsets and blue waters and she was not prepared for the dangers that lurked in harsh winters. That was his fault. He had not done enough to prepare her for that because she was never supposed to see it.

Mark said, "Baby, be careful," and then something slapped him in the face and knocked the next words aside. He'd meant to ask her a question, but he couldn't recall it now, and the snow was falling faster and the curtain of water was rippling like laundry on the line, and Lauren faded out of sight behind it all. Mark blinked and squinted and tried to find her but the snow was gone and then the water went with it.

He'd come to the surface.

No, that wasn't right. He'd never left the surface. His feet were on the ground and his ass was on a chair. These things were real, tangible. It was as dim here as it had been under-water. Some source of light was coming from behind him, painting shadows on a wall of boards in front of him. There was something wrong with the boards. The boards were melting. He tried hard to think of what that might mean, and then he thought *Fire* and fear overwhelmed him, because he knew that if there was a fire then he had to run, but he couldn't even get out of that chair.

"Settle down, damn it," someone said.

"The boards are melting," Mark said. "Look at them. They're melting!"

Another slap, and the fog that returned was gray, and Mark didn't mind it so much because at least he didn't have to see that wall melting in front of him anymore. His fear ebbed away and he became aware of a repeated question. Asked patiently but insistently.

"What did Ridley tell you?"

Ridley. That didn't make any sense. Ridley hadn't seen the reef. Nobody but Mark and Lauren had. The other divers were scared of going that far. Hell, Mark had been a little scared too. Lauren wasn't, though. He could see her blond hair fanned out wide in the current, could see those sleek legs in a smooth churn that drove her down effortlessly, and he remembered that he'd been scared of her in that moment. Scared for her, yes, but scared *of* her too, because nobody can hurt you worse than someone you love. Lauren was reckless in the way that you could be only if you'd never had true cause for fear. Mark didn't want her to be afraid, but maybe she needed to be. Fear protected you at times.

"She was just young," he said.

"What?"

"Just too damn young. Came from a different place than me, and I thought that was good. I thought that was perfect. But some people don't need to be older to understand what the world can do to you. She wasn't one of those, though. She wasn't."

"Sarah? You're talking about Sarah?"

The gray fog parted and Mark saw the melting boards again and felt panic again, but then the boards peeled away and there was nothing but water behind, shimmering curtains of water. Good. They weren't going to burn after all. You couldn't burn underwater, could you? Maybe in the right conditions you could. Things blew up underwater. Maybe in the right—

Another slap, then the voice, louder, and warm breath against Mark's ear. "What...did...Ridley...tell you?"

Ridley hadn't told Mark anything about Lauren. Why would he? He didn't know her. Wait. Wait one minute. He *had* said something about her.

"Dates were the same," Mark said.

"What dates?"

"When they died."

Hands fell on his shoulders, their grasp rough, shaking him, and when the voice returned, it had added urgency. Mark couldn't see anything but shadows now. One large shadow, looming above him. Too tall to be a man. Something bigger than a man, something worse.

"He knows they died on the same day? He's sure?"

"Yeah. Yeah, he's sure." Mark didn't understand the confusion about this. The dates were obvious; all Ridley had to do was read the newspaper. Maybe the shadow should learn to read. Mark started to laugh. The shadow didn't like the laugh, and he slapped him again. That was getting old. Mark was tired of the slaps.

"What else? Think hard, now, tell me the truth. What else did Ridley have to say?"

Mark wanted to please the shadow, which seemed strange because the shadow kept slapping him, but there was something in its voice that was so urgent, nearly desperate, that Mark wanted to provide the right answers.

"He said..." What had he said? They'd talked, hadn't they? Yes, they'd talked, and he'd said that the dates were the same, and that had bothered Mark. Mark got upset with Ridley then, he remembered that.

"He said *what?*"

"That I needed to go there."

"Where?"

Good question. Where was there? For a moment he was convinced that the right answer was the reef, but the reef hadn't involved Ridley, that had been just Mark and Lauren. Why did the reef keep coming to mind, then? Tanks. Tanks and rebreathers. Yes, he'd seen those with Ridley, that made sense. But Ridley didn't dive, he...

"Wanted me to go to the cave," Mark said.

"To Trapdoor?"

Mark nodded, happy to have been of help. "Yes, he knows about the cave. It is all about the cave with Ridley. Cave, cave, cave. That's all he wants to talk about." He started to laugh again. He got smacked again. He felt like crying. He felt like sleeping. Where was the water? Where was the reef? Where was his wife?

"Why did he want you in the cave?"

"That's what it's all about," Mark said.

The shadow went silent. Mark saw the melting boards again so he closed his eyes and tried to find the water. There it was. Gentle currents pushing and pulling at him, and somewhere up ahead was Lauren. Glimpses of her hair. Here and gone, here and gone. Why wouldn't she slow down and let him catch up? Going too fast was dangerous. It was reckless. It would get someone killed.

"Slow down," he whispered. "Wait."

"I'm thinking," the shadow said from somewhere behind Mark. The shadow had misunderstood; Mark didn't care if *he* slowed down. "I'm thinking that maybe Ridley was right. Maybe you need some time down there. It'll stir things up, won't it? Let's stir things up."

"Okay," Mark said agreeably. "Let's do."

Something was pulled over his head then, and the melting boards vanished and so did the water behind them. He'd never make the reef now. Lauren was up there ahead, and she was all alone.

Part Two

THE WORLD BELOW

15

Full consciousness had been with Mark for a while before he accepted that it had returned. It was difficult to believe that his mind was functioning, because the world he existed in now was stranger than what he'd experienced in the drug haze.

Blackness was all that he knew, but the hood was off his head, his eyes were open, and he believed he should be able to see. It took some time before he understood that the problem wasn't with his eyes—there was nothing but darkness.

What finally put him in motion was the cold. It wasn't bitter and wind-driven and there was no snow. The cold simply rose up and soaked into him. He ran his hands over his body and found his skin prickled with gooseflesh. He was naked except for his underwear, and at first he'd hoped that was an imagined condition, just as he'd hoped the blackness was. Another hallucination that would pass eventually.

It wasn't.

He extended his hands and swung them around, testing the blackness to see what was out there. His fingers made no contact with anything. He lifted one hand and held it directly in front of his face, then opened and closed it. He saw nothing, but there was a bizarre sensation that he *could*. He could visualize what the hand was doing, and so his brain seemed to accept it almost as if he had seen it.

There was a stone wall at his back and a stone floor beneath him but what was in front of him, or even nearby, was unknown.

Fear seized him then, a swift panic that made him get to his feet too fast, and he almost fell. His legs were numb from the long period of sitting, and all of him ached. He stood in the dark and tried to make some sense of it, of how he'd come to be in this place. Memories came at him in disjointed fragments, and that only exacerbated the panic.

Slow down, he told himself, *slow down and relax. You're alive, you're safe.*

Wasn't he? Maybe he was. How could you know when you couldn't see a single thing?

Where the hell are you? How did you get here?

He remembered the drive through the snow, the truck behind him, the van ahead of him, the men with shotguns. Three of them. Then he'd been in the van. Then he'd been somewhere in the snow with a knife against his throat and questions coming. Then...

He couldn't put that together. That was the point where memory turned to fragments and then to dust. None of the memories told him where he was now. Some sort of basement? No. The stone wasn't smooth like poured concrete. It was rough and smelled of soil and water, no trace of human interference. This was some kind of pit, some kind of...

"Cave." He said it aloud, and the sound of his voice made the darkness seem darker, made him feel smaller and more alone, more helpless. He shouted then, yelling *"Help!"* and *"Hello!"* over and over.

There was no response but an echo that made the place feel large and empty, as if he were a long way beneath the earth. He thought of Ridley Barnes, all those ropes and helmets and lamps scattered around his house. How far had

Mark been taken into this place? And from what direction?
Was the exit in front of him, or to the left, or to the right? Or,
hell, above? How did you even begin to search for it?

The panic he felt then was unlike any he'd known before.
A sensation of being trapped in someplace small and abandoned in someplace endless all at once. Anything would be
better than this blackness—being adrift on miles of empty
sea or being caught in a cage; either would be better, because
at least it would be known.

He moved his hands down to the stone floor and spread
his fingers wide and dug them in, felt his nails scrape against
the rock. He stayed like that, as if he were hanging on to
keep from being pulled away, and he closed his eyes, even
though there was no point—eyelids shielded you from nothing down here—and he tried to confine his concentration to
the physical sensation of touch, to the feel of the stone. It
was a known entity here in a world without many.

"All right," he said, and his words echoed. "All right,
Markus. Go ahead and open your eyes, and know that nothing will change."

Talking aloud provided some level of reassurance. He
opened his eyes, and while there was another stab of fear
when nothing changed, he contained it this time.

You ought to spend some time down there, Ridley Barnes
had said. *In the dark. Think about her, think about me.*

"Let's get out of here," Mark said, still speaking aloud because sound was comfort. "Let's go."

There was the challenge. Go where?

Moving in total blackness was daunting even if you had
an understanding of where you were. Without any, it seemed
impossible. But he had no choice. In this cold, if he didn't
find a way out soon, he never would.

Right or left? Or straight ahead? Every option seemed

the same. The only logic he could imagine was a process of elimination: pick one direction, head that way, and see what happened. Rinse and repeat and eventually he'd be moving in the right direction.

Unless there isn't a right direction. Because if this is a pit, and you need to go up...

He decided to move straight ahead first, because it occurred to him that it would be easier to find his way back to the starting point if he moved in a straight line. That way, if he ran into an obstacle, all he had to do was move directly backward until he found the wall again. This realization was the first thing approaching an actual plan, and he felt proud of it, as if the notion of crawling forward were a true breakthrough and not something instinctive to such brilliant creatures as earthworms and ants.

He began to crawl, and even though the impact was minimal, the stone was brutal on his knees. He considered standing but thought that would be more dangerous—by crawling, he was at least limiting how far he could fall.

He had gone maybe twenty or thirty feet when his left hand made contact with what seemed to be a wall in front of him. He ran both hands along the surface as far as he could extend his arms. He found no break in the wall. A dead end.

Unless, of course, the passage opened up a little to the left or to the right. It could be just ten feet away, and he wouldn't know.

His mouth was dry and his pulse hammered. He tried to calm himself with the reminder that he had no other choice but to keep trying. He was warmer when he was moving too, and that was important. That was critical. He could envision his mother in the snow of that Montana prairie, the blue tint seeming to come from within her flesh. Yes, it was important to keep moving.

He moved backward just as he'd come, but the going was slower because his feet weren't as dexterous as his hands and made poor guides in the dark. When he finally found the wall, he felt a sense of triumph. He'd achieved what he'd set out to do. Never mind that it hadn't actually taken him anywhere or changed his situation—he'd proved that he could move away from this spot and make it back again.

Now he was back to the old question: Right or left? He decided that right felt more natural, simply because he was right-handed. When he began to crawl again, he found that he preferred this path because he could keep the wall against his side. As he worked along the wall, he thought he heard sounds that weren't of his own making. He stopped and listened and what he would once have called silence now seemed filled with soft murmurs. Whispers of motion.

Snakes.

His brain treated that just as it had the opening and closing of his hand; because he could visualize snakes, it was almost as if he'd actually seen them. He crept backward, banging his knees painfully on the stone, and had gone about five feet before he stopped himself. He listened again, and now he wasn't sure there was anything. Sweat ran down his face despite the cold. He closed his eyes and took deep breaths and tried to clear the image of the snakes from his mind.

Doesn't matter if the place is crawling with snakes. If it is, they already know you're here, and they'll come for you if they want. Moving will make you more threatening, scare them off.

Sure. The mental commandments were easy to make, harder to obey.

Go forward, damn it. Go!

He began to crawl again, faster now, ignoring the pain

in his knees, and the amount of distance he'd covered from his starting position was encouraging, seemed to suggest this passage led somewhere.

When his right hand reached forward and didn't make contact with rock, he wasn't immediately scared. There had been small dips and drops here and there, and he assumed this was just another one, worthy of added caution but not cause for true alarm. Then he reached farther and still found nothing. He moved his left hand forward, and his left hand didn't come down on stone either. He was sitting on his knees, waving his hands in the air like a mime in a box. Where in the hell did the passage go? What was he missing? He reached down, trying to find out how far the floor dipped, and his hands kept extending through air. He was leaning so far forward that his balance was precarious, and the pressure caused a fresh ache in his knees. He swore, edged backward, stretched out flat on his stomach, then reached again, determined to figure out which way the floor was curling away from him.

His hands found nothing. He reached until sharp rock bit into his armpits, and he still couldn't find the floor. The drop ahead was a decent height. He fumbled around until he found a loose stone and then he pushed it over the edge, hoping he'd hear an immediate smack of contact that would tell him it was just a short step down.

Instead, he had enough time to be aware of the sound of his own breath—several breaths—before the rock landed with a crack on the floor below and broke into pieces.

Only then did he understand what was directly in front of him: a cliff.

16

Ridley had been in his workshop all day, never once venturing outdoors, but he looked snow covered nevertheless, his shirt and hair coated with fine flakes of sawdust, when the sheriff's car pulled into the yard. He knew just from the height of the driver that it was the sheriff himself. It had been a long time since Ridley had dealt with Blankenship.

He went to the door, opened it, and said, "Everything okay, Sheriff?," working hard on his I'm-just-another-good-citizen voice. He needed more practice with that one. Never sounded right, not even to his ear.

Blankenship looked him up and down without saying a word, and then he reached out and brushed Ridley's shoulder with the palm of his hand, making a show of dusting him off. Ridley kept his hand tight around the doorknob, knowing the sheriff had touched him just to rattle him. Ridley was sensitive about personal space, something that Blankenship had learned during their interviews. Maybe the only thing he had learned.

"Been woodcutting?"

"Damn, you must be some sort of detective."

"One of those boards bite you back?"

"What's that?"

"Your face looks a little busted up."

"Caving," Ridley said. "Rough hobby."

"Must be. I've seen men lose fights and come out looking better than that."

"Those men probably should stay aboveground."

"I've always figured we all should, for as long as we can. You got an idea what brings me to your door?"

"I asked Novak to town," Ridley said, "but I didn't put on a wig and a dress and tell him I was Sarah Martin's mother. So you don't need to linger. If anyone has a right to press charges, it's me, and I'm not doing that. Storm like this, I imagine people need you on the roads, not wasting your time with me. Go help the innocent."

"What would you be pressing charges for?"

"Like I said, I'm not."

"But you think you could be." Blankenship studied Ridley's face. "Did you not get along with the fellow from Florida, Ridley?"

Ridley didn't answer.

"Oh boy, we are already there, huh?" Blankenship said. "I ask a question, and you stare at me like you're a mental defective, and we go round and round."

A trace of a smile slipped onto Ridley's face then. He controlled it, but not before Blankenship saw it and lights of anger went on in his eyes.

"Entertaining shit to you, is it, old boy? Glad to know that it pleases you. Not a lot of happy people working down in that cave right now, so I'm glad you're pleased."

Ridley lost the smile. "Working in what cave?"

Blankenship didn't respond.

"What in the hell are you talking about, working in a cave?" Ridley hated the interest in his own voice, the need, but he couldn't help it.

Blankenship was silent, watching him.

"All right, I get it," Ridley said. "You want to play my game while you've got the chance. Enjoy it, Sheriff. I don't need to let the heat out." He started to push the door shut, but Blankenship got his foot wedged in.

"Cecil Buckner found Mark Novak's clothes inside the entrance of Trapdoor. You don't know anything about that, I'm sure."

Ridley opened the door and stared Blankenship full in the eyes.

"Who let him into Trapdoor? Cecil?"

Blankenship shook his head. "Cecil didn't so much as crack that door once he saw the clothes. He waited for a deputy."

"Then how in the hell did Novak get inside?"

"Someone spent time and muscle working on that gate with a crowbar." Blankenship gave him an appraising look. "You're pretty handy, aren't you? Good with tools, stronger than you look."

"Nice line, Sheriff. But what you should have said was that I understand leverage. You've experienced that, haven't you?"

"Go to hell," Blankenship said. "I've no more interest in verbal games with you than I ever had. I want to see some cave maps. Immediately."

"Why?"

"Because nobody can find the son of a bitch, and you're the one who knows that cave."

Novak was off the maps. Interesting. Trapdoor was up to something. Trapdoor had come alive again. Ridley shouldn't have been surprised by this, but he surely needed to respect it. Trapdoor had responded to Novak. Ridley had hoped for as much, but he'd thought it would be a long process. He hadn't anticipated that the cave would show her power so swiftly to an outsider. Still, it had been quite some time since she'd had visitors. Maybe she'd gotten lonely.

"He was just supposed to sit there and think," Ridley said.

Blankenship's eyes hardened. "You *knew* Novak was headed into the cave?"

"I'm the one who told him to go. I didn't expect he'd make such an effort, frankly. But he seems resourceful. She's *more* resourceful, though. He probably didn't count on that."

"She?"

Ridley ignored that and said, "You're going to need me in there."

"I don't think that idea will be real popular."

"If you think he's actually in there, you're going to need me."

"To do what?"

"Find him. Let me guess, you've called Anmar Mirza already, haven't you?"

"He's on his way from Bloomington."

"Sure he is. And he's good. But he doesn't know that cave like I do, and he'd be the first to admit it."

"I don't need Mr. Mirza's opinion of you, Ridley. And I'm not about to grant you access to Trapdoor. What we're going to do is talk about Mark Novak."

"Not enough time for that."

"No?" Blankenship tilted his head back. "Funny observation. You seem to know he's at risk."

"If the man's naked and in Trapdoor, he's at risk."

"Naked?" Blankenship echoed in that stupid cop voice that suggested he thought he'd caught Ridley in a slip because he was some sort of master interrogator.

"You were the one who said they found his clothes, Sheriff."

"Could have been his jacket. Could have been his belt. I don't recall any specificity."

"Well, *was* it?"

"I'd have to check my notes."

"You're doing the same thing you did last time. You're asking the wrong questions of the wrong people, killing time above the surface while somebody does real killing down below."

"Who did that killing down below?"

Ridley didn't answer.

"Right," Blankenship said. "That shuts your mouth pretty fast every time, doesn't it? Well, we don't need to worry about what happened in the past—"

"The past is the reason he's here. It's the reason he's in that cave. You might not want to admit it, but your past is now your present. Any other notion is wrong. And you can't *afford* to be wrong, Sheriff. Not again. You think about that. You think about what happens if you pull another body out of there."

For an instant, Ridley thought that Blankenship might hit him. All he did, though, was say "*You* pulled the body out" through clenched teeth.

"I sure did. Maybe I wouldn't have had to if you'd gotten me down there earlier. So now I'll make you an offer. I'll go into that cave, but this time it'll be different. This time, I'll make a concession. I'll keep you right by my side."

Blankenship stood silently in the snow, and his silence made Ridley's pulse race. The sheriff was considering it. He was actually considering it, which meant only one thing: he wanted to track every move Ridley made in the cave in the hope that it would tell him things about the past, because the sheriff had never gotten over the lack of answers to what had happened in Trapdoor ten years earlier. And that meant only one thing to Ridley: a chance to go back into the cave. If he played this right, he was going to get to see her again.

"Scared to go down there with me?" Ridley said. "Scared of being alone in the dark with me, Sheriff?"

"You're a sick son of a bitch."

"That isn't a fresh verdict."

"You're not going back into Trapdoor. We saw how that turned out last time."

"We sure as hell did. You let the girl die," Ridley said, and Blankenship swung on him then, hit him with an open palm but a damned big open palm; it knocked him back a step and brought blood to his lips. Ridley touched his mouth with his hand, looked at the blood, and shook his head.

"I am growing tired of getting hit today."

"You're going to—"

"Have some fun with a police-brutality charge, if I want to. But I don't. What I *want* to do is what you *need* to do: pull that Florida boy out of Trapdoor while he still has a pulse. I've already said I'll keep you or any of your deputies at my side. The choice is yours, Sheriff. Remember that you had the chance to make it. Remember how things might have gone if you'd made a different choice ten years ago."

"There's a special hell for you," Blankenship said. His voice was choked. "There just has to be."

"We'll find out one of these days," Ridley said, but in truth he'd already found out. "Back to your choice, Sheriff. Time's wasting. Decisions need to be made, and you're the man who has to make them. The good people of Garrison County have voted on that. Make your choice."

"I don't need you, Barnes. I just need the maps."

Ridley smiled and tapped his temple with his index finger. "I've got them archived."

Blankenship's jaw worked and he turned away from

Ridley so he wasn't facing him when he said, "Get your damn gear, then. Let's you and me go for a ride. I'll be curious to see how being back in that place works on you, Ridley. Might just sharpen a few of those memories you claim to have lost."

Ridley managed to smirk at that, but he, too, was wondering how being back in that place might work on him. He'd suggested going in with the sheriff because he knew it was the only chance he had of getting in. Inside Trapdoor, though, back there in the dark, the sheriff might end up regretting being at Ridley's side. Depending on how the cave worked on Ridley, that might wind up being a very poor decision indeed.

17

Mark's technical understanding of hypothermia came from diving courses, but his visceral understanding of it came from memory, of carrying his mother over his shoulder, trying to rub warmth into unresponsive flesh. It was on that long walk that he'd sworn he would never return to the Rockies, that when he died, it wouldn't be in the cold.

Now here he sat, half naked and shivering, remnants of an unknown drug from an unknown needle in his bloodstream. He'd become his mother.

You can't run away from your family, she had told him when he'd left for the bus station, and maybe she had been right.

Then again, she'd survived the cold that day.

He started to laugh and when the echo returned it to him, the laugh sounded deranged. Sounded, in fact, like his mother's.

"Get it together," he whispered. "Keep your head."

He thought that he should have reached the place he'd started from by now; he had been crawling away from the cliff for a long time, longer than it had taken him to reach it. Or maybe not. Time and distance were hard to judge in the blackness.

Getting cold. You are getting too cold.

The cave wasn't frigid, it wasn't the sort of alarming cold of the snowstorm above, but it could be just as deadly. Your core temperature came down slowly but steadily. You had to be aware of all the ways you might lose heat. Down here with no supplies and no clothes, Mark couldn't fight many of them. Something as simple as keeping his skin from making contact with the stone was impossible. The only way to stay warm was to keep moving, and there was some danger in that as well. The more he moved, the more likely he was to sweat and breathe hard, which cost him heat, and the more he moved, the more glucose he sapped from his bloodstream. He needed the glucose, his essential fuel. All of this he had written in notebooks when he was studying for a diving-instructor certification, a course that he'd never finished. After Lauren was killed, he'd never gone back into the water.

He felt as if he were crawling against a breeze, and that confused him for longer than it should have. Of course there would be a breeze. Air didn't just sit because it was underground. It still moved.

His thought process seemed clogged, mud in the gears, and he tried to blame whatever drug lingered in his system, but the more frightening possibility had nothing to do with that. Mental difficulties went hand in hand with physical difficulties in hypothermia. Simple thinking became complex.

He searched for a word that should have been easy to find, the one that explained what that cold cave air was doing to him, a word he'd written in one of those notebooks. He had crawled for quite a while before he came up with the word: *convection*. You lost heat via convection when air circulated. You lost heat via conduction when you came in contact with cold surfaces. You lost heat via radiation when you didn't have sufficient clothing; you lost heat via evaporation when you sweat; and you lost heat via respiration when you breathed. Those were all the ways you could find yourself in a hypothermic state. Any one of them could kill you, and Mark was experiencing *every* one of them.

Stop thinking about all the ways it's bad. Just concentrate on going forward. On doing the one thing you can do to help yourself. There's nothing left of you now but the essential. The only resources you have are your mind and body. Don't waste them.

It was hard to follow his own commands. Whatever confidence and concentration he might have been able to muster in other circumstances was drained by the darkness. It was one thing to summon the hope of salvation when you were crawling down a mountain or swimming away from a sinking ship; it was another to call it up when you were trying to escape blackness by moving into more blackness.

There's a reason they bury people underground, he thought. *It's the place where they come to an end. And you're there now.*

So was Lauren. He thought of her casket being lowered into the earth, put into the blackness and sealed away. He was down there with her now. And with Sarah Martin. How sad it was that they'd put her back underground when her last moments had surely involved a desperate hope to return to the surface. In the end, they'd just sent her remains down to the very world she'd died trying to escape. How terrible.

Maybe not; maybe she was cremated and her ashes scattered somewhere high. You don't know. She could be aboveground. You should find out, if you ever have a chance.

Strange thoughts, dark thoughts. Everything here was dark, though. There was no choice about that. He thought maybe his hands weren't working as well as they had been earlier. Opening and closing a little slower.

Hands are just tired. That's all.

Everything was coming at him in a swirl; a thought would be there and then something would spiral in and replace it and later the original thought would shoot back. He tried to do some simple math, addition and subtraction. Exercise the brain, keep it focused. No, wait, exercising it might be bad. Hadn't he read somewhere that mental willpower drained glucose faster than physical exertion? That didn't seem possible, but he thought it was what he'd read. They'd done a test, something involving weight lifting and problem solving. He was almost sure of it. So what should he think about? What took the least amount of will?

Quitting.

Sure. But it was cold on the stone, and he was warmer moving. When moving stopped being appealing or when he could no longer feel a difference, that was when he would know...

He stopped crawling and cocked his head. Something had changed. There were more sounds here.

He tried to quiet his breathing—it was more panting than breathing—and get a bearing on where the sound was coming from. No longer did he fear snakes. Any sound seemed friendly. It meant there was something else down here in the dark, meant that he wasn't entirely alone. By now, this was only a good thing.

To the right.

Dripping and splashing. There was moving water somewhere ahead. And at some point, it had come from the surface.

He found the source in another twenty feet, a shallow creek, just a few inches deep, but enough. He cupped his palms and lifted the water to his lips and drank greedily. It was muddy and tasted of the earth, and fine bits of grit coated his tongue and his teeth, but it was also delicious.

He drank enough to slake the thirst and then forced himself to stop, not wanting to push it and not sure if he'd even be able to hold it down. For a brief time he felt nauseated, but that passed and he moved along the underground stream just far enough to determine that it was going uphill.

The only thing he could possibly do to make himself colder, to accelerate his course toward hypothermia and death, would be to slip into water. His core temperature would begin to plummet then, and he had no means of raising it.

He just wasn't sure that he had any other choice. Staying dry was the thing to do if you believed that rescue might be on the way. Mark did not. So far as he knew, he'd been left in this place to die. Getting out was up to him. And while getting wet would hasten the onset of hypothermia, he knew he didn't have much time on that front anyhow. The difficulty in concentrating and the loss of his fine motor skills had already arrived, but what concerned Mark more was not the symptoms he was noticing but the one he'd stopped noticing: shivering. At first blush, this might seem like a good thing, an adaptation to the temperature. That was a cruel prank of biology, though. The body never really *adapted* to a change in temperature. His body was reacting to the temperature, but reacting was very different than adapting. While shivering was an unpleasant sensation, it generated heat.

He attempted to check his pulse, but he had trouble feeling the beats because of numb fingertips. As he ran his hands over his body, trying to warm himself, he was aware of how muscular he felt. His chest and abdominal muscles and triceps were taut the way they might be after a good weightlifting session. This was the worst sign yet. An increase in muscle tone meant he was well down the road to hypothermia. In severe cases, the muscles actually began to mimic rigor mortis, the body dying around you even while you still drew breath.

"Got to stay moving," he said, and his speech was slurred. Getting wet and getting colder might speed things along, but he didn't have enough time left to worry about wasting it.

He crawled into the stream going against the current. There wasn't much force to it here, but the water sounded louder ahead, and that might be a problem.

He had nothing but problems, though. Might as well add another. He put his head down and crawled, and time and distance faded from him, and for a long while there was nothing but the cold. He splashed on, and the pitch of the slope became much steeper, turning his crawl into a climb. It took an enormous effort—several times he fell and slid back down, banging painfully against the rocks—but he wasn't certain how much distance he'd gained for all the work.

He stopped crawling twice, when he became convinced that he was not alone. That someone was moving with him, splashing along right at his side. The most alarming thing was that in those stretches, he believed he could also see this other person. A white figure in the blackness, shapeless and featureless. When he stopped and stared, though, there was nothing but the darkness and the feeling of the water and the cold.

Better hurry, Markus. Once the mind goes, you're done.

He almost laughed at that. He didn't feel as if his mind had been his own for a long time.

A light broke in the darkness then. A glimmer of white, and he thought, *That is the snow. That is the surface.*

Then the light went away. He blinked and stared, squinted. Closed his eyes and counted to five—he thought it was five, but he seemed to get lost on the way there—and then opened them again.

Nothing. No snow, no surface. For a moment, though, he'd been so sure.

He pushed on, wishing that he hadn't imagined the light. Wishing that it might return for him. He thought of the girl—*What was her name?*—who had died down here. Had she seen a light at the end? If so, depending on the source, it might have scared her. That seemed terrible, to be scared by a light. It was unnatural. Light was supposed to help you in the dark, it was supposed to guide you and protect you. How wrong, if she'd died fearing a light and hoping for blackness.

What was her damn name? He couldn't forget that. It was the reason he was here.

Sarah.

He wondered who'd said that. Where the voice had come from. It didn't matter, though—the voice, which came through the darkness in a whisper, was correct. Her name had been Sarah. He said it aloud to make sure that it felt right.

"Sarah."

His voice wasn't right but the name was. He couldn't believe he'd forgotten it. He couldn't allow that to happen again. Keep saying it, then. Keep on repeating it, and that way he couldn't forget it.

"Sarah," he slurred. "Sarah, Sarah, Sarah."

The cave walls returned the name to him each time— *Sarah, Sarah, Sarah.* He thought it was an echo but maybe not. Maybe it was whoever was down here with him; maybe whoever had told him her name to begin with was saying it too. He tried to determine whether that mattered and couldn't reach a conclusion. A rock caught his shin, hard, and this confused him. He stopped walking and looked down and, of course, could not see the offender.

When had he begun to walk? He'd been crawling for so

long because crawling was safer. He considered that and then he got it: He couldn't crawl here because the water was too high. He should have remembered that. Like the name. He should have remembered...

He felt a wild surge of panic, because she'd escaped his mind again. Damn, but she was crafty. She could slip right past you. He'd had her, though. He'd just had her, and he could get her back. It was...

"Sarah."

Yes. Keep saying it. Keep walking.

He moved on, or thought he moved on, using her name as fuel.

Splash. "Sarah." *Splash.* "Sarah."

The cave whispered it back to him every time, and he was grateful for that. The cave wasn't going to let him forget again. He'd remember her.

18

Ridley had expected to make a stir with his arrival and was almost looking forward to watching Blankenship have to deal with that, but when the two of them got out of the car and began to move through the snow toward the cave, Ridley wearing his helmet and carrying his backpack and a loose coil of rope, there was already a stir going on.

"We can hear him!" a uniformed officer shouted, rushing up, slipping in the snow. "Sheriff, we can hear him! But we can't figure out how to get to him."

"Let me in," Ridley said, shoving past him. "If you can hear him, then I can find him."

"That's the thing," the deputy said, following behind. "It's like his voice is coming up from under the rocks. It's creepy, to tell you the truth."

Ridley made for the cave, Blankenship struggling to keep up. A few heads turned toward them and someone said, "What in the hell is he doing here?" but Ridley ignored that and passed them and entered Trapdoor Caverns for the first time in a decade.

He stood on the wide shelf of stone where steps had been carved so visitors could get down to the tour boats. The passage beyond was filled with people and voices. It was bright and loud and crowded. It was everything a cave should not be.

Two people rounded the corner and headed to the entrance, fighting through the tangle of bodies. One was a deputy whom Ridley remembered well; the other was a woman who was clearly part of the cave rescue team, dressed just like Ridley. At the sight of him, they both stopped short. The woman—*Rachel? Robin?* He couldn't remember—said, "You sick bastard."

He remembered her then. Rachel. She'd been on the outside preparing to go back in when Ridley arrived with Sarah Martin's body. She'd fallen to her knees at the sight of Sarah Martin and cried as if the girl were her own daughter.

Ridley hadn't said anything to her back then, and he didn't now. The deputy moved up to Ridley with his chest puffed and was in the midst of telling him that he had better get the hell out of here or he'd be going to jail when he spotted Blankenship.

"Sheriff? You want me to get this guy into the back of a car? He's trespassing, bare minimum, and interfering with police business."

He was right in Ridley's face now, wanting a fight, pressing as close as he could, one of those idiots who spent hours building up their pec muscles, as if you won fights by bumping chests. Ridley thought about kissing him, tried to imagine what the reaction to *that* would be. The image made him smile, and at the sight of that smile, the deputy actually reached out and grabbed the straps of his backpack, like a school-yard bully.

"Step back, Dawson, damn it, step back," Blankenship said. "He's here because I want him here. Now get the hell out of my way."

"You've got to be kidding me. You *want* him—"

"Did I stutter? You want an explanation, you can come to

my office once this scene has been handled. Until then, get out of my way."

Ridley turned and looked up at the sheriff's flushed face and said, "Thanks, Danny."

"Just keep walking."

They moved past the deputy and up to the woman, who was mud-covered and sweating. She regarded Ridley with revulsion and kept her eyes on him even when the sheriff asked her quietly, "Can you take me to the spot where they're hearing his voice?"

"Yeah. It's not far." She finally broke eye contact with Ridley, turned, and started back along the passage. They followed and curled away from the bright lights of the entrance chamber, and minimal darkness encroached, allowing Ridley to breathe easier. After spending so many hours practicing, he felt as if he should be able to stay in control, but he hadn't been practicing in Trapdoor. This cave was different. This cave was so very different.

Finally they reached full dark, and Ridley clicked on his headlamp but dimmed it down until it was only bright enough to show his boots. The sheriff had a bulky Maglite that was exactly what you didn't want in a cave, always occupying a hand and always requiring you to aim the light instead of having the light follow the turn of your head. Ridley had given him a helmet but hadn't outfitted it with a light because the sheriff insisted on taking the big flashlight.

They wound through the cave alongside the water for a time and then they parted from it and entered the Chapel Room. Its benchlike slabs of fallen stone resembled church pews, and a tall formation stood in the center like an altar. The woman said, "They're in the Funnel Room," and knelt in front of a crawling passage that led out of the Chapel Room.

Ridley said, "You'll need to be on your belly for a bit, Sheriff."

Blankenship didn't answer, but his breathing changed. The entrance to the crawl was about the size of a garbage-can lid, and everything beyond it was blackness. It looked spacious enough to a caver, but to the inexperienced, it might look terrifying. Ridley didn't glance back at the sheriff to see his face, just dropped to his knees and said, "Let's go."

"Her first," Blankenship said. "You stay with me."

"Going to have to go single file in there, Sheriff. Not a lot of room."

"You just let her lead the way, and you stay back with me."

Ridley shrugged, ignored another withering glance from Rachel, and waited as she dropped to her hands and knees. She was a bigger girl, wide-shouldered, and she had to wriggle a bit to slip through. Ridley could almost feel Blankenship tighten up, watching. Blankenship was a large man. Not fat, but tall and broad.

Ridley gave her a five-count to get moving so he wouldn't be nipping at her heels, and then he slid into the tunnel, feeling more at home once the walls closed in and there was stone all around. Some said that Ridley's unique abilities in cave exploration were a product of recklessness, of taking risks that others wouldn't, wedging his body into any crack in the rock without hesitation just in case it might lead somewhere, but that wasn't so. Ridley just read caves better than most. Listened to caves better than most. They told you things, if you wanted to hear. Funny, considering that caves had been used for silencing things so often in human history. As places for hideouts, secret meetings, buried treasure, buried bodies.

He listened for Blankenship, but the only thing he could hear was the scrabbling of boots and hands on stone. The sheriff was scared, which was natural enough, but he was also holding his breath.

"Sheriff? You're going to want to take some deep breaths."

"I'm fine." The words shook.

"I know you are. But you also probably haven't been in a space this tight before, and you probably feel like you could use up your air if you breathe too deeply, am I right? A sense that there's a finite amount of oxygen in here, and we are going to use it all up?"

"Just move," the sheriff barked. "I'm fine."

But Ridley could hear him breathing now, deep inhalations. One of the best ways to rush toward panic was to hold your breath and worry about your air. It was a common mistake of first-timers in tunnels; they assumed that because they couldn't see wide-open spaces, the air supply must be limited.

When the sheriff stopped moving, Ridley stopped too and said, "Rachel, hold up."

He could tell by the way she stiffened that she didn't like hearing him use her name. Probably didn't like that he even *knew* her name.

"Sheriff? You okay?"

Blankenship's breathing had changed again, gone faster. It took a few seconds before he responded, and when he did, his voice was soft and unsteady.

"I'm getting squeezed," he said. "It's getting too tight for me."

"No, it's not," Ridley said. The sheriff ignored him and began to slither backward. Ridley spoke more firmly. *"Stop moving."*

The sheriff listened. Silence again, except for those uneasy breaths. Edging toward hyperventilating, but not all the way there yet.

"Now, I can't turn around to get my light on you, so you're going to have to use your own," Ridley said. His voice was measured and calm, a bedside manner. "I want you to do as I say, and to concentrate. Give me five seconds of focus. You going to do that?"

"Yes." The word was a whisper full of self-loathing. The sheriff hated that he was showing fear, and he hated even more that he was showing it to Ridley.

"All right. Look to your right side."

The beam of the sheriff's flashlight bobbed around, casting shadows. He was doing as instructed, at least.

"Good," Ridley said. "Now turn it to the left."

The light bobbed again. Here the walls on each side were nearly touching Ridley's shoulders, and the sheriff had broader shoulders than he did. So did Rachel, for that matter. One of Ridley's greatest assets in a cave was his size.

"Those walls," Ridley said, "haven't done anything in hundreds of years. They're not going anywhere. They're solid. Now lift your head up."

"I can't. Too tight."

"I didn't say *sit* up. I told you to lift your head. Just lift until you can feel the stone."

There was a pause and then a *clink* of plastic against stone as the helmet found the roof.

"Okay. It's right there on top of me."

"Sure it is. But you had to move to touch it, didn't you?"

"Yeah." Already the sheriff's breathing was steadier. The simple act of following instructions kept him from feeling alone, and that made a dramatic difference.

"Then you know it's not actually squeezing you," Ridley said. "You can move. But the direction we need to move is forward. You ready?"

"Yeah."

Ridley reached out and tapped Rachel on the back of the leg. He felt the muscle go taut. "Let's go," he said.

"Don't touch me. Don't you *ever* touch me."

"Let's go," he repeated.

She began crawling again, moving faster, and that was just fine. Speed would help the sheriff, because he would imagine he was getting closer to an open space instead of deeper into the tunnel. Ridley would have preferred to take his time and let Trapdoor talk to him, but the circumstances weren't right. He wasn't communing with the cave now; he was just passing through.

When Rachel entered the chamber and stood, Ridley said, "Made it, Sheriff. You might need to duckwalk in here, tall guy like yourself, but you'll be all right."

"Duckwalk?"

"Just watch me." Ridley rose to half standing, upright but bent at the waist, knees flexed. "You ever play baseball, Sheriff?"

"Yeah."

"Think of yourself as a shortstop going after a ground ball. You're moving laterally, you're bent over, but you're still fluid, still loose. Pretend you're closing on second base, but you've got to keep your eye on the plate, right? That's where the ball is coming from."

"I played third."

"Pretend you were a little more athletic, then."

The sheriff scrambled awkwardly to his feet and imitated Ridley's posture as best he could.

Rachel said, "Let's go. It's not a tour."

"You think it would be faster if he'd frozen up back there in the crawl?"

"I'm not freezing up," Blankenship said. "Let's move."

"Good man." Ridley followed as soon as Rachel went

into motion, moving in a side step, watching the sheriff's footwork. Blankenship crossed his feet over now and then but he did all right. Being as tall as he was, he was going to have one hell of a stiff back by morning.

They were almost through the chamber and closing in on the next passageway when Blankenship said, "I can hear him!"

"No, you can't," Ridley said. He'd been listening to the voices for a while. "Those are the people who are trying to find him."

They curled through the passageway and came out on the other side in a room larger than any they'd seen since the entrance chamber. This was the Funnel Room, so named because it was shaped like an upside-down volcano. In the center was a nearly perfect funnel formation, thirty feet in diameter at the top and about three feet at the bottom. There were six people in the room, five men and one woman; two of the men were down in the bottom of the funnel, clipped to ropes. You could make it up and down the funnel without the use of ropes and ascenders, but the rescue teams took their safety protocols seriously. They'd seen what happened to those who did not.

One of the men up on the ledge looked at Ridley when he entered and said, "You've got to be kidding me."

"That line has already been used tonight," Ridley said. "Hope somebody comes up with new material." He didn't look any of them in the eye, but that wasn't because he felt intimidated—looking these folks in the eyes required staring into the beams from their headlamps. He crouched on the ledge and watched the men in the bottom of the funnel. One was Cecil Buckner; the other was Anmar Mirza, the cave rescue coordinator.

"He's down there?" the sheriff asked.

"That's where you can hear his voice," Rachel said. "At first we weren't sure it *was* a voice. Pretty weak."

"Is he responding to you? Can you communicate?"

"He seems to be talking to himself."

Down in the funnel, Cecil said, "Quiet! Listen!"

Everyone fell silent and looked toward the base of the funnel, casting their beams downward. For a time there was no sound, but then it came, faint but clear, a drawn-out call.

"Saaaarraaah."

The sound whispered out of the funnel and echoed through it, the name clear as a bell.

Silence lingered until the sheriff broke it with a soft question. "Who's he talking to?"

"We're not sure," Cecil answered. "He's stuck on that name, though. It's all we can hear." He pushed back from the wall on his toes, letting the rope take his weight, and wiped sweat from his face. "To tell you the truth, it's kind of freaking us out. Those of us who were...you know, in here before. Back then."

They all looked at Ridley. It was impossible not to realize that; their headlamps followed their eyes. In the cave, there was no such thing as a surreptitious stare, because light couldn't lie. Ridley felt as if he should say something, felt as if he should be defensive and angry or dismissive and wiseass or any combination thereof as long as he was *something.* But he couldn't come up with a response. When the voice came again—*Saaarrraaah*—gooseflesh broke out across his arms, and his spine prickled with a fear he'd thought he would never know again.

I'll be curious to see how being back in that place works on you, the sheriff had said. The way it worked on Ridley was supposed to be private, though. Internal. If the cave called her name, Ridley should have been the only one who could hear it.

He looked around the group then with an urgent need

to make sure that they *were* hearing it. Because down here, your mind could warp a little. Down here, real things could become false, and imagined horrors could leave bruises.

Nothing was imagined about this, though. They all seemed to be hearing it. If he was imagining—

"Saaarrraaaah..."

—this, then he was as good as done. What happened next could be very, very bad. Could be the end of him. He knew that better than any of these suspicious sons of bitches. He'd lived it.

His heart was racing, and all those beams were lancing at him from different directions like searchlights, and he closed his eyes against them despite himself.

"Saaarrraaaahh."

"You think you can get to him?" the sheriff asked Anmar after the last echo of that hair-raising whisper was gone. "Do you need blasting equipment, something to get through the rock?"

Ridley kept his eyes closed, but he was glad the sheriff was talking, providing a moment of distraction. Ridley concentrated on his breathing, trying to get steady. It wasn't easy. He was waiting on that whisper again, although it wasn't a real whisper, more of a weak howl. A cry from someone who wanted to sound strong but was too close to dead to achieve anything near that.

He heard it again, weaker still: *"Saaarrrraaaah."*

Everyone went silent when it came, the way you did when the minister spoke in church. Even if you knew the message, you had to listen to it respectfully.

"Can you get to him?" the sheriff asked again.

"I don't know," Anmar Mirza said. "We've got to find him first. It sounds as if he's just a shelf below us, but how he got there...I have no idea."

"Could we drill it?"

"We go up," Ridley said. He opened his eyes, and though he shielded them with his hands, like a golfer reading the green before a putt, he wasn't bothered by the harsh beams from his audience this time.

"What?"

"There's nothing down there but solid stone floor. You could drill all night and not make any progress. So we go up."

"I don't follow you, Ridley." This was from Cecil Buckner, and he was the only person who'd spoken Ridley's name. The only one who didn't have pure contempt in his voice. Regardless of what he thought of the past, he understood this about the present: Ridley could help. Ridley had drawn the maps.

"Shelves," Ridley said. "The cave is built in shelves." He made a stacking gesture with one hand. "But they're not laid properly. It's like an old fieldstone wall—uneven, overlapping. What can always find its way down through one of those walls?"

"Water," the sheriff said.

Ridley nodded. "So we turn into water. To find him, we become water. He's below us, but we can't get there from here. We're sitting in a little catch basin. This is where water gets trapped. So we go up and we go sideways until we get off this shelf. You follow now?"

Several headlamps turned upward, putting a gloss of light across the ceiling.

"There's no passage up there."

"You didn't draw the maps, Cecil."

"And I didn't get to *see* them either. But there's no passage up there."

"There's a crawler. A chute that will take us to the shelf below this one. Down toward his voice."

"Has anybody ever been through it?"

"Only one," Ridley said. "And it's tight."

"Can you make it again?"

"Yes." Ridley slipped his backpack off his shoulders and unzipped it.

"I'll stay with him," Blankenship said, but the unease in his voice was obvious.

"We need an experienced caver with him," Anmar said. "With all due respect, you're not right for the job. I'll do it. I'll make sure that whatever happens in here today, there are eyes on him."

Ridley ignored them both, removed a drill powered by lithium ion batteries from his pack, then opened another compartment and grabbed a handful of expansion bolts.

"What are you doing with that?" the sheriff asked.

"Building us a ladder," Ridley said. "And we need to do it fast. It's wet down where he is, and it's cold. Time isn't on his side."

As if to confirm this, the whisper came again, softer than ever: *"Saaarraahh."*

19

Mark met Sarah Martin in the water.

She came to him only after he quit fighting ahead, when he finally stopped moving and let the current take him.

There wasn't much current to speak of, because he'd made it back to water that was only up to his waist. Wading through waist-deep water was chore enough for a strong man, though, and Mark had stopped being strong long before, and he'd stopped being a man somewhere along the streambed, someplace where the water ran high and every now and then he'd stepped into a hole and was completely submerged, choking, close to drowning.

It was her name that brought him back to the surface on those occasions. The repetition of her name had felt critical to his memory once, but after a while, it became equally critical to his forward motion. He'd fallen into an unconscious cadence, saying her name with each step, and eventually he began to feel as if he could not do one without the other. Name, step. Name, step. He felt as if he had to say the dead girl's name in order to move forward, had to remember it. The past drove the present, always.

The next time he forgot her name, he froze. Her name had been right there on his tongue, he'd said it at least a thousand times in a row. But then...

What was her name?

He stumbled on the rocks, and the water pushed at his legs, and then he gave up because he could no longer remember, and once you forgot the past, there was no point in pushing to the future. The two were intertwined. He understood that now in a different way than he had before.

And so he knew it was time to quit.

The water caught his weight and carried him away from this hopeless place and back to the one where he could have made different decisions, chosen different paths. He let himself drift, and for a long, beautiful moment, he believed that was how it would feel forever—an endless slow drift through the blackness, going backward, always back, and that was good because it was where everything he wanted waited for him.

When he hit rock with his shoulder, the beautiful dark path was gone, and pain replaced it. The impact was so jarring and painful that it temporarily cleared his mind and he was aware of the water, the stone walls, and the blackness again.

He was not aware of the cold. In fact, he realized that he'd reached hot water. A hot spring, perhaps? It had to be. What began as a creeping warmth quickly became scorching, and he blamed the water and tried to escape it. There was a flat shelf of rock above him, and though it was not even chest high, it felt like it would be an impossible climb. On the fifth try, he finally made it, pulling his body out of the searing heat of the water.

The heat didn't leave him, though. It lingered, and the misery was terrible. He felt as if he were trapped inside a fire, one that would not burn over him and move on but was here to stay. He tried to brush the heat away from him, but his hands didn't obey his commands anymore. He thought that he was still too close to the water, and the farther from it he got, the deeper into the stone, the better. He slid and scooted and scraped along the shelf until he made contact with a wall, and there he stopped, and that was when he saw her.

She was sitting on a flat rock just across from him. There was an impossible brightness to her, as if light came from her pores. She wore jeans and a T-shirt and running shoes, and she sat with her knees pulled up to her chest, arms wrapped around them, as if to keep warm, which seemed a very strange thing to do down here where it was so damn hot. She didn't seem hot or cold, though, didn't seem bothered by the temperature in the least. Just comfortable. Watching him. Waiting. What was she waiting for? What did she want from him?

To remember.

Yes, that was right. He was required to remember her, to think about her in the dark. That was his instruction. No wonder she'd appeared; no wonder she was waiting on him. Knowing that you'd been forgotten had to be a unique and relentless pain.

"Sarah," he said. She didn't react, which was frustrating, because he knew that was right. That was her name. He thought that she must not have heard him. It had become loud down here, the water going from a trickle to a roar, and not only that, he seemed to be hearing voices from some other place, somewhere up above. Whatever they were saying, it wasn't the right thing, it wasn't pleasing to her, and it probably kept her from hearing him. He called her name again, louder this time, and still she didn't react.

He tried again, and again, and still she just sat there, knees held to her chest, her eyes fastened on him, watching and waiting. Unsatisfied by him but still hoping.

For what? he wanted to scream, but he was terrified of upsetting her. No—of disappointing her. What in the hell did she want from him? If not to be remembered, then *what?*

He leaned his head back against the stone, and though he could no longer see her face, he could still see the light from where she sat in the darkness, watching and waiting and hoping.

20

They'd put in seventeen expansion bolts by the time Ridley reached the ceiling. From the bolts hung seventeen etriers, short stretches of rope ladder. Ridley didn't travel underground with those, but the rescue team had, and he allowed them to be used because it would help others move up when he needed them. Not everyone was as skilled with single-rope techniques as he was, and he knew that when—if—the time came to move Novak down, the ladders would be a help.

He moved upward using a daisy chain attached to his climbing harness—a laborious process but a quick one if you were good. He'd secure a bolt above him, clip the daisy chain in, and use it to pull himself up until the bolt was at waist level. Then he'd reach up and install another bolt. A dynamic rope was tied to his harness, and this ran down to his belay man. If a bolt failed, the belayer would arrest his fall. Ridley understood that they preferred this approach and understood that perhaps it was safer, but he'd worked alone for so long that he didn't trust the idea. If he couldn't stop his fall himself, then let him fall.

He wasn't going to fall, though.

By the time he had the seventeenth bolt in, he was able to get his hands on the lip of rock just below the ceiling.

He hung there and caught his breath and rested for a minute while he searched the shadowed rocks for the right spot. He remembered that it had looked like nothing more than a large crack.

"How long now?" the sheriff asked, and the question put Ridley back into action, reminding him that there was no rest allowed. The sheriff was inquiring with the ground team, those still down in the funnel, as to how much time had passed since they last heard Novak's voice. The whispered calls had ceased when Ridley was on his twelfth bolt.

"Nine minutes," someone in the funnel said.

"Gotta move," another voice responded. "Clock is ticking."

If we're lucky, Ridley thought. *Could be that the clock has stopped, boys and girls.*

He'd been certain that the chute entrance was here, but now he was second-guessing himself, beginning to worry that they'd spent all this time climbing toward the wrong spot on the ceiling. Then his headlamp beam caught it, and he realized why he'd missed it the first time—it was awfully small.

"Entrance located," Ridley called, and he pointed toward it.

The sheriff's voice said, "I don't see it."

Ridley stretched and got his hand hooked into the crevice. "Right here."

One of the rescue-team members said, "No way we're getting through that. No way."

Ridley had to admit that it didn't look encouraging. It was the sort of space that most people wouldn't want to poke their heads into, let alone their bodies.

"I've been through," Ridley said. And then, more for himself than the rest of them, he added, "It opens up a little. Once you get going, it's not so bad at all."

But his mouth was dry and his heart was thundering.

"Give me just a second," he said, and then he closed his eyes and drank in the darkness, imagined he was folding it around himself like a shroud, then smoothing the shroud over each individual nerve ending. It was a burial shroud—the nerves were being put to permanent rest, one at a time, until all that remained within him was darkness and peace. In his mind, the nerves waved like blades of tall grass in the wind until he stilled them with the dark shroud.

"All right," he said. "I'm going in now. Anmar, you give me at least a minute lead time before you follow. If there's trouble getting through, we don't need two people on top of each other in there."

"Got it. I'll follow, but I won't breathe down your neck."

"Hang on," the sheriff said. "I don't want him going first."

There were a few murmurs of agreement. Anmar and Cecil were noticeably silent. Ridley called back and said, "Tell him, guys. Tell him why that is a bad idea."

Cecil's voice was soft and grudging. "It's about speed, Sheriff. He's fast, and he's been through it before, which is the big difference. If we lose speed, we might lose our chance."

The sheriff was still objecting when Ridley pulled his body up and reached into the gap with both arms. When his hands found purchase on the rough rock, he dragged his head into position, happy that there was a good foothold to help with balance, and leaned down so that the headlamp illuminated the interior, which looked like the inside of a stone air duct, and not a big one. The scene wasn't made any more appealing by the way the duct angled steeply down.

"Going in," he called, and then he lowered his head and pushed it forward. The helmet banged against rock immediately, and he twisted, hearing a scraping noise on all sides, and got his helmet through. His shoulders wedged tight. The sensation told him, *Stop, you do not belong in here,* but Ridley ignored the warning and wriggled forward. His feet were free now, kicking in open air above the ninety-foot drop, and he heard the sheriff say, "Good Lord." The belay rope tangled in Ridley's feet, and he wriggled again and got a few inches farther in, sure that he was solid now and would not fall. The rope was bothering him, and though he knew Anmar and the others would insist he keep it, he called, "Off rope," and, with difficulty, found the carabiner and unclipped it. He was untethered now, on his own. His head and torso were jammed into the crack in the stone, but his legs were still outside, and he knew that from down below, he must look like a rabbit being consumed by a snake.

His helmet scraped off the rock again as he used his elbows to pull himself forward. His headlamp had gotten jostled and was angled up a bit, which was a problem because the crawl was angled down. With the light pointed up, most of what lay ahead was dark.

He drove forward using his elbows. His feet left the air and found stone as he slipped all the way into the chute, thinking that it was going to be one hell of a hard thing to get Novak back up through here if he was in bad shape.

Don't do that, he scolded himself. The minute you began to worry about getting back out, panic could rise, claustrophobia could set in. One of the great myths of caving was that regulars couldn't be touched by claustrophobia. That was what the weekend warriors said, maybe, but people who'd spent a lot of time underground had seen others get stuck or had gotten stuck themselves or both. Real cavers understood real consequences.

But you're not going to get stuck. You've made it through here before.

Yes, he had. Ten years ago. And if a single piece of rock had fallen in that decade, he'd be worming himself right into a dead end.

Takes most rocks ten thousand years to fall.

Not all of them.

He paused there, the back-and-forth interior dialogue beginning to get to him, the worries about backing out of the chute into a ninety-foot fall—all of it swirling, threatening. This was where a cave could start to break your mind, and if you were brooding over these things in the dark...

That was what he'd practiced for all of these years, ever since his last descent into Trapdoor: control in the dark. He knew no panic. Not anymore. And no one would ever suffer the consequences of Ridley's panic in the dark again.

He closed his eyes, breathed a few times, and then continued on with his eyes closed. At this pace, you didn't need your eyes anyhow. Hell, at this pace, he could crawl over razor blades and just give himself a nice smooth shave.

Inch, inch, inch. The slope was getting steeper, and he knew that he was angling down behind the wall now.

When his shoulders caught, he wasn't immediately unnerved. He opened his eyes and assessed what little he could—not much to see except the backs of his hands—and tried to shimmy his shoulders around and loosen the grip.

It didn't loosen.

Well, now. Well. He was breathing faster, not all that different from the sheriff back in the entrance crawl, and he wet his lips and sucked in air and reminded himself yet again that he'd done this once before. Back when he hadn't known whether it was open, he'd gotten through. He took as deep a breath as he could manage with the squeeze on his ribs, braced his toes against the floor, and drove forward.

He moved a little. Just enough to wedge his upper body

in even tighter. He was upside down behind the wall now, and he was stuck.

Come on, Ridley, come on!

His face was pressed right against the stone. When he tried to wet his lips, his tongue licked across the rocks and brought the taste of wet earth into his mouth.

There'll be a day when you're too old. When your heart can't take it. There'll be a day…

"This ain't that day," he whispered, his lips brushing the stone. He braced his toes again and drove forward and, finally, earned a bit of relief. The steel bands around his chest loosened just a touch, and after some more scrabbling, he got to the point where he could use his elbows. The point where he could lift his chin off the stone floor. This must have been what he meant when he'd said it opened up a little once you got going.

And there it went, widening enough that he could lift his head and extend his arms. It was amazing just how *free* he felt. A few inches made a world of difference down here.

"Anmar? You good?"

"Working through it. Son of a bitch, this is tight."

"It gets better."

The idea of bringing Novak through here reared up again. He was taller than Ridley, but he wasn't stocky, thank God. Muscled but lean. That was good, because they weren't pulling anybody of girth through this crawl. Trying to get him through that squeeze Ridley had just left behind was going to be hell anyhow. He wasn't sure they could make that with Novak.

The chute bent slightly to the right and widened, and now he could hear water. Soft drips and trickles. The last time— the only time—he'd made it down here, he'd found a chamber filled nearly to the ceiling with water. That had been after a series of strong rains, though, and the water table had been higher than it was tonight. He'd run out of time then, but he'd left the cave and told Pershing MacAlister that he thought he might be on the verge of a breakthrough, a discovery that would take Trapdoor into the ranks of the longest caves in the country. There had been great excitement that evening, sitting on the deck of MacAlister's place and sharing beers and musing about the possibilities. Then the cave turned into a homicide scene, and then Pershing shut it down for good.

Sarah Martin had been there that night. She'd come down with Evan Borders, had sat on his lap and listened to the caving talk, looking impossibly young. That was the last time Ridley saw her alive. He thought. He hoped.

But it wasn't. You know that it wasn't.

It depended on your definition of *see*, he supposed. After the light died, when he'd met her in a blackness that was darker than any night in history, he hadn't seen a thing.

"You good, Barnes?"

Anmar's voice shook him back into the present.

"I'm good," he called. "Almost to the bottom."

The water sounds were louder now, and Ridley could see a yawning gap in the rock just ahead. His headlamp beam reflected off murky water beyond. The chute was tall enough here that he could rise to his knees, and the sensation was a sweet relief. On his hands and knees, he slipped through the gap, looked left, and saw Mark Novak's body on the rocks.

"Novak?" Ridley said. *"Novak!"*

There was no response. The body was motionless, and Novak was naked except for water-soaked underwear. His skin had a faint blue tint against the beam of Ridley's lamp, an almost ethereal glow, like a ghost.

"Shit!" Ridley shouted. The cave threw the word back at him, mocking.

"What's wrong?" Anmar cried from somewhere in the chute.

Ridley cupped his hands around his mouth and shouted, "Get back up there and tell them to have a medevac unit ready. Not an ambulance, a helicopter."

"You can see him? Is there a chance?"

Ridley was about to say no, was about to resign himself to bringing a second corpse out of Trapdoor, when Novak lifted his head to look in the direction of the sound, then raised a hand to block the glare from Ridley's headlamp. Ridley dimmed it immediately.

"You're alive." He said it with true surprise, because he hadn't anticipated that Trapdoor would release Novak once she'd gotten him this far. He'd hoped she might—it would be a shame to lose Novak so early—but he hadn't counted on it. In fact, this was the most fascinating development he had encountered underground in years. Trapdoor had allowed Novak in, and then kept him alive? There was an element of trust there that Ridley hadn't expected. Perhaps the old girl didn't mind the occasional visitor.

And perhaps she didn't appreciate that locked door at the entrance.

Ridley entered the water, which rose swiftly to his knees and then to his waist, and an odd thought passed through his mind: *You've been here before.*

He pivoted away from Novak, who was struggling to get upright, and stared at the water-filled passage ahead. They were off the maps now, at least the maps that everyone else had seen, but Ridley remembered this room, and he remembered the swim he'd made to get here.

He'd lost his first light in this room. Since he adhered to

the rule of three, he hadn't worried over that too much, because he'd been equipped with two backups. At that time, he hadn't understood what Trapdoor thought of light, just how strongly she resisted it. At that time, Ridley Barnes had yet to meet the dark man.

"You came close, Novak," he said. Anmar was struggling down the chute, sweating and gasping, a smashed backpack of first-aid equipment with him. He looked at Ridley and then at Novak, who had managed to get himself into some semblance of a sitting position but was staring at them with uncomprehending eyes.

"I lost her," Novak said. His voice was a dying man's rasp to which Trapdoor refused to even grant an echo. "I almost caught up to her, but then I lost her."

Anmar said, "We're *never* going to get him back up through there. It's too damn tight."

"Don't need to," Ridley said. He brightened the headlamp once more and pointed across the eerie aquamarine waters that carved through the stone and led away from Novak's resting place. "He was nearly out himself. Wouldn't that have been something, if he'd made it out alone? I wouldn't have thought it possible."

Again he wondered why Trapdoor had granted such favors, but Anmar interrupted his thoughts.

"What are you talking about, we don't need to? I thought that chute was the only way down here."

"Of course not. You have something to warm him up and keep him covered? More covered than he is, at least?"

"Yes."

"Get to it, then. We're going through the water, and we're going to need to hurry."

Anmar stared at the place where the water vanished around a bend of rock.

"You think that water passage goes anywhere good?"

"It'll take us right out to the place where they used to end the boat tours. It's a cakewalk for the medics from there."

"How in the hell do you know that?"

"Because I swam it once. The water table was higher then, and it required diving equipment. It's lower now, and we'll be able to find air. There's not a chance in hell we'd get him back up that chute. Time is the ticket, and we can get him out of here in a hurry if we go through the water. It's not far at all, and it's easy going. Trust me."

"How long has it been since someone did that?"

Ridley turned to him, let his glance linger for just a moment, and didn't answer the question.

"Clock's ticking," he said instead. "Let's move."

21

When Mark woke, he was in a bed with metal rails and there was an IV tube in his arm. He felt an incredible thirst and indescribable muscle aches. There was a call button beside him that would summon a nurse, and he considered it but didn't punch it, trying to take stock of his circumstances and recall how, exactly, he had ended up here. Events existed in his memory like scattered snapshots, all out of chronological order and some badly out of focus. The road back from Ridley's house—that was where it had started. A truck behind him, a van up ahead. Men with black masks and black shotguns. A field of windswept snow, and then...

A cave. That memory frightened him more than the others, even though it was among the out-of-focus set. Blackness and cold water. He'd been left there. He'd tried to find his way out of the dark.

And apparently succeeded? The hospital room told him that he had, but the foggy memories offered no confirmation, not even a hint.

He punched the call button then, and the door opened within seconds, and an overweight brunette woman with kind eyes looked at him and said, "My goodness. Let me get the doctor."

She was gone before he could even ask for water.

* * *

The doctor was a short, slender man named Mehir Desare, and as soon as he introduced himself to Mark, he told him that he owed him some thanks.

"If all continues to go well, you're going to get me in some medical journals. We're not supposed to confess that we desire that sort of thing—it's quite self-important and shameful to admit—but the truth is the truth, you know."

Mark nodded, though he wasn't following at all. Dr. Mehir Desare smiled at him over steepled fingers as he sat on a stool beside the bed and said, "Don't you want to know how we did it?"

"Sure," Mark said. His throat hurt when he spoke.

"You arrived to us with a core temperature of 24.8 Celsius—that would be, oh, 76.6 Fahrenheit, you know—quite low. *Quite* low. The EMTs had done a fine job with you, the very best they could, and still they had not succeeded in bringing your core temperature up any higher than that. A grim situation."

The doctor paused as if to make certain Mark appreciated the drama.

"Grim," Mark echoed, and Dr. Desare nodded.

"To rewarm you, we used ECMO, extracorporeal circulation. Do you know what extracorporeal circulation is, Mr. Novak?"

Mark didn't, but he considered the adjective for a moment and then said, "Out of body. Whatever you're talking about that kept me alive, it came from outside of the body."

"Indeed. The technique involves oxygenating the patient's blood outside the body via mechanical means. Where your system stops, ours begins. Consider it a pinch hitter for your circulation. Oxygen-depleted blood—or, in your case, chilled blood—is diverted from the body, rewarmed and en-riched with oxygen, then pumped back in. We weaned you from extracorporeal circulation when your own system indi-cated that it was ready to get back into the game. But you were kept alive thanks to an out-of-body experience."

Dr. Mehir Desare smiled at that, pleased with the little joke, but Mark was shuffling through some of those out-of-focus snapshots of memory. Shotguns. A van. Walking a plank that couldn't have been a plank. Then—

The wall was melting.

Then he'd been alone in the dark. Or had he been alone? He felt as if someone had been with him. But the image that came to mind—

Sarah Martin was watching me. She was lit from within and she was watching

—was not one he wanted to dwell on. Or even remember.

He thought then of his mother, of her skin turning blue on the wind-whipped prairie. A spirit quest, she'd told him when she was conscious again. By that point, she was so out of her head that she'd begun to believe her own con. She thought she really was a Nez Perce. *You're fucking German,* he'd told her, and when she insisted he was wrong, he'd held up his hands and said, *You're right, Mother. You're not Ger-man. You're a fraud, that's all,* and then the nurse had asked him to leave, and he never went back to the hospital. Last words. He had a way with them, certainly. He tried to think of the last thing he'd said before he'd ended up in the cave. If they hadn't gotten him out in time, what would his last words have been? He couldn't come up with anything.

"We administered some drugs to protect the brain and now you are"—Dr. Desare consulted his watch—"twenty-eight hours into your stay with us."

More than a day.

"How long was I in the cave?" Mark said.

"You remember the cave? Excellent!" The doctor was jubilant. "Memory function of the kind you're displaying is exciting. There was some concern about neurologic deficits. We'll be conducting tests, but at this juncture I'm pleased with your general cognitive ability."

"Deepest thanks," Mark said, and the doctor laughed.

"It might not seem like the highest of compliments, but we were worried. As for how long you were in the cave, I can't say. Are you up to seeing visitors, by the way? There's one waiting rather impatiently. A man from Florida."

Jeff London had arrived.

22

Jeff looked good, fit and rested, which came as no surprise. He worked out with religious fervor. He'd probably been doing push-ups in the waiting room. His hair was still thick but starting to go gray. His tan face was weathered. Still, he could have passed for forty without much question, and he was fifty-five.

"Rumor has it someone finally figured out how to thaw you out," he said.

"They pumped my blood out, warmed it up, and then let me have it back. Pretty good deal, don't you think?"

"Most people who know you wouldn't have given your blood back once they took it, that's for sure."

The hospital room might have seemed the wrong venue for the exchange of wiseass barbs, but the barbs were needed. From the way Jeff let his eyes drift, though, Mark knew the good humor wouldn't last long.

"Why in the hell did you force your way into that cave?" Jeff said. "Even in the annals of *your* decision-making, that one stands out as poor, which is really saying something."

"Force my way into the cave?" Mark stared at him without comprehension. "You haven't been told what happened?" He realized then what should have been obvious from the start—*nobody* had been told what happened. He'd felt it would be clear somehow. He'd been put in the cave and he'd been rescued from it, and so it seemed someone should have understood the basics. The rescue effort had been organized. He had vague flash memories of uniforms and lights and official questions. Amid all the confusion, he'd gotten some comfort in that—the police had been called, and that meant they understood what had happened. The idea that he had gone into the cave willingly was astonishing.

"I've been told you pried open an old gate and went wandering," Jeff said. "I don't believe that you chose to take your clothes off for the trip, though. It's been a point of contention between me and your friend the sheriff. The appearance of things suggested you went into the water after something. Your clothes were folded in a tidy pile right beside some sort of underground stream, like you'd taken them off before you waded in so they wouldn't get wet."

"Jeff...I was *abducted*. Three guys with shotguns."

"They took you to the cave?"

"Yes. Well...not directly. I mean, two of them left. I think. But I had a hood over my head, and I can't say exactly. But there was...I was somewhere else first."

"How'd you get into the cave?"

"I don't know."

"What do you mean? Did they knock you out?"

"Yes. Well...they must have. Because I don't remember how I got in there. There's a gap in my memory for a stretch, so they must have. I was up on the road, I was driving, and they stopped me and put me in this van. All of them had masks. All of them had shotguns. Then they put a hood over my head so I couldn't see anything, and we went...somewhere. There was one guy asking questions."

"The hood was on you the whole time?"

"No. It came off, I think."

"You *think?*"

"I don't remember!" He was watching Jeff's eyes, seeing the skepticism in them, and panic began to rise at the idea that even his friend didn't believe him. Jeff reached out and put a reassuring hand on his arm.

"All right, Markus. We'll get it straightened out."

"Straightened out? Someone tried to kill me! What do people *think* happened?"

Jeff pulled a plastic chair up close to the bed. "They think you went in there and got lost. The last report of you before that was from Ridley Barnes. He told the police that you came by and kicked the shit out of him. After tying him up with his own rope. That didn't happen either?"

"That actually did."

Jeff rubbed his eyes. "Beautiful."

"But then I left, and there was a truck behind me. It turned and blocked the road, and then the van came. Three people total, two in the van and one in the truck." Mark sat up with excitement, ignoring the aches that throbbed through his body. "My rental car. They took it. Didn't it occur to anybody that it would be hard for me to get to the cave without a car?"

Jeff studied him for a few seconds before he said, "Your car *was* at the cave. Parked up on top, pulled off the side of the road. The caretaker saw it, and that's when he went looking for you and found the damage to the gate and your clothes in a pile inside. Then he called the police."

"What?" Mark eased back in the bed in disbelief,

grateful that he could lie down. "I was left inside, Jeff. I don't know how or by who, but I was left inside."

"What *do* you remember about it?"

"Waking up in the dark and the cold. I couldn't just stay there, so I started to crawl. I was looking for a way out. There was no light. I can't explain just how dark it was." He remembered seeing the dead girl, Sarah Martin, and he knew that he'd better not tell Jeff about that.

"I was delirious at some points," he said. "Obviously, that can happen with hypothermia. But when it comes to how I was stopped on the road, I'm not confused. Not even a little."

"Okay. Well, we're going to need to figure out how to prove it, Markus. Because right now, we've got big problems. And I don't mean just the obvious ones. I mean back home."

"I don't follow."

"While the docs worked on you, I worked *for* you. I met with the sheriff, met with the state police, got your things out of the rental car, and generally did all the pushing I could to find that woman who told you she was the dead girl's mother."

Diane Martin. The first time that Mark's reality and the one everyone else participated in had separated.

"People are lying about her," Mark said. "I don't know why. I don't see how one man, who appears to be a town pariah, can exert so much influence. But he's doing it. The story the hotel clerk told? Total bullshit, Jeff. That woman was pretending to be Diane Martin! I can't say that clearly enough. If you've ever believed any words that came out of my mouth, it better be those."

The look on Jeff's face then was chilling—not because he was disturbed by what he'd heard, but because he apparently didn't believe it.

"How is he getting them to lie, Jeff? How in the hell is Ridley Barnes getting so many people to lie?"

Jeff wouldn't meet his eyes.

"What?" Mark said. "Damn it, you *do* believe me, don't you?"

Silence for a beat, and then Jeff took a deep breath and faced him again. "I talked to the bartender who served the two of you. His version of events closely matches the hotel employee's. He said he overheard you talking *about* Diane Martin, so unless you and this woman lapsed into the third person, it's hard to use his story to validate yours. I've also seen the security tapes from the hotel lobby. There's no audio, but your interaction with the woman…it certainly matches the clerk's story better than yours. There's no anger. You shake hands, talk a little, all pretty relaxed, and then you walk out the door together, happy as could be."

"That's not what happened," Mark said, although how he intended to argue with the video, he wasn't sure. He just needed to argue because doing anything else was to accept…what? That he was losing his mind?

"Fine. But it's what *appears* to have happened, and credible witnesses are backing that version. You've got to come up with the best explanation you can. And finding that woman will go a long way toward it. I don't want to keep you in Indiana, but…you're going to *need* to provide some better answers than you have."

Mark swallowed—a painful task—and said, "Let me guess. Board of directors isn't pleased."

"They weren't pleased before all of this. Now, with that frigging attorney calling everyone on the board individually and threatening to sue—"

"Hang on. What attorney?"

"One Danielle MacAlister, Esquire, of Louisville, Kentucky. Her father owns the cave. Based on my conversation with Miss MacAlister, *she* owns the universe. Of all the caves to wander into, you picked the wrong one. She came at us aggressively. A lot of talk about criminal trespassing."

"Trespassing!" Mark barked out a laugh at the absurdity of the claim. "I was—"

"I know. You were left there. But you can't prove it. Just like you can't prove that woman was really lying to you. And the board was already uneasy with your recent conduct. I'd just gotten that out of the way when this blew up."

"Am I going to be fired?"

Jeff hesitated. "Nobody wants to say that you're fired. Not right now, when press calls are flooding in. The board has decided to revisit the issue next week. Until then, you're suspended without pay, pending internal investigation."

Mark took the news in numbly. "What's your read?" he said. "Do I even have a chance?"

"Before this? Yes. With the current story, though? Without a better *explanation* for it, at least? I won't lie—the votes will be against you. There are some people who think you're going off the rails."

"I was kidnapped," Mark said. "Doesn't that mean anything? Doesn't that give some credibility to my *story,* as you call it?"

"You're going to need a witness."

"I'm going to need a witness? I was attacked by three men and put in a van and beaten and drugged and left to die!"

Jeff rubbed his eyes again as if weary of Mark's repetition. "I understand all of this. And I believe it, because I know you. But here's the scenario that the rest of the world knows right now: You wandered into town and claimed that you'd talked to a dead woman, then you claimed that someone had impersonated her, and both claims have been blown out of the water. Then you left the sheriff behind and went after Ridley Barnes. You're damn lucky he's not pressing charges, frankly."

Mark didn't say anything, and Jeff nodded at the silent confirmation.

"Then you fell off the grid," Jeff continued, and he lifted a hand before Mark could voice objection. "You were *forced* into the situation, but right now we can't prove that." His face was grim. "We're going to need to. If you want to hold on to your job, Markus, you are going to need to give me something real."

"It's all real," Mark said. "We'll prove that."

"Sure we will," Jeff said.

Mark recalled a hospital in Wyoming where his uncle Ronny lay dying of lung cancer, evidence that forty years of chain-smoking and no visits to doctors wasn't a recipe for a long life. Mark had told him they'd do some fly-fishing on the Lamar as soon as Ronny got out. *Sure we will,* his uncle had said with a wan smile, and they'd both known it would never happen. He was dead three weeks later.

"I've got to fly out tonight," Jeff said. "We're in trial on the Texas appeal. I've got to testify, and I don't know how fast things will move. When I can be back, I will be. Two days, maybe three. You have any idea when they're going to release you?"

"Not yet."

"All right. If it's before I get back, call me. I think we're going to need to make some good friends out of the police down in Garrison. I know you probably hate the idea of setting foot back in that town, but if you come home now, no evidence of anything you're claiming, then I'm afraid—"

"That it ends with the lie," Mark finished for him. "And you can't keep a crazy man employed."

Part Three

PRESSURE POINTS

23

His belongings were in plastic evidence bags, but they had been released to Jeff, apparently without any objection from the police. Legally, no crime except trespassing had been committed. Mark had willingly driven to Trapdoor, parked, and walked down to the cave. This was exactly what he'd been asked to do—visit the cave, spend some time down there in the dark.

Do some thinking.

Jeff was gone when the nurse finally brought the bags into the room, all of the things that had been removed from his unlocked rental car after they'd hauled him out of the cave on a backboard and carried him to a waiting helicopter. His wallet was untouched, every card and every dollar still inside, and his laptop was still in his travel bag, along with the thick folder from Ridley Barnes. Everything seemed just as it should be, at least until he went through his pockets with a growing unease.

"There was something else in my pockets," Mark said. "A diving permit."

The nurse raised her eyebrows. "Diving permit?"

"It's a little plastic disk. Like a poker chip almost."

"I'm sorry, that's all they gave us. I'm sure you can get your diving permit replaced," she said without interest.

Mark thought of his first trip with Lauren, of the sunset over the Saba reefs, of how many times he had touched that old tag as a reassurance that he had been made whole once and could be again.

"Sure," he said. "We'll get it all replaced."

He lay alone in the hospital room, one light on and shadows heavy in the corners, and read Ridley's case file for the first time.

The Diane Martin impersonator might have lied about what mattered most, but she'd been honest with regard to the way the case had developed. Evan had been the first suspect, his father also in the mix, before Ridley came to the surface with a body and a stream of bizarre statements that turned into silence and never changed. Evan's story hadn't changed either—he never backed off the claim that they'd heard noises and he thought someone had entered the cave with them so he'd told Sarah to hide while he checked it out, and she'd hidden a little too well.

Carson Borders had been a target of the investigation in the early days, and it was clear that the police had sweated Evan long and hard over the whereabouts of his father. He said he had no idea where his father had gone, and the police couldn't turn him up either, but with good reason—Carson was dead by then. Five years earlier, he'd given information about a gun- and drug-runner from Detroit named Lamar Hunter in hopes of receiving an early release. He hadn't been granted it, and Lamar hadn't forgotten about him. Prison guards at Pendleton testified that those last five years behind bars had been plenty rough for Carson, but Hunter was too smart to kill him inside. He'd promised Carson that he'd never see his family again, and apparently Hunter had made good on that promise. Evan swore that he hadn't seen his father after he was paroled, and while police had initially been suspicious of that, they couldn't come up with any evidence that Carson had made it back to Garrison. He'd vanished almost instantly upon his release. Photos in the case file showed thirty-one teeth, nicked and scarred by pliers, in a simple plastic sandwich bag. The teeth, along with a candy cane, had been mailed from a Detroit postal code in a plain brown envelope that arrived at Carson's son's doorstep on Christmas Eve.

There were references to Diane Martin in the file, plenty of them, but no indication that she had died. At the time the case file was assembled, she'd been very much alive and a factor in the investigation. The world created by the case file included two highlight-reel moments:

1. Ridley Barnes had been hired to map Trapdoor's passages the summer before Sarah Martin disappeared inside the cave; and
2. Dan Blankenship, then a chief deputy, had been removed from the search scene and, later, the investigation due to a "conflict of interests as a result of a personal relationship with the victim's mother."

The sheriff of Garrison County, the one Jeff had just identified as someone Mark was going to need to become awfully friendly with, had a personal attachment to the dead woman Mark had claimed to meet. It didn't seem like a promising start for a friendship. Mark remembered Blankenship's fists opening and closing, the way he'd said, *I told you this thing could cause pain. Would* cause pain.

They hadn't been together when Sarah went missing. By then, Diane Martin was engaged to Pershing MacAlister.

A missing item from Sarah's person, identified by both her mother and Evan Borders as something she was wearing the night she disappeared, was a sapphire necklace that was actually her mother's and that had been given to Diane by Dan Blankenship. The sheriff's voice had broken when he'd described Diane's last moments, that trip to her daughter's bedroom, the children's Bible in her hand. Mark had thought it was just that the case had struck an emotional chord, but he'd been wrong.

Mark flipped through the case file until he came to a photograph of Ridley Barnes taken the day he'd appeared with the body. He was a decade younger but didn't look much different. The wild hair was brown then, not gray, but not much else had changed. He was still whip-thin and fit, with hollow cheeks that seemed designed to draw attention to those oddly bright eyes. In the photograph he was dressed entirely in black but so covered in mud that the clothing looked like some sort of camouflage pattern. He was staring at the camera with distrust, like a primitive warrior who thought the device might steal his soul.

The final entry in the report was a supplemental written by the Indiana State Police summarizing the difficulties of getting the cave to reveal its secrets, a challenge exceeded only by the task of getting Ridley Barnes to reveal his.

Mr. MacAlister resisted sending Mr. Barnes on the search and was overruled by Chief Deputy Dan Blankenship of the Garrison County Sheriff's Department. Blankenship insisted that sources, including Mr. MacAlister, had stated that Mr. Barnes knew the cave better than anyone else and would be the most capable of conducting a full search in a timely fashion, the report read. *This was before the chief deputy was removed from the scene.*

"Good Lord," Mark whispered. Blankenship had made

the call. Blankenship had sent Ridley in, despite objections from the landowner. Mark doubted the sheriff had gone to sleep one night since without thinking of that decision.

Mr. Barnes has been mapping newly discovered passages for the past several months, the report continued. *He declined to produce any of the maps but said he would lead the search team. Once underground, however, Barnes separated from the search team, citing a lack of sufficient speed, and proceeded alone. He was not seen again until he arrived back in an area known as the Chapel Room with Sarah Martin's body. At that time, he was unable or unwilling to answer questions as to where she had been located. He was judged to be suffering from hypothermia and he was taken to Garrison County Hospital for treatment. In subsequent interviews, Mr. Barnes refused to provide any further detail as to his experiences in the cave once he left the larger search team, maintaining that he has no recollection of the events and had grown confused in the darkness. It is true that when Mr. Barnes returned, he no longer had a functioning light, although he had three of them at the start of his search. The location of Sarah Martin's body when he discovered it and her condition when discovered has never been established. Subsequent searches of the cave have been conducted prior to and after its closing, all with permission and cooperation of the landowner, but the experts involved were unable to determine what route Barnes took. One caving expert who was interviewed suggests that as much as 90 percent of the cave system may remain unexplored and unmapped. The system is a complex web of passages that are subject to being rendered unnavigable due to shifts in the water table, and all experts interviewed agree that the shifting conditions of the "wet cave" create a situation in which the possible routes taken by Barnes may sometimes be as good as invisible due to high water. An unusually dry summer preceded Sarah Martin's disappearance in the cave, although it began to rain that night and continued to rain heavily throughout the following week, causing swift and significant changes in the cave's water levels. To re-create the circumstances of Mr. Barnes's journey without his cooperation is essentially impossible at this time.*

Mark closed the file and dropped it back into the bag and turned off the bedside light, which did little to darken the hospital room, then closed his eyes and sought sleep. It was a fruitless search. He was exhausted physically, but mentally he was alert. Not just alert. Afraid. Mark was no stranger to horrors, but this one was unique. To say *This is what happened* and find neither trust nor support was a terrifying thing. How was it happening? Three men should be in prison for what they'd done to him, but the police weren't even looking.

You're going to need a witness, Jeff had said.

There had been three witnesses to his abduction. None of them were likely to corroborate Mark's version of the events.

But who were they? Where had they come from?

He turned the light back on, found the phone, and called Jeff.

It was an hour before he got through to him, fresh off the plane in Texas.

"I want Ridley's phone records," Mark said. "Whoever came for me, they were sent by Ridley. There's no other option. They came on fast too. He made a call, and there will be a record of it. The records can't lie."

The videotapes did, a voice in his head whispered. The

voice had become familiar in the hours since Jeff had left, and its tone had shifted from warning to mocking. *The people lie, and the videos lie, and you tell the truth, Mark? My, my. That'll be a tough sell.*

Almost on cue, Jeff said, "That'll be a tough subpoena to get, considering there's no legal case in progress and the only person who has grounds for charges here is Ridley, and against you."

"I didn't suggest a subpoena."

Silence.

"Jeff, I've worked with you for years. I'm well aware of what can be gotten, and how. You can get them, and we both know it."

"And we both know that it's illegal."

"We're talking about saving my job here."

"And risking mine."

Mark lowered his voice. "This is all I have, Jeff. It's not just a job, not just a paycheck. You *know* that."

"That's the same thing you told me the last time you jeopardized it. I listened then. I'm supposed to again?"

"Last time I made a mistake. This time I was forced into one. There isn't a chance we're going to take this case; it doesn't even meet the rules of the damned bylaws, we couldn't take it if we wanted to. Yet you sent me up here, and now everything I have left in my life is at risk, and you won't run a fucking *phone record* for me?"

Jeff didn't answer. Mark let the silence roll for a few seconds, and when he finally spoke, he had better control. "I know I've got no right to ask this of you. I know I keep pushing you for help, and your face told me what your words didn't when you were up here—you're starting to wonder about my story, aren't you? To wonder about *me*. If I can be trusted."

"I trust you," Jeff said in the way a man might say *I love you* to his ex-wife on the day they signed the divorce papers.

"I need you to understand this from my point of view. After listening to you and hearing what work you've done to verify my story and what you've found, I'm beginning to have trouble trusting *myself.* Think about that for a minute." Mark took a deep breath—which hurt; everything hurt, and he was still in bed—and said, "The only thing I can say is that Ridley is engineering all of this somehow. But he didn't know I was headed to his house until I showed up. No one was following me. They came at me after I came at him. So if Ridley didn't make any calls, Jeff? If his phone lines were silent between the time I left his house and the time I was stopped on the road? Then I need to go home. Without a job, because I won't deserve one. I'll deserve a room with padded walls."

Still Jeff didn't speak.

"You're the one who told me I'm going to need to prove my story to keep my head above water," Mark said. "It starts with those phone records. If you don't want to do it yourself, I understand. Give me the right contact, and I'll do it. You shouldn't be involved anyhow."

"Bullshit I shouldn't. It's my fault you're up there. You shouldn't have been there to begin with. You know that and you always did. I had an idea that it was what you needed. It was the wrong idea."

"You wanted me up here because of the date," Mark said. "You wanted to push my buttons, rattle me."

"Yes. I thought—I *hoped*—that if you spent even a little time looking at an unsolved case that bore any similarity to Lauren's, it might…give you a little perspective. Remind you that you're not alone in the world. That others have suffered the same losses. It was a terrible idea."

Two days ago, Mark had been enraged by the move. Now he couldn't summon any emotion over it, let alone anger.

"If you feel any responsibility for this, then do this one thing," he said. "Get those records. If Ridley didn't make any calls, then it means..."

"I'll do it," Jeff said. "But Markus? You're going to need to file this favor with all of the other things you can't remember."

"That'll be easy enough."

It took him less than an hour. Technology might have done a lot of good for the world, but it had done nothing good for personal privacy. If you floated around the investigative and intelligence professions for long enough, you began to understand just how laughable the illusion of privacy was; if a pro, or even a dedicated amateur, wanted someone's information, he could find it, and fast.

Jeff's phone-records contact was a retired FBI agent who'd specialized in computer intelligence and who now lived in Georgia and had an ax to grind with the government and a hard-core pill habit to support. His information came at a price, but it came fast, and it was reliable.

"Ridley was on the phone a total of four times to a total of three people in the two days you were in town," Jeff said. "One was a dentist, one was a bakery, and two calls were with a guy named Evan Borders."

"Evan Borders. Ridley *called* that guy?"

"You know the name?"

"He was the other suspect in Sarah Martin's murder. He was her boyfriend, the one who took her into the cave."

"Evan Borders called Ridley shortly before noon, at home," Jeff said. "Ridley called him back shortly after one."

Mark let out a breath that came more from his soul than

his lungs. "That's right after I left. They bookended me with phone calls, basically. Ridley picked up the phone just after I left."

"Seems like a strange choice. Two lead suspects trading calls?"

"Sure does. But it's real." That word had taken on new meaning in the past day. "Ridley engineered all of this. He wanted me down in that cave. He asked me to go, and when I didn't, he put me there. I don't understand how he's got the influence that he does, but I'll figure it out. I'll get him."

"Step lightly with that boy."

He asked Jeff for all the call times and numbers—Bishop was the dentist, and the bakery was Haringa's—and he wrote them down, thanked Jeff, and then hung up. There was only one light on in the hospital room, and he lay there in the dimness and stared at those names.

Evan Borders. The kid who'd brought Sarah Martin down to Trapdoor was in communication with her suspected killer a decade later.

Evan was going to require a visit, Mark decided. No phone call there, no discussion with the sheriff beforehand. Mark wanted to see Evan's face.

More important, he wanted to watch Evan see *his* face.

24

They released him the next day, after Dr. Desare had reviewed his test results and proclaimed him maybe not *the* luckiest son of a bitch in history, but on the short list.

"Go back home, and get some rest," he'd instructed. "Your body took a beating. Don't underestimate that. Some rest in the warm sun will be just right."

It sounded just right, but it wasn't an option. Mark had four days before his professional fate was decided for him, which meant three days to get some evidence for his side of the argument.

All of that evidence was in Garrison.

He arranged for a rental car to be dropped off at the hotel. This one was a Ford Edge. Charming names Ford was coming up with these days—Escape and Edge. They might be great marketing hooks, but Mark wouldn't have minded seeing a Chevy at this point. He eased behind the wheel like an elderly man; each movement required planning and brought pain. He thought he'd known soreness before in life, but it had just been redefined. As he drove out of the parking lot, he felt alone in a way that surprised and chilled him. More alone than even the worst days after Lauren's killing. Then, he'd had the support of those around him because they believed him. It had seemed a small thing then, to be believed.

Such a small thing.

You're going to need a witness, Jeff, his closest friend, had said, unwilling to look him in the eye.

To fill the silence of the car on the highway, he streamed music through the car's Bluetooth system. It was music he'd never allowed anyone except Lauren to hear him listening to. The songs had traveled with him from Montana, over time changing from one format to another and then another, the sound fuzzed with white noise by now. The original had been a cassette recorded by his mother at a powwow they'd attended one summer. It was drum and chant music, and the performances had been the one element of the weekend powerful enough to distract Mark from his shame even though his mother was recording it for use in her con. When Mark stole the tape, he'd been trying only to remove a bullet from her arsenal. He'd fallen in love with the sound, though. The power of the drums, the haunting cries in a tongue he could not understand but somehow felt he knew. The music was everything his mother was not: Authentic. And brave.

His uncle Ronny had caught him playing the tape once and viewed him grimly. Mark thought he might catch hell for stealing it, because his mother had searched frantically for weeks after discovering it was gone. Instead, Ronny had said only *Don't mess with that shit, Mark. You don't know what it is.*

Maybe he didn't. He knew what he felt when he listened to it, though. Stilled and angry, calm and fearless, all at once. There was a hypnotic blend of fatalism and perseverance to the music, a sense of an understood mission.

He listened while he drove south, listened until the drums began to enter his blood like a pulse. By the time he reached

Garrison, the pain and fatigue had retreated from the front of his mind, and his hands were steady on the wheel.

The downtown square snuck up on him in the way it can only in a small town—you ran right into the heart of the place without encountering any arteries along the way. The stretch of town that had been built up, where the hotels and chain restaurants were, was farther south, edging toward the interstate that was still miles away, trying to snuggle up as close as possible to something that connected the town to the rest of the world but not quite making it. Mark parked on the square, where he had his pick of empty spaces, their meters standing like hopeful ushers at a play that had overextended its run, the staff now outnumbering the audience. With piles of shoveled snow climbing the meter poles and not enough foot traffic on the sidewalk to even create slush, the only word for the town was *forlorn*.

As soon as he stepped out of the car, the wind caught him, and while he'd shrugged it off on his first visit, he couldn't afford to now, not in his present condition.

Coffee seemed like the best substitute for sleep, and there was an old-fashioned diner on the square with a few booths on one wall and a long lunch counter. When Mark pulled open the door, a bell jingled, and ten faces pivoted in unison to look at him. Seven customers—all older men—and three employees. Mark walked up to the counter and asked for the largest coffee to go that they had. The old men were watching him with undisguised interest the way you could only when you belonged and the object of your stare did not.

"Where's the best place to pick up a warm jacket around here?" he asked the girl behind the counter.

"Easton's Mercantile," she said. "Three blocks south, can't miss it. Big old stone building. Used to be the biggest store in town. Now they sell hunting gear and work boots, things like that. They'll fix you up."

One of the men, a guy with a gray goatee, slipped a five-dollar bill out of his shirt pocket and slid it across the counter.

"Take his coffee out of this, Donna."

"You don't need to do that," Mark said.

"I'll even buy you a cheeseburger," the man answered, "if you don't mind telling us why in the hell you felt the need to tell that tale about Diane Martin."

The remark seemed to add silence to the diner, but the truth was nobody had been talking anyhow. They were all just watching Mark.

"My picture made the paper, I take it," he said.

"Oh, sure did. Takes an unusual man to tell a story like that."

"Wasn't a story, old-timer. People in this town have lied to me and then about me. I'm back to set the record straight."

Mark met all their eyes, moving through the diner one un-friendly face at a time. "You all seem like the types who do a solid job of spreading the word in this town. Why don't you spread this one, far and wide: whoever put me in that cave made one hell of a mistake in letting me come back to the surface."

Easton's Mercantile—or *Merchantile,* according to the an-cient spelling that was carved into the limestone building— had morphed into a work-wear and sporting-goods store, with racks of shotguns and shelves filled with shells. Mark's eyes lingered on the oiled black-pump shotguns, remember-ing the three that had been leveled at him in the snow.

At the moment, Mark was wearing a pair of running shoes that he'd left in the hotel room before it all began, and he picked up a pair of waterproof steel-toe Wolverine boots to replace them. The weight of them felt good, and uncomfortably familiar. It had been many years since he'd worn real boots, but for many years before that, that had been all he'd worn. From the clearance clothing rack, he chose a pair of wool base layers and a couple of heavy canvas shirts. Then he moved to the jackets. The gray, hooded Carhartt was there, a twin of Ridley's and a cousin of the one Mark's mother had given him that Christmas. *Rugged and durable, kiddo. Just like you.* He grabbed it.

On his way to the cash register, he walked past a cubby filled with knit caps and ski masks. He pulled one of the masks out and looked at it, remembering the three of them advancing toward him through the snow. Then he added it to the pile.

Mark traded the running shoes for the boots before he even left the store, then slipped the jacket on and stepped outside, feeling warm for the first time in days and also feeling as if he blended in better, which wasn't a positive, because he did not want to be a part of this place. No choice about that, though. Not until he had some answers. He glanced back into the window of Easton's Mercantile and saw that rack of Mossberg pump guns, sleek and black and all too familiar.

No, he was not quite done in Garrison.

25

There'd been a poker game in a Montana town called Silver Gate on a blizzard-blasted week when Mark was fourteen. His uncles had brought him along with them to a bar and old boardinghouse called the Range Rider where they entertained the crowd by walking in their cowboy boots across the massive log beams that spanned the ceiling, usually for dollar bets, sometimes just for the hell of it. A slip from those timbers would have meant a broken back, but they'd never fallen.

The poker game that night was supposed to be good fun, but there was an out-of-towner and obvious cheat working the cards, a man who treated warnings with a wink. He'd given a false name, gotten up to go to the men's room, and never returned, hustling out in the middle of the night on a snowmobile, which was a problem for him because there wasn't far to go in Silver Gate on a night like that. "He got while the getting was not good," Larry had said ruefully, and then he and Ronny had passed a bottle of bourbon back and forth in the silent mood that their nephew knew better than to test, and eventually Ronny had said, "So we don't know who he is, but we know people who know him. He mentioned a name or two, if not his own."

When Larry had nodded, it was almost with sadness.

"They'll bring him to the surface," he said. "It's the only way."

It had been far from the only way. But it hadn't been ineffective. They'd crossed paths with three men and broken nine fingers before they got the name they wanted. They'd gotten it, though.

"It's a matter of physics," Ronny said as they made their way to the stranger's cabin, fourteen-year-old Mark at the wheel of the old Ford Sport Custom pickup, using the granny gear to claw through the snow while his uncles took turns on a flask. "You apply enough pressure, Mark, and eventually things start to leak. Ask any man who ever worked a pipeline. This world? It's run by pressure."

The pressure was on Mark now, and he had a limited window to adjust it. There was a proper way to work a case and there was a desperate way, and the former was no longer an option in Garrison. You fell back on more basic instincts when you had to, but Mark didn't feel so bad about that. In their own ways, his uncles had been fine detectives. If you judged the results instead of the process, they'd been damn good.

The rental house that Evan Borders currently called home was probably close to a hundred years old, with a deteriorating stone foundation, vinyl siding that bubbled in most places and curled apart at the corners, and an aluminum porch roof that had pulled loose from one support and hung at a precarious angle, dumping melting snow onto the steps below. Three plastic bins lined the base of the porch, each one overflowing with Busch cans floating in the snowmelt. There was a vehicle parked in the weeds beside the house, an old Jeep with oversize tires and a roof rack of lights. A shame. Mark had been hoping for a white Silverado or a panel van.

Mark pulled his car in across the street and sat with the engine running, looking the place over and hearing echoes of the various warnings. *Let's get to it,* Mark's mind said, but his body didn't agree. Mark didn't often have a pronounced size advantage, but he generally had a strength advantage, and ever since he was a child, he'd had one of the greatest advantages you could carry into a fight: he didn't mind getting hit. You learned a lot about fighting when you didn't disappear after the first punch, and in the circle of towns that Mark had passed through, there'd been a lot of first punches. That came with the constant string of new neighborhoods, new schools, new shames.

All of these things were supposed to be gone from him, of course. They had been, for a while. A few good years. But now he sat outside of the house of a man who possibly had held a knife on him, and then a needle, and what he wanted wasn't the sight of that man in handcuffs or a jail cell. What he wanted was blood. What he needed was the truth.

Whether Borders was the guilty man or not, there was a chance that Mark's walking onto his front porch was going to start a war. And today, when Mark could exhaust himself just by walking up a flight of stairs, that would end badly for him.

Still, some part of him wanted it.

The frame of the storm door was bent, keeping it from closing, so he pulled that open, blocked it with his heel, and pounded hard on the main door. A police knock, the kind that suggested you had a short window of time to open it yourself or it would be opened for you. Evan Borders had probably heard that kind before.

The door opened fast, and Mark's focus from the start was on the other man's eyes, because he knew they would tell him more than anything. Mark wasn't sure he'd be able to recognize anyone from that snowy road, not with the way they'd been dressed and had their faces covered, but he was damn sure anyone who had been there would recognize *him*.

Evan Borders took the detective work out of the equation fast. He said, "Hey, hey, the man himself. Novak, right?"

"I'm a familiar face to you?"

"Familiar face to anybody who reads the paper. You're one famous fella around here."

Mark looked into those eyes, trying to place them. Blue, and that seemed to fit, but he couldn't be sure. His size eliminated him from two of the three possibilities—if he'd been there, he'd been the man who waited in the middle of the road, the one who hadn't worn gloves. Mark looked at his hands, wondering if he'd have better luck recognizing something there. Again, it was impossible to tell. Evan was wearing an old T-shirt with the sleeves cut off, exposing tattoos on both biceps, a snake surrounded by flames on the right arm, a crucifix on the left. Perhaps that was an attempt at irony.

"Figured you'd drop by," Borders said.

"Why's that?"

"Because you weren't shy about throwing my fucking name around town, and even around the newspapers." His eyes were flint. "But then, after somebody decided to chill you out, I wasn't sure if you'd hit town again. After a thing like that, some men would head south."

"I'm not one of those men."

"Too tough, eh?"

"Or too stupid."

Borders smiled a mean smile and said, "That one would get my vote."

"I understand you and Ridley did some chatting the same day I took a beating."

"No shit?"

"None whatsoever."

"Yeah? So what of it, boy?"

Boy. It echoed in Mark's mind, familiar for reasons un-known. A simple word, but still, something about it taunted.

"Well?" Evan said.

"Mind telling me why?" Mark said. "Man's believed to have killed your girlfriend ten years ago, but you call him up at home same day I arrive asking questions? Seems odd."

"Those feel like police questions. You ain't police."

"If you don't answer me, the police'll be asking the same questions eventually. I'll see to it. You could save yourself the hassle."

Evan Borders smiled. "Appreciate you thinking of me that way, though I understand that the police have questions for *you.* Me? I've got nothing to hide, and I'm telling no lies, not like you. So you ask me an honest question, you get an honest answer in response. I called Ridley Barnes to of-fer my services. You might recall that it was snowing that day? Maybe you don't; you got an unusual memory, is what I hear."

"I remember the snow."

"Well, that's progress. During the winters, I plow snow. I was plowing all day; you can ask my cousins and our clients if you don't believe that. Plenty of witnesses on my side. Doesn't sound like you're too familiar with witnesses. I asked Ridley if he needed help 'cause I was out near his place, and turned out he didn't. He called me back and told me that. Now, I'll go ahead and answer your next ques-tion, which is whether I can prove this. Unlike you—notice how many differences there are between you and me and the stories we tell?—I sure can. I was working with two other people, and I got a client list a mile long that the police can check if *they* want to. You don't get that list, because I'm already being more generous than I need to be. Point is? I know what I *was* doing that day. What you were doing crawling into that cave? Boy, I got no idea on that front. Nobody in town seems to."

"Did you actually have feelings for Sarah?" Mark said.

Borders worked his tongue over his teeth like he was preparing for the taste of Mark's blood.

"You don't need to say her name. No more than you needed to say mine to that reporter. Saying too many names in this town will eventually get you in trouble."

"I'm just trying to put myself in your shoes. If I had feelings for a girl who was killed, last person I'd offer to help— clearing snow, of course, there was nothing more to it— would be the man people blame for her murder. But that's just me."

Evan Borders reached in the pocket of his jeans, removed a plastic container of chewing tobacco, and methodically worked a dip onto his fingertips and tucked it between his lower lip and his gums. He sucked on it for a few seconds and spit into the snow, all the while looking patient and thoughtful.

"Listen," he said, "I could invite you in out of the cold, but I'm not going to. Still, I'm a nice guy, right? Considerate. I'm aware that you've spent more time in the cold lately than you probably cared to. So I'll hustle things along, let you go on back to your car and get warmed up again. Looks like you need it. Don't mean to offend you, but you should be in bed, my man. Get you some chicken soup and some ginger ale, right? I don't have any to offer or I would, of course."

"Considerate," Mark said.

"*Exactly.*" Borders leaned his lanky body against the

door frame and crossed his arms over his chest. The muscles bunched against his skin. "And out of consideration, I'm going to save you time. I'm going to answer the rest of your questions with one word. That word is—"

"I don't have any other questions."

Borders raised his eyebrows. "No?"

"Was hoping you could do me a favor, though."

"A *favor,* he says. No shit? You toss my name around, stirring up old shit that you don't know a damn thing about, getting people to look sideways at me all over again, getting whispers started again, and then you come to me for a fucking favor? That's bold, brother."

"It would take only a few seconds of your time," Mark said.

"Well, let's hear it, my man. What *favor* can I do you?"

Mark reached into the pocket of his jacket, pulled out the black wool ski mask, and unfolded it methodically. He extended it to Evan Borders.

"Try this on, please. Just for a few seconds."

Borders stayed where he was and though his expression didn't change, one of the muscles in his arm trembled.

"Get the fuck off my porch," he said, his voice low. It was a classic threatening line, the get-out-of-my-face type of thing that a million assholes who thought they were hard would utter in a million situations, but it felt different coming from him. It felt real.

"Won't even try it on?" Mark said. "A considerate guy like you?"

Borders straightened, took the mask in his hands, and then, in a blink-fast flash, pulled it down over Mark's head. He'd turned it around so the eye- and mouth holes were at the back, leaving Mark blind again, just like he had been with the hood over his head. He tensed his abdominals, expecting a punch, but none came. He reached up and grasped the mask but didn't pull it off. Instead, he rotated it until it was in the proper place and he could see Evan Borders again.

"Feels good," Mark said. "Nice and warm. The last time I asked you for one, you weren't as generous."

Evan Borders leaned close to him and said, "You walk your ass back to your car now. You get in it, and you leave. And the next time you feel my name on your lips? You keep them shut. Garrison hears enough lies from Ridley Barnes. Don't need to add yours to the mix."

"If he's a liar, then why are you his cavalry when trouble comes?"

Evan Borders stepped back into his house and slammed the door.

Mark kept the mask on as he walked to his car.

This world? It's run by pressure.

The dials were beginning to tighten down in Garrison, and Mark was going to keep tightening them. He'd see Ridley Barnes again, but there was no need to rush for him. When he did see him, he wanted Ridley to have had plenty of time to consider Mark's presence back in town.

26

They made him wait an hour for the sheriff, at which point he began to whistle. Mark wasn't much for whistling these days. Uncle Ronny had been great at it, could imitate a harmonica if he chose, but most of that had been lost on Mark. Still, he had volume, and although it took all of "The Battle Hymn of the Republic" and the beginning of the marching song from *The Bridge on the River Kwai,* folks eventually decided the sheriff could see him after all.

Blankenship opened the door, gave Mark a sour look, and said, "I thought you were supposed to be back where the sun always shines, Novak."

"'Sun don't shine on the same dog's ass every day,'" Mark said.

The sheriff blinked at him.

"You don't know that line?" Mark said. "Son of a bitch, sheriff, that's Catfish Hunter's finest material, borrowed in the movie *Hoosiers.* I'd have expected more from you, being from Indiana."

"Get in here," Blankenship snapped, "so you can get the hell out faster."

Mark followed him back to the same office where he'd started this thing. The last time, he'd cruised through the department without noticing it, but now, with his labored breathing and heavy stride, he had the chance to take a good look at the place and all of the hostile, watching eyes. It was like the diner only with everyone in uniform.

"Why are you back?" Blankenship said when they were in his office.

"Because a very serious crime occurred in your county. A felony. A handful of felonies, in fact. You don't seem to be aware of it."

"This would be the tale you told about how you ended up in the cave? I spoke with your boss. He gave me your, um, take on that."

"You heard about a kidnapping and attempted murder in your county and didn't so much as bother to check in with the victim?"

"I also heard from a member of your board of directors. A Greg Roche? Name familiar?"

Mark said, "I know Greg," and hoped his face didn't show more than that. Greg was the reason Innocence Incorporated existed. A well-known prosecutor who'd worked high-profile cases and was appointed U.S. district attorney for Florida, Greg Roche had had one of the more famous change-of-heart moments in American law after he'd been presented with evidence that one of the death-row cases he'd prosecuted had resulted in the execution of an innocent man. He'd formed Innocence Incorporated then, bringing Jeff London on as his first investigator. Greg had also been Lauren's moral guide, a man she respected more than anyone else in the profession. The board of directors operated, theoretically, on majority rule, but Greg's vote counted the most.

"He was very interested to know my take on you, what your conduct had been, how you were representing the organization." Blankenship inserted a pause. "I got the impression that you're in a little bit of trouble with your own team."

"You got the right one. That's exactly why I'm back. I can't afford to leave here without the truth. I need your help proving it."

Blankenship shook his head. "I gave you the benefit of the doubt with your story about Diane Martin. I'm not wasting time on you again unless you have some evidence."

Mark nodded. "Understood. I don't have the evidence yet. I intend to gather it."

"Terrific. You step wrong here, and I mean *at all,* and I'll arrest you. To tell the truth, if it had been anyone other than Ridley Barnes that you'd bloodied up, I already would have. Ridley, though? He deserved what you gave him."

"Speaking of Ridley, I understand that he's the one who found me in the cave."

"He was the first one to you. The rescue team had located your general area, but Ridley was the one who determined how to actually reach you."

"Because he knew where I was. Have you considered that?"

"I have."

"And yet you show no interest in pursuing how I ended up in that cave. You tell me that I need evidence, but you don't have evidence to prove me wrong. Don't you want that?"

"After your opening act in town, no, I don't. You told a savage and sick lie, Novak."

"I would hope," Mark said, "based on your personal relationship with Diane Martin, you would have some interest in finding out who's pretending to be her."

Blankenship moved his large, heavy-knuckled hands around his desk as if looking for something to fill them with before they found their real target: Mark's throat.

"Let the dead have their peace," he said softly. "What is wrong with you?"

"You and I might understand each other a little better if you looked into my background, Sheriff."

"I've done so. I know what happened to your wife. I'm sorry. If that's the straw that broke the camel's back of your sanity, I am truly sorry. But the verdict is in: You lied. Why, I don't know. But I do know that you lied. And as for the next story? The three men who you say came for you? Well, Ridley doesn't have three friends in this world."

"I had the same notion, and I was proven wrong. Painfully. So I'd be careful in underestimating the reach of Ridley Barnes. I'd also like to know whose call it was to bring him into the cave looking for me."

"It was mine. He knows the place better than anyone alive. The only person who could solve my problem was him, whether I liked asking for his help or not."

"He's Captain Quint himself, eh?"

"I don't follow."

"Really? That might be the saddest thing I've heard yet. *Hoosiers,* sure, but you don't even get the *Jaws* reference? My goodness, Sheriff. Disappointing. Mind if I ask you another question about Ridley's, um, assistance in my situation?"

"Fire away."

"You called for him when you wanted Sarah Martin found, and that didn't go well. But when I went missing, you said again that you needed him, because he's the best."

Blankenship looked at him for a long time, the stare dim, as if he didn't want to allow himself to see Mark in focus. Or maybe as if he were trying to see someone else.

"He knew the cave best," he said finally, and his voice was hoarse. "Everyone said that, even Pershing admitted it; Pershing had hired him to explore the place! Pershing said he didn't trust Ridley, that they'd had disputes over the cave, but I didn't care about the cave, I cared about *her*." He thumped a hand on the desk. "Every caver I talked to, and I didn't give a damn what Pershing had to say, every *expert* I talked to told me that Ridley Barnes *had* to be involved because he was the only one who really knew the place, and I needed someone who could reach Sarah."

He choked on the last words and took a moment to collect himself.

"So why did I let him go after you?" Blankenship said. "Honestly, I wanted to see him in there. I wanted to watch him, watch where he went. I wanted him to go to the right place."

"You mean the place where she was found."

"Yes. No such luck. But it saved your dumb ass, so you can thank me and then go on your way."

Mark nodded. "Here's what I'd do if I were you," he said.

"This ought to be good."

"You might want to nudge around my story about those three men with shotguns, Sheriff. If they came for me the way I said, then Ridley called them. And if I were you, sitting there with a cold case still waiting to be closed? Well, I'd want to at least have a look at who Ridley might have called. I think you might find that *real* interesting. I think you might want to have a different kind of talk with me then. More cooperative."

"You talk like you already know what I'll find."

"Give it a look, Sheriff," Mark said, getting to his feet and trying to hide the wince of pain that the motion caused. "Then give me a call. Maybe we'll talk some more. Maybe you'll give me a little more credibility than you think."

"I don't need to study your credibility. You made up a

strange, sad little story, and two witnesses and a video disproved it. You've done absolutely nothing to help on the Sarah Martin case. From my perspective, you're not much different than Ridley Barnes."

"All due respect?" Mark said. "I need you to understand that I don't care about Sarah Martin's case, Sheriff. Never did and still don't. I wanted to come and go and stay gone. Now all I want is to know who fucked with me and why. When I know that, I'm gone. But people aren't helping me do that. You've got an aptly named little town, don't you? Everyone closes ranks fast when a stranger arrives with questions. Then they put guards at the walls."

"If you don't want to be here, go on home."

Mark ran a hand over his face, feeling the stubble from several days without shaving. He'd stayed clean-shaven in Florida, but not before that, when he was living in places where the cold could nip at your skin. His beard was growing in fast now.

"The hell of the thing, Sheriff? I just spent a lot of dollars on winter clothes. I'm in no rush."

The courthouse had gone up in 1903 according to the plaque on the front door, and based on the smell of the interior, it had been cleaned maybe once since then. Every footstep echoed on the wide, scarred floorboards, which had a little give, as if the joists were considering calling it a day. The courtrooms were on the ground floor, and the second floor held the county offices, with old frosted-glass doors labeled in gilded trim *Auditor, Clerk, Assessor.* Mark went to the clerk's office and asked to see the criminal records of Evan Borders and Jeremy Leonard.

"There's another Leonard," he said. "I think his name is—"

"Brett." The gray-haired woman with bifocals who stood

behind the counter said it without hesitation. "Sure. I hope you got some time on your hands, because there's plenty of paperwork."

Apparently Evan Borders and his snowplowing cousins were no strangers to the county court system. The gray-haired woman retrieved three stacks of folders, asked Mark to have a seat at a long wooden table beneath an arched window through which downtown Garrison looked almost charming instead of imposing, and told him to let her know if he had questions.

"They make for good reading, I'm sure," she said, handing him the files.

It wasn't quite as good reading as Mark had hoped. Evan's first encounter with law enforcement—barring any juvenile issues, which wouldn't be accessible in the public record—had come when he was twenty and arrested for marijuana possession and disorderly conduct. From then on, he'd visited more or less annually, but the charges never ranged into felony territory. He'd been arrested for assault once after a bar fight, but those charges had been dropped, and the other offenses were run-of-the-mill alcohol and disorderly conduct issues. Trafficking in stolen goods once, but that had also been dropped. He was like countless other small-town ne'er-do-wells, in and out of the local jail often but never staying long. If there was one thing that stood out, it wasn't his penchant for fighting but the consistent refusal of his victims to press charges. It seemed that those who ran afoul of Evan's temper were interested in seeking distance rather than justice.

Jeremy was thirty-two, the oldest of them, and Brett was twenty-seven, and the cousins were all cut from the same cloth, with one notable exception: Evan's violence involved only men. In the probable-cause affidavits, there were no females mentioned, let alone victimized. The Leonard brothers couldn't claim the same. Jeremy had been charged with statutory rape, which was pleaded down to a misdemeanor, but three years after that, he'd been charged with sexual assault after he'd bound a girlfriend's hands with duct tape in a "game" and then slapped her around and locked her out of the house, naked and in the rain.

Mark read that affidavit and felt his throat tighten and his breathing slow. The Leonards were the right kind of boys, that was for sure. If they'd been in a bar in Florida, he would have locked eyes with them, and he'd have known. He had teeth scars on his knuckles from men just like them.

Jeremy had gotten two years in prison for that one and was back out in a year with good-time credits. He and his brother had run into trouble together after that, had been arrested for robbing a pawnshop, which had led to Evan's charge of trafficking in stolen goods. Jeremy had gotten another six months; Brett got probation.

The most recent charge against either of the Leonards was an open case with a trial date set for April. Brett was out of jail after his father had posted a $10,000 surety bond in a date-rape case. An underage girl who'd been drinking at a bar called the Lowland Lounge had gone to the hospital the morning after a night of drinks and dancing with Brett Leonard. She'd woken in her own home, naked and sore, with vaginal bleeding and one black eye. She didn't remember how it had happened, but unlike so many other girls who woke in the same circumstances, she didn't let shame or fear keep her from going to the hospital. A blood test had shown the presence of a narcotic called ketamine.

The gray-haired clerk interrupted Mark, saying, "You need some help?"

Mark blinked back into the present and shook his head. "No, thank you. I think I've got the gist."

She frowned. "The gist is, those boys are bad news."

"Seems that way." Mark lowered his head again and flipped through the most recent case file until he came to an address of record for Brett Leonard, on Tower Ridge Road. Jeremy's was the same, albeit from a year earlier. It seemed they didn't drift far from each other. He wrote the address down, then went back and studied their booking photos. Jeremy was a bigger kid, six two and two hundred and fifteen pounds. Brett, the ketamine artist, was five inches shorter and fifty pounds lighter.

Mark's fingers drifted to the bruise on his forehead that the muzzle of a shotgun had left a few days earlier. A bigger, stronger man had slammed the muzzle into him, but he remembered being more concerned with the bantam-size man in the black mask, the one whose hands had seemed nervous near the trigger. He also thought of the witnesses he'd accused of lying, of his version of events that seemed so real but had no support.

Ketamine.

27

Rarely did the police arrive on your doorstep bearing good news, but Ridley found such good fortune when he answered a thundering knock. He was hoping for the visitor he didn't dare expect—Mark Novak—but when he saw that it was the sheriff, he was far from disappointed. Next to Novak, Blankenship was the best option.

"Lose somebody in Trapdoor again?" Ridley said, opening the door.

"Who'd you call after Novak left your property?"

Ridley cocked his head as if the question presented a difficulty

"Who did I *call?* My goodness, how in the world am I supposed to remember that? It's been days, Sheriff."

"It's easy enough for me to learn," Blankenship said. His long face was pale.

"Then why don't you go learn it instead of asking me?"

"He came up here at your request," Blankenship said, "but he's back for some other reason. What went wrong, Ridley?"

Ridley's already slow breathing nearly stopped. Novak *was* back? This was spectacular news. Ridley had been pleased with what he'd seen of the man, but the surface world exerted a unique set of pressures, and most people crumbled under them. The surface world should have sent Novak running from this place, not brought him back to it.

"I didn't call Novak after he left," Ridley said. "As I remember it, you came for me. Needing help."

"Who did you call, Ridley?"

Ridley sighed. "I'd love to help you. I really would. Best as I can remember, I called my dentist, and I called the bakery to order a pie. Maybe that's why I need the dentist, right? Have to cut out the sweets."

The sheriff didn't match Ridley's smile. The sheriff rarely did. Ridley could remember the way Blankenship had looked as chief deputy, his shoulders not yet stooped, his hair not yet gray. His eyes not yet haunted. He remembered in particular the way he looked when Diane Martin passed by. Blankenship always stood straighter then, sucked in what little gut he had, pulled his shoulders back. He'd been a comical presence, large and awkward and obvious.

"I'm doing some research into your boy," Blankenship said. "I can't quite figure how you found him or what he wants with you, but I will. That letter was a mistake. I'm not sure that you wrote it, of course—he probably handled the words for you—but you wanted him to wave it under my nose. That was a mistake."

"You ever read about the rapture before that note?" Ridley asked.

"I've read the Good Book plenty of times."

"Wrong book," Ridley said. "Wrong rapture. I'm talking about what happens to the mind when it's left alone in the dark. I'm guessing you probably never considered that. Or tested it."

"Did Novak enter that cave of his own free will, Ridley?"

"I can't speak to the will of another man. I wouldn't trust anyone who claimed to be able to either."

"Who did you call, Ridley?"

"Why my phone activities are of interest to you, I have no idea. On that day, not only was I the victim of a crime, but I came to your aid. If not for me, Sheriff, you might have lost another one in Trapdoor. That would have hurt you, I think. Am I wrong?"

Blankenship was staring at the ropes in front of the dark and cold woodstove. He looked like he was about to say something, but Ridley beat him to the punch.

"Tell me," he said, "did you ever discuss that situation with Pershing? I know there were some hostilities between you, or jealousies, however you prefer to phrase it, but I hope such petty things wouldn't have kept you from an honest exchange."

Blankenship's pallor drained to match the old ashes in the stove. "You know why I'm still the sheriff?" he said.

"A poorly educated electorate, I've always assumed."

"You," Blankenship said. "You're it, Ridley. You'll step the wrong way someday, I believe in that because I believe in God, and when you do? I'll be here."

"Have a fine afternoon, Sheriff. Next time you need my help, and you always seem to, you'll know where to find me."

Ridley closed the door and stood on the other side of it, his palm pressed to the wood—his hand was trembling faintly, and he hated that—until Blankenship had returned to his car and driven away. When he was out of sight, Ridley went for his own keys and hurried to his truck. He wasn't supposed to visit her unannounced, but he needed her now, and she understood emergencies.

Novak had returned, and Ridley needed to get his mind right before he saw him. He'd long ago given up the hope that he could achieve that alone, unguided in the dark.

28

Mark hesitated before deciding on the next person to call because all his hopes for a possible explanation of things rested on the conversation. Eventually he chose a medical examiner in Gainesville who had testified for Innocence Incorporated on a few cases, Arthur Stewart, and told him he had a simple question—he wanted to know about ketamine.

"Ever-evolving applications for the drug. Developed as a human anesthetic years ago," Dr. Stewart said. "Then it became a popular animal tranquilizer. Now some psychiatrists are using it to treat depression. Real-world guys are using it for date rape."

"Right. What are the effects?"

"There are plenty of them. Ketamine is a highly dissociative medication. Memory goes, and suggestibility of the victim is high, but physical performance isn't compromised as dramatically as with other tranquilizers. There are reasons it's a popular date-rape drug."

Memory goes. Mark let out a long breath. He might have something more than a desperate plea for Jeff London.

"When you say suggestibility of the victim is high, do you mean that someone who has been given it could be convinced to believe a version of events that wasn't true?"

"Possibly, although you'd have to see on a case-by-case basis; it's not a hard-and-fast rule. The imagination runs wild too. Hallucinations are common, which makes victim accounts extremely unreliable and makes the investigator's job harder."

"Hallucinations," Mark echoed, thinking of how clearly he'd seen Sarah Martin watching him from the rocks.

"Absolutely. It's called conscious sedation. Even if you know what is happening, you're unable to do anything about it. You're along for the ride."

"Suppose rape wasn't the goal," Mark said. "Suppose misinformation was the goal; would it be as effective?"

"I'm not sure that I follow. You mean, would it aid someone in lying to a victim?"

"Yes."

"Absolutely."

"And it's a pill or a liquid?"

"Both. You can inject it or snort it or, as is most common for criminal use, add it to a drink."

He spoke the words crisply but the images they conveyed were foggy and soft around the edges. Diane Martin's face, open and honest and imploring even as she told lies. Her eyes, so compelling, so haunting. Mark had looked into her eyes and he had known her pain. The greater violation was that he had believed she'd also known his. He tried to recall whether he'd left the table at some point, gone to the restroom or taken a call, given her any opportunity to be alone with his drink. He didn't think so. Then again, what he thought had happened no longer carried much weight. Memory and reality had taken different paths away from that meeting, and Mark had traveled along the wrong one.

"All right, Dr. Stewart," he said. "Thanks for the help. One last question, though, and this is important: How long would traces linger? How quickly do you need to test for its presence?"

"It *can* linger for up to two weeks, depending on the dose, but I'd want the test done within a few days, if at all possible."

Mark was four days removed from his meeting with Diane Martin now, and three days removed from the cave. He thanked Dr. Stewart again, hung up, and followed the GPS directions in search of Brett and Jeremy Leonard.

He'd been on the road for more than a mile before it felt familiar. He was in a tunnel of leafless trees, hemmed in, and up ahead, snow-covered fields stretched out, and a four-way stop loomed.

He pulled off the road and onto the shoulder and left the car running with the hazard lights flashing. Opened the door and stepped out into the snow and nodded when the wind rose to meet him. That was right. That was how it had been. No snow blowing in with it today, but the same arctic chill.

He walked down the middle of the road, looking at the pavement even though there would be nothing to see. The crime that had occurred here had been a clean one. No shots had been fired, no glass had broken, no evidence left behind to mark the road. He walked the pavement anyhow, just in case there was something. The intersection where the truck had turned sideways to block the road loomed ahead, and he thought then of an intersection in Cody, Wyoming, that he'd once thought of as the worst road in the world.

When Mark was thirteen, his uncles had retrieved a stray dog of indeterminate breed and presented it to him as a gift, against his mother's wishes. His uncles had named the dog Amigo, for reasons that probably had more to do with tequila than logic. Amigo was a goof, but he had fine energy and was well muscled, and when he laid out to run, he was *fast,* a true burner, and thus a wandering boy's best friend.

The only problem with Amigo—at least, the only one Mark saw—was that he pulled at his leash. The concept of being tethered was foreign to him, and what resulted was a war of wills.

It was on one of the more beautiful afternoons of spring that Amigo began to kick at the collar with his hind leg as they made the walk home. Mark responded by giving the leash a few gentle tugs, thinking that he needed to distract the dog from his itch, and then the third tug met no resistance and there was the tinkle of metal on asphalt. The collar had come free. For one long second, Amigo held his place, looking at Mark as if to see what the problem was. The choice Mark made then was the worst one possible: he lunged at the dog in the hope of recapturing him.

When Amigo hit full speed, he looked like a greyhound, his hind paws nearly catching his front as he exploded ahead. Mark compounded the mistake of the lunge by doing the only thing that he knew to do when a dog bolted—he ran after him. Amigo, absolutely delighted, raced ahead, the game of chase now fully approved.

There was a stop sign up ahead, and the road on the other side had a speed limit of thirty-five but nobody paid that number any mind and the average had to be fifty miles an hour. Mark ran after the dog as hard as he could, heart thundering and legs throbbing, but Amigo outpaced him effortlessly, gaining distance with each second and then pouring on speed as he approached the stop sign that meant absolutely nothing in his world. A Dodge pickup with oversize off-road tires and a lift kit roared downhill. Just before Amigo reached the intersection, he turned and looked at Mark with his tongue lolling and ears pinned back and an expression of utter, oblivious delight. Then he faced forward again, dipped lower, and ran on, through the stop sign and out in front of the truck.

Mark could see the rest as if it were written before him. The lift kit on the Dodge afforded extra height that exposed its undercarriage plain as day, including the axles that would corkscrew Amigo and thrash his body and throw it, mangled, out onto the other side.

Mark fell to his hands and knees and heard the horn blare and knew he owed it to his dog to watch—it seemed required—but he couldn't. He dropped his head and looked at his bleeding hands on the gravel and although he'd promised himself when he turned twelve that he would never cry again, he sobbed into the dust of the road.

He was still crying when he felt the dog's tongue. Amigo was lapping at his salty tears with the expression of delight still on his face, the game of chase everything he'd hoped for and more. Up ahead, the Dodge rested in a ditch just in front of the stop sign, trailed by black streaks of parched rubber, and a bearded man screamed obscenities at Mark from inside the cab.

Mark never walked Amigo on that route again. It was, as he told his mother and uncles—and, many times over, the dog—the worst road in the world.

He hadn't heard of the road to Cassadaga in those days.

They'd been in Cooke City, Montana, when his mother was arrested, and the cop told them that they couldn't take the dog. Mark, then fourteen, punched a grown man for the first time in his life that day. A police officer, no less. When his uncles heard the news and finally came to get Mark, they told him that Amigo was doing well, and the last time they'd seen the dog he'd been lounging in front of Miner's Saloon. *He's the town dog now,* Uncle Larry had said. *It's just as well. With your mother's habits, well, that's no way to raise a dog.*

If he'd understood the irony of that statement, he hadn't shown it.

For years, Mark dreamed of that hopeless run and the inevitable death that he was supposed to see, more a captured memory than a dream, always waking with a gasp when the dream dog's tongue touched his tears.

He missed the days when that dream had qualified as a nightmare.

He reached the stop sign and turned and looked back to where his rental car sat with the blinkers on, and he remembered everything that had happened here but he could not prove it. It was bad, but there were worse things, and he was well aware of them. At least he knew what had happened on this road.

From his vantage point in the middle of the intersection, he could see a weathered sign that he'd missed on his first trip, when all of his attention had been on the truck in his mirror. If he'd looked to the right at the stop sign, he would have seen it—a billboard advertising the *Amazing Trapdoor Caverns!*, only two miles away, on the left.

The Leonard brothers' home was "three point two miles ahead, destination on left," his GPS informed him.

Neighbors.

There were places where this wouldn't matter. He'd lived in enough one-stoplight towns to know that. But Garrison had a little more size to it, and Trapdoor wasn't on a major artery.

He walked back to the car and drove ahead slowly. The gated drive to Trapdoor appeared on his left and then fell behind in his mirror and the road curved sharply and then straightened out again and he saw that he was approaching the farm that could be seen from the banks of the creek near the cave, its rolling fields spread out over the bluffs.

Mark pulled into the gravel drive. The farmhouse was dark and the only vehicle in sight was a truck that looked as if it hadn't been moved in days.

No one answered his knock at the door, but instead of returning to the car, he walked up the drive and toward the barns, searching for any sign of life. He went from one outbuilding to another, knocking on doors, opening them, calling out. The only answers were the echoes of his own weary voice. He was winded from the walk, and even the echoes knew it.

He reached the stable last. It was set farthest back from the road and was clearly the newest of the buildings, styled to look like a high-end Kentucky ranch, home to Thoroughbreds. From the moment he entered it, memories slapped at him like storm-tossed waves. Nothing drove memories through you faster or harder than the senses. He'd learned that in a crippling way after Lauren was killed. He could be doing fine, getting through a day with a feeling of emotional control, and then something as simple as the smell of the right soap or the distant sound of the right song threatened to bring him to his knees.

The stable was all of this, heightened. He'd worked in a dozen of them, all in the West, and when he'd arrived in Florida with no money and needing a job, he'd known damn well that he could find the best pay at a stable, but he had gone to gas stations instead. He didn't want to remember the West. Not then, not now.

But here it was.

He put one hand on the steel rail of a stall gate and closed his eyes, drinking in the smell so pungent, it almost seemed to have a taste. The senses brought him another memory then, unbidden, as the thought of his family had been, relocating him in time and place once again. What he remembered was a smell that had been familiar but that he couldn't identify: the scent of the hood they'd pulled over his head in the field, rough as burlap, stinking of something earthy.

It had smelled of horse feed.

He opened his eyes and looked around the stalls and now he was entirely in the present.

There are a million feed sacks around here, he told himself. It was farm country. It could have come from anywhere.

But the Leonards didn't come from anywhere. They came from this place, and they ran with Evan Borders, and Evan Borders had once been a suspect in the murder of his teenage girlfriend Sarah Martin, and Evan Borders had exchanged calls with Ridley Barnes in the minutes preceding Mark's abduction.

He heard the sound of an engine then and walked out of the stable in time to see a pickup truck rattling in. A white Silverado. Like feed sacks, there would be plenty of them around here.

He waited outside the barn as the truck was parked and the driver got out—a large, bald man with a gray beard.

"Can I help you?"

"I was looking for Brett and Jeremy Leonard," Mark said, approaching the truck.

The man's face went from cordial to wary. "Those are my boys. What do you need with them?"

This obviously wasn't the first time someone had arrived in search of the Leonard boys.

"Wanted to ask them about clearing some snow," Mark said. "I was told they do that?"

"Oh, sure." The elder Leonard was relieved now. "I can

just take your name and address, get you put on the list. 'Nother storm due this evening is what I'm hearing. Be good to get on the plow schedule. I'm Lou, by the way."

Mark shook his hand but didn't give his own name, just said, "Good to meet you, Lou," and then he followed the older man inside the house. They walked into a kitchen that smelled of bacon, and Lou Leonard grabbed a notepad and a pen.

"It's my plow truck, but I don't get out there much anymore. That's a young man's game, you know? Takes a toll that you wouldn't think, all that time behind the wheel. And, hell, my eyes aren't what they used to be. When I was out in the last storm, I was struggling, to be honest. Was damn happy when the boys took over."

"Your boys, they work with Evan Borders?"

"Time to time. Evan's sketchy. Some days he's on time, some days he don't show up at all."

"Why do you keep him on?"

Lou Leonard sighed. "Family ties. That's my nephew. His mother left when he was a child, and I didn't blame her, though I'm not proud to say it. She'd found the wrong man. Carson was in a bar when he wasn't in a jail, and then he got sent up to Pendleton for a good stretch and Evan was in the wind, and I took him in so the state wouldn't. He lived with me while his daddy was in prison. You try to look out for someone that doesn't have anybody else. Some people call it foolish; I call it Christian."

"You said you were out in the last storm?" Mark asked.

"For a bit. I'm only good for a couple hours anymore."

Mark tried to keep his voice casual when he said, "What time was that?"

The old man gave him a curious look, and Mark said, "I was just thinking, it was blowing hard there for a while around noon. More than I could've handled."

"It was blowing hard," Lou agreed, and then he bent to his notepad again. "What was your name?"

"Mark Novak."

No reaction. For once, someone in Garrison didn't seem to be aware of who he was. He watched as his name was lettered in, and then Lou said, "Address?"

"I'm at Trapdoor Caverns right now."

This caught his attention. He looked up with a frown. "Doesn't Cecil clear the snow?"

"He's having some issues with the plow. It's a long driveway to work with just a snowblower."

"It sure is." But Lou was curious now, maybe suspicious.

"Your boys ever spend any time down in the cave when it was open?" Mark said. "I hear it was a popular place back in its day."

"For tourists maybe. I never cared for caves. Claustrophobic. Anyhow, we'll get you on the list, and when it snows, Cecil won't have to worry."

"Appreciate that." Mark turned to the window and waved a hand out at the fields. "Some beautiful horses there. You take care of them?"

"Yup. I never cared for horses much myself, but it's part of the job."

"What's the job?"

"Just what it looks like—tending the farm. All leased land now. People who own them horses are from Indianapolis. Had an idea about turning this place into some sort of a riding camp, training kids, crap like that. Poured money into the barn, but I ain't seen any dollars come back in from it yet. They don't need any, though. Funny how that goes—the people who own the land don't need the money from it; the people who live on it do. Ain't that the way all around?"

"I couldn't say. Your boys, do they tend to the horses as well?"

"Why in the hell are you so damn interested in my boys?"

"More interested in the horses, honestly. Look like nice animals. Well cared for."

"I suppose."

"Stable looks pretty well equipped too."

Lou tilted his head, eyeing Mark uneasily, and said, "What's it matter?"

"You ever hear of ketamine, Lou?"

"Nope."

Mark nodded. "Maybe your boys have," he said. "It's a horse tranquilizer."

Lou Leonard stared at Mark grimly. "What are you really after? What're they into?"

"I'll be real clear here," Mark said. "Your boys are going to want to speak with me. You're a smart guy, you get it. There are different roads I could take. The road *they* want to take? The road *you* want them to take? It starts with them coming to see me, Lou. Trust me on that."

"I don't know you. Sure as hell don't trust you."

"Sometimes you've got to gamble, Lou. I'll let you think on it." Mark gave him a little salute, turned, and left the house.

29

The black holes in Mark's memory hadn't swallowed his first visit to Trapdoor, and he noticed some changes there immediately: The gate at the top of the drive had been expanded with long strands of barbed wire, and the chains and locks were brand-new.

Mark pulled his rental car into the same place where they'd found the one that had been stolen, killed the engine, and sat in the silence for a few minutes, studying the property and trying to ignore the question dancing in his mind.

Is this the second time you've driven here or the third?

It was the second. He had to prove it, but he knew this.

Do you?

For the first time, he felt confident that he did. The ketamine explained what he could not. The proximity of the Leonards' farm seemed to go a long way toward explaining the rest of it, but he wanted to see how one would get down the bluffs to the cave entrance and whether they'd left any trace. He opened the door and stepped out into the snow. The waterproof boots held up well, and the jacket kept the wind from cutting him. All the same, each step was agony. He'd done nothing but drive and walk today, but his body felt pushed to its limits, and the physical aches were beginning to move toward mental, leaving him feeling feverish and a little dizzy.

He didn't make it nearly so far as he had on his first visit before he was interrupted.

"Unless you've got a badge, you better get the hell off this property or I'll call someone who does have a badge," Cecil Buckner began, boiling out of the garage as if he'd been lying in wait. He held a shotgun this time. Security at Trapdoor had been stepped up in the face of crisis, evidently. When he was close enough to see Mark's face, he pulled up short and squinted. "You got to be shitting me. You're *back?*"

"I've got some more questions," Mark said. "They're different this time around. I'd like to know how I got inside your cave."

"You ain't alone there, pal. I got my ass ripped good for it, like it was my fault."

Cecil propped the barrel of the shotgun in the snow and leaned on it as if it were a cane. Maybe it wasn't even loaded. Maybe he was just an idiot.

"I might know how to get us started answering them," Mark said. "What do you know about the family who lives in the farm up there?"

"The Leonards? Trash and trouble. Old Lou, he's not so bad, but those boys he raised are a different story." Cecil pointed in the opposite direction of the bluffs, off to the southwest, where the fields ran up alongside the road and a dilapidated trailer was barely visible. "Lou's sister lived right there, and she raised the only child in this county who could compete with his boys."

"Evan?"

"You know all the names, don't you? Yeah, that was his boyhood home. Nice place, ain't it? Now, you tell me, why in the hell would anybody want to rent to a family like that? It doesn't make sense. But Pershing—"

"Cecil?" A voice sharp as a gunshot snapped at them from the deck of the big house. "Who is it?"

Mark looked up and saw a woman framed in the doorway of the house. At the sight of her, Cecil went from cooperative gossip to guard dog in a flash, lifting the shotgun back into firing position and straightening up, like a sentry who'd been caught sleeping.

"It's that asshole who broke into the cave! I was throwing him out. You want me to call the police?"

There was a pause as the woman considered this information. From a distance, Mark couldn't tell much about her other than that she was young and slim and looked very cold on the deck. Outlined against the white landscape of the farm fields beyond, she also looked very alone.

"Bring him up," she said.

Cecil looked at Mark with a touch of pity. "That's Danielle MacAlister, Pershing's daughter. You're going to wish I'd just called the police."

The woman met them at the front door. It hadn't been a long walk, but Mark was winded by the time they arrived.

"Trespassing and breaking and entering could already be established, but now you're back," she said. "Perhaps stalking begins to apply."

She was young, maybe not yet thirty, wearing jeans and a button-down shirt, sleeves rolled up to expose thin forearms that were adorned with bracelets. An attractive woman, certainly, but if she had any charm to match her looks, it was well hidden. She had the bearing of someone used to being the boss but without the age that usually went with it.

"The breaking-and-entering charge might be useful,"

Mark said, "but it won't be levied against me. I was brought into the cave against my will. If you're scrambling for legal grounds, you might want to spend a little time brushing up on your own liability. I nearly died in a cave that you own and claim is secure."

"It's been secure for ten years, and I hardly think I'm liable when someone pries bars apart so he can—"

"I'm not really interested in the charges," Mark interrupted. "Go ahead and file them. I'll deal with them as they come. That's the least of my problems. I'm going to find the people who put me down there, and I'm going to find out why Ridley Barnes has such clout in a place where he's supposedly loathed and what inspired him to try to hire detectives to put him in the electric chair."

She'd wanted to continue the hostility, had been bracing for further argument, but something knocked her off stride.

"What do you mean, he tried to hire detectives to put him in the electric chair?"

"Ridley Barnes requested an investigation in Sarah Martin's murder so that he might know whether or not he killed her. We've seen a lot of odd requests, but that was a first."

Danielle MacAlister paused, then said, "Give us a few minutes, Cecil," dismissing the caretaker without even glancing his way. He gave a sullen nod and shuffled off, casting one look back at Mark as if to say, *I told you the police would be better.* She told Mark to come inside, and only when the door was closed behind him did she speak again.

"Ridley Barnes wants the case reopened?"

"That's right. I came up to discuss things. I knew nothing about what had happened here. It was preliminary talk, nothing more, at least until people began to involve me in elaborate lies and then tried to kill me. I owe your caretaker some gratitude, by the way. If he weren't alert on the job, I would have frozen to death down there."

She didn't seem to register those words. "Ridley Barnes *wants* the case reopened," she echoed, and then gave a bitter laugh. "That twisted bastard."

"Tell me about him," Mark said. "Please. Or put me in touch with your father so I can talk to him."

"You won't have any luck," she said. "My father is not very lucid these days. He had a bad stroke two years ago and has been in assisted living ever since. He might tell you stories about Trapdoor, but they're likely to be a product of his own imagination."

"He won't be alone in that regard."

She considered him in silence for a few seconds and then said, "I shouldn't be talking to you, but I'll go this far, despite my better judgment. You tell me about Ridley, everything *you* know about him, and I'll offer the same."

"Fair enough," Mark said, "but why so interested, Danielle?"

"My father was engaged to Diane Martin," Danielle MacAlister said. "Sarah and I would have been stepsisters, Mr. Novak. Instead, by the next summer, Sarah was in a casket, and Diane had left my father. Meanwhile, Ridley Barnes is free and clear. Do you still have any questions as to why I'm so *interested?*"

"No," Mark said. "No, I don't think so. Let's talk about Ridley."

He told her. Everything that she asked and that he could answer, he told her.

"I've got to defend myself against the lies that have been told," he concluded when she seemed to have run out of questions. "But more than that? There are people who should pay for what happened here, but I'm not one of them. I won't play that role."

She listened to that in silence.

"Okay," he said. "That's what I can give you. Every answer I have, you've heard. Your turn. Tell me about the Ridley Barnes you know."

She hesitated, then turned from him. "Follow me. I can *show* you Ridley. I can show you where the whole ugly mess began."

30

The basement was unfinished with walls of rough concrete block, cool and dimly lit. Metal stools without backs sat before an old workbench with a set of steel vises. An ancient La-Z-Boy recliner was in the corner of the room beside a minifridge from the same era, unplugged. Twin file cabinets stood against one wall beneath a bare lightbulb with a pull chain that produced dim light. The walls were lined with maps.

"The basement was my father's sacred ground," Danielle said. "Where all the grand plans were made. Where he looked at those maps and dreamed of success."

"What was success, in his mind?"

"Something bigger," she said with a wave of her hand. "Isn't that always the way? The small want to be big, the big want to be monstrous, and the monstrous..." She ran out of orders of magnitude, leaving *monstrous* to be the end of the growth cycle.

Mark walked to the wall and studied the hand-drawn maps.

"Chronological order, from left to right," Danielle MacAlister said. "The first ones were done by a group. You'll see the names on there. Then you'll see what it turned into."

Mark moved from left to right, passing across the years of Trapdoor. Many of the maps—most, even—were redundant, the only difference being changes to dimensions of chambers or passages, with few new discoveries. Most of the discovering in the early days had been done by Pershing MacAlister, Tyler Spatta, Dave Everton, and Joseph Anderson. Their names were noted on all the maps, and each was signed by the party who'd created the physical drawing— MacAlister had less skill but paid more attention to detail; Anderson had crafted far better images, but MacAlister had gone back through and corrected his measurements. The artist and the engineer working in tandem.

"Who were these three?" Mark asked. "Beyond your father, who are these guys?"

"Local cavers. When the place was first discovered, he recruited a team to help him explore it. Then he came across Ridley Barnes, who was supposed to be the best caver in the area and the most experienced with exploration teams. The others were willing to work with him, but Ridley had his own set of rules. He wasn't going to volunteer for the job, like everyone else had, and he was going to work alone. I don't know how much you understand about caves?"

"Next to nothing."

"Okay. Well, cave exploration, or digs, the trips to try and find new passages, they're incredibly dangerous if not done properly. People *always* work in teams. For a man to insist on working alone is beyond foolish. But that was Ridley."

"Why did your father agree to it, then?"

She sat on one of the stools in front of the workbench. "He got protective."

"Of what?"

"The potential, I suppose. He had a theory that there was something truly massive waiting to be found in there.

Something that would make the existing tour cave portion look like child's play. Ridley promised him secrecy—I've reviewed the confidentiality agreements and contracts they signed—but in exchange, he was paid for his work, and he was allowed to do it alone. For nine months, Trapdoor was Ridley's full-time job. He said it was the happiest he'd ever been in his life. That ended two weeks before Sarah was killed."

The final sets of maps were signed by Ridley and drawn with remarkable skill and attention to detail and scale; here, engineer and artist were combined in one man. Here, also, the rate of discovery accelerated. The original chambers and passages remained, but every so often an entirely new section would appear. Seeing the cave grow on the maps this way was a bizarre, fascinating thing, like watching a chronological series of fetal ultrasounds, except that the cave had always been there and needed only to be discovered.

Some of the chambers had names—the Funnel Room, the Chapel Room—and others did not. The stream flowing through the middle was labeled Greenglass River. Danielle, following his index finger as he traced along, said, "Ridley came up with that name. Most of the names are my father's ideas. The Chapel Room and Greenglass River belong to Ridley."

Outside the mouth of the cave, Greenglass River changed to Maiden Creek.

"Maiden Creek? That's really what it's called?"

"Yes," Danielle said. "Supposedly named after a beautiful young pioneer girl who drowned in it while running from the Indians."

Mark felt a cold that had nothing to do with the temperature. His face must have showed it, because Danielle said, "Why is that a problem for you?"

Because when my mother decided to be an Indian, she

named herself Snow Creek Maiden, he thought, *so if I'm standing beside Maiden Creek in the snow, maybe Ridley is right. When dangerous things stop feeling like coincidences, what's the term for that?*

But all he said was "That's a sad story, if it's true. Probably isn't, though. Most of the legends aren't. Here's a novice question, but I don't understand how it could take so long for these new portions to be found."

"Then you don't understand caves. My father didn't either. Ridley Barnes did. It also wasn't that long, really. My father bought the acreage for the timber rights but hadn't cut a single tree before the cave opened up."

"What do you mean, opened up? He had to go looking for it, right?"

She shook her head. "He bought the property in August and intended to begin timbering the following summer. That winter, it just sat. The next spring was a wet one, with high flood levels. The creek spilled over its banks and flooded a small pond that was on the other side. The level in the pond kept rising too. Then the pond vanished into the ground."

"Completely?" He was trying to envision it, trying to imagine what it must have been like to walk out into daylight and see that while you'd slept, the earth had changed.

"Completely. Where it had been, there was nothing but a gaping sinkhole with a small gap in the stone at the base. The ground just opened up and swallowed the pond. Hence the name—it swung open just like a trapdoor. A couple of the locals grabbed flashlights and ropes and went in and eventually called my father. Back then, the entrance was so small you had to squeeze to get through it. When my father realized there was a large cave beyond, he blasted the stone out to get the entrance you see today, and it looks like it has always been there."

Mark kept moving around the walls of maps as he listened, and as he studied the dimensions and details, he tried to find a room that approximated the one where'd he found himself. None of them did. There were some drops and cliffs, but nothing that looked as sheer as what he'd encountered. *Maybe it wasn't that deep at all. How do you know when you didn't see it? You also heard snakes. Without a doubt. But those weren't real. And what about Sarah Martin, sitting on that ledge with light emanating from her pores? Was that real?*

He finally reached the last one, an elaborate and painstaking sketch, dated May 2004.

"Ridley didn't find anything new that summer?" Mark asked.

"Oh, he did. He claimed to have made extraordinary finds that summer. He was *getting close,* he kept telling my dad, he was always *getting close.* But he never turned over the maps."

"According to the case reports, Blankenship was removed from the investigation because he had a relationship with Sarah's mother. But she was engaged to your father."

Danielle winced. "Both are true, ugly as that sounds. Sarah's father was killed in a bad trucking accident when she was twelve. Blankenship was the deputy who'd informed the family. He stayed in touch with Diane throughout, and eventually, he fell in love with her. Fell hard, I believe. Sarah told me that. But then Sarah began to work out here. Diane had a terrible fear of cars after the accident. She wouldn't let Sarah get a driver's license, so she would drop her off and pick her up every day. It was humiliating to Sarah—you know, the worries of the sixteen-year-old—but it also meant Diane was around every day." She sighed. "I'd love to tell you my father is this wonderful, noble man. I think he's a good man, and

I love him. But he has his weaknesses. Diane would have been his third wife, and I think there was another one who was almost in the mix. My mother was his second. My father liked to play the savior role. People accused those women of being gold diggers, but they were wrong. He liked to find women he could dazzle. Women he could introduce to a different type of world, a different lifestyle. Diane was one of those."

"So Blankenship was the jilted one in all this?"

"He felt he was, at least. He was also the one who called for Ridley over my father's objections. I don't think he's ever really recovered from that. How could someone?"

"Why did your father object?"

"Ridley was a disturbed man. We all knew that, because we'd been around him. Blankenship hadn't. He just thought he was getting an expert. That much was true, but he hadn't heard the way Ridley talked about the cave, talked about its power, talked about it like it was a person. And I think my father had an even darker concern that he didn't give voice to."

"What was that?"

"Ridley made some odd remarks about the girls who worked here. About me, and about Sarah. He said once that Sarah looked like his sister, but it was not a casual comment. It was creepy. It just felt *off*."

Mark remembered the chill he'd felt when Ridley said that Sarah had caught his eye.

"I understand that Blankenship was told Ridley could move fast in the cave, but I've always wondered how much of that decision to overrule my father came from testosterone rather than logic."

Probably a lot of it, Mark thought. Put a woman between two men, and anything that was even a cousin of logic would usually drown in the tidal waves of testosterone.

"At any rate, Blankenship was removed from the scene, and Ridley came. The rest ... well, you know the rest."

"I know the result. That's all."

"Then you know as much as everyone else. Nobody knows the rest except for Ridley Barnes."

"What do *you* think he did?" he asked.

"I think he killed her. He was supposed to *lead* the team, not *leave* the team. And the way he talked about the cave as if it were alive? It always gave me chills. He referred to the cave as 'her' or 'she' all the time. 'The old girl,' that was one of his favorites. Then he began to talk about his discoveries of new passages as if the cave had guided him. 'The old girl was whispering to me today, Danielle. She's starting to tell me her secrets.' I will never forget those words. So disturbing, particularly with the look in his eyes. This ... hunger. He'd gotten possessive about access to the cave too, wanted limits on everyone. Ironic, because that's just the way my father was. Trapdoor has that effect, I suppose. Another reason I'll never open the door." She looked at Mark with distaste. "Not that the locks stopped you."

"I didn't go in that cave of my own free will. And if you feel so passionately about Ridley's history, then you really should believe me."

"Maybe. If that were the only part of the story, I probably would, in fact. But that's *not* the only part of the story, is it? You also claimed to have seen Diane. I can believe some things about Ridley Barnes, and most of them are uniquely evil, but I don't believe he summoned poor old Diane Martin from the grave."

"She wasn't summoned from the grave. She was impersonated, and then people lied about it to make me look like a fool and keep the police from searching for the person who did it."

"Why would they do that?"

"People lie for different reasons. For money, sometimes. For power."

"Ridley is in no position to grant anyone money or power."

"There are other reasons. Fear, for one. You don't think Ridley can wield fear? Sounds like that's what he's good at."

She didn't answer. Instead, she reached out to one of the vises mounted on the workbench and ran a fingertip along the inside. It came back dry and clean, but she rubbed her fingers together and laughed.

"It still smells the same."

"What's that?"

"This room. Nobody has done any real work down here in years, but it still smells like sawdust, don't you think?"

It did. There wasn't a trace of sawdust in the room, but the smell was certainly there. She returned her focus to him. There was an intensity to it that, combined with her youth, made her painfully familiar. She looked like Lauren had when they were discussing a case for Innocence Incorporated. Danielle's face was more angular, with higher cheekbones, and her hair was auburn instead of blond, but the body type was close, and the combination of intelligence and intensity was identical. She was an attorney too. A young attorney, full of confidence, ready to conquer.

He looked away from her and reached automatically into his pocket for the Saba dive permit, forgetting that it was no longer there. He removed his hand and gazed around the room at that mess of maps, slowly developing, like an old Polaroid, revealing more and more.

"Do these maps show where I was found?" he said.

"No. You were off the maps."

"But not off Ridley's."

She shook her head. It was silent for a while, and then she broke the quiet by saying, "So people lie for different reasons. I'll grant you that. But if this woman impersonated Diane Martin...that's more than a lie. It would mean she's a little more invested, don't you think? It would mean that she has a stake in Ridley."

"Agreed."

"That's why I have trouble believing you," she said. "I can't imagine who in the world would have a stake in Ridley Barnes."

"Four people," Mark said. "Three guys on the road, and then the woman who pretended to be Diane."

Danielle frowned and shook her head. "Somehow the woman is harder for me to believe. The idea that he'd be able to recruit some locals with guns? I believe that. But a woman, *any* woman? Unless he paid her by the hour, I can't see it." She folded her arms across her chest. "I've given you more than you deserve, Mr. Novak. More than I should have, probably. But I'll admit that you've made me curious. If you have other questions, I'll consider answering them. Emphasis on *consider*. Because until you find a way to explain that story about Diane Martin, or prove anything else that you say, you feel just a little too much like Ridley himself for comfort."

31

She held a towel filled with ice against the side of his face and ran her fingertips lightly over the swollen skin. "Ridley," she said, "it was a mistake. It was too much."

He took a few breaths through his mouth—it was still painful to breathe through his nose, thanks to Novak—and said, "He's still here, at least."

"And how's that going for you?"

"We knew he wouldn't take it well. We always knew that."

"There's a difference."

"Easy thing to say. But if you imagine how he felt…"

"Trust me, I did. Before I saw him, and after. And during. Especially during."

"He was going to leave."

"Maybe not."

"He would have. I'm sure of it. And you know I can't allow that. He's too special."

She moved the ice away. "A mistake," she repeated.

"That's what he called it too."

"Unanimous, then." She replaced the ice, a little lower now. He closed his eyes against it and spoke with them squeezed shut.

"Now the sheriff is back around. I shouldn't be surprised,

but I have trouble with him all the same. I have struggles."
He opened his eyes. "He asked questions about how Novak
ended up in the cave, and I almost had to tell him."

"What would you have told him?"

"The truth."

"And what is the truth?"

"The cave sent forces to the surface for him. It was bound
to happen. He's special. The cave knows that. The cave
wasn't going to let him leave here without a visit." Ridley
shook his head with frustration and confessed the thing he
did not want to tell her: "I drew a knife on Novak."

The ice lowered again. Her eyes on him now were horri-
fied. Julianne's eyes usually held only sympathy or sugges-
tion. This reaction to him was jarring.

"You did *what?*" she said.

"Nothing happened. But it just..." He struggled for
words. Looking her in the eyes, he often did. "It just found
its way there."

"A knife just *found its way* into your hand?"

He fell silent, sucking air in through his mouth, and
closed his eyes.

"Talk me down," he said. "Please."

"It won't be easy right now. With the adrenaline? It won't
be easy."

"I can focus," Ridley said.

"Maybe we should stay up here for a while. Here on the
surface of the mind."

"I don't need that."

"Some people might disagree. Some people might hear
the story you told, hear about the knife in your hand, and
think that you cannot carry control back to the surface with
you."

"I have control!" The statement sounded ludicrous when

shouted. He took a breath, steadied himself, and repeated it again, lower and softer. "I have control."

"It's about trust, Ridley. You've always understood this."

"I trust you."

"I'm not the concern. Mr. Novak is your concern, isn't he? This will have been a waste unless you put real trust in him, Ridley. You'll need to turn over more than a case file."

After a short silence, the ice returned to his face. He tried to concentrate on only that sensation, tried not to think of the things that he wanted to think of, the things that could raise odd smiles at the wrong times. Knives and blood; shadows and screams. *No, no. Don't think those thoughts. Just the ice. Just concentrate on the ice.*

Her voice floated toward him then, softer and lower.

"Tell me your awareness of this space. Tell me what you feel."

"The ice. Only that."

"The ice, yes. You feel it on your skin, don't you?"

"Yes."

"And below the skin, on your nerves. Do you feel the ice on your nerves?"

"Yes."

"Follow the cold then. Down from the skin, down into the nerves. Let it go. Let it travel. Then travel with it, but only when you can see your path."

Silence. He kept his eyes shut, trying to visualize it, seeing his nerve endings like sea grass, loose and shifting. Saw the ice spread through them, slide down, find tunnels, and seep into them.

Then her voice again. Softer. "Let's imagine the way down. Do you mind if I touch you?"

"No."

Her hand moved to his and turned it over, and she began

to tap rapidly and rhythmically on the inside of his wrist. Then she moved to his face, her fingers avoiding the swollen areas Novak had left. The sensation, jarring at first, quickly became pleasant. So much tension—and things worse than tension—seemed to evaporate at the touch. It was like turning on windshield wipers, the way ahead suddenly clear again, the clouded vision gone.

"What do you see?" she asked as if she understood.

"Stone walls. Stone all around."

"Yes. And what does it smell like?"

"Damp. Old water."

"Yes. Tell me what you feel now that is different than before." The tapping never disrupted her voice. They could move at distinctly separate rhythms but in perfect harmony.

"Cool."

"Too cool? Cold?"

"No. Just right. Just right."

"Yes, it is. Yes. Look farther now, out ahead. What does it look like ahead?"

"Darker."

"Is the dark bad?"

"No. No, it's good."

"You're right." Her voice became softer still, fading, receding. "Now imagine a version of yourself that stands ahead, already there in the dark, already waiting. Perhaps he has always been here. Perhaps he watches over you from this spot. Go to that version of yourself now. Become that version of yourself. Now look back from that spot. What does that version of you see now, from this spot, that you did not see before?"

"That it's dark behind me too. That I've always been in the dark."

"What does that mean to you?"

"The darkness is within me. I don't have to search for it."

"Are you still moving?"

"I'm moving," he said, and the ice was harder to concentrate on now, his own voice farther away too, remaining with hers, wherever hers was. "I'm going farther down the tunnel. Farther down..."

A glimmer then, a flash of steel and a spray of crimson mist, and Ridley winced against it, trying to close eyes that were already closed. He had to hold the right visual. The wrong ones were dangerous. *Don't take those tunnels. Find the right ones.* He breathed deeply, slowly, and imagined himself returning to a chamber with many options. Imagined going down another passage now, one that led away from that glint of steel and blood. Here there was nothing but darkness and cool. Good. Follow it on, then. Go down, go deeper.

And keep going.

32

The exhaustion that had settled into Mark while he was with Danielle MacAlister peaked as he walked back to his car, every muscle ache amplified by the uphill walk through the snow. Cecil Buckner came out of his garage, where he had the bay doors open and appeared to be tinkering with a snowblower, and stood with his hands on his hips.

"Ain't she a treat?" he called.

"She was more cooperative than most."

Cecil shook his head. "Be careful with her, buddy."

Mark stopped. "Why?"

Cecil turned to look at the big house. There was smoke rising from the chimney now. Danielle had started a fire. Snowflakes had just begun to fall, joining the thin trail of smoke. When Cecil spoke again, his usually booming voice was softer.

"Everybody's got an agenda. Don't you forget that."

"What's hers?"

Cecil wouldn't take his eyes off the house, as if he was afraid someone would see them talking. "I couldn't say. But she sure as hell hustled up here once you got inside the cave, didn't she? First time I've seen her in almost three years too. I've *asked* her to come up and she says, 'No, thanks, keep up the good work,' *click.* But you got in and the police got called, and now she's camped out at that house. Staying the week, she says. For what? I says. But she won't answer that."

"What's her father like?"

"Aged and addled now. I haven't seen Pershing in five years, at least. Back when he was around, when the cave was open, he was popular with some, I suppose. You want to know what Pershing was like, you just close your eyes and picture the nineteenth hole at a country club. Any country club. They've all got one like him. Old-timer camped out at the bar acting like he's not an old-timer, telling bawdy jokes, silver hair that wouldn't slip out of place in a cyclone, a big tipper when people are watching, ten percent when they aren't. Tell me, buddy, ain't you met a guy like that somewhere along the line?"

"A few."

"Exactly. You got a sense of him, then. Some people take to that, others don't. He rubbed some of the cavers the wrong way because of how he treated Trapdoor, like personal property."

"Well, isn't it?"

Cecil frowned. "Yes, except there's a certain understanding with caves. A respect. It's a small community of people who care about them, and Pershing didn't get that. He just saw it as something like an oil well, a lucky piece of ground that was worth some dollars. Nobody else's business."

"Now he doesn't care about the dollars?"

"I field offers for this place on a regular basis. State officials, parks people, some private buyers. They come down here and talk to me, and I relay the messages. The answer is always a firm no. The MacAlisters don't want to sell *or* open the cave. But if you're not going to open the cave, why not unload it and make a couple million? I suppose he has the money not to care, but I don't understand it, and it surely doesn't sit well with people around here."

"Why do they care so much?"

Cecil rubbed his thumb and index finger together in the universal gesture meaning "money." "When the ground opened up and the cave came into view, people thought it was manna from heaven. The town was going to become a tourist economy, don't you know. Then that girl got killed, a sad deal to be sure, but no reason to shut the whole show down. But Pershing did shut it down, so there's the sense that he didn't ever give a damn about this place or the people in it. I don't know if that's right or wrong; all I know is that in the past ten years, I'm the only person in Garrison who's been making a living off him."

"How'd that come to pass?"

Cecil pointed at a massive tree beside them. "See that red oak?"

"Yeah."

"That's what I know. Trees. My family moved up here from Carolina in the early 1900s. Came for jobs at the resorts over by French Lick. But back in Carolina, they worked with timber. Until it was all cut. That's the problem with the way they handled that job back then. Cut off the hand that fed them, eventually. Then you had to move on. My family moved here. The knowledge of these trees, hell, that goes back to men I've never even seen in pictures. My family loved trees. That might sound strange considering they've always cut them down, but it's true. My father was in the timber business, and I came in behind him. Pershing was just a buyer. My job was to scout property for him. I chose this one for those trees. A lot of red oak, some walnut stands. Good hardwood. Turned out to be the most valuable find anyone ever made for him, but not because of the trees; they didn't count in that equation. The cave was where the money waited. Still waits. Anyone who opened that cave now, if it's everything Ridley Barnes claimed, would be a hero."

"Have you dealt with Barnes much?"

Cecil pulled off his knit cap and ran a hand over his bald head, his mouth twisting as if he'd tasted something sour.

"Dealt *with* him? Shit. I s'pose you could say that I've dealt with him. Crazy bastard showed up a few times over the years, trying to get in. Caught him once when he was set to go to work on those doors with a damned arc torch. Last time I threw him out, he took to begging. Got down on his knees like he was about to blow me. The man is everything people say, and then some. But the dealings I had *because* of him, those were the real bullshit matters."

"What do you mean?"

Cecil pulled the cap back on. His eyes had never left the house. "You heard what he had to say about his time in that cave before he found her?"

"I've read most of it, at least."

"Then you heard about the dark man."

"Yes."

Cecil gave an unpleasant smile. "You haven't been around town long, but let me ask you, how many black faces you seen?"

"Just you."

"There you go. I'm not completely alone in Garrison, but closer to it than not. Tell you just how, um, politically correct our local police are. They heard the phrase *dark man* and brought me in for questioning. No bullshit, it was that fast. Dark man." He shook his head, still in disbelief a decade after it had happened. "So I got grilled like a suspect while Ridley was being treated for hypothermia and, at that time, like a hero. For a few hours. Then they realized he was talking about some sort of damned ghost or phantom and thought the cave was a person and that the girl was alive but, no, maybe she was dead, she either said something or she didn't, maybe it was the cave talking to him, and he didn't remember her having handcuffs on, but maybe she did. Got to scrambling all over the place and then he just stopped talking, period. But not before he explained that the dark man lived in the cave and always had and couldn't die. He was eternal, that's my understanding. So me, this dark man, I got thanked for my time and sent on my way. But I haven't forgotten that. Shit, would you?"

"No," Mark said. "I wouldn't."

Cecil nodded and spit into the snow. "There ya go. As for Miss MacAlister up there? If I were you, I'd be careful with her, that's all. With that family."

"They seem to have been good enough to you."

Cecil's cockeyed grin held no humor. "Seem to, right? But that's another question you might think on before you throw in with the MacAlister family, buddy. You might ask why in the hell it's worth paying a caretaker to live down here if you have no intention of opening the cave or selling it. Why not seal the fucker down, pour some concrete in that entrance, and be done with it?"

"You're the caretaker," Mark said. "You tell me."

Cecil shook his head. "I can't, honestly. I keep expecting to get my walking papers. They never come. I stick on because, well, I like the place. I live for free, I hunt for free— there are fine deer in these woods, I take a buck every season—and what work there is ain't so bad. Painting and roofing and general repairs. I like working with my hands, I like my solitude, I like this place. But I'm providing maintenance on a forgotten property and one without any future. There are times I wonder about that. But then?" He spit into the snow again. "Then I remind myself to be grateful for the job. It's a paycheck, and it's a fine place to live. Better than any I had before. Long as I can get away with it, I'll stay here. But there are questions." His eyes remained on the smoke wafting from the chimney and joining the leaden sky. "There are certainly questions."

Mark was so tired when he reached the car that he wanted nothing more than to start the heater and sleep with his head on the steering wheel. Instead he drove through the blowing snow back to town, back to the same hotel where it had all begun.

The same clerk was on duty, the one who had looked the sheriff directly in the eyes and lied to him. When she saw Mark, she walked into an office and shut the door. A moment later, the door opened and a fat man with a receding hairline, pleated pants, and a stern expression appeared. Management.

"What do you need, sir?"

"A room, please."

"I'm afraid we can't do that."

Mark raised his eyebrows. "The sign says *vacancy*."

"It's not an issue of space."

"So what's the problem?"

"Let's not play dumb, please. The last time you were here, you caused some problems. You frightened my staff. You're not welcome back."

Mark leaned on the counter, a move the man apparently took as a show of aggression, because he backed up fast.

"I didn't cause any problems, and if your staff member was frightened, she was frightened by whoever convinced her to lie. Either way, I just want a shower and some sleep."

"Please don't make this difficult. I don't want to call the police."

"Call the police? I'm just asking for a damned room!"

"They have some across the street," the fat man said, and then he, too, turned and walked into the office, leaving Mark alone in the lobby where once he'd believed he'd met Diane Martin. He stood there for a moment, then gave up and shouldered his bag. He walked back out into the cold and across the parking lot. The only other options were the kind of motels he hated, where the doors opened directly to the outside. The crime scene–tape doors. There was one across the street.

The clerk there was a bored-looking woman with dyed-blond hair and long, bright red acrylic nails. She didn't seem happy that Mark had interrupted her television viewing with his arrival, but she rented him a room without question or curiosity.

According to the thermostat, the room was warm, but Mark's body argued that. He cranked the heat up and fastened both the dead bolt and the flimsy chain and then sat on the bed, thinking of Danielle MacAlister and the information she'd provided and the questions he could have asked, should have, while she was talking. It had been a surprise that she was that willing to talk. From Jeff London to Sheriff Blankenship to Cecil Buckner, nobody had given him the idea that she'd be cooperative.

Why had she been, then? There was something wrong with that. He'd intrigued her with the information about Ridley, yes, but had he hooked her enough for an attorney, no matter how young or inexperienced, to begin to tell the family stories to a stranger, let alone a potentially problematic stranger? No. She should have been more guarded than that, and she'd intended to be when he walked into the house. Then she'd pulled a one-eighty during the conversation. Why?

He leaned back on the bed as warm air smelling of burned dust swept out of the small heating unit, then he closed his eyes and fell asleep on the grimy comforter before even removing his boots. When Jeff London called, he didn't hear the phone ring.

His dreams were filled with maps. Obstinate, senseless maps. Frustrated in his attempts with them, he laid a compass down on the paper, trying to get his bearings. It was the compass his uncle had given him for his tenth birthday, a plastic device with a rotating bezel and a signal mirror to be used in case you needed rescue. To see the compass, you had to lift the top of the case, exposing the mirror. In the dream, when Mark set the compass on the map, the needle began to spin, true north impossible to find. Any true direction impossible to find. As the needle spun faster, the bezel began to move, too, going counterclockwise, so the magnetic needle and the guide were turning in opposite directions, spinning faster and faster. Something moved in the signal mirror then, and when Mark looked at it, he saw that the mirror was filled with Ridley Barnes's face. As the spinning compass picked up even more speed, Ridley smiled.

33

The drive to Stinesville usually took more than an hour in good conditions, and it took Ridley two hours in the snow. The county roads hadn't seen a plow yet, and though the accumulation was minimal, the changeover from rain to snow had allowed for a thin layer of ice. The rubber on the tires of his old truck was thinner still. He nursed the truck along, a tow chain jingling among the sandbags and cinder blocks that he'd tossed in the back to add weight over the rear axle.

The snow was blowing harder in Spencer, and the town streets were empty and unusually dark, none of the neon glowing at him from the gas stations along the highway. A power outage, evidently. He turned east and drove with the wind at his back, as if being offered up to the world by the storm itself.

The old family land was down a gravel road marked by sets of massive ruts left behind by an oversize four-wheel drive. Ridley decided he'd rather hike than shovel his tires out, and he left the truck on the side of the road, slipped his backpack over his shoulders, and stepped out into the wind. His breath was coming fast, fogging the air in quick puffs like antiaircraft fire. He didn't like this place, never had, never would. It was where he'd buried the darkest parts of him. Or where he'd tried to.

He walked down the road, his boots occasionally catching gravel but more often just snow, and above him the naked branches of the ash and walnut trees weaved and creaked. Shadows flickered ahead, dancing from one side of the drive to the other, and once he was certain that he saw his father among them. He kept his head down after that. His mother was the only one who belonged here—they'd scattered her ashes on an autumnal wind beneath a sky so blue that it hurt to look at—but it seemed unlikely she'd make an appearance. She'd been a quiet presence in Ridley's life and when his father was around, not much of a presence at all.

He wasn't certain who lived in the old house now. It had changed hands a few times, he was aware of that. He didn't care much. He'd sold the place as soon as it was his to sell, used the money to send his younger sister through two years of college. She lived in Rhode Island now, and he didn't hear from her often. Christmas cards always came, but they bore no message beyond whatever the card company had thought to offer. Once they had spoken on the telephone with some consistency. That had ended about ten years ago. He hadn't fought it. She had children who would ask questions about their uncle if they knew he was out there. You had to be understanding of something like that.

The house seemed to be occupied, with two vehicles parked outside, but the windows were dark, lights either lost to the power outage or turned off ahead of sleep. The outbuilding where his father had once taught him how to work wood with chisels and how to take a punch without tears had collapsed in on itself, the remains looking like something that had been subjected to a long, slow squeeze. A sapling was growing through a hole in the roof. Ridley skirted the building in a wide, looping arc, keeping his distance from whatever lingered there.

Fifty yards beyond the outbuilding, right where the field grass began to give itself over to brush at the edge of the tree line, the strip pit announced itself in a series of rock slabs burped up by the earth and then forgotten. The ash tree whose roots had once provided a chin-up-bar-style exit had died and fallen on its side. Someone had taken the time to limb it with a chain saw but had left most of the massive trunk and root ball untouched. They loomed above the pit now like bulwarks hastily erected against an invading army.

You didn't need a rope to descend into this pit, but Ridley wanted to work fast, and the ropes allowed for that. He freed them from his pack, scraped the snow clear beneath one of the uneven spots of the trunk, and then slid the rope around it and cinched it. A good anchor, and an easy one.

He was wearing a headlamp but hadn't turned it on yet, performing all of the tasks so far with ease, because the night didn't seem the least bit dark to him. Not aboveground, where the white snow held starlight and traces of a rarely seen moon. He glanced at the house, sure that he'd heard a whisper, but there was no sign of movement, and when he heard the whisper again, he knew that it was his own name, and he knew who was calling for him. He kept his eyes away from the remains of the woodshop, slipped into the strip pit, and began to rappel down into the darkness, closing his eyes against memories of outstretched hands scrambling to catch him before he could make it deep enough.

No hands chased him today. He went about ten feet down, until the neck of the pit narrowed, and then he clicked on the headlamp, keeping it to the dim red setting that was designed to protect night vision. He wasn't worried about his night vision but he didn't want to draw attention to himself if anyone in the house got up to take a piss. You could see the pit from the bathroom window. The bathroom window had been the place where Ridley usually reentered the house late at night. His sister, the one who now lived with her family in Rhode Island, had always unlocked it again after their father passed out. She'd been very young in those days, but still she had remembered Ridley, and stayed awake for him. The only one in the house who would.

He hated making this return, thought now that this had been a terrible idea. It had made some sort of karmic sense, leaving as much evil in this place as possible, but he should have known he would have to come back for one piece of it or another at some point. The world above didn't just let you put things away and move on. It sent you back for them in time, or—far worse—brought them back up for you.

When the walls of the pit began to squeeze his thighs, he let the rope go slack. This was the place where his father had never been able to follow, not even with his most diligent efforts. He was a bigger man and he drank too much and exercised too little. Ridley remembered being on a date, back in the days when such things had been possible in his life, during which the woman noticed how little he ate and said, "What are you watching your figure for?" It had been a joke, and she'd laughed without knowing why when Ridley said, "Ease of escape." That had not been a joke. They hadn't had a second date.

He wriggled his legs down and through and now he was essentially sitting on the bottom of the pit, his legs stretched out but his face and torso pressing against stone. He paused to shed the bulkier outer layer he was wearing, balled it up, and pushed it into the rocks, and then he began to dig with his heels, slowly drawing his body down into the gap beneath the stone. By the time you were done with this

maneuver, you were lying flat on your back, your face staring straight up to the top of the pit, your arms pinned against
your sides, useless for protection. Ridley's father used to
throw rocks or, if they were available, beer bottles at him until he disappeared from sight. It had been a very good thing
that the old man did most of his drinking from cans; the
glass littered the rocks and laced your flesh with cuts when
it was safe to emerge.

He'd experimented with a headfirst approach a few times,
not wanting to have that experience of staring straight up
into daylight and what waited there, but the feetfirst approach was faster, and when Ridley took to the pit, speed
was usually of the essence.

He slid into position now and took a deep breath, bracing
himself for the tight slide that waited. Above him, the snow
whirled down through the blackness, and a few stars glit-
tered. It was beautiful, and he wanted to lie there and drink it
in. He lingered too long, though, and his father caught him,
bounding up to the lip of the pit and leaning down, leering at
him with a wolf's smile.

Ridley closed his eyes and used his heels to drag himself
under the stone and out of sight.

That squeeze beneath the stone pulled you into a tomb of
rock. If you were brave enough—or scared enough—you
could keep pulling yourself forward with your heels, though,
and eventually you'd come out into a small chamber. Ridley
had a sense now of just how small it was, but in his boyhood,
the place had seemed impossibly massive, big enough for
treasure chests and pirate hideouts. High enough to allow
you to sit upright if not quite stand, about eight feet in diameter, and, best of all, accessible only through an opening
the size of a small oven door, easily sealed with a rock

if you needed protection. He had spent more hours in that small chamber than he could count. He hauled himself toward it again, pausing once to lift his head and kiss the stone roof for luck, the way he always had. It felt like kissing an old tombstone, but the taste was damp and earthy and comforting.

Once inside the little chamber, he sat up and took a few deep breaths. This was the place where all bad things became good, where all negative energy became fuel. His sister had called it the Batcave, but she was wrong, it was more like Superman's phone booth, a place where you transformed. There was an old metal ammunition box tucked in one corner, a relic from the Army Navy store in Bloomington, a gift from Ridley's parents on some long-ago Christmas. It had held his sacred things when he was a child, and still did. He opened it, paused to examine a rusted Swiss Army knife and a few arrowheads and the dusty remains of a letter and a poem he'd written to a girl from school but never delivered to her locker. At the bottom of the box was the most recent addition, a DVD in a plastic case, labeled with a date written in black Sharpie: *December 13, 2013.*

Ridley extracted the DVD and slipped it into the cargo pocket of his pants then restored the other items to their proper places and closed the ammo box and put a flat rock over the top of it and leaned another against that. Of all the hiding places he had, this was the poorest construction, but he believed it also had the smallest risk of a human encounter. This was the place where he'd intended to leave as much evil as possible, here in the chamber room, where the evil might in time be transformed into something else, something good.

Foolish, childish notions.

The DVD rode along in his pocket as he slipped back out of the chamber, found his rope, and began to ascend. There was no sign of his father. He climbed on toward a howling wind and a sky that was just beginning to flush around the edges.

34

Mark slept for nearly twelve hours but woke feeling groggy instead of refreshed. And stiff. When he climbed out of the bed, every muscle seemed to protest the movement in rapid-fire shrieks, like a disorganized and off-key choir. He limped to the bathroom and ran the shower as hot as it would go, then stood beneath the water until it went cold, which didn't take long. He toweled off and dressed in the same clothes he'd worn the day before and then stretched, or performed at least an approximation of stretching. It felt as if sleep had battered him rather than soothed him. He was cold but clammy with sweat too. Rest and warm sunshine, Dr. Desare had advised. Sure. When he pulled the curtains back, the landscape was covered with a fresh layer of snow, and the sky was an unbroken gray.

He was hungry, though, and when he considered it, he realized that he hadn't eaten in nearly a day. Breakfast in the hospital, coffee in Garrison, that was it. The recipe for recovery. He grabbed his bag and put on his jacket and stepped out into the winter morning. This hotel wasn't one that had a breakfast option, so he'd have to head into town. Or maybe he could walk across the street and see if they'd let him at least buy breakfast. Maybe if he sat there long enough, he'd have the chance to visit with Diane Martin again. Wouldn't that be nice. He had questions for her again, but they were...

He stopped in his tracks halfway to his car. He was standing in the parking lot of the low-rent motel, facing the higher-rent one that had sent him away. They shared an access road, if not clientele. You drove in the same way from the highway, and the road dead-ended just beyond the hotels and the restaurants. If you were visiting one or the other, you had to come in the same way. The parking lots were divided by the access road.

He turned back and paced the exterior of the shotgun-style motel until he found what he'd expected—security cameras were mounted under the eaves on both entrance doors. He stood beneath them and squared himself with their angles. Both were positioned to show anyone entering the motel, but they might pick up the parking lot too. And if they did, they surely picked up the access road beyond. The entrances to the parking lot of the nicer hotel, the national chain that had refused him the room last night because they didn't want more of his brand of trouble, were in plain view.

He left and got into his car and drove down the access road to the first gas station he found. Inside, he ran the Innocence Incorporated credit card on a cash advance. The machine limited him to four hundred dollars. He went to the next gas station and did the same thing. This time he got five hundred. In his own wallet, he'd had just over a hundred, bringing him to a grand, total. He could make another withdrawal somewhere else, but he was afraid of pushing it to the point that the fraud protection kicked in and killed his card. Besides, if it was the bored blonde again this morning, he thought that a grand might be enough.

* * *

She was in the office, and the television was still running. One of those shows where paternity tests were the bread and butter, everyone shouting at one another and the audience hooting at it all. Mark looked at her and considered whether or not to show his ID. Sometimes, the PI license helped. But in this town, his name was pretty familiar, and not in a helpful way. He'd lead with the cash.

"Your security cameras work?" he said.

She turned for the first time, regarded him with annoyance and contempt. "*Yes*. But there's a sign in the parking lot for a reason. Anything happened to your car, it's not our liability."

It was a response that begged the question of just how often cars in this particular Four Seasons were vandalized, but that wasn't Mark's interest. It was, however, an entry point that he hadn't considered, and one that he liked.

"Exactly. But you've got working cameras, to protect yourselves. Your buddies across the street? I stayed there last week, my car got busted into, and they said their cameras don't show the parking lot. I think they're lying about that."

"Wouldn't surprise me. You know it's one of those Pakistani chains. Or Indians, I don't know. Saudis?" She shrugged. "They own 'em all, mostly. You wouldn't *believe* how many hotels they own. Ain't many locals like us left."

Mark agreed that her establishment was one of a kind, then leaned on the counter and said conspiratorially, "I want to sue their asses. I don't even need a copy of your security videos to do that, I just need a look."

She frowned, torn. On the one hand, she clearly liked the notion of causing trouble for whatever Middle Eastern empire opposed her, but on the other, the task smelled like work. "I really shouldn't do that for you. You know, the legalities and whatnot."

"Sure." Mark reached into his jacket pocket and removed the wad of cash, glad for the first time in history that ATMs didn't dispense anything larger than a twenty, because it made the stack of bills look more substantial. "Or you could put this in your pocket, let me look at those videos, and I'll get the hell out of here and you won't see me again." He nodded across the street. "But *they* will. And so will their attorneys."

She looked out the front window. Other than her car and Mark's, the motel's parking lot was empty. She looked at the cash on the counter. There were at least fifty bills in the stack.

"It won't take me long," Mark said.

She used one of the laughably long acrylic nails to fan through the bills, then did the math—or gave up on doing it, one of the two—and said, "Come around the desk."

The cameras were standard cheap technology, adequate for the motel's liability insurance and little more. They fed back into a computer hard drive much like a television DVR, and a simple software program allowed you to enter the date and time of your choice. The blonde didn't know how to operate it, but Mark figured out the intricacies in about two minutes. He'd seen plenty of similar systems before. She sat and watched with the bills clutched in her hand.

The cameras captured what he'd hoped for, and more— the view of the parking-lot entrances across the street was clear, and you could see the cars well. He had to scroll through only twenty minutes before he saw his own Ford Escape pull in, and he watched himself stride through the parking lot. The view gave him an unexpected chill. When he'd walked into that place only a few days ago, he was generally regarded as an honest man. By the time he'd checked out the next morning, he was about to hit the news as an unusually disturbing fraud.

He accidentally fast-forwarded right over Diane Martin's arrival and had to go back to find her. When she appeared in the parking lot, his chill turned to rage. There she was, striding purposefully over the pavement on her way to destroy his career and threaten his life. Calm as could be.

He backed the video up farther and found the car she'd arrived in—an older Honda Civic, red—and discovered that she'd given him the most generous of gifts. She'd turned into the first entrance of the parking lot instead of the second. This meant that the back end of her car had faced the cheap motel squarely for a few precious seconds.

He zoomed in, his breath trapped in his chest. They weren't high-end cameras, and you could save a lot of money on cameras if you didn't care about the zoom. As he clicked, the image pixelated, but it held just clear enough. He could make out the license plate.

"Got a piece of paper?" he asked, and while the blonde was rummaging for a notepad and pen, he took his cell out of his pocket and snapped a few quick photos of the screen. When she gave him the notepad, he wrote the license plate down along with the arrival time of the vehicle and then tore the page free.

"That'll do," he said. "Thanks for the help."

"Sure thing," she said, and when he was back on the other side of the counter and had his hand on the door, she added, "Good luck chasing dead women."

He turned and stared at her, and she gave him a wide smile. "I'm not quite the yokel you want me to be, mister. But I do appreciate the cash."

Mark opened his mouth to speak, but she waved him off with those bright red nails. "Don't you worry about me, honey. It's an interesting little story, but I know how to run my business. Two things I'm real familiar with: cash and keeping my mouth shut. You go on your way now, and try to stay aboveground."

35

Jeff had called three times the previous night, but Mark had slept through them all. When Mark called him back, Jeff was on his way into the courthouse in Austin, and the concern in his voice was evident.

"The last time you started missing calls, they had to chopper you to a hospital, Markus."

"Sorry. I was asleep. Doctor's orders."

"Where are you?"

"Garrison."

"Shit, you went without me?"

"You're still in Texas. I can't really afford to wait. You're the one who made that clear. It became even more clear to me when I learned that Greg Roche is calling around. Not having someone do it for him—making calls himself."

He could hear Jeff take a deep breath. "Greg's concerned, yes."

Mark closed his eyes. If Greg was concerned now, that meant Mark's firing was imminent. But Greg couldn't know what had really happened in Coleman, the full scope of Mark's visits there and the offers he'd made, or Mark would already have been fired. Even Jeff didn't know all of that. The organization was dedicated to the opposition of capital punishment, and if its executives ever learned that Mark had been trying to arrange a prison hit—even if the target was guilty of murder—he'd be fired, and he'd face charges. Greg would see to that; he'd have to. The integrity of his organization would require it, and neither Jeff London nor anyone else would be able to prevent that train from running Mark down. The only saving grace was that nobody on earth knew what he'd really been after in Coleman. He was counting on that to save his job at least long enough for him to make one more pass through the prison. The one that counted.

"Good news is, I'm making progress here."

"Yeah?"

"Yeah." Mark told him about the conversations with Evan Borders and Danielle MacAlister and then of the reference to ketamine in Brett Leonard's recent charges.

"That could go a long way toward helping you," Jeff said. "They take any blood when you were at the hospital?"

"They took plenty of it, but all they did was warm it up and give it back to me. There were no drug tests conducted as far as I know. I already talked to Arthur Stewart about it. There's a chance something might show up at this point, but he thinks it's slim. Right now, I've got another priority." He told Jeff about the motel surveillance cameras and the license plate. "You get any questions about those cash withdrawals, come up with something good to cover me. Meanwhile, I need that plate run."

"Read it to me and give me ten minutes."

Mark gave him the number and hung up to let Jeff run it through DMV records. While he waited for the response, he drove to one of the gas stations he'd already visited, grabbed a handful of protein bars, a large black coffee, and a bottle of Advil. The aches and stiffness hadn't loosened as the morning wore on, and that clammy sweat that signaled a fever had lingered.

"You strike out, bro?" The guy at the cash register had red eyes, an uneven beard, and blue-ink tattoos on his hands.

"What?"

The guy smirked. "You was in here, what, twenty minutes ago, loading up on cash, and now you're loading up on caffeine and painkillers? You strike out or somebody sell you the wrong shit?"

"I'll take a paper bag," Mark said. "Leave you the plastic ones to put over your head."

The kid laughed like that was a hell of a joke and shoved Mark's protein bars and Advil back across the counter. He put them in his coat pockets and walked out, sipping the coffee and wondering if there was anyone in this town who *wasn't* watching him. Back in the car, he looked at himself in the rearview mirror as he prepared to drop a few of the Advil and thought that the kid at the gas station hadn't made a bad call. With his gray pallor, dark circles under his eyes, a four-day beard, and beads of sweat on his forehead despite the cold, Mark looked every bit the part of someone who would be hunting for a drug buy in the early-morning hours.

When Mark answered the phone, Jeff began without preamble.

"Owner is Julianne Grossman, white female, blond hair, age forty-four, of Garrison, Indiana. Previously of West Baden Springs and Evansville."

"West Baden Springs. Why does that sound familiar?"

"Little town with a big hotel. Had a bunch of tornadoes blow through a few years ago. Made national news for, like, a minute. I ran her through a basic profile report once I had her name. No criminal records, nothing in PACER, but there was one interesting detail. Your girl used to have a professional license in Indiana. Doesn't anymore. Her profession was once recognized and licensed by the state. Now it isn't. You can just hang out your shingle, apparently."

"What profession is that?"

"She's a hypnotist," Jeff said.

Mark had the coffee halfway to his lips. Now he set it in the cup holder. "You're kidding."

"Nope. I can look for more on her—all I did was a basic preliminary public records search—but that's what turned up. You think she hypnotized you?"

"No," Mark said. "Absolutely not, no chance." He could see his mother's face, one of the prettier images he had of it. She'd been leaning against the couch, sitting on the floor close to the fireplace with a blanket wrapped around her, on a night after another go-round with local police that had led to a rapid packing of the car. Her dark-colored contacts were out, so for once her blue eyes actually showed. She'd been staring into the fire with a deeply thoughtful expression when she said, *Maybe spirit readings are out, Mark. Maybe I should try hypnotism. It does sound complicated, though.*

"What's her address?" Mark asked Jeff. He scratched it down on the back of one of the ATM receipts, thanked Jeff, and ended the call. For a moment, he sat there and watched the rain and considered Jeff's advice about calling the sheriff. Then he entered Julianne Grossman's address into his GPS and put the car in gear.

Part Four

THE TRUTH OF
YOUR SINS

36

The gray skies opened up again as he drove, but this time it was rain, which helped melt the snow despite the low temperatures. The address for Julianne Grossman led him out of town and a short ways up into the hills, where the trees grew tall and dense. Mark turned into the driveway, a steep gravel track that led straight back down the hill and into the trees. Branches littered the ground, casualties from the recent storms. They crackled beneath his tires. At the base of the drive was a small, narrow house with weathered siding painted a deep red, like an old-time lake cottage. A carport with a sagging roof protected a red Honda Civic.

When Mark cut the engine and opened the door, a dog slipped out from under the wooden porch and peered at him, and at first he thought it was a fox, with its near-orange coat and upright, pointed ears. Its hackles rose and then it dipped back under the porch, and as Mark walked through the rain and up the steps, he heard a low growl from under the boards, like a troll under a bridge. Welcoming place.

When he knocked, the growling under the porch went up in pitch. A moment later he heard soft footsteps, and then the dead bolt ratcheted back and the door opened, still secured by a thin chain latch, and Mark saw her face.

Mark said, "Why, hello, Mrs. Martin. I was hoping we could discuss your daughter's case again."

To see her was startling as hell for him and should have been worse for her, but she simply said, "Hello, Mr. Novak," as if he were an expected and welcome guest.

"Mind if I come in?" he said, moving his foot against the door. "Get out of this rain?"

She unfastened the chain and opened the door wide. She was wearing loose-fitting white pants that billowed around her legs and a pale blue sweater, both of which made her blond hair seem like the darkest part of her. Mark had an eerie flash of the hallucination he'd had of Sarah Martin in the cave. Then, worse, of Lauren underwater.

"Yes, please come in. The last thing you need is more time in the cold. It's excellent that you found me. So much better than the alternatives."

He stood in the rain, staring at her. "You're kidding me, right?"

"Not at all. It's critical that we speak, but the fact that you found me under your own power is so much better."

"You can drive yourself to the sheriff's department and I'll follow, or we can call them here to get you," he said. "I'll leave that one up to you."

"And why would I go to the sheriff's department?"

"You impersonated a dead woman, a murdered girl's mother, and you think that's viewed as harmless fun? I assure you that the sheriff will be eager to make your acquaintance."

"I'm afraid you're mistaken," she said, no trace of distress in her voice or face. "I never impersonated anyone."

"You called Sarah 'my baby,' you lying bitch."

"You're upset, and that's fine. In your defense, though, I'd like to say that—"

"In *my* defense?"

"—that you *were* speaking with Sarah's mother at some points. There was a channel open, a conduit. Just as it was when you talked of your wife. It was extraordinary to see."

He pushed through the door, grabbed her by her shirt, and shoved her into the house. She flinched more from surprise than fear, his face inches from hers, and then met his eyes with a questioning look, waiting for his next move.

"True things," he said. His voice was a whisper. "That's all we're going to talk about."

He heard the clicking of paws on the porch floorboards and the growl became a snarl as the dog rushed up the stairs and at him. He released Julianne Grossman and turned as the dog rose up on its hind legs as if to strike, then hesitated in midair, dropped back to the ground, and danced away, head dipped, chagrined. When Mark looked back at Julianne Grossman, he saw that she had one hand lifted, palm out, a silent command that the animal had obeyed completely.

Mark was nonplussed, ashamed by both the burst of physical aggression and her calm in the face of it and even by the self-control the dog had exhibited, superior to Mark's own.

"Follow me," she said, and then turned her back to him as if she had nothing to fear from anything.

As dark as it was outside, with the cold rain falling from an overcast sky, the cottage seemed to trap light. Everything had a bright, airy feel and was clean and ordered, as if not a single dust mote could be tolerated. The living room was small but neatly furnished with a couch facing two rocking chairs; the walls were lined with books. Crystal prisms hung in the window, reflecting light that shouldn't be there, and there were maybe half a dozen unlit candles.

"Sit," Julianne Grossman said, indicating the couch. She

took one of the rocking chairs, crossed her legs elegantly, and looked at Mark, waiting. He didn't sit.

"You want true things," she said. "Everything I've told you is true. It's a matter of perception. But I understand your reluctance to believe."

"Stop," Mark said. "Just shut the hell up. I've met better frauds, Julianne. I was *raised* by one. Spare me the psychic bullshit. It's offensive to the dead and to those who cared for them."

"For a skeptic," Julianne Grossman said, "you entered trance most willingly. I didn't even really have to work at it. Your unconscious mind seemed almost *eager.*"

Mark started to respond but whatever words he'd intended didn't come. The word *trance* lingered in his mind, and he found himself coughing instead of speaking. His lungs scorched.

"We're going to the police," he said when he was done, "and we're going to call a few reporters on our way. They don't believe I talked to you."

"Not true. They don't believe you talked to *Diane Martin.* And you're hardly prepared to prove them wrong by producing me." She had an eerie calm, and he was reminded of the one tell he should have picked up on—she'd been too composed when she spoke of her supposed daughter. Far too composed.

"If the police were to search your house today, would they find any ketamine?" Mark asked. "Because I can arrange that search."

"They certainly would not. I'm not a fan of narcotics. They make my work far more challenging. It's harder to reach the unconscious if there are synthetic barriers in play. Would you like to hear a recording of our meeting, Mr. Novak?"

"I don't need to hear it. I was there."

"Let's see about that," she said, and then she stood and walked away, vanishing down a corridor. When she returned, she held a digital recorder in one hand.

"I don't need to hear something you've had days to tamper with," he said, but he felt a knot twisting in his gut.

"I actually think it would be prudent for you to get a sense of what really happened before you begin making calls to the media." She played with the buttons and then Mark's voice became audible.

What's your concern in the case, Julianne? I don't understand how it affects you personally.

There was faint static and background noise, but even so, there was no doubt that it was his voice and that he had called her Julianne. The knot twisting in his gut morphed into a sharp, ice-cold blade.

Julianne Grossman pressed pause. "Now, I'm not a detective, but it doesn't sound like you had much confusion over my identity."

"How did you alter that?"

"I didn't alter a thing."

"Slick trick, but I'm the wrong person to try it with. My company has contacts with the best audio forensic experts in the world. It'll take them twenty minutes to blow that bullshit out of the water."

"There's *that* option," she said, "or we could listen to a bit more, and maybe you'll reach a different understanding."

She returned her attention to the recorder, advanced it to the place that she wanted, and then played it. This time it was her voice, that strange cadence even more eerie over the static.

This has been a good conversation for you, hasn't it? Yes. Yes, it was beneficial, wasn't it?

Mark, sounding as if he'd overdosed on quaaludes, responded: *Yes.*

There are ways it might have been an even better conversation. So much better. For you, and for Sarah Martin. You know that there are ways, don't you? There are always ways. So much beyond what we know. So much beyond what we say. But you feel those ways, don't you?

Yes.

Of course. Of course you do. And the ways that allow you to feel close to her are the best, because it matters so much that you feel close to Sarah, doesn't it?

Yes.

Some of those ways feel out of reach now, don't they? They feel like something beyond you, beyond your potential. But they are not beyond your potential, Mark. You're feeling that now, aren't you? You're understanding that your potential has changed. That all the old approaches can be improved upon. Tell me what you think about your old approaches?

They can be improved upon.

Mark felt like rushing at her again; hell, he felt like hitting her this time, knocking her onto the floor and taking that recorder and smashing it until it turned to fragments and then until the fragments turned to dust. He couldn't move, though. He stood, frozen, listening to the voice he knew was his own speaking words he didn't remember saying.

To feel closer to Sarah, would it have helped you if you had spoken to her family, do you think? Would that have helped?

Yes. It would have helped.

Think back on this conversation, then. Recall all that was said and all that was beneath the words. Because you know that there were things beneath the words, and you know that what was beneath the words mattered most, and always does, and always will. The words we say are not what matters most, are they?

No. The words do not tell the story.

The words *Don't embarrass me with this shit* knifed through Mark's brain, and he winced. Julianne watched him in silence.

So you know this. And you know that what was beneath the words you heard today could have come from someone close to Sarah, could they not? They could have come from her mother, perhaps. Do you think that is true?

Yes. That is true.

Would you like to remember the conversation that way? So that you can focus on what counts, and you can open your mind to new approaches?

Yes.

Then you will. You will remember that you spoke to Diane Martin, Sarah's mother. You will remember her pain. You will remember her desperate thirst for truth. You will remember that what is beneath the words is what matters, and what was beneath the words came from Diane Martin. Do you remember this?

Yes.

Who did you speak with today?

Diane Martin.

And what mattered?

What was beneath the words.

Exactly. All of this you already know, and so all of this you will remember.

"Stop it," Mark said. His voice broke. "Turn that damn thing off, turn it off *now!*"

She stopped the recording. Her face was serene.

"It's jarring to hear, I'm sure. But if you—"

"How did you do that? Did you drug me? I'll have a blood test done, and if—"

"No drugs. You might do some Internet searches later on something called the Erickson handshake induction. You'll see some obvious frauds, and some things that once would have made you laugh. But now? Now you won't laugh."

Down in the hotel lobby, she grabbed your wrist. It looked like a handshake at first, but she took hold of your wrist. It was a strange contact.

But it couldn't have been that simple. There was no way. You didn't just take hold of someone's wrist in an unusual manner and then ask him unusual questions and through those means convince him that his reality had changed. It couldn't be done.

"It was ketamine," he said. "You didn't hypnotize me, and you know it. There was a drug involved, and that's easy enough to prove."

"Then feel free to prove it."

"How long have you known Jeremy and Brett Leonard?" Mark asked. "What about Evan Borders?"

Her face appeared genuinely puzzled, but she was a fine actor. "I've heard Evan's name, but the others are new to me."

"Sure they are. I'll find out where you got the drug and I'll connect you to them, but it won't be necessary for that stupid damned recording anyhow. People will hear that and they'll know that I was set up. You just proved my story with that alone."

"But what if they heard *this?*" she said, and she played another segment.

I had a snitch in Coleman prison down in Florida. He told me that he'd heard a rumor that someone in there had killed Lauren. And so I offered him ten thousand dollars and free legal assistance for his appeal if he... if he confirmed the rumor.

And how was he going to do that?

By any means necessary. And if it was confirmed, he had another hundred grand coming his way, though even he didn't know that, because we didn't get far enough along.

What was the other hundred grand for?

Killing him.

You would have arranged a man's murder? You would have been comfortable with it?

If I could prove that he was the one who'd killed my wife? Absolutely. Without hesitation, I'd have had him killed. My only regret would be that I couldn't do it myself.

Mark couldn't speak. The plan that he'd had for the inmate in Coleman had existed only in his own mind. He'd had no fear that someone might find out about it, because he'd never voiced the plan to a soul.

Or so he had believed. They'd talked about it, but he hadn't said... Even as he thought about it, though, it began to feel familiar. Feel vivid, in fact. He could see that table in the bar, could see her face, the face he'd believed was Diane Martin's, and could recall her composed acceptance of the news when he'd delivered it. Yes, it had happened. How in the hell had he not remembered it?

"What are you thinking, Mr. Novak? You've grown very quiet. What's on your mind?"

"You own me now," he said.

"I don't like that term."

"But it's the truth. You distribute that recording, and you can blow my life up. You know that and so do I. So what do you want? What in the hell do you want from me?"

"I want you to put Ridley Barnes in prison."

He stared at her. "What? I thought you were working *with* him."

"So does he," Julianne Grossman said. "That's why I had to go to the regrettable lengths that I did with you, in fact. Ridley does not trust easily. You have to prove yourself in the most severe ways to reach his inner circle. I've done that, I've broken my own ethical code to reach that point of trust with him, and I won't waste that now."

"Why do you care so much about Ridley Barnes?"

"Because I listened to him confess to the murder of Sarah Martin, Mr. Novak. Is that reason good enough for you?"

37

For a long time there was no sound but a ticking clock in some other room of the house. Julianne Grossman sat and waited and finally Mark said, "When did this happen?"

"During a trance session with Ridley last month. I make my living by using hypnosis to help people through their difficulties. Most of the time, that involves addictions or fears. I help people quit smoking, lose weight, gain the confidence to handle public speaking. Ridley came to me with a different problem; he said that he didn't remember whether he'd killed a child, and he wanted to know."

"You believed him."

"At the time, yes."

"And now?"

"Now I believe that Ridley Barnes is a wickedly smart sociopath. I believe that he killed that poor, sweet girl and got away with it and that too much time has passed and he's grown bored. It's important to me to keep him occupied. Do you understand why?"

"You think he'll kill again if he's not."

"I fear it's a very real possibility."

"That's a determination a good psychiatrist might be able to make," Mark said. "Not a hypnotist. And if you'd had true concerns about Ridley and any conscience at all, you'd have spoken to police about this. They're not aware of any confession, so I don't think that you've told anyone about it."

"No, I haven't spoken with police."

"So you're full of shit," Mark said. "If you'd heard it, and believed it, and cared as much as you claim, you'd have gone to them. Anything else is a lie."

"You're an experienced investigator. You should understand just how much value a confession given under hypnosis means. It's all but useless in the courts now, which is a true shame. One of the most valuable tools for witnesses has been removed due to ignorance and a few dishonest practitioners."

She wasn't lying about this. At one time, police departments in Los Angeles and New York had maintained dedicated hypnosis units. There had been a brief flash point of excitement about the technique, but that had been all but obliterated in appellate courts. Arguments of implanted memory and coercion, along with scathing questions over the expertise of the hypnotists, had created an environment in which neither prosecutors nor defense attorneys saw much gain in introducing anything procured through hypnosis. It carried all the legal problems of the polygraph multiplied by the potential for human error and human fraud. The once-booming study of forensic hypnosis was not a popular approach anymore.

"I tend to agree with the courts," Mark said. "You realize the recording you played for me does absolutely nothing but prove that point? If you could convince me you were Sarah's mother, what's to stop you from convincing Ridley to confess?"

"You're part of the game now," she said, "and I played a role in bringing you in. For that, I don't apologize. I need the help. I apologize for the methods, because I realize they were hurtful. But I need the help."

In the silence, all Mark could hear was the ticking of that unseen clock.

"Can you turn that thing down?"

"The clock?"

"Yeah."

"It bothers you?" She smiled, and he felt a surge of annoyance, because she seemed to understand why it bothered him—a childish, irrational fear that she was somehow going to be able to claim his mind against his will, use the ticking of the clock to lull him into a trance.

"It bothers me because it's all I can hear," he said. "And you're supposed to be talking."

"I've done my talking, Mr. Novak. You can run screaming to the police or to the media all you'd like, but I promise you this: the moment you do, Ridley's belief that he has me as an ally—and right now he believes that firmly—is gone. And the best chance at seeing him answer for his crimes goes with it."

"So you're going to extort me into helping you?" He gestured at the recorder that was still in her hand. "I'm supposed to trust someone who'd rather blackmail me than approach honestly?"

"I've already told you that this was about gaining Ridley's trust, not yours. I understand why it would be counterproductive for our relationship."

He almost laughed. "Yes, it could be viewed as counterproductive. I'm hanging on to my career by a thread, and you're the reason!"

"The purpose our meeting served is already paying dividends. I filmed my early sessions with Ridley until he decided he didn't like that. This morning, he returned one of those videos to me. Because of you. Because of what he feels your presence means to the cave."

"Means to the cave?"

"You'll understand that soon enough. Now I'll make you an offer. You feel blackmailed, you feel taken advantage of, all of these negative things. You fear the recording in my hand, don't you?"

Mark didn't say anything. She already knew he did.

"I'll turn it over to you," she said. "You can destroy it or do whatever you'd like with it, provided you give me twenty minutes of your time. If after those twenty minutes your concern is still with the recording, you may take it and go. I hope that won't be the case."

"What are we going to achieve in twenty minutes?"

"You're going to watch a video."

She had no television in the living room, so he followed her down a narrow hallway and into a small bedroom that had been converted into an office of sorts. Bookshelves filled three walls—most of the titles had to do with hypnosis, mindfulness, or spiritualist topics—and the other wall was occupied by an ancient oak desk with a high-end Mac computer. The computer felt out of place in the room, the lone intruder. Julianne sat at the desk and fed a DVD into the disk drive. Then she turned to Mark.

"You're the first person other than me to see this. That's all I'm going to say about it."

For a few seconds the screen was a bright, empty blue, and then it filled with an image of Ridley Barnes sitting alone in a straight-backed chair with a small pillow tucked behind his head. His eyes were closed. Mark recognized the room as Julianne's living room. She advanced the frames until she reached a place that satisfied her and then she stood up, stepped back, folded her arms, and let the video play.

The first voice that came, off-camera and soft, was Julianne's. Mark recognized the familiar, lulling cadence.

"Tell me more about Trapdoor. You've been there for a while, haven't you?"

"Yes," Ridley said. "Longer than I planned. Longer than I was ready for."

"Tell me what you see," Julianne said.

"Nothing."

"Why can't you see anything?"

"Darkness." Ridley's voice suggested that speaking took effort and he wanted to do as little of it as possible.

"Is the darkness all around?"

"All around." He nodded slightly. His back was rigid, but his neck muscles seemed so loose that they were barely capable of holding his head upright, requiring the support of the pillow.

"Why is it dark?"

"Lost my lights. Too long down here. Too long."

"Why do you think it has been too long?"

"Tired. I'm tired. And..." His head rocked again, as if he were struggling to free his own thoughts, and then he said, "And it's dark. It should never be dark."

"Right. It shouldn't be dark. So why is it?"

"Because my lights are gone."

"Where did the lights go?"

"Burned out. I've been down too long."

"Why did you stay so long?"

"Because I can hear her."

Mark felt his breath catch. He'd been watching the video with skepticism, or trying to, but there was something in the surreal sound of Ridley's answers that felt authentic.

"What do you hear?"

"Crying." Ridley's voice wavered and nearly broke. "She's crying. And I know she's right there, but I can't find her."

"You hear other things. There are other sounds. Tell me what they are."

Ridley's hands began to tremble and then the rest of his body joined in a single shudder.

"She's asking me to stop."

Mark felt a prickle along his spine.

"To stop what?" Julianne Grossman's voice said.

Silence. Ridley's eyelids fluttered but he didn't speak.

"What is the thing that she wants you to stop?" Julianne asked.

"I don't know."

"She wants to be found, doesn't she?"

These were the kinds of moments she'd mentioned to Mark, the moments that would render the video inadmissible in court. She was guiding him, coaxing him. An attorney couldn't get away with those tactics on cross-examination even with a coherent witness, and when the witness was hypnotized, it stood absolutely no chance. The opposition would call it memory implanting, and that would be the end of it. That didn't mean hypnosis wasn't a valid technique, though, and it didn't necessarily mean that she hadn't gotten the truth from him.

"I think so," Ridley said, his voice so soft that Mark leaned closer to the computer.

"Then why would she want you to stop looking?"

"She wouldn't."

"No, she wouldn't. She would want you to continue, yes?"

"Yes."

"You're certain of this?"

"I'm certain."

"Good. Very good. You know this to be true, don't you?"

"Yes."

"And since you know it to be true, then what does she want you to stop?"

"I don't know."

"Look around you. Tell me what you see."

"Nothing! Nothing, nothing. It's all dark, I can't see." His voice had gone high, had an edge of hysteria that raised the hair on Mark's arms.

"Tell me about the place. Use all of your senses. Tell me what you can feel."

"Stone and . . . and dampness."

"You're in the water?"

"No."

"What's the dampness, then? Are the stones wet?"

Ridley's body shuddered again, but he didn't speak.

"What do you smell?" Julianne Grossman asked.

"Blood." This answer came without pause, none of the previous hesitancy or sense of effort, just a simple, matter-of-fact statement. Mark's mouth had gone dry and though he wanted to see Julianne Grossman's expression he couldn't bring himself to look away from the image of Ridley on the screen.

"You smell blood. Yes. Good. Your memories are strong, aren't they? Because the senses hold memories, and you are using your senses. They hold more memories, don't they?"

"Yes."

"Smell the blood, then. Use your senses to find the source. Are you bleeding?"

"I don't think so."

"So where is the blood coming from?"

"I don't know."

"Is the dampness that you feel water, or is it blood?"

"I don't know." His voice was still high, and now it had an angry quality, as if the questions were frustrating him.

"Can you still hear her voice?"

"No."

"But she was speaking. Now she is not. Why did she stop speaking?"

Ridley's voice dipped again, soft and low. "She's too cold," he said.

"She told you that she's too cold?"

"No. I can feel it."

"How can you feel her sense of the cold? How is that possible?"

"Because I'm touching her. And she's too cold. She can't speak anymore. She won't speak anymore."

"Where is she?"

"In my arms."

"When did this happen? When did you reach her?"

"I don't know. Time is...confusing."

"Did you hurt her?"

On the screen, Ridley Barnes began to shiver. A single tear leaked down his cheek and into his beard.

"Did you hurt her?" Julianne Grossman repeated.

"Maybe." His voice was childlike.

"You need to tell yourself the truth. You need to be honest with yourself. Did you hurt her?"

"I don't know."

"Is the blood hers, Ridley?"

"Maybe. I don't know."

"Why are you touching her?"

"I'm moving her." Each word sounded weighted with guilt.

"Why?"

"Because she shouldn't be there anymore. Because they're all waiting for her."

"How long have you been with her?"

"Too long. Too long in the dark. She's too cold, and we've been too long in the dark."

"Is she alive, Ridley?"

"No. No, I don't think she is." More tears now, and the shivering was relentless. The neck pillow slipped loose and fell to the floor.

"Was she alive when you found her?"

"I think so."

"Why do you think so?"

"Because she talked."

"What did she say?"

" 'Please, stop.' "

"What did she want you to stop?"

"I don't know."

"Did you stop?"

"I don't know." He was shaking, and his hands were opening and closing. "I don't know, I don't know."

"Why did you go into the cave, Ridley?"

"To rescue her."

"Did you do that?"

"No."

"Why not?"

"Bad things happened. Things I didn't mean to do."

"What didn't you mean to do?"

"I didn't want to hurt anyone. I didn't."

"Of course you didn't want to. But did you hurt someone?"

"Yes. I didn't want to, but I did."

"Did you kill?"

"Yes."

"Did you kill Sarah Martin, Ridley?"

"I think so."

This proclamation, loud and shrill, put the first dent in Julianne Grossman's steady, unflappable voice. There was a silence, and when she spoke again it was clear that she was searching for the right words and tone, that the questioning was no longer as natural.

"Tell me how that happened."

"She was his responsibility. They'll all blame me but she belonged to him first."

"What do you mean, belonged?"

"If it's my fault, then it was his first."

"Who are you referring to? Whose fault was it?"

"The dark man's," Ridley said simply.

"Who is the dark man?"

"I don't know. How would I know?" He was getting edgy again, and his fingers were in motion, tapping on his legs like a nervous piano student fumbling through a bad recital.

"Did the dark man come into the cave with you?"

"Of course not."

"Then when did he join you?"

"He was always in the cave."

"That can't be true, can it?"

"Yes. Trapdoor sends him. He is the cave. He *is* the cave."

"Think about this. How can it be true?"

"It's true. *It is true.*"

Julianne was pushing too hard now, and Ridley was resisting. For the first time, a clear break had appeared, and even in his trance state, Ridley was beginning to view her as an interrogator and not a guide. She seemed to realize it because she changed tacks, but it was too late.

"Focus on the things around you," she said. "Don't worry

about how it all came to be. Return to your senses now. Only
the senses. Just tell me what you see, what you feel, what
you hear, what you smell."

"I don't want to be here anymore," Ridley said. "I can't
be here anymore."

"That's all right. You're fine, you're safe."

"No. Not here. In this place, no one is ever safe. Not
ever." The words had gone frantic.

"You're safe," Julianne said. "Can you say that? Say the
words and know that they are true. Say the words."

"I'm safe." He sounded like a blubbering child being
talked out of a crying fit, promised that his injury didn't hurt
as bad as he thought it did. His breathing had gotten so rapid
that he was hyperventilating. It was as if Ridley's mind had
blown a fuse, and whatever protection the hypnotized state
had once offered him was now gone.

"I want to leave. Please. I want out of the dark. Please."
Each word left him with a gasp.

"Then we'll leave it behind. We're going to count our
way back now, all right? We're going to start at one, and
when we reach ten, you'll be back where you are safe.
You will feel better, because you've asked yourself the right
questions, and you know that you need to ask those questions. When we reach ten, you will feel safe, and you will
feel peaceful. You will feel these things because you deserve
them, don't you? Yes. You deserve to feel safe and peaceful.
You deserve that. One... You know that you deserve peace.
Two... And when you return you will feel good, you will
feel alert and strong and clean, you will feel so much better
than before. Three... You know that you deserve safety.
Four... five... six." As she counted up, her voice rose in volume just a touch, a slow but steady increase, and even from
just the recording Mark could feel a shift in his own energy.

"You have done all of the right things, and you have asked the right questions, and you will feel better now than before, you will be a new and better version of yourself, because you have sought these things. You will feel the peace that comes with doing the right things...seven...eight...Let yourself feel warmth again. Feel warmth and see light. Everything will be brighter now. Everything will be safe. Nine...feeling the warmth...feeling so good and so peaceful...and ten."

Ridley's eyes opened on ten with an unseeing stare that focused quickly. His chest rose and fell in long, deep breaths. His hands were motionless against his legs; his body was still. For a moment, the screen held on his eyes, which were looking directly into the camera, and then the picture went black.

38

Mark let out a breath he hadn't been aware of holding. Julianne was still standing just as she had been, a few steps behind him, her eyes locked on the now blank computer screen, her arms folded.

"That was in December," she said. "I've continued working with him, but we've never gotten back to that place. Never so far. He's very guarded now. As I said, I have had to prove myself as an ally. I couldn't go to the police. You might disagree, but I know what would have happened. They would have dismissed me, then they would have been too aggressive with him, and the bond of trust I was forming with Ridley would have shattered."

"But there's been no gain to it," Mark said. He was still shaken by what he'd seen. He'd never watched anyone speaking under hypnosis before, let alone confessing to a murder. "Your trust hasn't led to anything good."

She turned from the screen to face him. "It's led to you."

He didn't answer right away. The clock ticked somewhere down the hall, and the wind drove rain against the windows, and Julianne Grossman stared at him as if she were waiting for an answer to a question that hadn't been voiced.

"What am I supposed to do?" Mark said finally. "What do you think I can do that the police can't?"

"Engage him in the way he wants to be engaged," she said. "That's the secret. He chooses who gets to play the game, don't you see that? He gave the police nothing. Ever. He gave me something, and once he realized that he had, he came back around. I had no idea how to handle it, nor did I have the skills. It's why I convinced him that we needed help to get his truth. When we found you...well, it was easier then. Because of your wife, you fit the role quite nicely."

Mark ran a hand over his face and it came back damp with sweat. He was dizzy and wanted to sit.

"Was Ridley playing with you, or was that legit?"

"Do you mean was he really in trance? Yes. I'm certain of that. I've been a practicing hypnotist for twenty-two years. I know when someone is faking, and I know when it is real. Ridley was in trance."

"And you've put him back in trance."

"Yes. But he no longer shows interest in recall or trapped memories. He speaks of the dark man, he speaks of the cave as if it is a person. He speaks of what the cave wants him to do."

"What do you make of the dark man?"

"He's a part of Ridley. A part he wants to deny."

"But that portion in which he talks about Sarah being someone else's responsibility suggests that she wasn't alone, doesn't it?"

"Not necessarily. I suppose he could be blaming Evan Borders for losing her, but I think he's blaming himself throughout. You just watched a chess match, and Ridley Barnes lost. To his own subconscious. I don't think it happens often, though. I think he usually wins."

"Even if I agree with everything you said, I don't see how I can help. This"—he pointed at the computer monitor—"is not what I do. A forensic psychiatrist might have a shot with him. I wouldn't."

"I disagree. He has a vision for your role. If you play it, I think we can have some success."

"What's his vision for me?"

"You're supposed to get him access to the cave. He's certain of this. The fact that you already went into the cave—"

"I was *forced* into the cave!"

"Fine. Either way, it has validated his vision of you. That the cave wants you. He's convinced that you can get him access to the cave. That the reach and clout of your firm can do that."

"My firm wants nothing to do with me."

"Access is controlled by Danielle MacAlister. She's more likely to listen to someone of your background than someone of mine. If you could gain her cooperation, Ridley would view it as progress."

"I'm not going back in that cave."

"Why not?"

"If you'd spent the quality time down there that I did, you wouldn't need to ask. But there's also simply no gain to it. Let's imagine it's possible for me to get access, which I doubt, but let's imagine it. What good comes of having Ridley in the cave?"

"For hypnotherapy, none whatsoever. We would ordinarily *never* expose someone to fear-inducing imagery. In somnambulism—that's deep trance—the imagery becomes very, very real. Ridley carries powerful beliefs about Trapdoor on both the conscious and subconscious levels. At the level reached in deep trance, he believes that Trapdoor is a source of special power. It's not that strange when you consider the experience he had there, his closeness with death and violence and questions of his own survival. Over time, however, those experiences have become more deeply associated with Trapdoor in his mind. It has become a mythological sort of place to him, capable of bestowing gifts on people and . . . and requiring gifts from them."

"Gifts," Mark echoed. "Can you elaborate on that?"

She looked at him for a long time before she said, "Lives. Deep in his mind, Ridley believes that the cave can grant them. Or demand them."

"Fantastic. If no good can come from it, why would you indulge him in the attempt?"

"Because he *already knows* what happened in that cave. And what other trance sessions have told me—when I'm able to achieve deep trance with Ridley, that is, he can be a challenge—is that he wants to show someone where it happened." She swallowed, and for the first time she looked afraid. Outside, the wind picked up and grew louder, and the dog began to howl along with it, as if concerned over the changes that were on the way. "In particular, he wants to show *me*."

"You truly believe that he would take you to where she was killed? That he would tell you the truth?"

"I can't say that for certain. But I know that I can't walk away from what I've heard." She moved to a closet set between the bookshelves and opened the door. On the back of it, carefully taped, were articles with enlarged photographs of Sarah Martin. Old newspaper items covering her disappearance and the discovery of her body.

"I knew her mother," Julianne said.

"Hey, that's funny, so did I! I wouldn't mention that around town, though. Just a bit of friendly advice."

When she turned back to him, her eyes were dark. "You think you were the only person who was hurt that night, and that's far from the truth. I've told you why I did what I did."

"Sure. To appease a sociopath."

"In part," she said. "But there are many more layers. You need to know all of them to make a judgment. That's your problem. You're too comfortable determining the shape of the world from the surface."

"Of the many problems facing me today, that's not a high priority."

"I'm sorry to hear that." She looked at the articles again, all those bold headlines announcing no leads, no arrests, and finally a "Ten Years Later, Still No Answers" anniversary piece. Mark thought about Lauren's case. Sixteen months in, no arrests. What would they write in ten years?

"Diane Martin came to me at the recommendation of a friend," Julianne said. "It was the year her husband was killed in a car accident. She was struggling with insomnia. She visited four times, and on the last visit reported that she was finally sleeping well. She said that she was dreaming vividly and that most of her dreams involved her daughter, and that in them, her daughter was always happy."

Julianne closed the door slowly. "I reached out to her when I heard about Sarah. I didn't hear back, but that wasn't surprising, because everyone was reaching out to her then. I offered to help her in any way that I could. I never heard from her again. When she died, though, it was from an overdose of sleeping pills."

"Maybe she didn't think your techniques would work again."

"Maybe she didn't know if she'd find any peace in her dreams." Julianne Grossman stepped away from the closet and looked Mark in the eye. "When Ridley came to me, I considered refusing. I suppose I should have. But my theoretical conflict of interest was dead, and, frankly, I was curious. I wanted to know what he would say. That's the truth of *everyone* in this town—we all want to know what he would say if he'd talk. Well, I got to be the lucky one." She turned away and took a deep breath. "Then I learned what is being done on her case: nothing. *Nothing.* Investigation has ceased. If he was honest in that confession, and I believe that he was..." She turned back to Mark. "I can't be the only one who knows. If he wants to bring me to the place where he killed her and tell me how he did it, I'm willing to take that walk. But I need help. I need someone who believes in what you just saw, someone who won't roll his eyes and say that confession was coerced, someone who understands that you can tell the truth without ever being aware of doing it. I need you."

"My only concern is my job," Mark said. "You've threatened my career. My life. The rest of this, the story you just told? It doesn't matter to me, Julianne. As much as I hate to say it, Sarah Martin doesn't matter to me, either. Let me be absolutely clear: *I don't care.* I just want out of this town with my life intact. That's all."

She crossed the room and stopped close to him, nearly touching him. The force of her stare seemed to hold his feet to the floor, making movement impossible. He struggled to keep the eye contact.

"Somewhere in the world," she said, "someone knows the truth about your wife. I wonder if they care."

He didn't answer. She pressed the digital recorder into his palm.

"There's your career," she said. "There's the truth you came back to Garrison to find. Do what you'd like with it."

39

Mark turned the wrong way out of Julianne Grossman's house and drove through the rain down an unfamiliar road until he reached a dead end and realized his mistake. Instead of turning around, he put the car in park and wiped sweat from his brow with trembling hands and then shook his head, as if he could clear his thoughts from inside it. Turned the AC on and cranked the fan up in hopes the cold air would sharpen his thinking. The digital recorder that Julianne Grossman had used to threaten his career was now in his jacket pocket. He pulled it out and stared at it for a few seconds, considering this supposed goodwill gesture. She could have made copies of the recording. She could be e-mailing them to his board of directors right now, and the sheriff, and anyone else who was interested; she could be burning CDs to distribute far and wide.

He pressed play and turned the volume up so he could hear the conversation clearly, and for the next twenty minutes he didn't move, just sat there with the air-conditioning blasting on him even though it was thirty-some degrees outside and listened to his own voice telling Julianne all of the things she had wanted to hear. He listened to the way she'd asked him, in a casual but still direct fashion, for his own permission before various points of questioning. The permission was always granted.

There's the truth you came back to Garrison to find.

He punched the power button and shut the recorder off.

If he shared the recording, people would know the reason he'd lied, supposing that they believed in hypnosis, but if he shared it, people would also know that he'd planned to murder a man. He could pull select clips, but sooner or later someone was going to want to hear the whole thing.

Some gift she'd bestowed upon him. Some peace offering.

He took out his cell phone and called Jeff London.

"Any progress up there, Markus?"

"Some." Mark had the recorder in his free hand and was looking at it as if it were a snake. "But not all good."

"I don't follow."

"You're not going to like where I go with this." Mark took a breath and said, "Jeff, do you believe in hypnotism?"

"What do you mean, do I believe in it? As in, does it exist? Of course."

"I mean..." He wanted to ask whether Jeff believed that someone could be hypnotized and never remember that it had occurred, but he couldn't bring himself to say the words. "If I told you I put any confidence in a confession a man gave under hypnosis, you'd tell me I was crazy, wouldn't you?"

"Not at all. I'd tell you that we likely couldn't get it into court, but I wouldn't tell you to discount it."

"Really?"

"Absolutely. I've got friends who worked with the old units at NYPD and LAPD. Some of those guys swear by them. There was that famous kidnapping case in California, the one where the bus driver accurately recalled most of a license-plate number under hypnosis. Another one, this was crazy, they were interviewing a victim who said she couldn't recall any information about the car she'd been abducted in, right? All she said, over and over, was that she didn't know anything about cars, so she couldn't help. Well, she was an artist. They hypnotized her and asked her to sketch the car. She drew it so accurately they got a make and model, located the car, and then found forensic evidence connecting the car not only to her but to other victims. *That* story really piqued my interest. You ought to see the sketches compared to what she said in the initial interviews. Her mind recorded so much detail, but somehow, because she didn't know cars, she had convinced herself that she wasn't capable of remembering it. Who gave you a hypnotized confession?"

"Ridley Barnes. But I never figured you'd put any credibility in things like that."

"Hell, I've *consulted* hypnotists," Jeff said. "Now, I lead with skepticism. Always. But you have to try any tactic in a dead-end case, and I'll listen to anybody once. If the facts stand up, I'll keep listening. Most times, with those types, they don't. But every now and then, something I'm hard-pressed to believe in will bear some fruit. I mean, I didn't send Lauren to Cassadaga on what I thought was a fool's errand."

Mark forgot the question he had been prepared to ask about Julianne Grossman's techniques. Forgot about Ridley Barnes and the cave and the Indiana rain that was turning to ice. He was on a sidewalk now, standing on concrete baked by a harsh sun, saying, *Don't embarrass me with this shit.*

"*You* sent her?"

"Of course. You knew that. We spoke to the police together."

"I knew that you understood where she was going. I just thought that it was her idea."

"What the hell does that matter? It was an assignment. She was on the job."

"But I thought it was her idea," Mark repeated, and he wanted Jeff to say that it had been, he wanted that even more desperately than he'd wanted Jeff to believe him about what had happened in Garrison.

"It wasn't her idea, it was her *instruction*," Jeff said. "But I don't see the difference. She was working for me. You want to blame me, then—"

"No," Mark said. "You don't understand. I didn't want her to go, because I thought you wouldn't have approved of her consulting a psychic. I thought it would have been...embarrassing. That last day, I was trying to talk her out of it to shield her from that. From your response."

"She went at my instruction. The only thing I would have had a negative response to was her not doing her job. That day, that was her job. I wish it hadn't been."

"She had a chance to tell me that. We *argued* about that. I was upset that she was giving the story any credibility, I said you wouldn't support it and she'd hurt her standing with you if she filed the report. Why wouldn't she have said it was your instruction?"

Jeff's voice softened. "Sounds like you were a little caught up in trying to protect each other."

"How so?"

"The original assignment was intended for your desk. She convinced me that was a bad fit for you, and she asked for it."

"*What?*"

"She told me that you weren't equipped to interview the woman. The one who said she was a psychic. The woman had identified a few things, and I thought it was worth the wild-goose chase. As I said, I'll listen to anybody once. So

I was going to send you, but then Lauren heard and said that you wouldn't do the interview well. I've never told you that because... well, because it seemed like an unnecessary addition of pain. I thought telling you that she'd stepped in for you would only hurt worse. But now you're asking. She told me you wouldn't do the interview well because you wouldn't think the woman had any credibility. That you'd scorn her, and if there was anything legitimate, you'd overlook it. She said that was a personal hang-up of yours and that she didn't want me to put you in that position. It would be hard for you, she said. *Unfair,* that was the word. She said it would be unfair to you."

Rain drummed off the hood of the car and ran down the windshield, putting a crystalline buffer between him and the clarity of the world beyond.

"She said it would be unfair for me." His words tottered out as if they were just learning to walk.

"It doesn't matter in any ways but good ones," Jeff said. He sounded as if he regretted having told the story. "She wanted to take care of you. Always. You know that."

"But I was the one who should have been on that road."

"Don't think about it like that. Think about it the way she'd want you to: she was looking after you, Markus."

"'Don't embarrass me with this shit,'" Mark said. "I said that to a woman I was more proud of than anyone I've ever known. 'Don't embarrass me.'"

"Pardon?"

"Nothing, Jeff. Let's get back to the point of the call."

What had the point been? Mark didn't remember, didn't care. He was glad when Jeff picked up the baton.

"Is anything about this confession, the hypnosis deal, going to help *you?*" Jeff said. "Because that's why you're there, right?"

I can't be the only one who knows. If he wants to bring me to the place where he killed her and tell me how he did it, I'm willing to take that walk. But I need help.

"Right," he said. "That's why I'm here."

"Well? Can this shit help you, or is it a dead end? You don't have time for dead ends. The board meets day after tomorrow, and this time you'll need to be here for it with whatever you have to offer."

Mark turned the recorder over in his hand. "I'm getting close," he said, and the drumming became a rattle as the rain turned to ice.

40

In all the time that he'd been working with her, Ridley Barnes had gone to see Julianne Grossman for every session. When her car pulled into his yard, tires skidding in the mix of rain and snow, he felt a black chill spread through his chest. He had carried his secrets to her. If they returned to his doorstep in a rush, he knew it was trouble.

"What's happened?" he said, opening the door as she jogged through the dampness and up the porch steps.

"He watched it."

Ridley stood stock-still, oblivious to the cold rain. "Novak? You played him the video?"

"Yes."

"He came to you?" Ridley said. "Today?"

"Yes."

"Was he alone, or was he with Blankenship?"

"He was alone."

Ridley let her in and closed the door and found himself feeling vulnerable and exposed as she looked around his house. That was laughable, considering he had let her probe the blackest places of his unconscious mind, but he felt it all the same.

"Do you think he will be a help?"

"I do. It's early to tell, of course. That's why I came

here—I wanted to let you know immediately, and in person. I didn't want there to be any surprises."

"And how did our friend Novak, the chosen one, react to my confession?"

"He seemed to believe it."

"Well, he should. That's not what I'm asking. Does he understand the importance of the cave?"

"He wants the same thing you do, though he's not fully aware of it yet. He wants to return to Trapdoor. I'm almost certain."

Ridley went to the woodstove and busied himself with stoking the fire just because he needed something to do, a place to direct the energy that was pulsing within him.

"He's not what I'd hoped," he said with his back to her. "He's too rigid. I don't think he understands the first thing about that place."

"Earlier you thought that the cave might have shown more of herself to Novak than to others."

Ridley watched the flames grow and then he added fresh wood and cupped his hands and soaked in the warmth as the fire crackled.

"Why are you here?" he said finally, still without turning.

"I was afraid he might be headed this way. I wanted to prepare you."

"I can handle him just fine. He's no different than any other detective."

"He most certainly is. You sent for him, Ridley. You asked him in."

"And you supported it. *Suggested* it, even."

"I did, and I do now, but with much more caution. Much more. Because I see real risk. For the both of you."

"What would you like me to do about that?"

"Challenge yourself," she said.

He looked over his shoulder. "I'm not hurting for challenges."

She nodded. "So you can bear another one, can't you?"

He didn't answer.

"You're going to need to trust him first," she said. "You're going to need to be vulnerable with him, Ridley, in ways that you don't like to be."

He returned his attention to the fire. A blackened piece of ash went up in an orange glow and licked toward the front of the stove as if it had eyes on escape. He grabbed a rag to keep from burning his hand and pushed the stove door closed, sealing in the flames, then adjusted the damper so that the fire could exhale.

"I can keep my control around him," he said. "That won't be a problem."

But he was thinking of Novak inside of Julianne's house, invading that safe haven, and his hands opened and closed on the rag. She had suggested getting involved with Novak, and it made sense to recruit someone from the outside. Now he had his doubts. Even while she was exhorting him to show control, she was removing some of it from him.

"I'm simply telling you that he'll need to be shown trust," Julianne said. "If you can't do that, then it may be better to send him away. If you still can."

If you still can. There was an accusatory flavor to the statement, an indictment, and he wanted to whirl around and shout that it had been her idea in the first place. The tension that had been growing in him in recent days was reaching a high-water mark.

"I won't need him if I can just get access to that cave," he said.

"I know you'd like that. I also know that you have some fear related to that place."

"That's the wrong word."

"It's the word you use when you're in a state of trance."

Once again, he found himself disliking her. Trance had been an intriguing gambit once upon a time, and certainly they had reached interesting places and had fascinating conversations. Lately, though, he wondered if she believed she had more power over him than she truly did.

"Nothing will go wrong," he said.

"Your subconscious disagrees. Your subconscious has disclosed, on multiple occasions, that you fear a return to Trapdoor will provoke a return to violence. That you may harm people."

She said all of this flatly, as if reading information off his driver's license. That was part of her approach with him, always had been—she listened to the discussion of violent deeds and the potential for worse and responded to them with detachment—but still, it unnerved him.

"I fear harming people?" he said, and he smiled in the firelight. "Well, that is troubling news, isn't it?"

"It isn't news to you. I came here because I wanted to tell you what had happened with Novak and tell you what I think."

"Which is that I should trust him."

"Yes."

Ridley nodded, and the motion cast rippling shadows along the wall. "I've trusted you. With Novak, I am only willing to wait. He's seen what he needs to see. There will be no further contact between you. Not until I'm convinced that he can, in fact, be trusted."

"We've already agreed that—"

"What was agreed to has been done. What he does from here, we'll just have to wait and see. He must come to me now. Not you. Only me."

"That may be out of my control, Ridley. He could return. He could return with the police."

"And you will send him away." He turned from the stove to face her. "Is this understood?"

Her expression didn't change. "I'll send him away. Until you're ready. And you will need to be ready."

"I lack many things, Julianne. Readiness is not one of them."

4 1

Mark drove to Trapdoor with air vents angled onto his face, blowing cold air into his eyes to help him stay alert. The road seemed to swim at times. Twice he looked at the GPS for guidance and realized that he'd never put in an address. He made the turns with confidence, though, as if the route were familiar.

The gate at the top of the drive was closed and locked. Mark left the car and walked down the slushy drive. The rain was beginning to mix with snow.

Cecil Buckner didn't spot him this time, or if he did, he didn't care to stop him. Mark made it all the way to the front door. When Danielle MacAlister opened it in response to his knock, her eyes went wide. "What's the matter?"

"Nothing's the matter. I just need some help."

"Well, get inside."

Once he was inside, dripping water onto her hardwood floors, he realized that her concern wasn't over his presence so much as his condition.

"I'm a little under the weather still," he said.

"You look awful. Sit down."

He sat on her leather sofa without removing his jacket. If there was a more comfortable couch in the world, he couldn't imagine it. Lord, he was tired.

"Did Cecil let you in?" she said.

"I walked down."

She didn't seem pleased to hear that.

"I'm sorry," he said. "Coming in like this. But I need some help."

She was looking at him with a mixture of sympathy and caution. "What can I do?"

"I need a copy of a map. One of the maps that Ridley drew."

"Why?" She folded her arms over her breasts in a protective fashion, and Mark observed that she wasn't wearing a bra and that she was in sweatpants and a T-shirt, and he wondered what time it was and why he didn't know that.

"I'm sorry," he said again.

"Do you need me to call someone, Mr. Novak? You don't look well."

"Just tired," he said. "I'm on my way back to a hotel, but I needed to stop here first. I'd like to have a copy of one of those maps. I need to get a sense of where I was. At the time, in the dark, it was hard to get my bearings."

"The maps won't show where you were found."

"But Ridley would know. Ridley could show me, because he's the one who found me, and he's the one who made the map."

"I suppose."

"I'll just make a copy," he said. "You can come with me, never let it out of your sight."

"You can have the original for as long as you need it."

He thought that she would have offered him just about anything as long as it ensured that he left her house in a hurry.

"I'll find the maps," she said. "Wait here, please?"

She went to a door that led to a staircase, but she passed

through the kitchen first and picked up a knife with a long, shining blade. She was afraid of him. He wanted to tell her that wasn't necessary. He meant no harm. He just needed to get a sense of Trapdoor. Down there alone in the dark, it hadn't been possible. He'd get a sense of it, and he'd ask Ridley to show him, and he would watch Ridley. He wanted to watch Ridley with those maps, and maybe—*maybe*—he'd ask what Ridley would think of giving him a tour, of showing Mark exactly how he'd gotten lost.

Danielle closed the door behind her and he heard her footsteps on the stairs and then he leaned back against the plush leather couch to wait. When his head settled against the cushion, he closed his eyes despite himself. With a couch like this, a man would never need a bed. Speaking of which, he was going to need a bed. His lungs hurt and his throat was sore and his body ached. He listened for her footsteps on the stairs and hoped that they wouldn't come too fast, that she wouldn't hurry. He just needed a few minutes with his eyes closed. It had been a long day.

When he woke, the room was dark except for a soft lamp in the corner, and he had no idea where he was. He closed his eyes again, wanting to retreat, but then the reality of his situation intruded and he straightened up fast, hoping that he'd been asleep for a minute or two, no more.

From the corner opposite the lamp, Danielle MacAlister said, "I've been debating whether to call the police or a doctor. I'm really not sure. In the end, I just let you sleep."

"You don't need to call anyone." He rubbed a hand over his eyes and felt radiant warmth from clammy skin. "I'm sorry. I'll get out of here."

"It's past midnight, Mr. Novak."

"You're kidding."

She shook her head. She was still wearing the sweats and had her auburn hair pulled back and tied loosely so that it fell over one shoulder, and the formidable, authoritative quality that she'd had before was gone and she looked very young. There was a tenderness in the way that she watched him that should have been sweet but instead was unsettling, because it had been a long time since anyone had looked at him that way.

"You've slept for a long time. It was obvious that you had a fever. You slept like a dead man until about an hour ago, and then your fever broke and you were covered in sweat. You started talking in your sleep a little. I think your dreams were awful until then. Then, when your fever broke, they changed."

He swung his legs around and put his feet on the floor. The room seemed to keep swinging when his own motion was done.

"Sorry," he said. "It's been a long day. I pushed it when I shouldn't have. You didn't need to let me sleep, though."

"You talked about your wife."

Mark retied a boot lace that was already tied just to give him an excuse to look away from her. "Did I?"

"Yes. It was actually very...sweet. You talked to her as if she were here. I know that she's not. I mean, obviously she's not here—I'm saying that I know what happened to her."

Mark looked up, and now she seemed flustered.

"I researched you, of course," she said. "It seemed prudent, after you'd trespassed on our property. I had to see who I was dealing with, that's all."

"Sure," Mark said. He wanted to know what he had said to Lauren in his sleep, what had been so sweet, but he couldn't bring himself to ask. He rose unsteadily, each bruise taking the opportunity to announce its presence.

"I'm sorry. I can't believe I fell asleep here. This was embarrassing."

"Where are you going now?"

"I'll find a hotel."

"It's past midnight, it's snowing again, and you're ill. All things considered, I think you should stay here tonight. There's a blanket and another pillow next to the couch. Just so you're aware, I will be in the room at the far end of the hall. I keep the door locked, and I have a handgun, and I'm accurate with it."

She spoke with a firmness that suggested she believed in her capabilities to protect herself, and no doubt she did. The young often believed in their own capabilities and their own safety. Too often.

"You won't need any locks or guns," Mark said.

"I'll make that judgment, thank you."

She left him then, and a few seconds later he heard the door close and the lock engage. He turned and looked out of the window behind him and saw nothing but blackness and a skein of ice on the glass. The wind came in shrieks and howls. He knew he should leave but the thought of that long walk through the snow and up the hill to his car seemed exhausting, and the motel where he'd paid for surveillance videos that morning held no more appeal. He took his boots off, stretched out on the couch, and didn't even bother to look for the blanket or pillow she'd mentioned. He was asleep again almost immediately, and though she'd said he'd dreamed sweet things of his wife, all he was aware of dreaming of now was Ridley Barnes, Ridley sitting in a straight-backed chair with his eyelids fluttering, then Ridley with a smile like a deranged clown and endlessly dark eyes. *I told you,* he said, *all you needed to do was spend some time down there. In the dark. Let's go back. Let's go back to where we both belong.*

And Mark followed, because in the dream he had no other choice. He knew that it was the wrong path, the dangerous one, and yet he followed Ridley out of the light and into the darkness. He was cold immediately, and then his clothes were gone and he was crawling in the dark again, crawling once more in an endless room, and though he was alone, he knew that Ridley was still with him, invisible but watching, always watching.

42

Mark woke before Danielle MacAlister. He rose from the couch and went into the kitchen, poured a glass of water, drank it gratefully, then chased it with another. In the pale light of dawn he could see that maybe two or three new inches of snow had fallen overnight. He'd slept deeply and he felt physically better and more mentally in control than he had when he'd arrived. That thought disturbed him more than it comforted him, though, as if his coming to Trapdoor hadn't been his own idea.

If you can get Danielle MacAlister's cooperation, Julianne had said, her unseen clock ticking loudly, and then Mark had driven to Danielle's house.

There was a laptop computer on the dining room table, and Mark went to it and opened it and got on the Internet and began to search for information on Julianne Grossman. He found no criminal or civil charges, but Garrison County and Orange County did not strike him as places where local records would be picked up by the major search databases. Small towns required local searches, even in the computer age. In general searches, all he found was that she had a website advertising her services and that her professed specialties were just as she'd claimed: help with addiction, anxiety, confidence building. She identified a number of hypnotherapy certifications that meant nothing to Mark but neglected to add any formal educational history. She appeared to be a local girl who'd gotten very interested in hypnosis very early. *As an agent for positive change, I will help you rewire your brain to transform!* she promised on the site.

He ran searches for the Erickson handshake induction she had referenced. He watched half a dozen videos of people supposedly put into immediate hypnosis with a few slight hand movements, and he said "Bullshit" under his breath. *You'll see some obvious frauds, and some things that once would have made you laugh,* she had told him. *But now? Now you won't laugh.*

She was right about that much. He wasn't laughing.

"Make yourself at home," a voice from behind him said, and he turned to see Danielle standing in the kitchen.

"Sorry," he said. "I shouldn't have—"

"It's fine." She waved him off and turned her attention to the coffeemaker. She was dressed in jeans and a formfitting long-sleeved shirt, and she stood barefoot on the hardwood floors. Her auburn hair was loose around her shoulders, and the sight of her, so natural and comfortable in her own home, drove thoughts of Lauren at him like a spear. There had been other women since Lauren, but not many, and he'd never lingered long enough to see one of them at home in the morning. Watching Danielle MacAlister go about making coffee was, in its own way, a more intimate moment than any he'd shared with a woman since Lauren died.

"Last night you wanted maps," she said. "Do you still?"

"Yes."

"Well, we can go downstairs and pick one out."

He closed her laptop and came into the kitchen. "Why are you cooperating?"

She set the coffee to brew without answering, then

watched it for a few seconds. When the pot began to fill, she turned back to him.

"You've been told that I wouldn't, I take it?"

"That seems to be the family reputation."

"It better be. The property is my family's and there's no small amount of liability risk with a cave. Your situation is the perfect example. If you'd died in there, someone might have sued us, even though you'd trespassed."

"That explains your defensiveness. But I asked about your cooperation."

She took a breath, pushed a stray strand of hair out of her eyes, and said, "Ridley Barnes talked to you."

"Correct."

"Ridley Barnes hasn't talked to anyone in ten years."

"You want to know what he says to me."

"And *why*. Yes. If you bring Ridley a map and he sits down and looks at it and talks to you about the cave? About *anything?* My God, would I love to know what he has to say and why he's decided to say it. It's fascinating. He hasn't spoken to anyone about Sarah, at least not as far as I know."

"He speaks to Evan Borders."

She stared at him. "What?"

"They exchanged calls the day I ended up in your cave. I found that interesting, to say the least."

"Ridley talks to Evan." She said it as if she were trying to believe it.

"At least that day. Did you know Evan?"

"Oh, yes. He's very different now than he was back then."

"How was he back then?"

"Funny. He was an entertainer. He liked to get you laughing, and he was good at it. That's hard to remember now."

"He wasn't telling many knee-slappers when I met him, that's for sure."

"Evan is another casualty, in my opinion. He wasn't killed, but whatever happened that night took what he was, what he could have been, and snatched that away. Then he became what the town probably expected him to be all along—like his father. One of those people who just seem destined for bad luck and trouble, you know? But when he was a kid…" She shook her head. "There's a reason a girl like Sarah Martin ended up in that cave with him. You see him today, you wonder how it would be possible, because he seems…"

"Threatening," Mark offered, and she nodded with what seemed to be real sorrow.

"He's angry white trash now, right? That's what people who don't know him would say. Isn't that what you'd say?"

Mark thought of the bins overflowing with Busch cans, of the rental house that was waiting on a teardown. "He's trying to play the role, at least."

"*That's* my point. He was given a role, and it was given to him that night in the cave."

Mark understood something about being given a role and about the way you could play a different one if you cared to try, but he didn't want to argue with her. He was about to ask another question when he was interrupted by an electronic chime. Danielle leaned over and punched a button on an old-fashioned intercom screen that was mounted on the wall above the kitchen counter.

"Good morning, Cecil."

"Miss MacAlister, I think that asshole from Florida came back."

Danielle smiled at Mark, then pushed the talk button again. "I'm aware of this. He's actually standing here with me now."

There was a pause, but Cecil's voice didn't betray any

less hostility when he spoke again. "I didn't know he was on the property. From the snow, looks like he has been all night."

"It's under control, Cecil. Thanks."

The intercom light blinked off. Mark nodded at it and said, "That's connected to the garage?"

"Yes. And he has a radio." She shook her head and poured coffee into two mugs and passed one to Mark. "He's quite the watchdog, our Cecil. Always vigilant. Only took him twelve hours to notice your car."

"Yet your father has paid to keep him here for ten years. Even Cecil seems confused by that."

She drank some of the coffee without looking at him and said, "Let's go downstairs and get your map."

They were back in the unfinished basement room with the map-covered walls when Mark said, "Why do you still have this place? Why let it sit for a decade?"

"That wasn't my choice. It will be soon enough, I'm afraid. My father isn't well."

"Will you sell it?"

"Absolutely."

"So why hasn't he?"

"He promised Diane Martin he would keep the cave closed," she said. "That was when they were still speaking. Whatever they had, it fell apart fast after Sarah died. Selling Trapdoor would have made him feel like he was profiteering when he should be suffering, I think. So he put that gate up, put the locks on, and left it to sit like some sort of monument to the dead. Any thought of selling it ended completely when Diane overdosed. He never came back to Garrison when he heard that. Not once. I'm the only person in the family to have stepped onto this property in the past four years, and I wasn't any more eager to do that than he was. For my family, Trapdoor became a very bad place, very fast. There's nothing but a lot of regret here."

She sat down on the old recliner, and dust rose from the cushions. She pulled the wooden handle on the side of the chair and the footrest rolled out with a protesting creak.

"You know this was the first place I ever made out with a boy? Not kissed, I'd been kissed before, but I mean really...you follow."

"I follow the mechanics, sure. I don't follow why you're talking about them."

"It felt terrible. Not the make-out session, that's not what I mean. At that age, you don't know what feels good yet."

"Then why'd it feel terrible?"

"You're a detective," she said.

"That's right. But apparently not a very good one, because I don't know why we're talking about this."

"Do some detecting, then," she said. "Why does a girl feel terrible for kissing a boy?"

Beside them the furnace kicked on and the exposed ductwork above began to hum. Mark looked at her and said, "Evan Borders?"

"You *are* a detective." She wiped her face with the back of her hand.

"When he was dating Sarah?"

"Yes."

"You were competing for him?"

"Oh, no. I had no interest in Evan. He was a sweet kid, cute and funny, but he was Sarah's."

"So you kissed him..."

"To hurt her," Danielle said. "I wanted to *really* hurt her, you know? In the worst possible way."

"Why?"

"Because I was seventeen years old and my father couldn't keep it in his pants and he was getting married *again* and Sarah was delighted about it. She was just thrilled. She'd talk about it all the time, she'd write me notes, send these cute little messages all with the same theme: we were going to be sisters. But I didn't want to be her sister. I wanted to be her friend, and I wanted my father back with my mother. She was so clueless about that, so obtuse, and it drove me crazy. I wanted to punish her. And what's the best way for one teenage girl to punish another?"

"Through her boyfriend."

"There you go. I knew it was an awful thing to do, of course. That was the point. I was *trying* to be awful. Because she needed to be punished, you know, for daring to act as if it were a good thing that my father was marrying her mother. For daring to want to be my sister."

She wiped at her eyes again. "That was the last weekend I was here. I went back to Louisville two days later, feeling very self-righteous about what I'd done, about teaching that little bitch a lesson. But that's all it was, understand? A lesson. A temporary thing. I'd see her again in a few weeks, and we'd get over it. Of *course* we'd get over it, because we were seventeen years old and we'd be family for the rest of our lives, right? The rest of our lives. It would be a footnote by the time we were twenty, something we laughed about by the time we were forty."

She put the footrest down and got out of the chair, returned to the file cabinet, opened it again, removed a photograph, and handed it to him. There were nine teenagers pictured, four boys in T-shirts and five girls in tank tops that said *Trapdoor Caverns.* They were standing in front of the entrance to the cave, everybody smiling, the sun on their faces. In the back row, Evan Borders looked relaxed and charming, a kid ready to cruise through the world. Just in front of him, kneeling with their hands on their slim, tan thighs, were Sarah Martin and Danielle MacAlister. Their heads were close together, their smiles wide. Sarah was just a few weeks away from another photo shoot, this one in the county morgue.

"Look at those eyes," Danielle whispered. "She had eyes that *shone*. Eyes that belonged to some pop love song. And when Evan came by? Her eyes took on a luminescence when he passed through. She was always smiling too. Immune to the petty and melodramatic things that you'd get between kids. Because she was trying to show her maturity that summer. Trying to act older to impress Evan. To impress *me*. I can't lie about that. She looked up to me, and I knew that. How awful then that I was the one who was petty and melodramatic. I was the child to her. My God, her father had *died* a few years earlier, and I was so dramatic about a *divorce* that I wanted to punish Sarah? How awful is that?"

She stepped away from Mark and sat back down on the ancient, creaking recliner. The day was young but she looked as if she wanted it to come to an end already. The question Mark asked then wasn't a detective's question at all.

"What was the last thing you said to her?"

She looked at him with surprise. "Why does that matter?"

"Don't you remember? I think most people do when they lose someone. Or if they don't, they come up with something. They need to remember, whether it's accurate or not."

Her chest swelled with a deep breath, and then she said, "I told her that she'd never be my sister, and I hoped she was classy enough not to take my family's last name for her own." She managed to say it without looking away from Mark, but it was evident that the statement was a bloodletting.

"You were right," she said. "People remember. I wish that

I didn't, though. What was the last thing you said to your wife?"

"Told her that I loved her."

"Do you know what I would give to be able to say that same thing?" Danielle asked, and Mark looked away.

They were quiet for a few moments. Danielle sat in the recliner and gazed around the room as if she didn't recognize it.

"You asked why we let this place sit," she said. "Understand now? Trapdoor seemed so pure once, seemed so *magical.* Right up until my father proposed to Diane Martin. And do you know what? Diane was lovely. She was a lovely woman, and her daughter was the same, and I *knew* that. Even when I went out of my way to hurt her, I knew that. I just wanted to be allowed to be angry about it. He was my father, and he'd left my mother, and I was *entitled* to my anger, and Sarah didn't get it. But my anger wasn't supposed to last. I understood that even then. The fight would pass, and we'd be fine. We were seventeen. You get another chance then, always."

She tucked her feet beneath her so she was sitting curled up on the oversize chair, and she cried without making much of a sound. He didn't say a word, because he understood. She needed to weep for Sarah, for her father, for Evan Borders, for an unspoiled summer that had been swallowed by darkness. To weep not for the way things had once been but for the way things had been supposed to go and did not. People believed that they were haunted by bad memories, but that wasn't the truth. The most sinister hauntings were from unrealized futures.

Mark watched her and wondered why he hadn't told her the truth. Because it was none of her damned business, that's why.

Then why'd you ask her?

What he'd told her wasn't a lie. He had said the words into the phone, whether they'd been heard or not. Maybe they had been. How could he know?

You know.

Of course he did. *Don't embarrass me with this shit.* For so long, he'd known what he'd meant—his wife was willingly pursuing a fraud's foolishness. He had known that without question, because it was the truth and the truth didn't require questioning. Then Jeff London provided his addendum, and the old truth remained but another emerged beside it: Lauren had gone to Cassadaga to protect him. To cover for his weaknesses.

She told me you wouldn't do the interview well because you wouldn't think the woman had any credibility, Jeff had said. *That you'd scorn her, and if there was anything legitimate, you'd overlook it.*

Mark went to the wall and removed the tape from the last map Ridley Barnes had drawn, the one from the summer of Sarah Martin's death.

"Are you going to see Ridley?" Danielle asked.

"Maybe. First I've got another stop to make. We'll see how it goes."

43

The dog that looked like a fox was back in the yard when he pulled in. It kept its distance but watched him with total focus and a regal stance, like some sort of mythical guardian. He was wary of it as he walked to the porch, but the dog let him pass without a sound. It felt like the animal had made a conscious decision, one that could easily have gone another way.

Julianne Grossman answered the door and said, "You look better. You've slept."

"I'm going to need you to prove yourself to me," Mark said.

"I gave you the recorder. You've got everything you need."

"Not enough to prove that Ridley's confession was anything close to legitimate."

"I thought that was irrelevant to you. That you—to be absolutely clear—didn't care."

Mark said, "I can't get at the truth of Ridley in an hour. I should be able to with you."

It could have been a confusing statement, but she followed. "You want to be hypnotized?"

Mark nodded.

"This will tell you, what, whether I'm a fraud?"

"Whether I should believe that video confession of Ridley's was anything close to legitimate."

"It won't tell you that," she said. "You'll learn about yourself, not about me. But I get your point nonetheless."

"You're from here," Mark said. "Not Garrison, but close by. How did you come to do what you do? It's a strange profession for an honest person to pursue."

"You're very wrong about that. There are many honest hypnotists. Some frauds, sure. But I suspect there are fewer frauds in hypnosis than there are in banking or real estate. And I'm quite confident there are more in politics."

"How did you come to do what you do?" he repeated.

"My older sister struggled with alcoholism. Badly. She turned to a hypnotist, and everyone else thought she had lost her mind and was throwing away money. It worked. I was fascinated by that. I'd seen the wreckage of her life, and the idea that this thing had *worked*, and so effectively . . . it fascinated me. I read; I studied. I took classes." She paused, and her eyes drifted, which was unusual for her. "There was another reason too."

"What was that?"

She refocused on him. "There are always skeptics. Every day, I meet someone who doesn't believe in me. In what I do. People like you. The personal challenge of that, the emotional challenge? I've learned to embrace it. Now, I could provide references, you could interview people about me to your heart's content, you could go out and do your fact-checking work, but that's not going to mean anything to you, is it? You need to *feel* things to believe in them. Every skeptic must. You put faith only in your own judgments, your own experiences."

He thought of his mother with the dyed braids and brown contacts and self-tanning lotion, dream catchers scattered about.

"Yes, I put more stock in my judgment than in anyone else's."

She nodded. "That's an issue you're going to need to work on for the long haul, isn't it? But no matter. We can conduct trance. I think if we—"

"We'll conduct it just like Ridley's confession." Mark held out his phone. "We're going to record it with this, not your equipment. And we're going after memories, just like you did with him."

"What memories, Mark?"

"How I got in that cave."

She gave another of those measured, steady nods, but he could see intrigue in her eyes. "All right. We can do that. Come on in."

He stepped over the threshold.

"Take the couch, please," she said, and then she pulled a straight-backed chair close to him. He sat on the couch and tried to look relaxed, indifferent, crossing one leg over the other and folding his arms over his chest. She reached out and tapped his ankle.

"Let's try a different posture. Something not so defensive. You're guarding yourself."

He put both feet flat on the floor and moved his hands to his sides and was amazed at how instantly vulnerable he felt.

"You're going to have to be receptive," she said. "Your pursuit right now seems to be due to sheer skepticism. You want me to prove that I *can* hypnotize you. I'd encourage you to think deeper. A stage hypnotist could hypnotize you, but it wouldn't mean that person would be able to ascertain anything of value in working with Ridley Barnes. You want to get at your memories of that day, correct? The day you were hurt."

"The day I was attacked."

"And did that not hurt you?"

Mark wet his lips and gave a grudging nod.

"Can we vocalize that, please?"

"Yes, it hurt me," he said, and the admission was entirely unpleasant. *Try,* he told himself, *you've got to try. Think about Lauren, damn it. What she said you couldn't do. Do not show this woman scorn or contempt, and do not rule out the chance of something legitimate here.*

He was in his most receptive mood when Julianne said, "Can you give those emotions a shape?"

"Excuse me?"

"Tell me what shape they have. Those feelings, those hurts. What shape?"

He knew then that it wouldn't work. Not on him. "I do not have a *shape* for my emotions," he said.

"Then we'll start with a box," she answered, unfazed. "I think that's a fine shape for your emotions, Mark. I want you to imagine a box in the center of the room."

Lauren, baby, I'm trying, I really am, but this...

"Right there where the light goes through the shadow, do you see that?" Julianne said.

"Yes."

"Good. Imagine the box. When you're ready, I want you to describe it for me."

He stared at the place where the light met the shadow, and he tried like hell to imagine a box, to imagine there was anything there but weathered floorboards. He couldn't, but he didn't want to admit that, so he said, "It's wooden," simply because the floorboards were wood and that was the easiest visual to conjure up.

"What kind of wood?"

"Older," he said. He still wasn't visualizing anything. He just wanted to have an answer.

"A large box? Like a chest?"

"No." He wasn't sure why he sounded so damn confident about that, considering he was making it all up on the fly.

"So what size is it?"

"Um...maybe about a cigar-box size," he said, and there was a flicker of an image then, neither real nor imagined, just some spark in the synapses that gave him a vague sense of the thing that he was attempting to describe to appease her. He understood what a cigar box was, of course, he could picture that, and so the image flickered through and was gone and the empty floor remained.

"Keep looking at it," Julianne said. Her voice had gone lower and softer and he squinted at the floor intently and then thought of how he must look and felt torn between a desire to call the whole thing off and a desire to laugh wildly. Julianne's voice came again, though, saying, "The box needs to hold all of your focus. Really try. I know it's not easy, but I can see how hard you are trying. That is very good. That is excellent. Your focus is impressive. Keep your attention out there in the room. There's a box on the floor, and it is old, and it is made of wood, and it is a cigar box, maybe, or at least it is of that size. Focus on it. Focus."

Mark stared at the patch of light on the floor trying to imagine a cigar box and thought, *This is going to take a while.*

It did. There were times when he felt vaguely detached and removed, times when answering questions about an imaginary box seemed important, but then self-awareness would return and jar him, or his mind would simply wander, and thoughts of Florida and Jeff London would intrude, or images of Ridley Barnes on the video, speaking of the dark man. He'd say this for Julianne Grossman—she was patient.

She was incredibly patient. Over and over she asked meaningless, silly questions and listened to his meaningless, silly answers, and not once did her energy diminish. She managed to sound fascinated by his descriptions of the stupid damn box, and her voice came on and on in waves that rose and fell and broke over him and then washed back across him, and he was impressed by both her steadiness and her bearing, because it couldn't be easy. He knew that it was not easy. He'd conducted a lot of interviews. Controlling your focus and emotions was hard enough, but to keep that cadence, that rise and fall, rise and fall, the vocal equivalent of rocking a child, was impressive. He was curious how she did it and how much practice it took and wondered if she was aware of her breathing or if that became natural. She never took a breath at the wrong time, and he thought that was probably critical. Any disruption would break the spell. Although of course there was no spell, no trance. No hypnosis. He'd always been skeptical that it would work on him. He believed that it worked in some situations, the science and evidence seemed undeniable, but it wasn't for him.

Still, the cadence was effective. He had to admit that. The cadence was relaxing, soothing, and the way she held his focus by asking these ridiculous questions kept the mind from wandering. The visualization technique was smart, too, because it demanded stillness and focus that was truly draining. His vision had begun to ripple along the periphery. Yes, all in all, he could see how her techniques might be effective in time, on the right person. He just wasn't that person.

When he said, "I think it's a cave," he felt a sense of slipping, like he'd hit mental black ice. What question had she asked? He couldn't remember, but he'd given the answer, and she seemed pleased by it. And the cave was where they were supposed to be going, wasn't it?

"And what do you see?"

"Blackness," he said, an automatic answer that seemed logical, but it was also confusing, because what had happened to the cigar box? That was what he was supposed to be imagining. Maybe he should try a little harder. He focused but couldn't find the floor. He thought he heard distant drums. That didn't make any sense. He needed to clear his head. Needed to—

"If you would like, you may close your eyes," Julianne said, and he thought, *Thank God,* because he was so tired now, and the floor where that box was supposed to be had started to swim from the sheer effort of staring at it for so long. Shutting his fatigued eyes for just a moment sounded grand.

It's working on me, he thought, and there was some true and deep fear to that realization.

But not enough to keep his eyes open.

44

Ridley should have gone underground after Julianne's visit—he needed the solace—but he hadn't. Instead, he had stayed in the house listening to the wind blow snow against the walls, and he debated whether he could still view Julianne as an ally.

Always, she had listened to his needs, and always, she had attended to them. Or so he'd thought. As the snow accumulated and the dark hours passed and were replaced by the light, he considered the evidence against Julianne's integrity, and he was concerned.

There had been no shortage of people in Ridley's life who believed they could manipulate him, but he'd not sought any of them out. Julianne was his own find; he'd gone to her for help and she had provided not only help but a sense of possibility. What Ridley had once believed was beyond his grasp, Julianne had convinced him was in fact a reasonable goal.

She had also convinced him that Mark Novak would be of assistance in achieving that goal. The problem, Ridley realized as he tied knots with hands that had gone slick with sweat, was that *she* had located Novak. Ridley had done the writing, Ridley had reached out, but Novak had not been his discovery. He belonged to Julianne.

That was beginning to feel like a problem.

The decision to trust him with a video of Ridley's most vulnerable moment, an even greater problem.

The goal, as Julianne had always understood—or claimed to understand—was to grasp the full power of Trapdoor. She had been the only person who had listened to Ridley's explanations of the cave and not recoiled. She was the only person who had enough wisdom to refer to Trapdoor with proper respect. For all of these reasons, he had felt certain that she was the only person the cave would permit to join Ridley in a quest that had been building for ten years.

The rope slipped from his fingers and fell to the floor and he opened his eyes and stared at it in horror, trying to remember the last time he had dropped a rope while tying a knot.

The snarl of rope lay there like a symbol of the mistake that he had made, and he understood that he should never have written to Novak, but it was too late to fix that. Whether it was too late to give up on Julianne, he wasn't sure. He'd waited so long for someone like her and had nearly lost hope.

He wiped his hands dry on his jeans and went upstairs to his bookshelves, which were lined with studies on the power of the mind, from a 120-year-old volume on levitation to the latest neuroscience research. There was also a collection on jewelry and gemstones, and the highlighted portions all concerned the sapphire. If there was any topic Ridley would consider discussing with Blankenship—and he'd come close once, only to pull back at the last minute—it was the sapphire necklace. Ridley understood from the police reports that Blankenship had given the necklace to Diane Martin because it was her birthstone. A simple enough reason for a simple man, and Blankenship was nothing if not simple, but Ridley wondered if the stone might have been powerful enough to affect him nevertheless. The sapphire, Ridley had learned in his studies, provided spiritual enlightenment, inner peace, and—most critically—protection from harm. Whether Blankenship might have sensed a harm approaching the Martin household was something Ridley had long wondered.

Eastern cultures believed the stone warded off evil, but if you studied enough, you learned that the gemstone's power was so mighty as to be selective and that it would protect its first wearer even if it was sold or given away to another. Ridley thought this might explain why it had failed Diane's daughter, but Diane was dead now as well and there was no one left to ask about this except for Blankenship, who seemed too dull to receive the question properly.

And there was Julianne.

Ridley left the bookshelf untouched and went instead to the knee wall, pressed on the panel, and revealed the room hidden beyond. He retrieved the necklace with the broken chain and handled it carefully. The stone was small and unremarkable in color, but it was genuine. According to Persian legend, the entire earth rested on a core of sapphire, and the sky was blue because it reflected the color of that hidden core. According to Greek myth, Prometheus had been chained to a rock for stealing fire from the gods, and the rock was made of sapphire. Ridley believed both stories could be true. While he could not speak for the accuracy of all the sapphire's reputed powers, he understood that they must be great because Trapdoor had presented it to him and allowed him to remove it from underground. The necklace, he'd come to realize, was the most sacred of all his possessions—so sacred that he had taken the risk of keeping it with him rather than placing it in the ground near his childhood home, so sacred that he had never shared it with anyone.

Now was the time.

The sun was high in a cloudless sky as he drove to Julianne's, and, never a fan of bright light, he cursed the harsh white landscape, lowered the visors in the truck, and put on sunglasses. They dulled the glare some, but not enough. He was beginning to feel a real rage over the light when it occurred to him that the sky was sapphire blue and that this was perhaps a good sign. He would show Julianne the necklace and in this gesture of trust he believed her allegiance would be assured once more.

He felt renewed confidence as he turned onto the gravel road that led to Julianne's, and he thought the small sapphire clutched in his palm had warmed ever so faintly, just enough to let him know that he was on the right course.

That was when he started to make the turn into her drive and saw that another car was already there.

He came to a stop and then moved to put the truck in park. When he reached for the gearshift, the necklace slipped from his hand and the sapphire fell to the filthy floor mat, its brilliant shine lost in Ridley's own shadow.

The car was a new-model Ford SUV and while Ridley wanted to believe that it was not a rental and did not belong to Mark Novak, he couldn't convince himself of that. He reached into the glove compartment and withdrew a small pair of binoculars that he carried with him in the field to study terrain. He focused them on the front window of the house and what he saw chilled his blood.

Julianne was seated in a chair beside the couch, and on the couch, his posture slumped, his head drooping, was Mark Novak.

He was in trance. She had promised Ridley she would have no more contact with the man until Ridley commanded otherwise, and not only had she broken that promise, but she'd shattered it in the most irrevocable way—she was working with him, guiding him in the way she had guided Ridley.

He sat in the idling truck for a long time, and then he reached down and fumbled around the dirty floor mat until he found the necklace with the broken chain. The gemstone's power was not a lie. Whether it would grant him protection or not, Ridley couldn't say, but it had guided him and allowed him to see things clearly again, and this was critical.

He put the necklace into his shirt pocket, close to his heart, and drove away knowing that the time had come to set right his mistakes. He had trusted in something outside of himself and should have known better.

45

Mark felt incredibly relaxed as he listened to Julianne count upward to ten, though he became aware of the progression only at around five or six. Then, when he opened his eyes at ten, he felt exposed. The room came into focus in a disorienting way, and his first clear thought was that the light on the floor had shifted to another area. Some time had passed, certainly. His mouth was dry and he wanted to talk just to reassure himself that he had control over his own voice, but no words came to mind. There was a sensation of pressure on his right hand, and he looked down and saw that his index finger and thumb were curled together in a perfect circle, like a basketball player signaling for three points.

You did that to join the past and the present, he thought, and though the purpose seemed crystal clear he couldn't recall the specifics of the action or how long he'd held his hand in that fashion. He relaxed his fingers and flexed them, then looked up at Julianne Grossman. She was watching him with an expression of deep compassion, and he felt nothing but warmth for her in that moment.

"So," Mark said, his voice a croak. He worked his tongue around his mouth, trying to rid it of that dry sensation. "So, how about that? How good was I?"

Julianne smiled. "How do you feel?"

"Odd," he said. "And tired."

"Would you like some water? Sometimes trance can cause a strong feeling of thirst."

"I would love some water," he said, the word *trance* lingering in his mind, bouncing around. He'd actually entered one. She'd hypnotized him. He wasn't sure how to feel about that.

Julianne brought him a glass of water and didn't speak while he drank. Outside, the trees moaned in a strong wind, and he wondered how he hadn't heard them before.

"Okay," he said. "Did we get anywhere? Or did I just talk about the cigar box the whole time?"

Julianne said, "That's all you remember?"

He thought about it, and although he couldn't recall the specifics beyond that, it wasn't a troubling sensation.

"That's all," he said.

"You reached a state of somnambulistic trance," she said. "That's excellent, you know. For all of your initial resistance, in the end you made quite an effort."

"So what did I remember?" Mark said.

"It's all recorded on your phone, as you requested. But your descriptions of what happened on the road were... vivid. You talked about the way the men spoke, looked, and breathed. The way the wind felt. You said that you'd tried to make a trail of blood so that the police would have better clues than they'd had with your wife's case. You didn't want to make it hard on the police if you were killed."

Mark turned away from her and looked out the window. The trees were weaving and at the top of the driveway the dog was patrolling, nose up, sniffing the wind.

"That's right," he said, and his voice was thick. He hadn't remembered the attempt to leave a blood trail behind until now, and that seemed impossible. It had been so calculated; how could he have forgotten?

"After they put you in the van, they took you to another place," Julianne continued. "A field. Your head was covered by some sort of a hood that you said smelled like horse feed."

He nodded.

"At that point, you thought there was only one of them left. He was the one who cut you, the one who put a needle in your arm." She paused and then said, "Maybe that blood test you keep talking about wouldn't be a bad idea after all."

"Did I remember going into the cave?"

"No. You said that this one man, the only one left, took you somewhere to ask more questions. You said that it was probably a house, you weren't sure about that, but you knew that it was someplace where you couldn't feel the wind, though it was still cold even without the wind. Your memory of getting inside involved walking a plank."

"Walking a *plank?* They took me to a pirate ship? That ought to be easy to find."

Julianne continued without pause at his sarcasm. "You didn't remember much about the house except for a wall of boards that you said didn't look right. At times you thought they were melting."

This meant less to him. A vague sense of recollection, but not as clear as the blood trail.

"The questions this man asked you were mostly related to Ridley Barnes and the cave. He was very interested in the cave."

Listening to a recap of his own words when he didn't remember the words or the source of them was surreal.

"You don't seem to have any memory at all of how you arrived in the cave. There's a gap, which suggests that you were truly unconscious when you went from this place with the wall of boards to the darkness in the cave." She paused, gazing at him with interest. "The recollections of the cave troubled you. That was the only time you displayed any real resistance to trance. You said you encountered people in the cave who did not belong there. You would not identify them to me because you said they were not real."

"Sarah Martin," he said. "I was imagining things. Hallucinating."

"Interesting. Here you are willing to tell me that, but in trance you were not."

"Which means what?"

"That your subconscious has a greater difficulty dismissing the things that you saw."

"My subconscious can believe in ghosts, but I can't? That's what you mean?"

"Possibly? I'm trying to facilitate access. I'm not trying to interpret for you. You can consider the meaning of all this on your own. Before we ended the trance, I asked whether there was anything you could or should do to further help yourself understand what had happened in the cave. You said you should have looked at the maps by now."

"That's what I was going to do next. I want to look at a cave map with Ridley."

"That's not the way you put it during trance. You said repeatedly that you were looking at the wrong maps, and that was a problem. You were very insistent that you needed to look at different maps. At this point, you laughed a little and told me that your mother wouldn't have made the same mistake."

Mark felt a ripple of distaste, the first sense of regret over letting her probe around in his unconscious mind. It was easier to accept the notion that his subconscious believed in ghosts than it was to think he would give his mother any credit for logic.

"The creek name," he said, waving a hand. "That's all that was."

"The creek name?"

"It's nothing," he said. "My mother had a bullshit persona that connected to the creek name, which would be on maps. I get it. Don't worry about it. You just said yourself that you're not trying to interpret for me."

She gave a slow nod, but he felt like a specimen under a microscope.

"What was the deal with my hand?" He made the circle with his thumb and index finger again.

"That was done while we asked your subconscious mind to close the link between past and present."

Exactly what he'd understood, even though he hadn't remembered the moment.

"Well, I'm impressed, I'll admit that," he said finally. "Sadly, it didn't turn up much of value."

"I don't know if that's true. Many times the value of memory—of the unconscious in general—isn't readily apparent."

"Melting boards aren't going to get me far with the sheriff or going forward with Ridley. That seems readily apparent."

"I asked about going forward."

"Oh? Did I crack the case?" Mark was smiling until she answered.

"You seemed to take a macro view of the question. You told me that you would have to go to a place called Cassadaga, and then to the mountains."

She watched his smile fade into something hard and cold and said, "Cassadaga has meaning to you, I take it?"

"A little. But I won't be going there."

"What about the mountains?"

"I don't care for the mountains. If I can avoid them, I will."

"Why is that?"

"I've seen enough of them." He got to his feet and picked up his phone from where it rested, still recording, on the coffee table beside him. He stopped the recording, put the phone in his pocket, and looked outside. The sky was cloudless today and the sun was gorgeous on the snow.

"You're willing to go into that cave with Ridley if it can be arranged?" he asked her.

"Yes."

"And you honestly believe that he will say something of value?"

"He wants to show me the place. He's made that clear."

"It's a hell of a risk for you," Mark said.

"I understand that. Do you think you can get us access?"

He thought of Danielle MacAlister, crying in her basement chair surrounded by Ridley's hand-drawn maps.

"I think it's possible."

46

The sweat didn't start until he was back in the rental car, and he was out of the driveway before he allowed himself to use his shirtsleeve to mop his face. He had wanted the hypnosis to work, had wanted to see Julianne Grossman provide something that allowed him to believe in her, but a part of him—larger maybe than he'd expected at first—was terrified at the idea that she'd been able to take him to a place in which he'd communicated without awareness or memory of it. Mark had no conscious ranking of his personal values, but one had floated to the surface during his time in Garrison: control. He didn't just want it, he craved it. *Self-control*, he would have called it once, but that was a lie. The word was *control*, pure and simple, and though he'd sacrificed it willingly with Julianne this time, it still hadn't settled comfortably.

He was still sweating and so he put down the window and let the chill in. When his phone rang and it was Jeff London, he stared at the display with surprise. Only yesterday he would have picked it up eagerly. Now it seemed to confuse his purpose.

"Hey, Jeff."

"*Hey, Jeff?* I left two messages. Markus, I've got to sit down with the board *tomorrow*. Do you have anything, and

I mean *anything,* for me to show in your defense? I thought you said that you were making progress!"

"I am."

"Good." Jeff's exhalation was audible. "Tell me something I can use."

"I'm not quite there yet."

"I don't mean full resolution, I mean *anything!* What happened to the hypnotist? What about the ketamine? What can I tell them?"

The road rolled by for a few seconds before Mark said, "You know I've never broken a case?"

"What in the hell are you talking about?"

"Not one case. I never broke one open."

"Bullshit you didn't. Your work was critical on so many different—"

"Critical, sure. I made some finds. I passed them off to you. I never got to see one through. That's the point, isn't it, Jeff? To come in without the truth and stay until you've learned it?"

"The point is generating quality work product for the team."

"Did you ever solve one? I mean *really* solve one? Ever go from looking at crime scene photographs of a murder victim to seeing the truth come to the surface thanks to your own work?"

Jeff's voice softened. "A few times."

"How'd that feel?"

"Why are you asking this?"

"I need to know," Mark said. The wind had picked up again and it should have chilled him but the cold felt good, familiar in the ways he'd wanted to deny when he arrived. "I need to know what it feels like. Maybe you were right that it shouldn't be Lauren's case."

"I *know* I'm right about that. You'll drown in those waters, Markus. You've already come close. Don't go back in."

"Sarah Martin isn't Lauren. But she deserves it just as much."

"They all do," Jeff said. "It's the reason I sent you up there to begin with. I've already acknowledged that was a mistake. Don't double-down on it. Please."

Mark was now just two miles from Trapdoor, and the open fields came into view and with them the snow-covered, collapsing trailer and beyond those and far on the horizon the high bluffs where the horses had been visible on Mark's first visit. He hadn't heard back from the Leonard family. Maybe it was time to go see the old man again. Maybe it was—

"Markus? Mark?"

The urgency in Jeff's voice made Mark blink back into reality. "Yeah," he said. "Yeah, I'm here." But he'd pulled off the road and was staring at the trailer. "Listen, Jeff, I've got to go. I'll be back in touch fast. With something you can use. I promise."

He disconnected before Jeff could utter a response.

What had once been the drive to the trailer was so overgrown that small shrubs were visible even beneath the blanket of snow. The trailer still stood, but that was a generous term. The whole structure canted to the left, like a sinking ship listing to port. On the road-facing side, the roof was bowed in almost to its limits. The windows were broken and even the plywood sheets that had been fastened to them from the inside were pocked with holes and splinters. A corrugated metal ramp that had once served as a front porch was disengaged from the main building completely; at least three feet of air separated the top of the ramp from the front door.

Mark killed the engine and stepped out of the car. To the

east he could see the bluffs, no horses in sight today, and to the south he could see the tree line where the bluffs began their descent to Maiden Creek and the caverns its water had opened. He turned again, putting his back to the trailer, and looked to the west, his face into the wind.

The wind worked on you with a honed blade, coming over those fields with nothing to disrupt it. Mark closed his eyes and felt the wind and thought of Julianne Grossman's recap of his hypnosis session.

You said that it was probably a house, you weren't sure about that, but you knew that it was someplace where you couldn't feel the wind, though it was still cold even without the wind. Your memory of getting inside involved walking a plank.

He opened his eyes, turned back to the trailer, and studied that ramp, the way the connecting bolts were sheared, leaving it loose at the top. He walked down the drive and up the ramp slowly, and this walk he made with his eyes closed, paying attention to every other sense. The thin metal boomed with each step and flexed beneath his weight because it was no longer anchored to anything, the top end floating in the air. With his eyes closed, it felt very much like walking a plank.

There were hinges for a storm door, but there wasn't a storm door. The knob on the main door didn't turn. Locked.

He removed a credit card from his wallet and slipped it between the door frame and the door. It slid down past the dead bolt without making contact, which was good. Dead bolts were more time-consuming, though hardly impossible. Shimming a lock was a skill you picked up fast when you were regularly evicted from apartments. Mark's mother had been a hell of a lock pick.

He felt pressure on the card and then twisted the knob

hard to the left and flicked the card down. The door swung open, releasing a wave of dank air. On the other side was a strip of peeling linoleum and stained carpet beyond that. A skim of ice had formed on one portion of the carpet.

Cold even without the wind.

As Mark stepped inside, he heard a plinking noise and saw that water was dripping through the molded tiles of the drop ceiling, probably right below the place where the roof bowed severely. He stood on the linoleum square and looked around, wishing for a flashlight. Not that there was much to see. The trailer was vacant and had been for years, save for the occasional rodent. There were mouse droppings on the kitchen floor to the right, beside a chair that been smashed and left in shards.

He slipped his cell phone out and used its flashlight function and swung back to the left, where the trailer's only source of sound was provided by the steady plinking of the dripping water on the skim of ice over the carpet, and then he stopped scanning the place and stared at the far wall of the living room. It was covered in the faux-wood paneling that had once been popular and now made most people shudder, the kind that was supposed to give a room a log-cabin feel. There was clearly another leak behind the wall, because the paneling was peeling away from the studs, warped and bubbling.

He stepped over the ice and walked up to the wall. Ran his fingertips along the warped panels. Moisture had caused some to peel free and others to sag, although a few remained in place. The final effect was something you wouldn't want in your home but that Salvador Dalí might have appreciated—it looked like the wall was melting.

"Well done, Julianne," Mark whispered.

He'd been here before, and she'd gotten him to tell her

about it. During hypnosis he'd ranted to her about a melting wall. It made no sense unless you'd seen these warped panels through a semiconscious haze, which was exactly what he'd done. He dropped to one knee and looked at the filthy carpet, tracked back through it until he found what he was looking for: four faint impressions, the kind left behind by the legs of a chair. Yes, this was where he'd been. The chair would have faced the wall. It was probably the one in splinters in the kitchen. Evan Borders had taken some frustration out on it. There were red stains on the carpet. Mark's blood, probably. He lifted the cell phone higher and passed the faint glow over the filthy carpet. He turned halfway to the kitchen, froze, and then—slowly, as if rapid motion would scare off what he'd seen—brought the beam back.

There was a piece of plastic in the shadows on the floor. He slid forward and then lowered himself until he was resting on his hands and knees and could see the plastic squarely centered in the light.

It was about the size of a poker chip and bore the logo of the Saba National Marine Park. A diving permit.

Mark reached for it and managed to stop himself when his fingers were about an inch away. He closed his eyes again and breathed a few times and then he rose without allowing himself a look back and went outside in the hard white glare of the day and called the sheriff's office and asked for Dan Blankenship.

47

It took the sheriff just over fifteen minutes to arrive and when he did, he was alone. He was in uniform with the badge gleaming high on his chest and even had the brown trooper hat. Very Wild West.

"Let me guess," he said. "The door was standing open when you found it."

"You're good at this," Mark said.

Blankenship spit into the snow, trying to hold his trademark sour expression with Mark, but he was struggling. Something about the place excited him, and that was interesting, because the only importance Mark could attach to it was that this was where he'd been beaten, drugged, and interrogated—all crimes that Blankenship claimed he didn't believe had occurred.

"You've got unique law enforcement in this county," Mark said.

"How's that?" Blankenship answered.

"Fieldwork tends to be handled by deputies. But I get the elected official himself, and I get him solo."

"You didn't call 911, Novak, you called me direct. I always answer direct phone calls. Part of my duty to the taxpayers."

"That must be it," Mark said. "In Florida, we don't pay

state income tax. I've always suspected policing was a lot more hands-on in places where you did."

Blankenship almost smiled at that. He walked through the snow and up to the ramp and put one gloved hand on the railing.

"You said you had evidence, not just a story. Is that inside?"

"Yes, sir. You'll find a plastic dive permit on the ground in there that was previously in my pocket."

"The kind of thing you could have just dropped on the ground before you called me, in other words."

"Exactly that kind of thing. Only I didn't. And the dive permit doesn't belong to me. It belonged to my wife."

Blankenship turned away from the trailer and his expression softened.

"You carried it with you?"

"Every day, Sheriff. Every single day."

They looked at each other in silence and then Blankenship said, "Anything else?"

"Bloodstains on the carpet. They'll belong to me. Maybe not all of them, it looks like the sort of place that has seen some blood before, but I can point you to some of them."

"Stand where you are for a bit, all right?"

"Sure."

Blankenship went up the ramp, walking carefully, and then withdrew a small tactical flashlight and used it to illuminate the interior of the trailer. He didn't cross the threshold, but he didn't need to in order to see the living room.

"I didn't touch the dive permit," Mark said. "Sure wanted to, but I left it."

"You think it's worth bagging and tagging?"

"I doubt it, but that's why I didn't touch it. Two of them

wore gloves, but maybe they took them off at some point. Test it, but I'd like it back when you're done. Please."

The sheriff turned the light off and walked back down the ramp to join him.

"So this is where they brought you, eh? Three masked men. An abandoned trailer. And you just happened to come across it?"

"The search was a little harder than that."

"Yeah? How'd you get here?"

"I was hypnotized. By a woman named Julianne Grossman."

Blankenship was one of those rare older men who could still intimidate with sheer size, and he knew how to draw it up. His body seemed to inflate.

"There are some lines you don't cross," he said, each word deep and dark.

"I'm not *trying* to cross any, damn it. I came back here to find out who had fucked with me, and why. She's the woman who impersonated Diane Martin. Only it's a little more complex than that. If you know anything about her, maybe you understand what I mean."

He had Blankenship's full interest now.

"You know Julianne personally, or you just know of her?" Mark asked.

Blankenship didn't answer right away.

"What I was told," Mark said, "was that she worked with Diane Martin after her husband died. That's all I know. If she lied to me, then set me straight, please. Because I've got my own issues with Julianne."

The sheriff turned the flashlight over in his hands and hesitated as if he was trying to make up his mind on something. Finally he said, "What do you know about this place, Novak?"

"I know that I can see the cave from here, and that's where I ended up. I know that the Leonard brothers live at that farm way out across."

"The Leonards have gone to ground, by the way. Haven't been seen in a few days. You know anything about that?"

"I stopped by to talk with Lou."

"That would have done it. They'll be MIA for another week or two and then I'll see them again." Blankenship pointed at the trailer. "But *this* place? What do you know about it?"

"I've got a feeling it will help prove my story."

"You're telling me the truth?"

"Damn it, Sheriff, I don't know another way to say it."

Blankenship shook his head. "You weren't kidding when you said you didn't care, were you? You came back here for your own skin. You got no interest in Sarah."

"I wasn't kidding when I said it, but I'm starting to care." *You see, I saw her down there,* Mark thought. *And she's waiting, Sheriff. She's waiting, and she doesn't understand why it's taking so long.* But what he said was "What's so important about the trailer?"

"It's where Evan Borders lived as a child. This collapsing shit pile was home when his daddy wasn't in prison. Family land, going back more than a century. Carson—that's his father—ended up selling it off to pay for his lawyers and his habits. Didn't get much for his money. Tried to bargain his way out of prison in a different fashion and got a hit put on his head for that effort. All that remains of Carson's legacy in Garrison County is his son. And, I suppose, his teeth. The boys in Detroit were kind enough to mail those back."

"Would Evan have owned the cave?" Mark said. "If his father hadn't gotten into the legal troubles, would the cave have been theirs?"

"Yes. If it had opened up a little earlier, a little later, how-ever you care to look at it. Family land, like I said. But instead, it was going to be Sarah's family land. I always wondered about that. Seems irrelevant to some, I suppose, but I wondered."

"You were right to," Mark said. He remembered a rancher outside Billings who sold a few hundred acres of generations-old family cattle land that turned out to have vast oil deposits. He'd put the barrel of a twelve-gauge in his mouth six months after news of the discovery broke. He hadn't ever disputed that the transaction was fair and honest. The point was only that it had been made.

"I can tell you some things about Ridley," Mark said. "They've got nothing to do with what happened to me here, but I think you should hear them."

"We'll talk in my office," the sheriff said, and then he walked away from Mark and back up to the road. He had his radio to his lips by the time he reached his car.

48

The sapphire sky was cleansed of color by storm clouds just before dusk and then the sun went down somewhere behind them and full dark settled and Ridley knew that it was time.

He had two caving packs prepared, perfect twins, every tool in his own pack mirrored by one in the other. Julianne was not capable of using all the equipment, but still he'd outfitted her with the proper gear. Ropes, carabiners, and ascenders. Gloves, knee pads, elbow pads. A first-aid kit. Protein bars and glucose tablets and water bottles and an emergency blanket. Headlamps with fresh batteries.

He looked over all the gear, satisfied except for the missing tool, the one he never went into a cave—or anywhere, even aboveground—without: a Benchmade knife with black grips and a folding steel blade that was just a fraction under four inches in length. It was as close as he'd ever been able to come to the discontinued model that he'd carried for years and lost somewhere in Trapdoor in a transaction that was forever hazy—a knife in hand one moment, Sarah Martin's sapphire necklace in hand the next. When he thought of being back there in the dark with Julianne Grossman at his side, he wondered if maybe he should leave the knife behind.

He thumbed it open, the blade extending with a soft *snick,* the grip perfectly balanced in his hand. His mouth was dry. When it came to this tool, Julianne would not need a matching version.

He put the knife in his pocket, clipped helmets to the packs, slung one pack over each shoulder, and turned and looked around the house. The rooms were hard to make out in the shadows but he knew them well and he thought that his time here had been mostly good. Of the homes he had known on the surface of the earth, this was probably the best of them. He stepped outside and walked to the truck and put the packs in the bed and was in the driver's seat with the key in his hand when he stopped. He did not believe he would be returning to this place, and while he wasn't one for sentimental gestures, he felt that he hadn't left it quite right for the visitors who would soon descend on it. He left the truck and walked into the house and went upstairs. He pushed on the knee wall and watched it pivot open soundlessly. The seams were still flawless and there was not so much as a creak to the dowels. It was fine work and he wondered if anyone would appreciate that. He turned it until it was half open, and then he left the room and went back down the stairs and exited again. This time he remembered to leave the front door unlocked. If it was not unlocked, they'd kick it down, and Ridley had built the door and the frame himself and hated the idea of that beautiful wood splintering needlessly.

The roads had been plowed and salted and there was no fresh snow coming down but somehow his thin tires felt less secure on the road than they had only a day before. Only this morning, even. You could wear the rubber down for just so long before the wires started to show and then the withheld pressure you counted on to carry you along went from helpful to dangerous. He'd understood this since he was a boy and he was vaguely disappointed in himself for having allowed the tires to reach such a point, and in the winter, no less, when traction was critical and steady pressure was harder to hold. He'd gotten distracted somewhere along the line.

When he took the sapphire necklace out of his pocket, the stone was cold, and though he held it in his hand for most of the drive, it never warmed. Just before he reached Julianne's house he reached up and looped the chain around the rearview mirror so that it dangled in the center of the cab. For a short stretch, it caught the reflected light off the snow and glistened beautifully, but then he had to turn the lights off and the color went with them.

He drove the last half mile in the dark and parked on the shoulder of the road where he was screened from her house by the trees. In all of his visits he had never seen her dog indoors, and that was a problem because she appeared to be a vigilant animal. Ridley had always appreciated the vigilance and the fact that she was clearly a den dog, always burrowing, digging deeper, a creature who wanted to crawl beneath. Those were fine things and he would hate to see any harm come to the dog, but all the same he slipped his knife free from his pocket as he approached.

He was twenty feet from the house when the dog began to bark, and Ridley gritted his teeth and snapped the blade open and then closed it again when the animal retreated. In his past visits, she would cautiously advance toward him and the fact that she would not tonight made him curious as to what she smelled on him. How did she know? It was fascinating to consider. *If dogs could talk,* people would say, but they were always referring to the idea that the dogs would reveal something stupid or humorous; they failed to grasp just how much their worlds would change if dogs could talk. You were exposed in front of a dog in ways you never considered. The moment you hit the door, your dog knew whether you felt anger or fear, whether you'd wept recently, fought recently, had sex recently—and whether that sex had been with your spouse. *If dogs could talk.* Yes, wouldn't that be something? Ridley wondered how many people would have pet dogs in that world.

He went up the steps as the dog circled the porch and he knocked on the door with his left hand and opened the knife again with his right and held it so that the edge of the blade was facing forward. When Julianne opened the door he showed her the knife and said, "Please do not make me kill the dog."

She had the security chain fastened but they both understood that would not hold as long as she would need it to.

"Don't do this," she said. Her voice so soft, so familiar. "Please do not do this."

"Open the door."

She opened the door. She was an intelligent woman and he was grateful for that.

As she stepped away from the door, words poured from her.

"Please sit so that we may talk about the things that you are feeling. There is a chance of more snow again tonight, did you hear? I have not seen so much snow in a winter in a long time, and if you would like to sit on the couch, obviously there is negative emotion with you tonight, the emotion that you have, feeling very negative, and those feelings are very valid, so if you would like to sit, you may. If you would like to sit and leave the cold outside and we could—"

Ridley grabbed her hair with his right hand, the knife

tangling in the strands, and put his left hand over her mouth. Her words had been streaming at him in those unusual rhythms and with unusual thoughts, thoughts that did not match the situation. Ridley had studied enough to understand that this was one area where Julianne Grossman excelled. While she had weaknesses as a hypnotist, her ability with what was called neurolinguistic programming was remarkable. She jarred your expectations with thoughts and cadences and word choices, and eventually her suggestions ceased to feel suggestive and became more directive and then your mind belonged to her.

Ridley no longer wanted it to.

"You will have an opportunity to talk," he said. She was not struggling. She was aware of the knife just behind her brain stem. "But I can't allow you to have that now, because you are so good with words. You are so good at what you do. I respect that. You know that I have always respected that, don't you?"

Her eyes were locked on his and there was fear in them but there was something else also and he said, "Do not let the dog inside."

He had not turned to see the dog and he had not heard the dog but he knew that it was there and when she lifted her hand, he allowed the motion because the hand was for the dog and not for Ridley. There was an anxious whine from behind him and Ridley realized how close things had come to going very bad.

"Thank you," he said. "Use the same hand to close the door."

He maneuvered her toward the door in an awkward waltz and she pushed it shut. The dog barked twice when the barrier was closed.

"Out of respect for your talents," Ridley said, "I am going to need to tape your mouth shut."

He removed a thin roll of duct tape from his jacket pocket, and though it required taking his hand from her mouth, she didn't try to speak. He worked fast but he made certain to lift her hair high with his right hand so that it was not caught in the mess. He did not want her to be uncomfortable.

A phone began to ring in the house, but neither of them looked in the direction of the sound. He stepped back and re-moved his hooded jacket and held it out to her. She lifted her arms and allowed him to slip the jacket on her, as if it were a gallant gesture.

"Put the hood up so it covers your face, and we will walk to my truck. Please be mindful of your dog's life when we step outside."

He opened the door and nodded that she should go first. The dog was crouched with every muscle bunched, hackles lining her spine. She whined when she saw Julianne, a pleading sound, desperate for instruction. Or permission.

Julianne lowered herself to her knees and took the dog's face in her hands and then stroked along the hackles, trying to soothe her. Some of the tension loosened, but only some. The dog's eyes were on Ridley.

"Let's go," Ridley said.

Julianne pressed her tape-covered face to the dog's, and the dog lapped at her eyelids. Julianne had begun to cry.

"Let's go," he repeated, but he was careful not to pull her up because he didn't think the dog would allow that. He waited until Julianne rose and walked down the steps and then he followed. The dog walked close to her side all the way to the truck, and Ridley held the knife in a hand that was as tensed as the dog's muscles. He opened the passen-ger door of the truck and Julianne climbed inside. Ridley had to walk back around the front of the truck to get in, and for a few steps the dog was alone with him, but she was still watching Julianne. Ridley got in the truck and closed the door and then closed the knife.

"Very noble choice," he said. "The dog would have been willing to die for you, and you knew that and could have demanded it. But instead you chose to take your chances even if it means you die for the dog. That is a rare choice."

She was no longer crying, and she didn't look at him. He sighed, remembering all of the comfort he had taken in her once, and then he started the truck and turned on the lights and pulled away. The dog stood in the middle of the road behind them. When it became evident that they were leaving, the dog began to howl. Ridley winced at the mournful sound. He felt as if the dog knew that she had made a choice and that she now regretted the one she had made.

He hoped that the dog's memory was not long.

49

Mark was told to wait in the sheriff's office, and when Blankenship finally entered he was carrying two cups of coffee. He handed one to Mark without a word. The dynamic between them had shifted dramatically but Mark couldn't say why. The discoveries in the trailer meant plenty to Mark, but he had expected an uphill battle to convince Blankenship of that.

"When we have anything from that scene, I'll let you know," Blankenship said. He drank his coffee for a few seconds. The door was closed and it was quiet in his office.

"Before you talk," he said, "I probably should. I was pulled from Sarah's case once, and if we went by the book, you shouldn't be talking to me."

"My time in Garrison hasn't been very by-the-book so far."

"Ain't that the truth." Blankenship took his hat off and tossed it onto an empty chair beside the desk. His gray hair was thin. "Here's what you should know, at least in my judgment, before you talk to *me* about anything related to Sarah Martin. That girl haunts my dreams, Novak. She and her mother both."

He'd been staring at his hat, but now he moved his eyes back to Mark.

"I knew Diane and Sarah and Richard—that was Sarah's father—through church. Richard died in a car wreck when I was still working road duty. One of the worst I've ever seen. I drew the job of notifying the family." His voice thickened and he cleared his throat. "I stayed in touch a little. But with distance, you know. There's a job involved, and there's a respect involved. Both of them mattered to me. Both still do."

He seemed to be waiting on a challenge over that. Mark didn't offer one.

"You mentioned Julianne Grossman," Blankenship said. "I've never laid eyes on her. I know that Diane went to see her for help with insomnia after Richard was killed. I didn't really like that, to tell you the truth. Whole thing just seemed strange to me. Maybe I'm not much of a modern thinker, I don't know. But back then I didn't have as close of a relationship with Diane, and so I didn't say anything. Later...later I told her not to go back. I told her to go to a real doctor and get herself some pills. Same kind that eventually killed her."

He made himself look Mark in the eye when he said that. All Mark could do was nod. Blankenship returned the gesture. "So you understand that part. Okay. Time went on; I started to see Diane a little more. I was always real conscious of Sarah because I'd known her daddy and I knew what she'd gone through and I didn't want..." He hesitated. "I didn't want to *infringe* on that, you understand? I felt like her father, dead or alive, still had some jurisdiction."

He ran his big hand over his eyes. A quick pass.

"That cave opened up for business sort of in the middle of all this. People thought it was a big deal, there was some excitement around here about it. I've never liked tight places. But Sarah? She was fifteen at the time, and she was real interested. When they opened up the tours, we all went down and took one together. I wish you'd seen her that day." He shook his head at the memory. "The way a place can affect two people so differently, it's really something. I couldn't get out of that cave fast enough. You'd have thought she wanted to move in.

"The next summer, she wanted a job but didn't want to work at a restaurant or behind a cash register. I'd just heard this when I went out to talk to Pershing MacAlister about some issues at that cave. He had complaints about the locals, people vandalizing the cave, sneaking into it; he wanted me to cooperate with the newspaper and say we were watching the place. Spread the word. What I did then, well, I good-old-boy'd it, plain and simple. Asked whether there might be a summer job available. Man needed my help, and I asked him for a favor. You might not believe it, but I didn't often do those things."

Mark believed it.

"So Sarah got the job, and it was all my doing, ain't that something to consider? She never applied for it, never knew it existed. Never would have been down there again, probably. People would say it was such a small thing, getting a teenager a job, but I knew what I was doing. Using my position to get Sarah what she wanted, because Diane was what I wanted. I wasn't doing police work. Maybe you pay for choices like that. I just never could have imagined the ways."

His phone rang and he silenced it with one touch and without a glance. He drank some coffee and cleared his throat again. He had stopped looking at Mark.

"Things went fast between Diane and Pershing. That's all that need be said about that. It isn't my business, what happened between them. I told Diane that then, and I'm telling you now. The engagement happened, and I . . . I had to get used to another change in jurisdiction then. Diane and Sarah, they weren't..." He had to work to get the next words out: "They weren't in mine anymore. And that...that was a hard summer for me. Then came September, and the call came in, and that was the worst day of my life. Because I *knew*. Even while I was arranging the searches and telling Diane not to worry, I knew we weren't going to be finding Sarah alive. Don't ask me how. Sometimes you know."

He closed his eyes briefly, then opened them and spoke again.

"I sent Ridley Barnes in. You already asked me about it, and I walked out of here after you asked and drank whiskey for the first time in probably fifteen years. I sent Ridley in. Pershing tried to warn me that Ridley was not right, that he had mental issues, but I also had the caving people telling me they needed someone who knew the cave, and so I made the call. I believed it was the right thing, then. I've thought a lot about it, and I truly don't think I was trying to overrule Pershing. I hope to God that I wasn't. I couldn't live with myself if I believed that. Hell, I don't know, you can judge me how you want, and one day God will judge me in the way that counts, and I'll know then, won't I?"

He wiped at his right eye with his thumb, and Mark looked at the floor out of respect. He kept his eyes down until Blankenship spoke again.

"Now I'm going to tell you one last thing you should know," he said. "When Sarah went missing, at first all anyone understood was that she was lost."

"Right."

"Back then, I didn't know that Ridley believed that a hole in the ground was a supernatural place. That he told Pershing the cave made him stronger with each trip. Gave him *power* with each trip. Didn't know he'd said he had to work alone because the cave wouldn't *talk* to anyone else."

He pulled himself up to the desk and faced Mark again.

"Now you've heard what I have to say, and you're smart enough to understand how we go from here. You might want to talk to somebody else. Otherwise, whatever you disclose here, you're disclosing it to an officer who was removed from that investigation for due cause. You want somebody else, I can point you to the state police."

"I think I'd rather talk to you, Sheriff," Mark said.

"All right, then. Let's hear it."

Blankenship didn't say a word until Mark was through. Then he said, "Ridley confessed. On video, he confessed."

"Yes. But it wouldn't be worth a damn to the prosecutor. It would be blown up for coercion or false memory even if Julianne was accepted by the court as an expert, and that's discounting Ridley's options entirely. He might sit down with you and laugh in your face and tell you that he was putting on a show for her the whole time, and who could prove him wrong?"

"Do you think he was?"

"Not after this morning, I don't," Mark said. "I think she got him to tell the truth."

Blankenship rose and went to the window and looked out at his little town. Someone was shoveling snow off the sidewalk and the rhythmic scraping was the only sound for a few seconds. Then he said, "She really thinks that Ridley will show her something if he gets the chance to be alone in that cave with her."

"That's what I'm told. She's willing to do it, and she's willing to wear a wire or a camera. She says he won't allow anyone else along. It would be a damn difficult surveillance."

"It would be impossible. Ridley would smell anything out

of place down there, and you need light to move an inch. Or at least most people do."

"Could put recorders in the cave, but you'd need a lot of them, since we have no idea where he'd take her. Not practical. Any device has to be on her."

"Anything went wrong down there, I'd lose my badge. Hell, even if it went right, I probably would."

Blankenship's voice suggested he wasn't too concerned with that.

"It's a tough spot for police," Mark said. "She knows that. Ridley does too."

"*Damn* that man," Blankenship said suddenly, a near shout. "He killed her. He killed her but I can't prove it, Novak. I have known this for ten years. I cannot prove it. I have no crime scene, I have no witnesses, and I have no forensics that he can't explain away by claiming he found her body and dragged it through a cave. I have nothing."

Mark had a flash memory of his last meeting with the lead investigator in Lauren's case. *I have nothing, Mr. Novak. I'm sorry, but it's the truth. We'll get there, though. We'll get there.*

"I don't want to go back in that cave," Mark said. "I surely don't want to go down there with Ridley Barnes."

"Nobody's asking you to. It's a foolish idea, and nobody in his right mind *would* ask you to."

"No, he wouldn't. And let's keep it that way. Because when I come back up from Trapdoor, Sheriff, we'll both need you to have your legal distance preserved."

"No. Absolutely not. I'll handle Ridley."

"All due respect," Mark said, "but he's not going to open the door to you, Sheriff. Not in any way that counts, at least. Don't forget the essential difference in our approach here: You've been working on Ridley Barnes. As far as I've been concerned, Ridley Barnes has been working on me. Until today."

"Until today. Now you care?"

Mark nodded. "I do. And you're starting to trust me a little. The balance is shifting on Ridley. What scares me, though? What scares me is that he may already know that."

Part Five

A LITTLE DIFFERENT
IN THE LIGHT

50

It was time to see Ridley again face-to-face.

Mark had returned to Garrison determined not to make the same mistake he'd made on his first visit, when he'd had the blissful sense of going through the motions. He'd rushed into contact with Ridley then. He didn't intend to repeat the mistake.

The time had come, though.

He was driving along the icy country roads when Jeff called.

"Please tell me you're on a plane," Jeff said without preamble.

"Not yet."

"Mark..."

When Jeff London used the short version of Markus, it was the equivalent of anyone else using the full version *and* the middle name.

"I've got nothing for them yet," Mark said. "But I will. You tell them that, and—"

"*I can't just tell them things!* This is it. This is the end of the road. You've got to sit at the table this time. No pick-and-roll left to be run. You've *got* to understand that."

"If I leave here, Ridley Barnes is not going to answer for anything, and—"

"Ridley Barnes is not your case!"

Mark turned onto the winding road to Ridley's, grateful for the security of the all-wheel drive beneath him. "I was nearly one of his victims. If it's not my case, whose is it?"

"That's not the point, and you know it. There are victims and there are vigilantes. I thought we'd reached an understanding as to which side of that fence you were staying on."

Mark watched the lonesome fields pass by and didn't speak. They'd reached an understanding on this, yes. An understanding that was based on a lie: *I will leave Lauren's case to the authorities and I will not seek the death penalty.*

It had been an easy lie to tell then, when it saved him the only thing he had left that he cared about—his job. Somewhere along the line, somewhere during his time in this backwater Indiana town, he'd begun to tire of the lie. No matter what it gained him. No matter what it cost.

"I think I'm drifting a little too Old Testament for our line of work," Mark said.

"What the hell does that mean?"

"Eye for an eye."

"Don't start again, Markus. Damn it, do not start that again. Leave her case to the people who have the right distance."

"We'll talk about it. We'll also talk about this case. We never would have taken it. Sarah Martin's death wouldn't have qualified, because there was no capital-punishment element. No conviction, even."

"I'm well aware of that, and if you think you deserve yet another apology, then—"

"I don't," Mark said. "She does."

"What?"

"What if Diane Martin had been alive, Jeff?"

"She isn't."

"She might have been. What if I'd walked into her town and sat across from her and promised her the answers she deserved would finally be given to her. And then I walked away."

Jeff's sigh had some horsepower behind it. "I'm going to say this once, and you need to listen to it and comprehend it: I've been busting my ass for weeks trying to convince the board that you are still a trustworthy employee, that when you are given direct instructions, you follow them. Your instructions here are simple: Come home. First flight you can get on. Or drive all night, I don't care, but you better be back in town tomorrow. You're going to have to talk with the board at this point. I can't promise how that will go with you in the room, but I *can* promise how it will go if you're not in the room—you're done. And I won't vote against it. If you can't do something as simple as get on a plane when you're told to, Markus?" There was a long pause, and when Jeff finally spoke again, his voice was sorrowful. "Then even I can't trust you anymore."

It was a statement that demanded a response, but Mark couldn't even grant it his full attention. He was closing on Ridley's house now, and two troubling things were already apparent: Ridley's truck was gone, and his front door was standing open.

"Jeff," he said. "I've got to go. I'm sorry. Really, I am. But I've got to go."

He disconnected before he heard another word. He pulled into the driveway and parked in the place where Ridley's truck belonged and stared at that open door. Maybe it didn't mean a thing. The wind had been coming in gusts all day; it was certainly capable of pushing open a shut door, and maybe Ridley hadn't locked it when he left.

Mark doubted that, though.

He got out of the car and called Ridley's name but heard no answer. He wished he had a weapon.

He walked up the steps and called Ridley's name again and received nothing but silence, and then he pushed the door wide open and looked inside at the shadowed room. Everything seemed in place, no trace of disturbance, but the shadows teased his mind and suggested possibilities. He found the light switch and flicked it on and breathed a little easier when the shadows vanished and tangible objects took their places.

"Ridley!" The name left his mouth with more aggression than he'd intended. For some reason, the empty place and open door had summoned adrenaline. You weren't supposed to be scared of empty spaces. Ridley's house had other ideas.

He walked to the stairs and stopped himself from calling Ridley's name again. There would be no answer. He had proven that now. He found another light switch and illuminated the hall at the top of the stairs and then went on up. There was a single bathroom, clean and tidy but missing a mirror. The medicine-cabinet frame where it belonged was empty, the contents beyond the door exposed. Past the bathroom was a bedroom, and beyond that another room that was filled with bookshelves. There was a strange shadow to the left, something out of place. Mark hit more lights and saw that there was a false wall that had been turned into a door.

The chill he felt then was almost a prayer—*Don't let me find what I'm afraid of in there*—as images of chains and shackles and bones flickered through his mind, all the things a psychotic might store away in secret places. Then he dropped to one knee, pushed the wall back, and saw what it hid: maps.

Nothing else. The wall was lined with maps. Not the sort

that hung on the basement walls at Trapdoor, those hand-drawn illustrations of cave interiors. These were topographic land maps. Mark looked at them and thought of what he'd told Julianne Grossman during his trance: that he'd been looking at the wrong maps.

He pushed the wall back farther so he could see one of the topographic maps clearly. It was covered with notations and filled with pushpins.

Burial sites, he thought. *My God. If every one of those pins represents a…*

But they couldn't. There hadn't been that many missing people in Garrison County in the past hundred years, probably, and Ridley wasn't known to range far from home. So what had he been locating?

Mark climbed farther behind the wall, studying the maps. None of them were of Trapdoor. None of them showed anything that made them worth hiding, as far as he could tell.

Wrong maps. You said you were looking at the wrong maps.

He'd looked at every map he knew existed, and now he was looking at others, but still he didn't see where his mistake had been made, because he hadn't known these existed before.

You told me your mother wouldn't have made the same mistake.

But his mother wouldn't have known about Ridley's maps. Where was the joke there? Julianne said that he'd laughed before he said it. Hilarious stuff going on in his subconscious, apparently, but he couldn't imagine what it had been.

It took him a while but he finally found the location of Trapdoor on the map. He traced the outline of Maiden Creek with his index finger and came up to the road and the place where the trailer stood and then he stopped and for a long moment he didn't move or make a sound.

There had always been other maps, and they'd always been available to him. They were the ones that counted too. Everyone else cared about the ones Ridley had not shared, but those mattered only when they were paired with others: the ones of the surface, the ones that showed ownership.

He left Ridley's hidden room and walked back down the stairs. In front of the cold stove where Ridley had once sat with bright eyes and told Mark that someone needed to speak for Sarah Martin, Mark sat and called Jeff London.

"Call back after a hang-up," Jeff said. "Let me guess— you're in trouble. What can I do for you?"

The bitterness in his voice was valid, but Mark couldn't worry about it. Not now.

"You got a computer handy?" he said.

"Hell are you talking about?"

"I need to know whether Garrison County has a GIS database."

GIS stood for geographic information system, computer-mapping technology that had its origins in nuclear-war fears during the 1960s but was now common for local property records.

Jeff was silent for a moment. When he spoke again, he sounded near desperate, a broken man asking a priest to explain to him once more why he should believe.

"What do you think this can accomplish?" he said.

"Ridley wants the cave," Mark said. "I can't explain how much it means to him. He believes it's something more than a cave. But he's no fool. He understands access. He understands that someone owns it. And that he isn't that man."

"Tell me why that matters."

"I'm not sure."

"Markus—"

"I'm almost there!"

This time the silence went on so long that Mark thought Jeff had hung up. He actually pulled the phone away and looked at the display, saw the ticking seconds. A countdown of trust. It had to blow at some point.

"They have a GIS database," Jeff said. Speaking in measured tones now, clinically. Like Dr. Desare when he'd explained how Mark had been brought back from the dead. "Who do you want me to search for?"

"Ridley Barnes."

Pause. "One property. Five acres, with a single residential structure valued at—"

"I'm standing in it now. I don't need the specs. Try again. First name Pershing, last name MacAlister. M-A-C."

Pause. "Nothing."

"There has to be."

"There isn't."

Mark rose from the chair but didn't move away from it. "Put in the word *Trapdoor*. See if it hits." Mark could see his reflection in the window. With the woodstove in the background, the image reminded him of different places, a different man. Howling blizzards and small towns. Broken fingers and pickup trucks crawling through the snow. Exposed lies. Blood and justification.

"Eleven properties," Jeff said. "The name is Trapdoor Caverns Land Trust."

"*Eleven?* Eleven unique properties. You're sure? No duplicate records."

"I'm looking at the parcel map, Markus. Eleven properties, roughly following the basin of something called Maiden Creek. Sound right?"

Too right. Mark wet his lips and said, "Can you see who owns the trust?"

"Nobody owns a trust."

"What do you mean?"

"A land trust is its own entity. Like a corporation. It doesn't have owners, it has beneficiaries. Those names aren't public. Obviously, we can find them, but as far as the public record is concerned, Trapdoor Caverns is its own legal entity. Trapdoor can buy and sell land. So far, it has only bought."

"How recently?"

"Let me see." It was quiet for a few seconds while Jeff looked, and then he said, "Each parcel was transferred to the trust from Pershing MacAlister in October of 2004."

"The month after Sarah was killed."

"That makes sense, though. They shut the place down after she was killed."

"You said you could see a parcel map," Mark said. "What does it look like?"

"*Look* like?"

"Yes. What does the shape of the Trapdoor land-trust property look like?"

"Like a snake. It follows the creek, then curls out and away. I don't know what shape it has. It looks like a suburban subdivision, maybe. Winding roads and cul-de-sacs. What are you hoping to hear?"

"Exactly that."

"Markus, what are you talking about?"

"Ridley mapped it from below," Mark said. "But the cave's not worth anything unless you own what's above it. I'm sure of that, Jeff. I'm from oil country. Surface ownership extends to the core of the earth. Ridley was working from the bottom up."

"Which matters *how?*"

"How fast can we get ahold of that trust document?"

"Not very. Private and sealed legal agreement. We'd need a subpoena."

"There has to be a faster approach than that."

"Sure. You can find one of the parties involved and ask if you can see a copy. Short of that cooperation, you'll need a subpoena. But you still haven't given me an answer. Why do you think this matters? What does it have to do with Sarah Martin?"

"I'm close," Mark said, as if that answered the question. He was circling through the fog, waiting to land. Instruments were out, only instinct left. He was close. You either landed or crashed.

5 1

Ridley questioned Julianne Grossman's authenticity on many things, but he couldn't deny the power of her presence. Her energy was palpable in the truck, even though she couldn't speak and chose not to move. She sat there in his jacket with the tape over her mouth and she stared straight ahead, and still he could feel her like a pulse. He was relieved that he had silenced her.

On the road to Trapdoor they passed the tumbledown trailer that had once belonged to Carson Borders. The headlights caught a glimmer of police tape. Ridley hit the brakes so hard that the truck fishtailed and what was left of the tires was put to shrieking work. They held on to the road, but just barely.

The truck was across both lanes when it stopped but Ridley didn't care to move it. He kept his foot on the brake and stared at the trailer. The snow all around it was mashed down and trampled by tire tracks and boot prints. A perimeter had been cordoned off with tape.

"What is this?" he said, but of course Julianne was unable to answer. He thought she might know and he was tempted to remove the tape to ask but afraid of the result. The point was to make it into Trapdoor, and it was more than logical that the surface world would try to prevent him. Perhaps the scene at the trailer was not even real.

"Do you see that?" he asked Julianne.

She was eyeing him warily but she nodded.

"I don't mean the building. I mean the rest."

Again she nodded. He thought she was being sincere. "Okay," he said. "All right, that's very good."

He took his foot off the brake, but he was shaking now.

"The thing to remember," he said, "is that this doesn't matter. All of this, what we see up here? It doesn't mean a thing. What matters happened *down there.* We can't see any of what matters. Not yet. That is what we *must* remember!"

He had started to shout and he didn't like that, because it suggested a lack of control. He concentrated on his breathing until they reached Trapdoor. Just beyond the closed gate, he pulled off the road and into the snow and killed the engine. He took the sapphire necklace down from the rearview mirror and put it in his pocket and then he got out of the truck and took both backpacks out of the bed. He opened Julianne's door, took her hand, and helped her out of the cab. He would never have admitted it but the touch of her hand was comforting. He doubted that she felt the same about his.

"There's a garage up ahead and to the left," he said. "That's the caretaker's quarters. We'll walk there. Don't run."

She didn't run. He put one of the backpacks over her shoulders, and she moved to cooperate, no sign of resistance. They walked on the other side of the tree line and parallel to the drive, went as far as the back corner of the garage, and then Ridley whispered, "Hands, please. Only for a little while."

She offered them reluctantly, and he tied them without ever having to take his eyes off the house. This was why you practiced. You never knew what would be asked of you.

"All right," he said. "Quietly ahead. Quietly. And, Julianne, you might see some things that will suggest that all of your efforts have been wasted. That I've lost control again. Don't be fooled. I'm in control." He extended his hands, palms down, like a child waiting to play a slap game. They showed no more movement than the ice over the creek.

He nudged her forward and they walked around the garage and up the exterior stairs that led to the apartment above. He was entranced by her movement. He'd anticipated that she would struggle to walk, that fear would make her clumsy. Instead, she glided along in perfect step, matching his energy and joining it, like a dance partner.

Maybe you're wrong about her. You don't know what she really said to Novak. You've made assumptions.

No, no, no. He had trusted once and would not again. The surface world was false and she had come from it.

At the base of the steps that led to Cecil Buckner's apartment, Ridley paused and studied the windows, looking for any indication that Cecil was up and moving. He wasn't at the window, but Ridley could see his socked feet resting on a coffee table, a can of beer beside them. He was clueless and unprepared, as he should be. Despite his proximity to Trapdoor, Cecil had never learned to listen to what she might tell him, the warnings she might whisper. The very notion that he was entrusted to be the cave's caretaker was offensive.

Ridley positioned Julianne in front of him, withdrew his knife, flicked the blade open, put it to her throat, and shoved her forward. He walked with his chest pressed to her back and guided her up the stairs. He reached around her then and knocked on the door with his free hand.

The beer had vanished from sight but now it returned to the coffee table and Cecil's socked feet went into motion and the door was opened. His eyes took in the scene fast.

"Ridley," he said. "What in the hell ... Ridley, no, don't—"

"Let us in."

Cecil took a step back, too willingly, and Ridley saw that his eyes were drifting right, and so he released Julianne and stepped around her and punched Cecil once in the face and kicked him once in the groin, and the bigger man fell to the floor in gasping pain without ever reaching the shotgun leaning against the wall just to the right of the door.

"Your choice, Cecil," Ridley said. He guided Julianne inside and closed the door behind them. Cecil was writhing on the floor.

"I know this is not the way it is supposed to go," Ridley said, "but I'm going to need to get in to see her tonight. There simply is no other choice at this point. It has to be done."

For a time Cecil didn't answer, just gasped his way back to breath, a string of spit hanging from his lips. He got slowly to his hands and knees, looked up at Ridley, and said, "You stupid son of a bitch. You'll end up in prison. Ten years free, and you'll still end up in prison."

"There's a lot left to play out before that," Ridley said, "though I acknowledge the possibility. I always have."

Cecil breathed through his mouth, his eyes flicking around the room in search of options.

"Keep your attention on me," Ridley said. "There's no need to delay. I just need the keys."

"All you had to do was wait, you freak," Cecil said.

Ridley nodded with sorrow. "I tried to. You know that. But it was easier for you. You never had any *questions*. And if you did, they were about me. Now, imagine *being* me and having those same questions."

"You'll end up in Terre Haute waiting on the electric chair."

"The keys," Ridley said, beckoning with his hand. "Otherwise, you'll watch everything that happens to her and it will happen in your home and before your eyes. And you will know that you made a choice that might have stopped it. You'll live with that."

Cecil rose unsteadily.

"I'll give you the damn keys, though if you were only smart enough to wait, they'd have been yours anyhow. Now that will never happen. You understand that, don't you?"

"Where are the keys?"

"Right behind your head. Hanging on the peg."

"Get them for me."

"They're only a foot away from you."

"Get them for me."

Cecil shuffled forward, walking in pain, and extended his arm to reach around Ridley for the keys. When he made his next move, it was with speed that Ridley hadn't anticipated. Cecil had been a fine athlete in his day, his name still in the Garrison High record books for tackles, and his muscle memory had lasted through the years—he got both arms around Ridley and drove him back into the wall. Julianne was trapped between them, in danger from Ridley's knife, which was the reason he hadn't been prepared for the assault. He'd expected Cecil would value her life more than this.

He couldn't allow her to be hurt, not yet, not when they were so close to the place where he would need her, and so he dropped the knife and stumbled backward. All three of them hit the floor hard. Ridley rolled and Cecil did exactly what Ridley had expected and went after the shotgun. Ridley stepped over Julianne and grabbed the back of Cecil's head just as he reached the gun. Rather than pulling him back, Ridley drove him forward and slammed Cecil into the wall. The shotgun clattered to the floor just as Cecil's nose shattered.

Cecil threw a high, powerful elbow that might have found Ridley's face if Cecil hadn't slipped on the hardwood floor. This was why Ridley kept his boots on even in his own home. Traction was something you could never take for granted.

Cecil was a tall and muscular man, bigger and stronger than Ridley, but he did not have traction and he did not have momentum. Ridley banged Cecil's face off the wall one more time and then threw him to the floor. It could have ended there, should have, but Cecil landed near the knife and made the mistake of reaching for it.

Ridley raised his boot and smashed it down on Cecil's hand and felt the bones break. Cecil cried out and rolled away, clutching his wrist to his belly as Ridley picked up the open knife. He felt in control at that moment, aggressive but focused, the goal clear: incapacitate Cecil and enter the cave.

Two changes occurred. Fast. One: Cecil reached for the shotgun again, even after he should have known better. Two: The knife spoke to Ridley. It was open and in his hand. In its designed position. Ready to do what it was meant to do, but more than that, what it had already done on a night he could not fully remember.

Night, was it night? Maybe day. Darkness. Certainly darkness. Down there, all days become nights and neither matters. And you held the knife like this and you—

Cecil's fingers scrabbled for the shotgun and missed. Ridley pulled the big man's head back and saw wide white eyes, and then Cecil's chin rolled up and back and his throat was exposed. Ridley was ready then, ready to slash the knife down to do what it was intended to do, what *Ridley* was intended to do, when Julianne howled from beneath the tape over her mouth. The trapped sound was soft but its intensity was not.

He looked back to where she lay on her side on the floor, a helpless spectator, and he saw only terror in her eyes. It was the way Ridley's sister had looked at their father on many occasions. Whenever Ridley saw that look come into his sister's face, he had interceded. It hadn't gone well for him, ever, but he'd always done it.

Julianne took a gasping breath that made the tape over her mouth bubble, and the look in her eyes made Ridley cringe. All she saw was horror, and she blamed Ridley. She was afraid of him, and that was a standard part of his days now and had been for years, but it had never been desired. He had never wanted to cause fear. People feared him, yes, but it wasn't a product of his intentions. Actions, perhaps, but never intentions.

He slid off Cecil Buckner's back and swept the shotgun across the floor. Cecil didn't struggle. His eyes were on the blade that had nearly carved through his throat.

"You can wait here in peace, or they can find your body," Ridley said. "Now put out your hands."

Ridley was even faster with the paracord this time, binding Cecil's hands and then his ankles, then connecting the two with a fast hitch. There was no need to pull Cecil's feet as close to the back of his head as Ridley did, but the knife was no longer involved, and it seemed that Cecil should be forced to consider that and appreciate it. His life had been saved by the look in a stranger's eyes. Would he ever know that? Ever understand how close he had come? Ridley doubted it, and so he pulled the cord tighter, pulled until Cecil's heels came close to the back of his skull, and his spine was pushing its limits. Cecil shrieked in pain and Ridley found the tape and wrapped it quickly over his mouth to silence that aggravating sound. When he was finished, Cecil was bound with his hands and heels pressed together, his body arched backward. The paracord cinched tighter as he struggled. Soon he would realize that. He would remain in that position until someone came to free him. Ridley hoped that it would take some time and that Cecil would use the time to think, but he wasn't optimistic about that possibility.

He straightened and took the keys—there were three key rings on different pegs and he took them all—and considered the shotgun briefly but decided against it. A gun was not a caving tool, and when he entered Trapdoor, he wanted the cave to know that he was pure of heart.

"We're close," he said, and then he used the open knife to guide Julianne back toward the door.

52

Mark was driving too fast over the icy roads when he called Danielle MacAlister, but the Ford held steady in its lane.

"You said your father bought his land for timber rights," he said.

"Well, hello, Mr. Novak. Nice to hear from you again."

"You said your father bought his land for timber rights," he repeated.

"Correct."

"He never did any cutting."

"The cave redirected him, obviously."

"But he owns property in all directions and most of it is open field, no timber at all. There's a local who rents it for horses. The cave maps that Ridley drew are guides, but they'd have nothing to do with ownership. Those would be standard maps. Parcel maps. Ridley stopped drawing the underground maps at one point. Stopped sharing them with your father, at least."

"We've already discussed this."

Mark made a turn, felt the tires slide, and corrected for the skid. "I disagree. You told me what you wanted to share. I have new questions. I'm on my way to see you, in fact."

In truth, he wasn't even sure of his questions. The

property mattered to Ridley. The property mattered to Pershing MacAlister's family.

"You're making a mistake," she said.

"Explain how."

He could hear her breathing. For a moment he thought she was going to offer something, but all she said was "I've taken enough of your questions. You have no legal authority. If you come here, it's trespassing. I can have you arrested."

"Tell Cecil to open the gate. It's what he's there for. To keep an eye on things, make sure there's no trouble."

"Do I have trouble, Mr. Novak?"

"If you didn't think that you did, you wouldn't have come up here. You damn sure wouldn't have stayed."

"You broke into our property and got lost in the cave. That's why I'm here."

"It's not why you stayed. You stayed to know what Ridley was telling me."

"You've already earned that confession once. I'm not hiding that interest."

"What are the stipulations of the land trust?" Mark asked. "The property just sits there untouched, forever, is what Cecil told me. Your father felt that strongly about it?"

"About a girl being murdered on his property, a girl who'd been about to join his family? Yes, he felt strongly about it. He didn't want to let this become a sideshow, an exploitation of tragedy."

"Your father sounds like a shrewd businessman. But rather than bring a concrete company down here and just fill that entrance in and call it a day, he makes the decision to pay a caretaker to live on the property. For ten years, he does this. He'll do it for another ten? Twenty?"

"I don't know." Her voice was tight.

"How do you not know? It's your property."

"It's in a trust. The environmental stipulations of the trust might preclude that sort of—"

"No legalese, no stipulations. You're an attorney, you know what it says. What will the situation at Trapdoor be in ten years?"

"Probably not what you think, but it's none of your concern. I've been patient enough with you and I—"

"Show me the trust documents, then. You won't even have to talk to me this time. Just show me those documents and I'll be on my way."

"You won't see me if you come here. I'll send for Cecil. It's his baby now. I'm done with your questions, Mr. Novak. If you come here, you'll need to deal with Cecil."

"This is why he's worth keeping on for a decade, Danielle? To keep trespassers away from the cave and questions away from your family?"

The line went dead.

Mark didn't call back. Just kept driving. Snow was falling again. The conditions and his speed would have bothered him when he arrived in Indiana but they felt familiar now. Muscle memory. Sometimes the things you thought you'd left behind circled back for you.

53

The door was in sight and the keys were in hand but still the surface world wouldn't grant Ridley access without resistance. He and Julianne were no more than fifty feet from the entrance when the security floodlights went on.

The footbridge and the gate were instantly illuminated, and the light spread out almost far enough to reveal Ridley and Julianne. They were in the farthest reaches of the shadows. He stopped walking and grabbed Julianne's arm to bring her to a halt. The lights had come on without warning, as if tripped by a motion sensor, but he knew that the lights here didn't operate on motion sensors. Someone had turned them on, which meant someone had seen them.

There was the sound of a door opening and closing—not just closing, *slamming*—up at the big house just above them, and then a flashlight beam appeared.

Ridley pushed Julianne farther from the light. This required leaving the creek bank and moving out onto the ice itself. They'd made it three steps when there was a single loud crack followed by an uneasy yawning sound all around them as the stressed ice fought to hold. Ridley stopped moving. If the ice broke beneath them, it would draw that flashlight beam their way, and then he would have to act fast.

Water bubbled up beside Julianne's foot but the crack

didn't spread. The ice sheet creaked and strained but it held. Ridley kept his eyes on the house, and a few seconds later the source of the flashlight appeared: Danielle MacAlister, walking with hostile purpose, walking toward them. Ridley's jaw clenched as he reached for his knife. He did not want Danielle to be part of this but he could not allow her to disrupt him either. He simply couldn't.

He had put the knife to Julianne's throat and was ready to push her into the light, ready to show Danielle the consequences that awaited, when Danielle turned away from the creek without breaking stride.

She wasn't coming to the cave. Wasn't coming to confront them. She was following the driveway.

When it was obvious that she wasn't approaching them, Julianne did a strange thing. Despite the knife at her throat, she leaned her head against Ridley's shoulder. A gesture of relief, which made some sense, but almost intimate as well, and even more fascinating, the relief didn't seem to be entirely on her own behalf. She seemed relieved for *him* as well.

Maybe you are wrong about her.

No. She had a knife at her throat, that was all. Of course she did not want him to be forced to use it. Her relief was only a product of self-preservation.

Still, he felt a connection to the touch that suggested they were in this together. Did she understand now? She was an intuitive woman. Did she realize that he'd told her only the truth, always?

Ridley looked at her face and then back up at Danielle MacAlister, who was walking away from them, toward either Cecil's apartment or the front gate. If she was headed to Cecil's, that meant he was about to be freed and the police called. Trapdoor would be a scene of chaos soon, and that couldn't be allowed. All Ridley needed was time. They wouldn't understand that, though. Never had.

"I need to stop her," he whispered. "I have to."

Julianne lifted her head from his shoulder, twisted to face him, and shook her head. Slowly and emphatically. Then she tilted her head pointedly to the right. Toward the cave. He followed the gesture with his eyes, saw the door, so close to them now. When he looked back at her, she flicked her eyes down at the keys in his hand, then back up to him. Held the stare.

She was right, he realized. There was no need to intervene with Danielle MacAlister. Not when they were this close and he had the keys. Let Danielle call the police, let them come for him. Once he was inside the cave, they wouldn't catch him. Once he was inside, he could stay as long as he wanted, as long as he needed.

"Yes," he said. "We'll go ahead. That's all that needs to be done."

Julianne nodded. He felt his trust for her returning despite his better judgment.

"Step carefully," he said. "We need to stay in the shadows."

Staying in the shadows required walking under the footbridge instead of across it, and that meant they'd have to cover the rest of the distance over the ice, which had cracked once already. The creaking and groaning sounds were all around them, but Ridley preferred that risk to climbing back onto the creek bank and standing exposed in the floodlights.

They moved slowly across the slick surface. Once, there was a sharp crack like a gunshot, and Ridley braced himself for the fall. The crack had come from a tree branch, though, not the ice. The weak limb snapped and its load of snow fell to the earth with a sound like the release of a held breath. He nudged Julianne forward again. They passed beneath the bridge and then made it up onto the rocks. He looked back up the drive and could no longer see Danielle's flashlight. It didn't matter. He just needed to get inside.

Cecil had better have told the truth about the keys. If he lied about that and I do not have the right keys, then God help them all. I've come too far to be lied to.

The first key he tried fit the lock. He exhaled and turned the key and heard the bolts slide back. When he pulled the door open, it scraped on the stone and sounded terribly loud, but he didn't allow himself to look back, just shoved Julianne through. He saw no way to lock the door from the inside and he didn't have the time to waste, so he left it standing ajar. He walked Julianne ten steps inside the cave and then he paused and took a deep breath.

"All right," he said. "It should go easier from here. She will understand why we've come. I'm sure of that."

Almost as if in response, a gunshot thundered from somewhere outside the cave. Julianne went rigid and Ridley spun and stared back at the entrance. He saw nothing but snow and ice.

Cecil is free, and Cecil is shooting. I could have killed him. Should have killed him. She stopped me.

Julianne's hand found his. Squeezed. He looked at her fingers as if he weren't sure what they were. She tugged him forward, tilting her head again, indicating the black depths that lay before them.

"Yes," he said. "Yes, we will just leave them behind. We will leave them all behind."

She nodded and tugged again. This was wrong—he was supposed to be the guide, not her. But he also knew she was right. There was no reason to retreat to the surface. Not now. He walked ahead, moving quickly and without light because he did not need it here. This was the old tour route, the ground carefully scraped free of any obstacle, any potential lawsuit. Pershing had shown no respect for the cave in the way he had cleared the tour route.

They went far enough that the entrance disappeared from view and total darkness descended and then he stopped and drank in the wonderful smell of the place—stone and water and power. Traces of blood, yes. But the power was there.

Julianne seemed aware of it too. Her body had stiffened and she was pivoting her head as if straining to see in the dark.

"It's remarkable, isn't it?" he whispered. "You'll see so much more of it than most. More than anyone else alive. I'll take you farther, I promise. The tours they ran, those were like making people pay admission to admire a mansion's front porch but never letting them get inside the door. I'm so excited to show someone else what lies beyond. Nobody has seen these places but me, do you understand that? And she was mine. She was going to be mine."

His own whispers returned to him in a soft echo and he felt a pang of regret, thinking of all that this would cost him.

"What's done is done," he said, and then he pulled his helmet free from his pack and put it on and turned the head-lamp beam to red, the night-vision setting. A crimson glow covered Julianne's face. He slipped his knife out and opened the blade, and her eyes went a little wide but still she did not resist. Not once had she made a move to run or fight him. She had demonstrated nothing but trust in a situation where he had expected no trust. It took courage, but he understood the manipulation in the technique. She was trying to create a sense of partnership so that he might let down his guard.

He leaned as close to her as he could, nose to nose, his eyes on hers, her face awash with red light, their exhaled breath creating mingling tendrils of fog.

"I'm giving her up for the truth," he said. "No one will ever understand what that means. No one but her. I had hope for you, even for Novak. Misplaced hope. But we're still here. And the lie you told me once will need to become the truth now. Do you understand me? Do you understand what that means?"

She nodded.

He moved her hair away from her neck gingerly and brought the blade up against her flesh and made a soft "Now, now," like a parent removing a splinter from a child's finger, as he sliced through the tape. He peeled it loose and her lips parted but she didn't speak. She just breathed. Her breath fogged in the red light like bloody vapors.

"I told you that I would show you everything I could," he said. "And I do not tell lies, Julianne. I do not tell lies. For a long time, I thought that you did not either."

"I want to help you," she said.

Ridley smiled. "Sure you do. And now you have your chance. We're here for the truth. Your job is to help me remember. Can you do that? I have faith in your abilities, if not in your integrity."

She gave an unsteady nod. None of her usual confidence. Trapdoor could do that to you. Trapdoor could turn the brave to weak in a flash.

He put the knife back in his pocket and retrieved the sapphire necklace and pressed it into Julianne's palm. He held her hand tightly, the stone between them.

"That was around Sarah Martin's neck," he said. "Then it was in my hand. I want to know how that happened. That's your job. That's your life."

54

Ridley's truck was pulled off the road just in front of Trapdoor.

Mark parked behind it. His headlights caught the rear window and showed an empty interior. When he cut the engine he felt as if he could hear his own heartbeat. He got out of the car and approached the truck. There was no one inside, and the dusting of snow across the hood and windshield told him that it had been parked here for a while. He'd been on the phone with Danielle MacAlister not five minutes ago. The truck had been here longer than that.

He started to walk around the gate and then hesitated, turned, and went back to his car. Opened the door and found the map he'd peeled off the wall of Danielle's basement, the last map Ridley had turned over to the MacAlister family. Folded it and put it in his pocket.

"You won't need to go inside," he said aloud. The reassurance felt necessary. His mouth was dry just thinking of the place. Something in the stillness of the night whispered otherwise, though, whispered that Ridley hadn't left his door wide open and his truck here because he intended to skip stones over the frozen creek.

Twin tracks of footprints leading away from the truck said that he hadn't come alone either.

Mark thought about calling Blankenship. But what was there to report? The appearance of trespassing, which Mark was about to do himself? He'd come here to confront Danielle, not pursue Ridley. Suddenly both were in play.

He followed the tracks away from Ridley's truck. The size difference was apparent. Ridley was traveling with a woman or a child.

Julianne?

Mark wished for a gun.

The tracks led along the driveway but behind the trees, as if whoever left them had wanted to approach unseen. They led all the way up to the garage. Mark was thirty feet from the base of the exterior stairs when he saw the blood.

There were vivid splashes of red on each riser of the steps and on down into the yard. There the footprints continued but the blood died out, washed clean by the snow. Two sets of tracks led to the garage. Three led away. And one of them had left bloodstains. That set of tracks came from the biggest footprints.

Cecil went after them, Mark thought. *Ridley roughed him up and probably got what he came for, but Cecil went after them.*

He followed the tracks as far as the blood went, then stopped and stared ahead. The frozen creek was lost to shadows but the footbridge and the cave entrance were illuminated with floodlights. He could see a figure on the footbridge, descending toward the cave. Cecil Buckner. Mark shouted at him, but Cecil didn't hear; he stepped through the open door and vanished. It was not a good sign that the door was open, and Cecil didn't appear to be the one who'd unlocked it. Ridley had gotten in ahead of him.

Trapdoor was open for visitors once more.

Mark glanced up at the big house, where even more lights

were on and Danielle's car was parked in front. Did she have any idea what was happening here? Or was she waiting, clueless, as her bloodied caretaker staggered after Ridley Barnes into the cave? Mark took out his phone and called her as he doubled back toward the drive. Five rings, voice mail.

He came out of the woods beside the garage, intending to run up to the big house and tell Danielle to call the police just as she'd threatened to, when something moved in his peripheral vision and he pivoted to look.

Motion again, and this time he saw it clearly—a scarlet bead fell from the top of the stairs and hit the snow below. Another fell, and then another. Mark lifted his head to look at the apartment. From this angle, he saw that the door was ajar and the wood in the center of it was splintered, puckered with small holes and jagged fragments.

Numbness crawled up his spine and spread along the back of his skull.

Too much blood. That is too much blood.

He went up the steps slowly, taking care to avoid the blood, which grew thicker with each riser. Now he could see a stream of it working through the cracked-open doorway. He felt just as he had when he'd opened the hidden door in Ridley's house, certain of the horrors that waited. This time, though, he wasn't going to be rewarded with maps.

He pushed the door open, which allowed more blood to rush out and pool against his boots, and he saw what remained of Danielle MacAlister.

She lay on her back in the center of the floor, close to the door. She hadn't been standing that close to it when she'd died, though. The impact had blown her back several feet. It was a shotgun wound. Twelve-gauge at least. Maybe a ten. Fired at close range, the load heavy enough to obliterate most of her left side and shoulder and rip a hole through her throat. Her right hand was curled toward her throat, as if she'd tried to close the wound.

Mark stood absolutely still and looked at her and thought, *I will kill you, Ridley. I will find you in whatever hole you're headed for down there, and I will kill you.*

There was paracord on the floor, snipped into several lengths, and a pair of kitchen scissors lay in Danielle's blood. A few feet farther on was a long piece of duct tape, tangled and stuck together.

Was this how Ridley had brought Julianne inside? It didn't have to be Julianne with him, but Mark felt certain it was. She was the only one Ridley wanted. She was the fated one in Ridley's warped mind, the one who had to join him belowground. He would have brought her here and demanded access. Because of this, she was possibly still alive.

He called 911 from the doorway. He wasn't very aware of the words that he offered, but they seemed to make sense to the operator. He heard snippets of her questions back to him: Were there any other victims? Was there an active shooter? He answered as best as he could. Told her that he believed the shooter was in the cave and that he might have a hostage. Told her that someone else had probably gone in after the shooter. He said Ridley Barnes's name several times. Heard his voice rising when he said it. There were too many questions. Why hadn't Cecil called them? What was he thinking following Ridley into that cave, where Ridley held every advantage?

The same thing you are. He wants to end it himself. Not wait on the police. He *wants to end it.*

The operator was still talking but Mark had stopped responding. His eyes were on the gun cabinet in the corner of the room. He stepped over Danielle MacAlister's body without looking at her and went to the cabinet. He set the phone down while he opened the cabinet. Two shotguns and a lever-action .22-caliber rifle with a scope. No handguns. He wanted a handgun if he was going into the cave. Easier to move with, easier to shoot with. The shotguns were bad options. A wide spray pattern in a contained space was likely to hit more than the intended target, and Ridley was not alone. Mark didn't like the .22 either, but at least it gave a shooter a chance to deliver in a tight window. Down there, it was going to be tight.

He removed the .22 and checked it for ammunition. It was loaded. The scope was a cheap infrared model, one that projected a red dot onto its target. Cutting-edge technology when Mark was a kid, now available at every Walmart. There was a flashlight at the bottom of the cabinet, resting against the stock of one of the shotguns. Not a big light. A small Maglite, probably powered by two double-A batteries. It was going to seem very weak in the cave, but there was no time to look for another option. Cecil had made the right decision, trying to stop Ridley before he got deep into the cave. If he was allowed to get far enough, there'd be no catching him. Not in Trapdoor.

Mark put the flashlight in his jacket pocket and shifted the rifle to his left hand. The voice was still coming from his cell phone. Loud and urgent. He picked it up and put it back to his ear.

"Sir? Sir, can you hear me?"

"Yes."

"Sir, we have officers en route. I need you to stay where you are and stay on the line until they arrive."

"Tell them to go to the cave. There's nobody left here but the dead. The live ones are in the cave. For now, at least, there are live ones left."

"Sir, I am instructing you to stay where you are and stay on the—"

Mark disconnected. The phone began to ring again almost immediately and he silenced it. He left the apartment with the .22 in his hands, walking around Danielle MacAlister's body.

"I'm going to kill him," he said to her. Maybe somewhere, somehow, the promise mattered. Mark wasn't sure, but he felt it needed to be said. Just in case.

He walked down the stairs and followed the tracks out to the creek as far-off sirens became audible and fat, soft snowflakes wafted down. Ahead of him, the gate to Trapdoor stood open, and the darkness beyond beckoned.

55

The cave was as it should be, still and silent and soothing. Ridley had permitted Julianne to use the full strength of her headlamp for navigation, an undesirable intrusion but one he would not deny her because it allowed them to travel faster. They were walking on a ledge beside the deepwater channel. The channel was runoff from Maiden Creek that formed an underground tributary that Ridley had named the Greenglass River. In 2004, Pershing had run boat tours into the cave on the Greenglass, and Ridley hated those. He'd been in a boat in the cave only once, and he hadn't lasted long in it that time, gone just far enough to ferry himself and his gear to the regions of the cave that fell off the maps, regions that had been dismissed by previous searchers because of the high water. Nobody could believe that Sarah Martin would enter a passage filled with water so high that she barely had clearance to breathe between the surface and the ceiling. All that Ridley had known was that they hadn't found her yet and that people did strange things during spells of panic.

Back then, he hadn't understood that people might do strange things in Trapdoor simply because the cave coerced them.

They walked in silence, and Julianne was honoring his demand not to assault his mind with words. The tape had been a valuable teacher. Perhaps she was even savvier than that, though, and knew that what Ridley needed from the cave was found in trapped whispers that came from beneath the water and behind the walls and out beyond the black.

The boat tours—fifteen dollars a pop in the old days, and ten for kids—had gone three-quarters of a mile back into the cave, a mere taste of what the Greenglass had to offer. Still, it was fascinating to have the experience of floating along beneath the earth, watching that green water reflect the light, seeing the dips and darts of the blind cave fish, listening to the slow, steady drips of stalactites—all of that was a new world to most.

It was also a world that extended far beyond what anyone understood. During the summer of 2004 Ridley had believed he'd learned most of what the cave had to offer, but at some point in the search for Sarah Martin, after the food went but before the batteries did, he'd found himself in spectacular new territory. Afterward, in total blackness, carrying a hand-cuffed corpse, he couldn't say what he had passed through.

When they reached a wide chamber where the ceiling climbed to forty feet and rock formations jutted out of the water like abandoned pilings from a collapsed dock, he nudged Julianne to the right and into the walking passage that led to the Chapel Room. The Chapel Room was the first grand feature of Trapdoor, with a high domed ceiling and gorgeous stalactites that hung like prehistoric icicles over a series of descending rock ledges that had once been the ground formation of a waterfall but now, left high and dry, resembled empty church pews. Ridley paused when they entered the room, considering stopping there and sitting and taking this spot to engage Julianne in the talk that must begin soon, but he shook that off and led her deeper.

"There are passages all around us," he said, breaking the

silence. "Above and below and on each side. Some are navigable, some aren't. Some go places, some don't. Picture a bowl of spaghetti, and each strand is a passage. That's what it's like down here."

Julianne said, "May I speak now?"

"Not yet. Thank you."

The simplest route out of the Chapel Room led to the right. The fastest was straight ahead, the crawling passage that had given Blankenship so much trouble. You could get to the same place in far less time through the crawler. Ridley was impressed by the way Julianne forged ahead once they were inside, the walls squeezing, the ceiling lowering She was much smaller than Blankenship but size didn't necessarily affect claustrophobia. There was much ahead that she would not be capable of doing, though, passages that required technical expertise, but he was counting on Trapdoor to cooperate once his mission was clear. Trapdoor would simply have to. Not only was Julianne incapable of following him as far as he'd gone on that last trip; he was incapable of guiding her. He didn't remember the turns he'd made, the paths he'd chosen. After he'd pulled on his wetsuit and slipped into the water, things had gotten away from him fast, and now that trip existed only in splashes—of water and of blood—and in whispers. Oh, maybe some screams too. Yes, there had been some screams.

Once, he thought he heard something and came to a stop. Killed his light and listened. All he could hear was Julianne's breathing and, up ahead, the soft sounds of moving water. He turned the light back on and kept crawling.

They came out of the crawling passage into the Funnel Room and Ridley guided Julianne away from the basin and toward a high ledge at the far wall. The stalagmites here were taller than a man. Where the floor and ceiling sloped steeply toward an angled meeting point there was a shallow stream that bubbled up at one end and had carved a small portal through the wall at the other.

The only sound beyond his own breathing came from echoing drips of water that were carving new crevices that would later become new passages and, later still, spectacular chambers. The drips had a leisurely pace as they went about their work, and why not? They had literally all the time in the world.

Julianne disobeyed the order of silence to say, "It really is incredible."

Ridley didn't answer. He was looking at the stalagmites and remembering when they had started to move. There had been a time, in a room not so far from here, when the rocks had begun to move around him. At first he'd believed it was a trick of shadow, but then the rocks had grown hungrier and he could hear them sliding in from behind and cutting him off up ahead, circling him, drawing ever closer. He'd taken to the water then in a hurry—in a panic, fine, he would admit that. He had panicked when the formations moved; who wouldn't?

It was then, entering the water in the panic, that he'd lost his first light.

He wiped sweat from his face. He was sweating freely, though not due to either temperature or exertion, and his mouth was so damn dry. "Yes, it is a special place," he said.

Up ahead, the stream trickled through an opening in the wall about the size of a truck tire. Ridley pointed at it.

"That's where I went into the water for Sarah Martin. It's where I came back from the water with Mark Novak."

"They were found in the same place?"

"No. She didn't want me to go that way for Novak. It was too easy. She wanted to have some fun with me. She made me earn him. I had to climb up and crawl down, that was all she would give me, but once I got to him, she gave me an easier out. She was done with Novak by then, I guess."

"When you went in after Sarah, this is where you left the group?" Julianne was ignoring the directive of silence, but he didn't care to stop her. It was time to begin.

"Yes," he said. "This is where I left the group."

Julianne stared at the opening. "It's tight. And the water doesn't look deep."

"Not here, but you crawl through for about fifty feet, and it gets much deeper. Crawl a little farther than that, and you begin to swim. When the water table is high, you're bouncing right off the ceiling. The best way to explore this section is with diving equipment."

"What's that in the water?"

He followed her gaze and, sure enough, saw something floating. That was odd. He walked closer, with Julianne trailing, and trapped the object in the beam from his headlamp: it was a remnant of crime scene tape. The rest had been torn free when they cleared out of the cave ten years ago, but this short length had been missed, and now it undulated slowly in the water, like a dying snake. Or a long strand of a girl's blond hair.

"A welcome mat," he said. "She knows we're here. I think maybe she even knows why."

Julianne had taken a few steps back, but she said, "This is good. This is perfect. I hadn't dared hope for anything so perfect."

"Why so pleased?"

"It's ideal visualization. That narrow opening is a literal portal."

Her voice was natural again, just as if they were inside her living room for a scheduled appointment. As if she'd never had a knife at her throat and tape over her mouth. He was both pleased by that and disarmed by it. He needed her to be a willing, focused participant, but her calm suggested that she believed she could gain control again. She simply had to learn that down here, neither of them would have control.

"A portal is exactly what it is," he said. He thought he saw one of the rock formations moving, shifting as if leaning down to overhear them, but he didn't turn toward it. He knew better. "This is where your work begins."

"You wish to enter trance here."

"A form of it."

"There's only one form I know."

"She knows others. She'll guide the process. You'll facilitate, but she will guide. It won't be what you're used to. She won't allow that."

"There are many reasons you don't want to leave here now," she said, "and it is obvious that whatever trust you had in me has been damaged, but for your own well-being, I would like you to listen to me when I say that trance here is a dangerous thing for you."

"Remaining on the surface is far more dangerous." Ridley dropped to his knees on the stone and removed his backpack and began to assemble the special equipment he'd brought for this portion of the journey. He had a white wax candle and a small crystal base, and he fit the candle into it carefully and withdrew a pack of matches and struck one, tingeing the damp air with sulfur. The wick accepted the flame immediately.

"This isn't how we do things," Julianne said. "Not with candles and crystals, Ridley. You know better than that."

"Things are different here. Do you have the necklace?"

"Yes."

"Good. Hold it in both hands, please. And turn your headlamp off."

She removed the helmet to turn off the lamp. She was clumsy with the equipment, and he watched that with dismay, because he knew they would have some traveling to do. At least she was not scared of tight spaces, or hadn't been so far. Trapdoor could breathe new fears into you swiftly, though.

When her headlamp was off, he was relieved. The candlelight was softer and it shifted and breathed and it was natural. Ridley's mouth was the driest it had ever been. He freed a water bottle from his pack and drank heavily. It made no impact.

56

Mark had spent hours in a cave in a way few people alive could relate to, and yet he'd never experienced one in anything but blackness.

In the light, it could take your breath away.

The deepwater channel with its odd coloration set the tone, but it was the way the cave expanded as it descended that really created a sense of awesome power, a promise that there was so much more here than you would have guessed.

The small flashlight seemed weaker with each step. He thumped it against his hand and adjusted the focus, trying to coax more light out of it. The sense that it was dimming was an illusion, though, created by the size of the cave and the totality of the darkness.

He walked on a ledge to the right of the water because it was the only option.

Drops of fresh blood painted the cave floor. Cecil was wounded, but he wasn't bleeding badly. Just a steady drip. Mark's flashlight caught something reflective and glistening up on the stones. A strip of duct tape, sliced neatly in half. A twin of what had been on the floor in Cecil's apartment, only without any of Danielle MacAlister's blood on it.

He stepped over it and moved ahead.

For a while he did not need to attempt any tracking or

even consider it because there was only one path. Then, in a spot where the water channel opened up into a wide pool, he saw the looming blackness of a tunnel on the left and another one on the right, and for the first time there was a decision to be made.

He dropped to one knee, removed Ridley's decade-old map from his pocket, and got his bearings. He'd been walking along the Greenglass River and now he had the choice of scrambling toward the tunnel on the left or bending toward the one on the right. According to the map, the tunnel on the left emptied out into a circular room named Solitude. There was no indication that there was a way out of Solitude, but of course Ridley had stopped recording the passages at some point and it was entirely possible that there were numerous ways ahead from the supposed dead end. All the same, Mark found himself guessing that Ridley had gone right, toward the Chapel Room and then the Funnel Room, where Mark had been told they'd begun the search for him, Ridley traveling up when everyone else was looking down.

His turn was the right choice—Cecil's blood was visible again, meaning that he, at least, had come this way. Whether he'd had visual contact with Ridley at the time was another question. Inside the cave, Ridley held all the advantages—knowledge of terrain, technical expertise, every level of comfort one could have on his home turf—but he'd hindered himself by bringing Julianne along. The things that Ridley could do down here alone using his ropes and wetsuits and challenging high walls and narrow tunnels, he would not be able to do with Julianne, or at least not with any speed. That meant if Mark kept up a good pace, he stood a chance of finding them fast, but moving quickly would be a struggle because he was beginning to feel the return of the unease with the cave now. As he entered the tunnel that led to the

Chapel Room, he was positive he heard a sound behind him, and he whirled and banged the rifle barrel off the stone walls. The flashlight illuminated nothing that could have moved or made a sound. It was only in his head.

Mark knew he had to hurry to catch them, but he wanted to go slowly. No, that wasn't even the truth. He wanted to get *out.* There was a bad feel to the place once the walls of the tunnel narrowed around him and the ceiling angled down and he saw that he was going to have to crawl.

You may only be making this worse, he thought. *An amateur chasing a pro in a place like this, it could be a disaster for everyone.*

True, but that was not enough to make him leave. It would take them a long time to get caving experts in here, and who knew what the police would want to do at that point? Caving experts were still civilians. The police might decide to enter themselves, and they'd be just as slow as Mark. Maybe slower.

Cecil was out there ahead, and Mark wanted to catch up to him, at least. Together they would have a better chance. Mark understood the adrenaline, the desire for immediate pursuit, but Cecil had scarcely entered the cave when Mark arrived. He should have seen Mark's car pulling in and known that someone was here, someone who maybe could help. If nothing else, Cecil should have asked Mark to call for reinforcements while he went after them.

Decisions made in battle often lacked clarity and logic, though, and Cecil had certainly been under fire. His home had been ransacked, his employer brutally murdered, and Ridley had a hostage. Mark hadn't even thought to check the phone in Cecil's apartment and see if it worked. He'd called the police from his own cell. Perhaps Ridley had taken away Cecil's ability to call out. The only chance for Cecil then would have seemed the hero's play, trying to stop Ridley alone. After seeing what Ridley had done to Danielle, that took real courage.

Mark stopped crawling and rested his bruised knuckles on the stone, the .22 in his left hand, the flashlight in his right. He leaned against the tunnel wall as sweat dripped from his forehead and his heart thundered. Adrenaline coursing, the same thing he was busy ascribing to Cecil. He'd been telling himself he couldn't pause, couldn't slow, that it was all about speed now, and Ridley had had a head start.

Speeding in the wrong direction wasn't worth a damn, though. Speeding in the wrong direction was a good way to die.

Did you see things right, Markus? Did you see the truth back there?

He'd seen brutality, a murder victim awash in blood, and he'd identified her killer without pause. Ridley was the threat, and Ridley was on the property, ergo...

But why hadn't Ridley killed Cecil, then? If Mark's perception was right, it meant Ridley had been armed with a shotgun in Cecil's apartment and had used it on Danielle. Why Danielle? And why let Cecil live?

Maybe Cecil fought back. He resisted; he escaped.

Fought back well enough to avoid death, but not well enough to kill Ridley? Cecil was a large and powerful man. He had no shortage of firepower in that gun cabinet. If he'd been able to gain the upper hand even for a moment, why had it ended with Ridley and Julianne already out of sight in the cave, and Cecil limping after them?

Something was wrong in there. Something didn't make sense in there.

Danielle's body had occupied Mark's focus. Her body

and the blood. So much blood. It had been hard to consider much else. But there had been other things. Paracord, the kind that lay in neat coils all around Ridley's house. Duct tape, more of which Mark had seen in the cave. The tape had been different, though. The tape on the floor in Cecil's home had been pulled off and lay in a tangled clump. The tape in the cave had been sliced perfectly in two. The latter made sense. Ridley was a knife man. Ridley and that ever-present Benchmade. His reflex weapon, the one he'd drawn on Mark.

Far more important, though—Ridley was also a rope man. He cared for them, worried over them. Ridley was a knot master. He'd have untied the paracord, not cut it. Rope men did not cut their ropes if they could possibly avoid it. And even if for some reason he had decided to cut it, Ridley would never have needed to find a pair of kitchen scissors for the task. He'd have used the knife, just as he had on the tape in the cave.

That wasn't his work. Someone else cut Julianne loose.

Or they hadn't cut Julianne loose at all. There was tape left behind in the cave but no rope. Why would there be? Ridley would have untied it and kept it. Rope was valuable to him. So who had been cut loose in Cecil's apartment? The work had been awkward—all the lengths of cord hacked into pieces. That was the product of someone who didn't understand the knots at all, who simply kept cutting until all the cord was loose. Had Ridley bound Danielle up, leaving her to be hastily freed by Cecil?

Not Danielle. There wasn't enough time for her to go through all of that. I'd just spoken to her. So that leaves…

Cecil.

Which meant that Danielle had freed him.

So who had pulled the trigger on her?

I'll send for Cecil. It's his baby now, she had told him just before she hung up the phone. He'd thought that meant that she was going to ask Cecil to block him from the property. That the trouble Mark represented was about to be Cecil's baby. It had seemed obvious. She was calling her caretaker in to do his job. But maybe she wasn't calling him in for the obvious reason. Maybe she was calling in Cecil for another reason entirely—to answer for himself.

It's his baby now.

For the first time, Mark was fully aware of the cold in the cave and of the darkness ahead and behind. There were three people belowground with him. He'd thought one was an enemy.

Maybe he had two.

57

Julianne sat on the stones with her legs crossed. Her helmet was beside her, and she held the sapphire necklace in her hands. Her face was obscured by shadows in the flickering candlelight, and Ridley couldn't make out her eyes. He wanted to see them and find the comfort that they held, but he couldn't afford to sacrifice the darkness. The truths that he wanted out of Trapdoor had all been lost in the dark. He would have to find them there.

"We'll start with an offering," he said. He set the knife on the stone near his right hand, blade open.

"No," Julianne said. "No, Ridley, that's not how we start."

"Things are different here." He reached into his backpack and pulled free a roll of papers.

"What is that?"

The pages were larger than normal, the long format of legal documents.

"This is a trust document," Ridley said. "Dated October second, 2004. You know what's special about that time and this place. I don't need to explain it to you. All that matters to you are contained in a few lines."

He knew the document so well he could have recited the lines from memory, but still he flipped through the pages. They deserved to be read once more.

"'To be executed ten years from the date of this agreement or at the time of my death, whichever comes first,'" he read aloud, "'with the stipulation that all terms of this agreement are rendered wholly null and void if the circumstances of my death are determined to be the result of criminal action.'"

Julianne was staring at him with an expression he'd never seen on her face before.

"What is this?" she said. "Why was this agreement made?"

"Let me finish. Let me read the beautiful line, the one that gave me hope and patience for so long." He worked his tongue around his mouth in a fruitless attempt to bring moisture to it, and then read, "'At which time all holdings of Trapdoor Caverns Land Trust will become the property of Cecil Buckner and Ridley Barnes.'"

Julianne didn't speak. Ridley took a deep breath and shook his head. "How much that meant to me, I can't explain. But those were in different times. Patience can hold you only so far in the absence of truth. Cecil doesn't understand that, because Cecil doesn't have the same questions. I'll trade for the truth. It's a bargain I hate to make, but I'll trade the trust for the truth."

He was speaking more to the cave than to Julianne now. He fed the title page of the document into the candle flame. The flame chewed around the edge of the paper and flared brightly but then died, leaving one charred corner. He shouldn't have been surprised.

"She has no use for documents," he said. "Certainly no use for talk of ownership. I always understood that. My request was that I be referred to as a *steward* of Trapdoor Caverns. That was the role I wanted. Apparently, it was not the right legal term, but it's all I wanted to be."

He set the partially burned document aside and took the knife in his hand. "Now it's about to be your show," he said. "Are you ready for that?"

"Let's talk more about this."

"No." He shook his head. "We will talk about Sarah. Where she was found, how she was found. You'll have to trust the cave. We're so much closer to the truth now. All you have to do is open the door for me. You're the only one who can do that."

For a long time she was silent, but when she finally spoke, her voice was perfect, the cadence he'd come to know and require.

"If you would like to face the water and focus on that portal, you may do so," she said.

He turned obediently, and now Julianne and the candle were in his peripheral vision, a flickering in the corner of his right eye. He could see the shadow line of the stream and the place where it disappeared. He turned to look at her. With the blackness at her back and the candlelight before her and those pale clothes and her blond hair, she seemed to glow.

"I'll need total darkness," he said.

"Even from the candle?"

"Yes. I'll need it the way it was back then."

She hesitated, but then she leaned her face close to the candle's warm, soft light, parted her lips, and exhaled soundlessly, and the candle extinguished and they belonged to the blackness.

"All right. Let's work our way toward that day together, shall we?" she said. "Always together. Never alone. Remember that you are never alone here."

Not a problem, Ridley thought. *Not in Trapdoor.*

"You may focus on that spot," Julianne said. "On that portal. It may be the place where the present ceases for you and the past begins. Take your time if you wish, and maybe you will wish to let the water guide you. You may wish to remember all of the days we have done these exercises together and all of the progress you have made. Your confidence and your strength. Remember that you are required to follow it only as far as you wish."

He'd worked with her long enough to understand the double message here, the way she was using the word *remember* as often as possible, a guide that went beyond the surface message.

"Whenever you are ready, you may focus all of your attention on that portal," she said, her voice rising and falling in subtle shifts. "You may begin to consider all of the places that it can take you. All of the places that lie beyond. You may remember those now, if you choose. You may vocalize those, if you choose. The seeing is within your reach and yours alone. You know this, and you know that even though it is dark to me, it is not to you."

"Yes," Ridley said in a dried out whisper. "Yes."

"Would you like to approach it now? Would you like to pass through it and tell me some things about what lies beyond?"

"Yes."

"Listen to the water and to the other sounds that you might hear, sounds perhaps different than those that I can hear."

He knew what she could hear: the steady, tinny drip of water from the ceiling, plinking down into a puddle that was patiently working its way through the stone, unhurried by the passing centuries. It was a pleasant sound, not unlike the ticking of a clock. In its own way, that was exactly what it was.

"Allow yourself to pass through, if you wish. Give

yourself that permission now. Permission to go down that path. Moving forward, yes, but also backward. As far back as you choose. You know the path. You've been on it before. Follow it now, if you wish. Follow it and see where it leads. I will count down from ten to one, and when I reach one, you will be on the path as you once were before."

Ridley closed his eyes even though he was in blackness, and his head bobbed in rhythm with her voice, and his thumb worked lightly over the knife. Though it drew blood, he felt no pain.

58

Mark was on his hands and knees again, freshening the bruises from his last time in this terrible place. If you wanted to make it out of Trapdoor alive, you had to be willing to spend some time on your knees. There was no other option.

The pain from the bruises was bad but the memories it triggered were much worse. Each ache forced him to recall the way it had been down here before, when he was alone and shivering in the blackness. When he had called on every resource for survival and found that your resources didn't matter much when you were lost in the dark. You needed help from outside the blackness then. That had been the most unsettling realization of his life: *I cannot save myself.*

These memories should have made him even more grateful for the light, but instead he found a strange resentment of it. He maneuvered through the tunnel without needing to make any effort or even give any thought to avoiding the walls and the rocks, and he felt almost outraged by how simple it seemed. He knew what he'd earned in the dark, he knew how hard it had come, how much it had taken from both mind and body. That anything so arduous could be made so easy felt almost insulting, a mocking of what he had achieved.

The tunnel opened up, and the flashlight exposed a wide chamber with high ceilings and an odd, staggered floor that looked almost like bleachers, as if the water had carved seating for some grand performance. The Chapel Room, he assumed. There was no trace of Ridley or Julianne, but there was blood from Cecil. Less of it now, spaced out by larger distances.

Mark set down the rifle and withdrew Ridley's map once more and checked. Yes, this was the Chapel Room. Here again he had options—three passages, one that went up to a second level of the cave, one that went straight ahead, and one that curled to the right. The passages both directly ahead and to the right took you to the Funnel Room, the place where they had first heard Mark's voice. According to the dimensions on the map, the passage to the right was much larger, a walking passage with a twelve-foot ceiling. The passage ahead was labeled in Ridley's scrawl—*belly crawl, very tight.* The wider passage was a much longer trip toward the same destination, a distance of a quarter of a mile to achieve what the belly crawl would do in three hundred feet.

He stepped back and moved the light around and saw that what looked like one rock angled in front of another was actually a gap in the wall. The obvious opening was a dead end, but the hidden one led on. There was blood on the floor here. Cecil had taken the walking passage.

Mark hesitated and looked back at Ridley's map. For ease of access, he should follow Cecil's route. If he took the crawl, though, and he moved fast enough, he could pull ahead of Cecil.

He turned from the open passage and walked back to the crawl without allowing any pause for reflection. When he saw the opening, it did not look so bad: a gap at least three feet high and equally wide. Easy going. He dropped back down to his hands and knees then and shone the light into the tunnel and saw a shelf of rock ceiling so low that it didn't look as if a basketball could roll through.

"No," he whispered. "Not worth it."

That was when he heard a voice. Too soft to be understood but undeniably human. He ducked lower, listened. Heard the voice again and this time he recognized it: Julianne's.

She was alive, and she was speaking. Cecil Buckner, who had left behind a gruesome scene that made no sense to Mark, was heading toward her. How close Cecil was to her, Mark didn't know, but thanks to Ridley's map, Mark knew exactly how close *he* was—three hundred feet. One football field, that was all.

One football field that he would have to crawl over on his belly, his shoulders squeezed on each side, the ceiling brushing his head.

He lowered himself onto his stomach and crawled forward, once more pushing the .22 ahead of him with his left hand while holding the flashlight in his right. Five feet in, then ten, and he was feeling fine, he believed that the visual intimidation of the crawl was harder than the process.

Then his shoulders brushed the walls. No big deal. Just wriggle forward. He lifted his head so he could extend his elbows.

His head cracked off the stone ceiling, and when he lowered it, his chin bounced off the floor.

Terror now. A flood of it. Not even fifteen feet in and he felt trapped, felt as if he should scramble backward.

He closed his eyes. A bead of sweat ran down his forehead and over his eyelid and across his lips. He licked it away, tasting the salt. Opened his eyes.

Everything ahead of him was blurred. The passage was too low, too narrow, too dark.

But he could breathe. He could breathe and he could move.

He also knew where it led. He knew that because Ridley Barnes had passed through here before. More than once. He'd passed through it with enough calm and composure to not only see where it led but chart its dimensions. *Belly crawl, very tight.*

A voice became audible again. Julianne's. Soothing, composed. What she'd endured to this point Mark had no idea, but he'd seen Danielle MacAlister's corpse. He knew what waited ahead for her.

We'll all end up here, he thought. *It's just a matter of time. I'll join them all down here. Sarah Martin. Diane Martin. Lauren.*

He crawled ahead. Ten feet, fifteen, twenty. His breathing came too fast and his heart thundered. For the second time in this cave, he thought that he heard snakes, but there weren't any. This time he had the light to prove it. He paused for a few seconds and steadied himself and then pushed on. Again he tried to look up and banged his head and felt a shudder of pain all the way along his spine. There was a reason you were supposed to wear a helmet. He crawled on, shoving the rifle in front of him, and he was cursing his slow progress when he heard two voices, a man's voice joining Julianne's, and this time he could understand the words, and the first one that registered was *light.*

He clicked off the flashlight, sure that they were speaking of him and were aware of his arrival. The instant the light was gone he had no idea where he was. The totality of the darkness was like a physical thing. His thumb moved toward the switch again but he willed it down and did not touch it.

Instead, he crept forward slowly, moving as quietly as possible. He no longer believed the distance on Ridley's map. It had to be a lie. Mark had been crawling for more than a hundred yards. A half a mile at least. Two miles. The distance was as endless as the darkness.

The words became clear just as the walls widened and the ceiling lifted. Julianne and Ridley were speaking, and they were not far from him. It seemed they were in a room just around the bend, but that meant they were in total darkness. All that existed of them was their voices. It gave the situation an eerie quality of unreality. Ridley's voice had been low and sluggish when it first became audible but now it was sharp, his words racing.

"She's there and I can hear her and I know that I can't go back because it sounds as if she's hurting. Hurting and afraid but so close. She is so close and that means I can't go back, I have to go forward or I might lose her. And it's a problem because the light is getting dim; it's getting dark and so I have to hurry."

Mark shifted his hand so he could reach the rifle's trigger. Then he heard Julianne.

"Why is the light getting dim?" she asked, but there was no light in their room, and Mark finally understood what was happening. Ridley's rapid account was being spoken in the present tense but the story came from the past. He was talking about Sarah Martin.

Ridley said, "Batteries, batteries, I've been running this lamp too long, the whole time down here, and there's another one behind me but I can't go back for it now because I can hear her and I can't lose her, this is why I'm in the cave, I came for her, right? I came for her. The crawl is tight, very narrow, squeezes the shoulders, and I can't believe she came this way. I can't believe it. She was not skilled enough to get here, but she is here. No one else has been here, so how did she make it? Just a scared girl in the dark. How did she make it? She couldn't have made it."

"If you didn't believe you would find her in this place, what led you to it?"

"I take what the cave gives me. It's one of the only rules."

"Who makes those rules?"

"The cave. The rules have always been here, but you understand them better in the dark."

Mark was relieved that he'd turned off his light. He hadn't wanted to go dark in this place ever again, but if Ridley believed these were the rules, it was better not to disturb him. He wasn't sure whether to advance or wait. Without being able to see what was before him, he couldn't make a call on how to proceed. It seemed to be just the two of them, no demonstrated danger, but Cecil Buckner was circling from the other side.

"Continue along the journey," Julianne said.

"It's dark by the time I make the top of the crawl. Battery's done, it's dead, I've made it all the way now but I don't have light and I can't go back because she's so close. So I shout."

Mark didn't like the use of the present tense. It suggested Ridley wasn't recalling the past as much as reliving it. Still, he was entranced by it, because what Ridley was telling Julianne now was the thing he'd refused to share for ten years.

"What do you shout at her?" Julianne asked.

"That I'm coming for her. That she will be safe."

"Does she answer?"

"Yes. She asks me to stop. She says, 'Please, stop.' But that doesn't make any sense because she's lost and she's hurt and she needs help. So I keep climbing, and she says, 'Please, stop,' and I think that she is talking to me but it's to the cave."

"Why do you think it's to the cave?"

"Because the cave tries to kill me. And then I do the wrong thing. I fight it."

"How do you fight it?"

"With my knife. The dark man, he has me by the throat. I have no lights anymore but I still have the knife."

"Who is the dark man?"

"He belongs to the cave. He's always been here."

Mark thought, *Here we go, here we lose him, any chance of getting the truth dies with the madness of the dark man,* but Julianne countered Ridley beautifully.

"How can you fight someone who has always been here?" she asked.

"With my knife. I grab it and I slam the blade backward, again and again, and he's screaming now."

"Screaming because you are causing him pain?"

"Yes."

"But he's always been in the cave?"

"Yes."

"Do you see how these things might create a problem when considered together?"

There was a long pause. Finally, Ridley's voice returned: "He should be hard to hurt. *Impossible* to hurt."

She was getting him to confront his own fiction or hallucination or whatever it was. Mark could hardly breathe. There was no police interview that could have delivered this. No interrogation. He wouldn't have believed that before, but he was sure of it now.

"If he is eternal, it seems he should be difficult to hurt, yes," Julianne said. "But you're certain you hurt him?"

"Yes. I am certain. And then I have to make him stop. I have to silence him."

"Why?"

"Because when he screams, she screams, and so I need him to stop, I have to make him stop. So I do. It's a mistake, though. It is a terrible mistake. Because now he can't tell me where she is, and he's the one who knows. Who knew. I should have stopped when he screamed."

Mark could hear Ridley sobbing between the words now.

"I should have let him keep screaming, that is better than the way it is now, because he can't talk, and he's the one who knows where she is. And now I can't see and I don't know where to go. It's dark all around but I can still hear her. She's so close, but I can't see! And I think... I think he was providing for her, maybe? At least he knew how to find her. But now he can't go back. Because of me. So I'm going to have to find her in the dark and I will have to find her fast, because if I don't, if I don't..."

"What happens if you don't?"

"She dies," Ridley said, his voice dipping. "I need to find her before she dies."

Mark thought of that first confession—*I think I killed her.* This version had another layer: he'd removed her lifeline. She'd died because of his actions but not at his hand in this scenario. If it was true, if any of it was true, that meant someone else had died in Trapdoor too.

"Let's consider the dark man again, if you wish. Tell me what he sounded like, what he smelled like, what he felt like. Use all the senses. They have their own memories, as you know. Use them now."

"Blood," Ridley said.

"What?"

"He smells of blood. Then Sarah does. And then I do the wrong thing."

"What wrong thing?"

"I take her."

"What do you mean?"

"She belongs to the cave. She was never supposed to leave. That's why so much pain came. It's a penance. She wasn't supposed to go."

He sounded like a child now, his voice high and needy and desperate: *Understand me.* Mark shifted forward, trying to hear, because Ridley's voice had grown very soft. Mark had no idea when he should act. He didn't know where Cecil was, wasn't even certain that Cecil was a threat. Without any view of the room or sense of where Ridley and Julianne were, Mark could put her in more danger by entering the room. He thought of the scope on the .22 then, the cheap infrared. He could project a red dot into the room, but they'd see that. Useless. He needed to commit to the light at some point.

"You wanted to talk about the necklace," Julianne said. "You wanted to know how it found its way into your hand. Think of the necklace now. What is your first memory of the necklace?"

"She dies," Ridley said as if he hadn't heard the question. "I need to find her before she dies. I can hear her and I know that she is alive and I am supposed to find her. I am supposed to save her. It's why I'm here. The only reason."

There was silence from them, and Mark wondered if it was because Julianne was as stunned as he was, if she was beginning to fumble for the next question, the next bit of guidance. That didn't seem like her, though. She understood how to take things home. Why the silence?

When she spoke again, the trance cadence was gone from her voice, and sharpness had replaced it.

"Ridley, I am going to count to five. When we reach five, you will be gone from the past, you will be feeling so good, relieved of your burdens and so good, you will feel safe and"—*What in the hell is she doing?* Mark thought, and that was when he saw a faint light on the wall up ahead— "at peace. One. Feeling energized now, feeling good energy spreading through you. Two."

She was panicking, rushing through. That light bothered her, which meant it didn't come from the two of them. They were no longer alone. Someone had joined them in the cave; someone was approaching.

The caretaker had arrived.

Mark got to his feet as she said "Three" and then Ridley spoke for the first time in several seconds.

"Here he comes. I knew that he would. She's sent him to stop us."

The pale light intensified then and the world of stone lit up before Mark. He was facing a chamber with an angled roof and he could see Ridley clearly, Ridley with one arm wrapped around Julianne Grossman's throat, pulling her backward, stumbling among the rock formations, trying to clear the two of them away from the white light that was emerging from a tunnel twenty feet ahead. Ridley fell and Julianne fell with him and her skull smacked the stone with a crack that hurt just to hear. Ridley froze and looked at her in horror as blood spread through her blond hair. His attention belonged entirely to her and he didn't even turn to face the light when Cecil Buckner stepped out from the tunnel, wearing a caving helmet and holding a shotgun belt-high.

Mark flicked the switch on the infrared scope and put a red dot on the center of Cecil's chest.

"Put the gun down!" he shouted.

Cecil spun toward his voice, but Mark was on the ground, below the light. Cecil couldn't see him, but that didn't stop him from shooting.

The sound was enormously loud in the trapped space, like

a mortar round. Rock fragments exploded into the air, and needles of pain found Mark's cheek and neck as he pulled the trigger on the .22 and shot Cecil in the chest.

Cecil rocked back and fired the shotgun once more as he fell, this blast connecting with the ceiling, and then he was down on his back and the shotgun clattered over the stone and into the water. He sat up and fumbled for it. Mark worked the lever action on the rifle as he rose to his feet, and this time he put the red dot on Cecil's eye.

Cecil stopped searching for the shotgun. He moaned in pain as he put a hand to his chest and found it wet with blood, but he wasn't going to die from the wound. Not from the .22, which had hit low, missing his heart. The killing gun in play was still the shotgun, and Mark needed to claim it.

Ridley had been silent and motionless until Mark was almost to Cecil. Then he spun with such speed and agility that Mark nearly shot him out of surprise. But Ridley ignored him, splashed into the water beside Cecil, and came up with the shotgun. He pivoted toward Mark, his finger drifting to the trigger.

"Don't," Mark began, but he didn't need to bother with instruction, because Ridley simply threw the gun onto the rocks.

"Those don't belong here," he said. He sounded groggy, distant and uninterested. He stared at Mark as if he did not recognize him or even understand what he was.

"Same team, Ridley," Mark said. "I'm here to help you. And Julianne. Let me help you."

"You're not here for her," Ridley said.

"Yes, I am," Mark said, though he had no idea whom Ridley meant by *her*. Julianne, Sarah Martin, the cave? All of them? "Step back," Mark said. "Ridley, just step back."

"None of you belong here," Ridley said. "She doesn't

want any of you." He stepped over Cecil and moved through the water, heading deeper into the cave.

"Ridley! Stop moving!"

Ridley ignored him. He dropped to his hands and knees in the water and crawled toward a narrow gap in the wall. Mark had the choice to shoot him in the back to stop him or let him go.

He let him go. Ridley crawled through the gap and vanished into the darkness. Then it was just Mark, rifle in hands, and two people on the ground in front of him, bleeding into the rocks.

59

Cecil was terrified of his wound, pressing on it with both hands and giving a high, strange moan that echoed around the room. His eyes were wide and panicked as he watched the blood flow through his fingers.

"Help," Cecil said. He looked from the wound to Mark, his face desperate. Taking blood was one thing to him; watching it leave his own body another. "I'm dying. Don't let me die!"

Mark ignored him, set the .22 beside the shotgun, both weapons well out of Cecil's reach, and turned to Julianne. She was facedown, and blood ran through her hair and joined the water on its slow journey deeper into the cave, chasing after Ridley Barnes.

Her wrist showed a pulse, and her breathing seemed steady. The blood loss was the only immediate threat, or at least the only one Mark was qualified to do anything about. He removed his jacket to serve as a compress but he needed something to secure it. Ridley surely had brought rope with him, and his caving pack was still here.

There was rope, but once Mark had the pack open, he realized he didn't need it. Before Ridley Barnes had decided to try to kill Julianne Grossman, he had packed a first-aid kit for her. There was a packet of pads coated with a clotting agent, and there was a roll of three-inch-wide gauze. Mark took both of them and left the rest of the kit. All he was concerned with right now was stopping that bleeding as fast as possible. He pushed her hair out of the way as best he could and applied two of the sterile pads. When they contacted the blood, a sticky gel formed. He wrapped the roll of gauze around her head, keeping it tight. Blood stained the first layers but did not continue to soak through.

Through it all, Cecil had moaned and called for help, and Mark hadn't responded. When Julianne spoke, he almost dropped her head onto the rocks again.

"Worked," she said. Her voice was as thick as if her mouth were packed with cotton. "Worked."

He moved so he could see her face, and her eyes tracked him but they had a foggy look.

"Julianne? Julianne, do you understand where you are?"

"It worked," she said. "Detail. He gave…detail." She put together sentences like a climber clawing toward an icy summit.

"Just rest," he said. "Rest for now. We'll talk about it. But right now we need to get you out of here. That's the—"

Light splashed over the wall behind them then and Mark whirled and reached for the shotgun. He realized quickly that the light was coming from the tunnel that led back to the Chapel Room and not the one Ridley had vanished into, but that didn't mean a whole lot; Ridley was capable of circling back in ways no one else understood.

"Who's there?" Mark shouted.

The light's motion stopped and there was a pause before another voice responded. "Indiana State Police. Who are we talking to?"

Cecil stopped moaning. For the first time, he seemed aware of something beyond his wound. Julianne's face showed no response at all.

Mark said, "You're talking to Markus Novak. You're clear to approach. There are two wounded in this room, and there's one missing somewhere else. There are two weapons that I'm aware of, but they are not in play."

The light went back into motion and he turned to face Julianne, hoping she understood that rescue was here. She didn't look relieved, though; she looked concerned.

"We didn't end trance," she said. "That...that is dangerous for Ridley now. The worst possible thing. He doesn't know what is real down here...that could be very bad."

60

Ridley embraced the cold water, swam down until his hands touched the bottom, and then pulled himself forward along the rock lining the streambed. Only at the last possible second, when his head had begun to throb and his lips threatened to part despite his will, did he allow himself to break the surface.

The water-table line was high and he struck the limestone ceiling with enough force to snap his teeth together; the impact drove his face back into the water. Choking and sputtering, he rose again and this time he leaned his head back and got a fuller breath.

He treaded water there, in a place where he had anticipated it would be shallow enough for him to stand, and got his breath back as the cold found his bones. He saw motion to the right, perhaps a stalactite relocating from one side of the stream to the next, a process that not even a millennium could bring about in another cave but that could occur within seconds in Trapdoor. She was shifting around him, changing the rules; all night she had been changing the rules, and he was weary of that. What the cave had done tonight revealed her true character.

Something Ridley had always understood about Trapdoor was that she protected the past. The cave wanted to hold her secrets and so she had wiped Ridley's mind clear with blackness before she sent him back to the surface. Certainly there had been a price to pay for that, not one without pain—the hostile police, hateful neighbors, relentless media. And, of course, what memories the cave had allowed him to keep. Those seemed carefully crafted, snapshots of blood and scrabbling fingers and echoes of screams and then, far worse, echoes of whispers.

Please, stop

He had hoped that with ten years in constant communion with the world below—if not in this place, then close by, close enough that he could feel Trapdoor's heartbeat and know that his could be felt as well—a mutual understanding might grow. The cave would learn that Ridley wanted to atone for only himself, that he did not blame Trapdoor for what had occurred, and that whatever he might learn about the past, he would answer for on the surface, leaving the cave in peace.

Those hopes had vanished back in the Funnel Room, where Ridley Barnes had once entered the water with rescue on his mind and returned with a dead girl in his arms, and where tonight he had sat with an innocent—

an interloper, an intruder

—at his side. All that had followed had been hostile, and unnecessary. He'd come for the truth, and he deserved it. Instead, the cave had turned on him. He was enraged by that, because his intent had been clear and his respect unquestionable.

"She didn't belong to you!" he screamed into the blackness. *"She belonged up there! And you know it! You fucking know it!"*

He was gasping when he finished, the scream spreading pain through him like a fever. All he wanted to do was pass that pain along to the cave, the source of it all. Sarah Martin had belonged on the surface, and she had not deserved harm. Ridley had not deserved harm either, and still the cave had applied her power for vengeance, nothing more. When Trapdoor turned on a good and faithful servant who had sought only the right path, who had honored every request and kept every secret? At that point, even the righteous should be allowed to resist.

He bobbed too high in the water again and his helmet cracked against the stone and he was about to sink lower when he paused to consider his helmet and the potential it carried.

He'd instructed Julianne to join him in total blackness down here because he believed it was what Trapdoor had desired of him. Now he no longer cared what Trapdoor desired. *Problems with the dark man,* he thought, and he tried to recall what Julianne had said and what he'd said to her. The words didn't seem far off, but they were hard to grasp. There was a problem with the dark man.

He found the headlamp switch and pressed it, and the shapeless dark became a tunnel, its outer reaches within the range of Ridley's spotlight. The last time he'd passed this way, it had been only blackness. Now he could see. He could find his way back to where it had started.

He had to.

The lack of a wetsuit in fifty-eight-degree water put a ticking clock on Ridley, but the light allowed him to beat it. Maybe.

It was a question of preparation and performance now, and Ridley Barnes had been a long ten years in training.

He swam ahead. The light led the way, and Ridley chased behind it.

61

It snowed all night and then broke off just before dawn, and the clouds pushed east and left a hard, shining sun behind.

All of this happened as Mark sat in the Garrison County Sheriff's Department. He'd given three interviews to a total of seven police officers and still hadn't seen Blankenship. He'd asked about him several times but nobody had an answer and finally they'd left him here and told him to wait.

The state police had been the first ones into the cave, and they'd separated Mark from Julianne swiftly and handcuffed everyone, even the kidnapping victim. Mark couldn't say that he blamed them, though. It was a hell of a strange scene down there. The last he'd heard from Julianne, she was imploring the police to go after Ridley. They promised that they would, but Mark saw the looks in their eyes as they studied the water-filled passage Ridley had vanished into and he knew that nobody was going to be rushing after him. They'd send for experts, people with the right knowledge and equipment, and by then Ridley would have had quite a head start.

He'd been waiting alone for more than an hour when Blankenship finally entered the room. He crossed over to him and pulled up a chair and sat down heavily. Reached into his shirt pocket and removed something and spun it across the table to Mark. The object came to rest just in front of him: the Saba National Marine Park diving permit.

"No prints on it," Blankenship said. "I thought you should have it back as soon as possible."

"Thank you."

Blankenship nodded and he kept his eyes occupied elsewhere while Mark picked the plastic disk up and put it in his pocket.

"You got one back from him alive," Blankenship said. "I thank you for that. It could have gone another way. It has before."

"She's doing all right?"

"Docs say she's stable, and she's talking pretty well now. Same story as you gave me. Says he came to her originally asking for help with memory retrieval and that she heard a confession. Knew it wouldn't stand up in court and wanted to find help. She says he wouldn't have taken help from my kind of detective. She thought he would from yours." Blankenship's face showed only the sleepless night.

"Did she know what Ridley wanted from her last night? Before they got down there?"

"Not hardly. He came to the house. She was sure he was going to kill her. Then they got in the cave and he said he wanted to...to do her thing."

"He wanted to go into trance in the cave."

"I suppose that's what you'd call it. I suppose they made it too. She says they did. I don't know anything about that. I don't know what I believe of it, to tell you the truth."

"Believe more than you want to," Mark said. "It's a start. Trust me. I've stood in your place on that one. Any luck locating Ridley?"

"Not yet. We'll get him, though."

Mark didn't share his confidence, and, after seeing

Ridley's face in those last moments, he wasn't sure they should want him back on the surface.

"What about Danielle MacAlister?" he asked. "Was Julianne able to tell you anything?"

"Danielle MacAlister walked out of the house while Ridley and Julianne were heading toward the cave. Ridley started to go for his knife, then let her pass. They were just inside the cave when they heard a gunshot."

"Cecil."

"It would seem that way, yes. Cecil was talking for a time. Then he realized his story wasn't as believable as he needed it to be, and he asked for a lawyer. I was with him in the hospital while he told a weak story about going into the cave to try to make sure Julianne Grossman was safe."

"Bullshit. He went in to kill them. The only problem he had was that they were in the dark. That meant he had to show himself to them instead of the other way around. There's no sneaking up on Ridley Barnes in the dark. If Cecil wanted to clip him, he should have done it on the town square under a bright sun. My guess is he'd have found a sympathetic jury in Garrison."

Blankenship let that one pass and said, "You understand why he killed Danielle?"

"She was done with whatever story they'd been protecting, would be my guess. She went down there to prep him for my arrival and found him trussed up. Cut him loose, and then…"

"Paid for that mistake," Blankenship finished. "Yes. That's my read. Cecil has some risk in all this that I don't quite understand yet, some risk that made murder acceptable so long as he could blame Ridley for it."

"But what is that? What's he protecting?"

"You see the shit Ridley brought in there? The paperwork?"

"I saw it, but I couldn't tell you what it was. I was just aware that it was there. Looked like he'd burned some of it."

"Uh-huh. Well, it's a trust document. Interesting read. Deeds the property to Cecil and Ridley."

"Cecil *and* Ridley?"

"Yes. The document Ridley took down there has an effective date that is only a few months away, or when Pershing dies, whichever comes first. Fun thing about that? Pershing has to die of natural causes. It's the strangest damn protective order in history, essentially."

"Why is the cave willed to them?"

"Because Pershing gave Ridley the motive to kill Sarah."

"What?"

"Cecil puts the blame on Pershing. Pershing can't speak to defend himself, and now his daughter can't defend him either. But according to Cecil, Ridley reached a point where he wouldn't take money for mapping the cave. He wanted a piece of ownership. Pershing didn't want to grant that. So he drew Ridley up a nice little cartoon trust to keep him going with the exploration and keep him silent about just what he was finding. Only problem is that Ridley went down to the courthouse to inquire about it."

The disclosure should have felt like a triumph, but Mark's stomach turned.

"Ridley found out he had a handful of wooden nickels? And then Sarah went missing how much later?"

"Six weeks later," Blankenship said. He had trouble with the words.

"Why in the hell didn't Ridley tell anyone this?"

"Because they drew up the new trust. It contented him, apparently. This is what he explained to Julianne Grossman."

"But that came after Sarah."

Blankenship nodded and when he spoke again, his

voice had a honed edge. "So Pershing and Cecil knew the man was crazy, they played him for a fool, and then they got caught. All in the summer before... before Sarah. By the time I enter the frame, all of this has come to pass and she's missing in the cave and I pull rank and demand that they send Ridley in after her. Pershing put up some resistance, I'll admit that and already have, but the chickenshit never came *close* to saying what needed to be said. He didn't want to admit it in front of Diane, is what Cecil and Danielle told me. He also didn't think Ridley would hurt Sarah; he thought that she was just lost. But I'll tell you this right now—I was the one who dealt with Pershing, and he was scared of Ridley Barnes. Never said a word of the true reasons, though. Never said enough to convince me Ridley was a threat and had reason to want to hurt Pershing, hurt the family. So I let him in, and then Ridley went in there and *killed her!*"

Mark let him run out of steam and allowed a few seconds to pass before he spoke.

"I think you're almost there," he said. "But you're having trouble seeing past Pershing. I don't blame you. It's the reason they pulled you back then, but I don't blame you a bit."

"What am I missing, Novak?"

"The dark man that Ridley talks about like some sort of ghost or spirit of the cave? I think he was real. There was somebody else down there with him."

"Cecil, probably."

"I don't think so. If Ridley told Julianne the truth last night, the dark man from that encounter is a dead man now. Ridley killed him."

"I should have seen a crime report on him, then. This *dark man*. Somebody should have noticed he was missing."

"I think you've got his teeth," Mark said.

Blankenship went silent for a few seconds. "You think Carson Borders was down there."

"Maybe, yeah."

"Teeth came from Detroit. Motive for killing him came from Detroit. Connections to Ridley don't exist."

"His son is connected to it," Mark said. "Of that, I'm certain. Where's Evan?"

"Missing. Same as his cousins."

"You'll need to find him," Mark said.

"I'm not buying Ridley's version of what happened in that cave, whether he was hypnotized for it or not," Blankenship said, but the words came slowly and his eyes had a far-off look.

"You're wondering about it, though."

"No."

He was lying. Mark had seen similar lights in investigators' eyes before. He'd *felt* that light.

Blankenship's chest filled with a tired breath. "I suppose if Ridley ever comes back to the surface, I can ask him."

"You can't ask him," Mark said. "That's the hell of it, Sheriff. You've got to figure out his world to see where the pieces of your own got lost in it."

62

Ridley was freezing and wet and it was impossible to dry off down here in the damp air. The chilled water beaded all along his goosefleshed skin, and when he shivered water sprayed from him like a dog shaking dry. Even by Ridley's standards, it was far too cold, and that meant he was entering dangerous ground. He'd flirted with hypothermia before, but nothing like this.

He sat on a lip of stone, pondering problems that light alone could not fix. Ahead of him was a steep drop of at least thirty feet, and while he remembered it and knew that he was on the right path, he'd had climbing gear the first time through. He'd removed his backpack to work with Julianne, a critical mistake. He needed it now, but going back didn't seem like an option. He wasn't sure that the cave would allow him to pass back through the water again. He had to stay in pursuit until he found the dark man, but that meant finding a way down this wall. There were bolts in the stone and that surprised him because he didn't remember running any bolts when he'd come this way searching for Sarah Martin. He was almost certain he hadn't, but it was foolish to think that the dark man would have needed them. He could pass through as he wanted; the cave yielded for him, and surely he did not require mechanical assistance.

Ridley leaned forward, out over the lip, and studied the bolts. They were not the kind he used for the etriers. They were open U-bolts and there were only two of them, set eighteen inches apart and just below the cliff edge. Ridley was no stranger to visions, so he reached out and touched one of the bolts, feeling the steel under his fingertips. Very real. The steel was scraped, the base of the U-shaped portion nicked. Ropes would not do that. Metal would. He looked at the open bolts again and now he thought he understood. A quick scan of the room confirmed it—a caving ladder rested in the rocks just beside him, coiled up and tossed aside, waiting for someone's return.

Ridley had been using single-rope techniques for so long that the possibility of the ladder had not come to him as swiftly as it should have. The ladder was made of aluminum steps with strands of cable for the side supports so that it could be rolled up.

Ridley unfurled the ladder slowly and the feeling that descended upon him then was one he'd always feared he'd encounter in a cave, although he'd expected it would come from a roof collapse, a rock slide, something that left him trapped and hopeless. He hadn't expected it to come in the form of a ladder.

Police searchers could not have left this behind ten years ago. They hadn't made it this far. No one had. This was the province of the dark man, the heart of Trapdoor, and nobody but Ridley—and Sarah Martin—had ever passed this way.

None of this made any sense. The cave had created the dark man, and the dark man did not require ladders.

Ridley hung the ladder through the bolts, giving him a method of descending the wall, but he was so tired after that small bit of effort that he sat on the cliff with his feet dangling off the edge as he fought to catch his breath. He stared at the ladder as he breathed, so focused that his peripheral vision began to blur, almost as it did during visualization just before trance.

Look at it from above, and then from below. What do you notice about it now that you did not notice before?

There was blood on the rocks. These were old stains, streaks of dusty red that might have belonged to an ancient people. Ridley had shed no blood here.

The only thing that seemed less likely than the dark man requiring ladders was the dark man bleeding.

What do you understand now that you did not understand before?

The light was bothering him now and he wanted to reach up and turn the headlamp off and be soothed by the dark. He squeezed his hands into fists to still them. He needed to keep the light on, whether it was pleasant or not. He had to remember the things Julianne had taught him.

"What did you do, Ridley?"

He breathed the words into the emptiness, a question so familiar it seemed like part of his name now. It was the wrong question. He thought that he knew what he had done and that he always had. That meant he needed to ask a different question.

Why had he done it?

63

Mark's rental car was in the police impound lot in an alley across from the sheriff's department. Blankenship opened it for him and then said he was going back to talk to Cecil Buckner.

"You hang around town for me, okay? We'll need to talk again."

"I've got no place to go," Mark said. They had just returned his phone to him. The battery was dead, so he couldn't see how many calls from Jeff London had stacked up. By now the board of directors had already met. He wondered if they had any idea what was going on in Indiana at the moment. He had trouble bringing himself to care. What had once seemed paramount—appeasing the people in that room—now seemed inconsequential, with Julianne in the hospital and Ridley Barnes still belowground and the dark man with him in mind if not in body.

Mark pulled out of the impound lot and went through the alley and came out on a street that ran toward the downtown square and the courthouse where once Ridley Barnes had walked in with a few questions and a fake deed. What exactly had that day done to this town? What had that decision by Pershing MacAlister done?

"Never count out your sins," Mark's uncle had told him

the night they had Mark drive them through the snow to find the poker cheat. There had been blood on Larry's jeans by then, and they weren't even through with the search.

He started toward Trapdoor even though he'd been told to stay away. The town fell behind him and the fields opened ahead and he'd gone no more than half a mile before he saw the white truck approaching in his rearview mirror. He reached for the brake but just as he hit it, the truck turned off the road and the exhaust growled as it headed south, away from Mark and out of sight. He watched the mirror for a few seconds anyway, but the road behind him was empty now, and then he let up on the brake and continued out of town.

The next time, he heard the exhaust before he saw the truck. It came from his right, where a four-way stop loomed, woods on the right-hand side and fields and two pole barns on the left. The barns were closed and no one was in sight. By the time Mark reached the stop sign, he could see the truck tear-assing up the road in an effort to beat him to the intersection.

He brought the car to a stop and put it in park. Watched as the white Silverado fishtailed into the middle of the intersection, black smoke bubbling from the worn-out muffler. Mark opened the door and got out of his car and walked toward the truck with his hands in his pockets and his head high as Evan Borders fumbled out of the driver's seat with a gun in hand.

"No mask today," Mark said. "And no friends?"

Borders looked at him and then glanced at his gun as if confused by it, because it now appeared to be an unnecessary tool. "You were a long time with the police," he said.

"Lots to talk about. People keep dying in this town. They'd like that to stop."

"You're pretty relaxed for a guy without a gun."

"I'm getting used to the role."

Evan Borders nodded, looking over Mark's shoulder and back toward town. No traffic was coming from that way, but it was bound to eventually.

"You stay relaxed, then," he said. "We're going to take a little trip. You can drive."

"I'm not real interested in a trip right now."

"Bullshit you aren't. You want to know if Ridley makes it through. So do I. Why don't we take your ride? Police have eyes for mine. I'll leave it here where it's convenient for them."

The gun was pointed down. A car had appeared far off down the road, heading toward town, and Evan pressed the handgun into the pocket of the oversize farm jacket he wore and said, "Just get back behind the wheel and keep it in park."

He climbed into his own truck and pulled out of the intersection and onto the side of the road as the car came by. Mark gave the driver a nod and a wave as he passed, casual. By the time the car was gone, Evan was out of the truck and jogging toward him, the gun still hidden in his coat.

"All right," Mark said. "I'll drive."

"There ya go!"

Evan walked around the front of the car with a cheerful, buoyant stride, went to the passenger door, opened it, and fell into the seat.

"*Cold* today!" he said. "My goodness, the sun comes out and it gets colder? Crazy."

The muzzle of the gun was showing again, pointed at Mark, and Evan had a strange false smile, like a department-store greeter.

"Where are we going?" Mark said.

"Just drive toward Trapdoor for now."

"Bad location if you're hoping to avoid police."

"Why don't you let me give the tour?"

The route took them across the intersection and back into the winding hills. Evan watched it all as if he were seeing the place for the first time.

"What do you think of our town?" he said.

"One of those unfortunate situations where my experiences are tainting my sense of the place," Mark said. "Don't take that personally. It's not Garrison, it's me."

"Sure. You know, it's actually a hell of a nice little town. I've always enjoyed it. Haven't enjoyed all the people, and that's more than mutual, but I like the place. Growing up, kids were always talking about getting out of here. For what? I'd say. I don't like cities. Just can't take them. People talk about the beach too, someplace warm, but, you know, I like seasons. I like knowing the back roads and the trails that nobody else knows. Sound enough like a country song to you? It's the truth, though. I was always happy here."

Mark didn't say anything. He just drove. The gun was pointed at him but Evan seemed uninterested in it, or even in Mark.

"I never cared about money," Evan said. "That's the truth. I just needed enough to get by. Tell you something that makes me happy—cutting grass and plowing snow. You can see your work. See the mess that was there before you, and how nice and clean it is when you're done. How *orderly*. I always liked that feeling. People say a lot of negative shit about me, but I defy you to find somebody who says I did a poor job of cutting grass or clearing snow."

Mark drove on in silence.

"Wonder where I'll land," Evan said. "Man, I hope not in a city. I don't like crowds." He shook his head and sighed as if to redirect himself, then said, "So, the longer I've been waiting on you, more curious I've been getting. Who said what? You solved it all yet, Detective?"

"No," Mark said. "I didn't do much detecting either. I just put on enough pressure that things started to leak."

"Things blew up, is what happened. Didn't leak long. Now we're going to talk straight, just the way you wanted when you came around the first time."

"I came around then because I was curious if you'd tried to kill me. And you had."

"Oh, hell, I've never been a killing man. Not even a hunter. Kids would make fun of me for that. I just had to pretend I'm a lousy shot. You weren't going to die down there."

"The doctor had another perspective on that."

"Well, you wandered off. Shit, if you'd stayed in one place, you'd have been fine."

"My apologies. It was inconsiderate of me. What was supposed to happen?"

"I didn't really have a plan for that. I just thought it was time to send them back in."

"Send who back in?"

"Police, searchers, the whole damn show, one more time. Encore performance. See if anybody made it through and wait for Cecil to make a decision on pulling your ass out if nobody else did. Far as I know, only Ridley Barnes has made it through, but he doesn't remember how he did it. Word is he's taking another run at it right now; is that true?"

"He's in the cave," Mark said. "That's all I can tell you."

"Then he's making a run at it. He's not as young as he was the first time, and he damn near died in there then, so this will be a stretch."

The snow-covered farmland was falling away at the road's sides and the interior of the car had warmed and Evan seemed like an almost congenial presence as long as Mark disregarded the gun in his hand.

"Tell me something," Evan said. "Did you really remember the trailer? If so, I was given some bad advice. You weren't supposed to remember shit."

"It came to me," Mark said.

Evan frowned. He'd pulled the hood down from his jacket, and with his dark hair cropped short, he looked younger than he was; he could have passed for a college student.

"Well, not all of it came to you. So I guess I got my money's worth. Go on and pull in there now when we get to it."

"The trailer?"

"Yes. Nobody's been back since last night. You got 'em all distracted now. Of course, it doesn't take much in this county, there aren't that many police. What do you think of our sheriff anyhow?"

"You'll meet worse."

"I agree," Evan said, seeming to miss the predictive quality of the statement. "He's a good man. He wouldn't say the same of me, would he?"

"He hasn't yet."

"I didn't think so. You tell him I appreciate him, though. Always did."

Mark made a left turn and they were now just two miles from Trapdoor. The open fields came into view and with them the snow-covered collapsing trailer that Carson and Evan Borders had once called home, on the last of their family land.

"Almost done with it," Evan said. "Maybe I'll think different in a little while, but right now, I'm almost glad you blew into town. The wait has been too long for too many good people. Maybe it worked out well for me these past ten years, maybe not, I could argue either way, but there are too many good people in this place who cared about Sarah. Why in the hell did you come back, though? Close as you came to death down there, why in the hell make a return trip?"

"Somebody tried to kill me."

"Exactly. That's the point of leaving for good."

Mark shook his head. "That's the point of coming back."

"You *want* to die?"

"I'm in no hurry to. But somebody tries to kill me, I'm going to try to find out who he is and why I was worth it to him."

They reached the trailer and Mark pulled into the drive. There was crime scene tape around the front door and the ramp, and the snow all over was trampled. In the distance police vehicles were visible at Trapdoor.

"Congratulations, then," Evan said. "You're about to find out why you were worth it. Now we'll have to hustle. Only a matter of time before somebody stops in, and I'll need to be on the road before that. I hope you don't mind me taking your car. Nothing parties like a rental, right?"

Mark shut off the car and Evan nudged him with the muzzle of the gun. "Be good when you get out, now. You're close to what you came for."

64

Ridley walked alone through a forest that was so spectacular he could almost forget the pain.

In a room with a towering ceiling and stalagmites that rose like trees, triple his height or even greater, Ridley stumbled forward, his headlamp beam small in the vastness. The first time he'd been here, he'd hardly believed what he was seeing. The second time, he'd been unable to see and he had the girl over his shoulder.

Now there was no reason to rush ahead because the only cries of pain were his own. He could take his time to savor this place, and so he did, pausing and leaning against a rock formation that was as thick as an oak tree. He gazed around, painting the high domed ceiling with his headlamp beam. He had read about caves in places like Mexico and Russia and Vietnam that held unbelievable wonders—caverns with their own ecosystems, home to animals and trees. Son Doong in Vietnam contained a river and a jungle and even its own cloud system, and it hadn't been explored until 2010. There were wonders beneath the earth beyond anything most had seen on its surface, but Ridley would take Trapdoor over any of them.

Because he'd been the first one through. Or so he'd always thought. That was becoming hard to believe, though. There were things down here that did not belong.

He was sad about that, because he'd always viewed himself as an explorer of the first order, breaking new ground. But maybe there was always somebody who'd beaten you there. When John Colter returned from the West and reported his discovery of Yellowstone—a discovery for which he'd been mocked, with his outlandish tales of giant, boiling geysers rising from the earth—there had been Indians living there for hundreds of years. Maybe there was always someone ahead of you.

Once, Ridley would have cared about that more. Today, shivering and weak, he could only appreciate that he'd been one of the early ones. That he'd had the chance to see this at all.

The room he was in had ceilings at least ninety feet high that fanned out like a giant dome, vaulted like a holy structure. He considered lying down and soaking in the beauty of it and waiting until his light burned out again.

He couldn't do that, though. He had a purpose, although it was not as urgent as the one he'd had the first time he'd passed through. He needed to find the place again. Where the dark man had lain in wait for attack and where, just above, Sarah Martin had waited for rescue. They were not places Ridley wished to see again or had ever wished to see—no one had understood that when they refused his requests for a return, over and over again; no one had ever understood that it would be worse for Ridley than anyone else. Ridley had given up on being understood long ago. What he knew now was that he had to keep moving or he was never going to reach those places again, and he had promised himself that he would do that before the end of his life. He had sacrificed much for it and it would do no good to stop here, no matter how beautiful the spot.

He pushed away from the oak-size rock and moved

ahead, his steps sluggish. All around him, the massive formations spread their shadows, and Ridley's own was very small against them. His shadow was the only one moving, though, and he was grateful for that. Trapdoor had turned a benevolent eye on him once more and would not hinder his way through the wilderness. He did not understand the reasons for her choices. She gave and she took and the order of those choices seemed indiscriminate and arbitrary at best and, at worst, cruel.

But it wasn't his role to understand her. It was his role to get through her, that was all. She had been around for more millennia than he had years and he had no right to question anything that she did. You had to enter the darkness with some humility if you hoped to pass through it.

He traversed the full length of the domed room and then he faced half a dozen passages honeycombed in the far wall and did not hesitate before selecting one. He believed he'd tried several on his last time through, wasting valuable time, but the cave was guiding him now   it was either that or his memory, and Ridley's memory had long been suspect and often loathed—and he knew that he was on the right path. The tunnel led past a wide pool like a lagoon, and air moved over the water and carried a clean, undamaged smell that seemed to heal him as he walked, the smell doing more to ease the pain than any pill could. The cold, not the pain, was the real killer and he knew he was beyond the threshold there, but he believed he had enough time left to see it through.

He stumbled over a rock and fell to his knees too easily, his body unable to offer any resistance, lacking the coordination necessary to simply regain balance. The landing was painful, and he cried out without shame because there was no one to hear him but the cave, and she'd watched him come all this way and had to understand that he was hurting. It would do no good to cry out to her, but it would do no harm either. She simply watched and listened in silence.

He closed his eyes and fought for breath and for a moment he could feel the girl's weight on his shoulder again. He'd fallen many times with her, and each time he had apologized. Several times he had wept. Never had he stopped.

Sarah had been as silent and cold as the cave for most of the journey and Ridley did not hold great hope for her but he'd come too far to simply leave her behind and so he had talked with her and wept with her and he had carried her. For a long time he had carried her, so long that he had come to believe that he'd passed on and entered another life where there would be no pleasure, only pain and suffering and responsibility. But he'd understood the responsibility and so he'd bent to that task and he had never stopped carrying her through the darkness.

The surface world that had opened up to greet him was the same one he'd left behind, but it was no more welcoming than the underground one he'd shared with Sarah Martin. In many ways it was worse. *Tell us what happened* went from a request to a threat fast, and Ridley couldn't tell them what happened because he didn't remember all of it, and what he did remember, they refused to believe. When he spoke of things that sounded like magic, they were dismissed as lies and again and again people demanded the truth from him without accepting that he'd told the only parts of it that he knew.

His head fell forward, heavy with sleep, but his eyes snapped open and he shook himself awake. He couldn't estimate how long he'd been going. He guessed it was well into a new day now, but perhaps he was wrong. All he knew was that he'd not allowed himself to rest so far and that he'd left much distance behind him. He turned and looked back and wondered if anyone would ever believe that he'd made it in the dark the first time while carrying her. He'd told them this, and he'd been ridiculed and scorned and even marked for death by many, and he could have accepted all of those things if only they had accepted the truth of what he had done to bring her out.

He rose from the ground with an effort and walked on and he'd gone maybe another fifty feet and the ceiling was getting lower when he saw his old backpack.

This was where he had started to climb ten years ago. Where he had heard her voice, her cries, and left his gear to try the crawling passage that led up to the level above, shedding weight to gain speed, because she was hurting. Where he'd left his last light, the backup light, the one he had not been able to find again when he emerged through a different passage with the girl in his arms. The fact that it was sitting out in the open, so visible now with the light, was hard to bear.

But you're close. Yes. He was very close now. He just had to climb.

That sounded like an extraordinary task, but he reminded himself of what he had once achieved in this same place and he passed by his backpack and found the crawling passage and began to climb. He was slower than he had been on the first trip, but he allowed himself to be, for there was no hurry. The climb seemed endless but he doubted it was more than twenty feet, and it required no ropes, just dedication. Most of this stretch of the cave was that way. He came to the end and managed to shove his shoulders through and that was when he saw the bones.

The skeleton was intact and it looked quite beautiful. Its eye sockets were twin shadows, and one arm was extended and the finger bones were stretched toward the surface, as if it were begging for something.

Something glistened amid the bones, and Ridley reached forward and gingerly removed the object. Ten years of dampness had corroded the Benchmade knife a bit, but it still felt familiar, an old friend in his palm. He tried to close the blade but it would no longer shut, so he placed it back where it had been, as if the scene were a tableau the cave wanted to preserve.

Ridley sat back on his heels and looked at the skeleton for a long time.

What do you see that you did not see before?

"The dark man," he said.

But the dark man was white and shining now. And the dark man had once been human.

65

Only my father," Evan Borders said, "could sell the wrong part of his own land. If he'd just hung on to it, he'd have had the golden ticket he wanted. But he was in a hurry. You don't get rich by being slow, he told me. He was broke when he said that, by the way. So he sold it, and the other fucking entrance opened up within the year. How about that?"

"Other entrance?" Mark said.

Evan nodded. "You got it, brother. You're the one who's going to need to understand this shit and weigh it against whatever comes out of Cecil's mouth. That'll be intriguing."

"All right. Tell me what I'm weighing."

"First entrance to Trapdoor was the one on the property my father kept. But he was secretive about that, was scared to death to tell people, because he was looking at ten years in Pendleton if things went wrong during his trial, and that's a long time to let your oil well sit, right? He thought somebody would claim it, somehow. So he went looking for money and lawyers fast as he could."

"So Cecil connected him with Pershing."

"And that didn't work out so well all the way around. I'll say this much for Cecil—he never said shit about the cave, to the best of my knowledge. He had to scramble once the other entrance opened, though. The second entrance opened twenty months after my father found the first. Think about all the time the cave has sat down there, right? A thousand years, or is it a million, I don't know. Hell of a long time, just sitting there. And then one year it rains too much. One year out of all those. One wet year too many. For all those thousands of years, nobody would have killed over this land. Then something shows itself under the ground, and now we've got, what, three dead already, and Ridley down below somewhere. All because of the chance to take money out of the ground."

Mark followed him around to the northern corner of the trailer, closest to where the ground sloped off into a deep sinkhole, a farmer's nightmare. The trailer was raised on cinder blocks and skirted with a rotting piece of fascia. Evan pulled one of the fascia panels loose and crawled under, and Mark followed. There wasn't much clearance, maybe two feet at most. It was a belly crawl. Evan slid forward over the wet soil, pulled a flashlight from his pocket, and turned it on. The beam showed an elevated concrete ring with a rusted manhole cover over the top.

"What do you think that is?" Evan said.

"Somebody wants it to look like the septic tank, but you don't drop a trailer on top of your septic."

"That was a last-minute call. My father spent the days just before his trial out here with Cecil Buckner. They rented an excavator and did the job alone. He still didn't trust it, though, so they moved the trailer too. I suppose it worked. Not the worst idea in the world, really. Most people don't pause to study on trailers and septic tanks."

He crawled over and pushed the lid back. He had to set the gun down to do it; the lid was plenty heavy. When it had scraped clear, Evan rolled onto his right shoulder and waved for Mark.

"Not bad, right? Only my old man could think to hide his golden ticket in shit. More I think about it, more it suits him."

Mark crawled close enough to see, and then Evan lifted the flashlight and shone it down. The false septic tank spread out into a narrow and deep chamber of stone. Deeper than the light could reach. In the center, a long ladder made of steel cables and aluminum steps dangled. The walls sloped inward, forming a V, and it looked tight at the far end.

Mark glanced away from it and out at the fields that swept toward Trapdoor, and the distance seemed extraordinary. He'd made it all that way in the dark?

"This is where you put me?"

"Hell, no! You'd still be down there, your bones sitting alongside my old man's. You went in the main entrance, the one people know about. And not far in, either. But in your attempt to get out, you just went farther in."

"I thought I was getting close," Mark said. "I thought I was heading the right way."

"You were heading deeper into the cave."

It seemed impossible to believe, but if anyone would know, it was the man who'd left him there.

"The entrances connect," Evan said. "Only two people ever figured out how. My dad from this end and, apparently, Ridley Barnes from the other. Because Ridley got there, didn't he? Hard to kill a man if you don't get to him."

"Your father is the dark man," Mark said.

"The what?"

"He's down there," Mark said. "Your father's body is down in that cave."

Evan nodded.

"The teeth came from Detroit," Mark said. "The police seem convinced of that."

"That's because they were mailed from Detroit, yes. Cecil needed people to stop looking for my father. The longer they looked for him, the more trouble it would be. Good news was, there was already somebody in the game who'd promised to kill my dad. And his people were in Detroit. Cecil drove up there and mailed them down and damned if he wasn't right—it quieted the search awfully fast. Everybody had been waiting for my dad to get popped when he came out of prison, so when they finally had evidence that he had been, they were content with that. The old boy who put the hit on him, he wasn't one to miss. That's why, during the short time my dad *was* back in this town, he was stealthy about it."

"Cecil pulled your father's teeth out of his mouth?"

"No," Evan said. "I did that."

He didn't look away from Mark. His face was hard and his voice steady and dark. "Cecil offered. I didn't think that was right. I thought if anyone was going to treat his body like that, it should be family."

Mark tried to imagine what that had been like. How long had it taken? How easily did they come out? How often did Evan see those images when he closed his eyes at night?

"I was told he never came back to town after he was paroled," Mark said. "Everyone seems to believe that. How long was he really here?"

"If they believe it, then Cecil did his job. All summer, from the day my father got paroled to the day I came in here with Sarah, Cecil was hustling to keep my father quiet and invisible. It wasn't easy. My old man was fixated on the cave and he would drink and do dumb shit, call Pershing and make threats, go down there and tag the cave with paint like a little kid. Cecil would rip his ass and then put the blame on Ridley, and that was easy enough because Ridley

Barnes is the craziest fucking man who ever walked through this county. He's talking to caves, right? Got himself friends down there, rocks he thinks are people. You know how convenient Ridley Barnes was for Cecil Buckner? Damn, brother, you have *no clue* just how valuable that old boy was. He was like one of those loons who stand on street corners preaching about the end times and government conspiracies or whatever. People *expect* him to say crazy shit, do crazy shit. They don't expect him to say the truth."

"You took Sarah in there for your father?"

"I did not take her in there for him!" For the first time, his mask of good nature shattered and Mark could see the dangerous rage that existed beneath it. When Mark spoke again, he took care to keep his voice gentle.

"Then what happened?"

"Just what I said happened from the start. We went in there because Sarah wanted to, then somebody scared us, and she hid. Then she was lost. Every bit of that was true." He swallowed. "I just didn't mention that I met my father in the cave. When I left her to check out the noises, the drunk son of a bitch came in and screamed at me for telling her about the cave. Except I wasn't *going* to. I wasn't going to tell her anything that she didn't know, that everyone who paid ten bucks for a tour didn't know. I tried to explain that. I'll never know if she heard any of it or not. He laid me upside the head with a Maglite, and by the time I came to, they were both gone. So I went for help. I went to Cecil. I've spent ten years wishing I'd turned in any other direction. Hell, just gone right to the cops and let the old man go back to prison. But he was my father. I didn't like the man, but he was my *father*. And the only friend he had in this world was Cecil Buckner."

"What did Cecil tell you to do?"

"We went back and searched together. Didn't find them. He told me to call the police but to keep my dad out of it and said that he would do the same and he'd find my father and get it settled. Basically, he told me he'd fix it. Then as soon as I got away from the police, he came to me and said that they were figuring it out. That Sarah was fine, my father was just waiting for the chance to take her back to a place where they could find her, toward Pershing's entrance. Because it couldn't be *this* place, you know. The whole fucking dream would have died then. Even while Cecil was telling me that, though, he was seeing the angles. He knew that Sarah meant something to Pershing. My father didn't."

"You think your father would have brought her back out?"

"I honestly do. Maybe that's ignorant. But he listened to Cecil. Always. He trusted Cecil, because Cecil had earned it as far as my father was concerned. Cecil didn't give up the cave while my father was in prison. He kept quiet. My father considered Cecil a partner. More than that, he considered him a *boss*. You got in trouble, you asked Cecil how to get out of it. Well, we both did that summer. And you can see how well that worked for us."

Mark turned from him and stared into the unimpressive crack in the earth.

"This was the point of it all?" Mark said. "People died because of this?"

"People died because Cecil and my father wanted their dreams back. But don't write *this* off until you've seen it, brother. What's down there is special, and somebody will pay one hell of a lot of money for it. Wait and see on that. You can add a few more zeros to whatever number is in your mind. You can roll your eyes and shrug right now like everybody else, but trust me, by the time it's done, a lot of money will have traded hands over this place."

Mark believed him. The story wasn't a new one. People had been doing two things with the earth for centuries upon centuries: digging for their fortunes beneath it, and burying their dead within it. In Trapdoor, the two had collided.

"Pershing's land has the best entrance chamber," Evan said, "but he never had a clue what kind of cave was there. That's what Cecil kept telling my father. 'Be patient, be patient. This guy, Pershing, he'll get bored and sell his interest. Because it really isn't that special of a cave over there. Dozens like it have opened and closed already.' Problem was, Pershing wanted to keep exploring it. He was pecking on the borders. Still, you had to *work* to get through it from over there. Nobody but Ridley Bats in the Belfry Barnes could've done it. If what he says is true? If he actually brought Sarah out of there in the *dark?*" Evan shook his head. "If he managed that, they should build a statue of him and put it on the courthouse lawn. Because that is some heroic work, I'm not kidding you That's flat-out miraculous. I don't know if it's true or not. I suppose nobody ever will."

He fell silent and joined Mark in looking into the dark stones for a time.

"I understand why Pershing was willing to deal with Ridley," Mark said finally, "but what value did Cecil have? He was your father's partner, not Ridley's. Why include him in the trust?"

"Because Cecil kept Pershing clean. Kept his secrets, same as he kept mine. Cecil, he's damn good at tending secrets. Only man better is Ridley Barnes. Except that son of a bitch apparently just can't remember his." Evan shook his head. "When Ridley brought her body out...I couldn't believe it. I just couldn't. My father was feeding her, he was giving her water, he was keeping her alive and he'd never let her see him. He was always in the dark. She didn't know who he was, that's what he said. She didn't know it was him. So he was going to wait for the right opportunity and he was going to take her back. Was supposed to be within a day. That was the promise they made me. She'd be out by the end of the day. I didn't know he was writing ransom notes then. I'll tell you who did know: Cecil."

Evan wiped at his face and left streaks of dirt under his eyes.

"End of the day turned into a second day, and then a third, and she stayed in, and I was too scared to talk. I mean, if it had just been me going to jail, maybe. Thing was, that was my father who had her. And as damn foolish as it sounds—and it would sound even more foolish if you'd known the nasty son of a bitch—I couldn't tell the police it was my father. I just couldn't bring myself to do it. He'd done seven years in prison waiting to come back to this. It was family land, had been for a hundred and thirty years, and he was going to take it back. Besides, everything was going to be fine, right? Everything was going to work out fine. If everybody just stayed silent, it'd work out. Cecil told me that plenty of times.

"Then Ridley came out with her body, and Dad was gone. I figured she'd died from the cold, and he'd taken off when he realized what he'd let happen. Once he saw he was looking at murder, he bailed fast, and bailed for good. Cecil thought the same. It wouldn't have been unlike him. But then it began to feel like Ridley had killed her because he was so damn strange about it, saying he couldn't remember what had happened. Meanwhile the old man's gone. I was scared to come here; hell, scared to go anywhere. There was no trace of him, though. I told myself that was good, but you know what? You can't walk away from your family. You all walk together, whether you can see them there beside you or not."

"How long was it before you found him?"

"More than a year. I told Cecil, and he said to leave him where he lay. Said the facts of the situation hadn't changed—I brought Sarah in, my dad grabbed her, I lied to the police about it, and she died. I'd still go to prison. He was telling the truth about that much. I would have gone then, and I will go now. I'm an accessory, always have been. Didn't have to be, but I made the wrong choice and trusted the wrong people. I thought she'd come back out safe. I was promised that she would. I had the chance to be something different, and I didn't take it."

He fell silent. The two of them lay there in the wet earth under the decaying trailer and Evan Borders stared into the cave entrance as if willing it to turn into something else. A door to the past. A second chance.

"You think Ridley's still down there?" Mark asked eventually.

"If he's still alive, he's still down there. We'll let you go take a look."

Mark had no desire to venture down that flimsy ladder into the narrowing walls and the blackness.

"We'll go together," he said. "Show me how to get to him."

Evan laughed. "Sure. I have no idea how to get to him. And I don't want to. It's time for me to roll. They probably won't let me get far now, but I'll give 'er hell, right? Make the run I should've made ten years ago." He offered Mark the flashlight. "Go on."

"Just drive," Mark said. "I'll give you some lead time. But give me the chance to get the right people here."

Evan shook his head. "Let's not make it complicated. You make it to the bottom of that ladder, and you're on your own.

I'll leave it for you. You can climb right on back up if you want. But you're going to start at the bottom whether you choose to take the ladder or not. I'd be careful walking up on Ridley Barnes down there, though. It usually goes bad."

Mark made it only three steps down before he hesitated. The ladder swayed with every step and each rung flexed as if it were about to break.

"It ain't so bad," Evan said. "But if I were you, I'd put the flashlight in my teeth so I could use both hands, at least."

Mark put the flashlight in his teeth and bit down on the rubber handle so he could have both hands on the ladder. The climb felt long, thirty feet at least, maybe forty, and still his feet hadn't touched the ground. When he heard a grinding noise, he looked up to see Evan sliding the manhole cover back in place.

"With any luck," Evan called, "you'll be talking to the police before I am. We'll see. But if you do, you tell them something. Tell them I loved that girl. People won't believe it, but it needs to be said."

He shoved the lid all the way over the top then and sealed Mark in the blackness.

66

Mark's feet touched stone but still he clung to the ladder, feeling around carefully to make certain it was the floor and not just a ledge. He had to be fifty feet down, and it was a straight descent. He tried to imagine Carson Borders taking a look at that crack in the earth and deciding to rappel down to see what he had. How many tries had it taken him?

He stepped away from the ladder and took the flashlight out of his mouth and for the first time he saw the room around him. There was nothing impressive about it. It had the size and feel of the cellar in an old house, cold and cramped, with a low ceiling and smell of old moisture. There was an opening about twenty feet across that looked like a tunnel. Mark considered it and then looked up at the ladder, wondering if the best course of action was simply to climb back out and call for help.

That was when he heard the moaning.

The sound seemed far away, but it was clear, a low wail of pain or anguish or both, and the way it whispered through the cave and echoed raised the hair on Mark's arms and neck.

"Ridley?" he called, and even in the cramped room, his voice sounded small.

I'd be careful walking up on Ridley Barnes down there, though. It usually goes bad.

He turned from the ladder despite his desire to keep one hand on it and moved toward the tunnel, toward the sound. The walls were narrower here but the ceiling was about the same, so all he had to do was stoop. He'd gone no more than twenty paces when the cave opened up to his left and spread out in an immense chamber filled with bizarre and glorious rock formations. The stalagmites rising from the ground were far taller than him. He stood transfixed by the size of it for a moment and then took a few steps into the room, awed by its scope and grandeur. Carson Borders had seen this beneath his own land while police were investigating him for drug dealing and robbery, had gone away for seven years and sat in a cell knowing that it was there, waiting.

Mark was turning to his right when he saw a flicker of light in his peripheral vision to the left. He turned back and lost it in the beam of his own flashlight, so he turned the flashlight off, and there it was. A faint glow in the farthest reaches of the room, coming from the opposite direction. Another tunnel.

He turned his light back on and picked his way through the rock formations, and the second light grew brighter and brighter and then he rounded a corner and nearly walked into thin air.

He was standing on a ledge, and some twenty feet below him was a stream, not as wide as the boat channel at the main entrance, but close. Ridley Barnes sat on a shelf of stone beside it. He was wet and he was shaking and he looked at Mark without much interest.

"This is where she was," he said. He angled his headlamp down and Mark saw water jugs and tin cans and a spoon and the remains of a blanket.

"This is where you found Sarah?"

Ridley nodded. "There's a body back there. I don't know

who that is. I would like to know. I came a long way and I think that I deserve to know."

It didn't sound as if he was talking to Mark.

"It's Carson Borders," Mark said.

Ridley cocked his head as if surprised that the answer had come from Mark and not the cave.

"Carson."

"Yes."

"Carson kept her down here. You know that?" He looked at Mark then, swinging the headlamp to face him. His long gray hair was plastered against his neck in wet tangles. "You're sure?"

"I'm sure. I just heard it from his son."

"No teeth," Ridley said. "The skeleton had no teeth. You're right. That's Carson. Who took his teeth?"

"Evan."

It was a thought that would have revolted most, but Ridley took it in stride, nodding as if it made some sense to him.

"Nobody would look for him then."

"Exactly. He'd been holding her down here. He told some people he was going to let her go, but he wrote ransom notes while he said it."

Ridley thought about that for a while in silence, then indicated the old cans and water jugs. "But he was caring for her. You can see that much. She was alive and she had food and water. So long as she had him, she was all right." He spoke through chattering teeth.

"You don't know that, Ridley. She was abducted by a violent man who was fresh out of seven years in prison and didn't want to go back. You don't know how it would have played out."

"I know how it *did*. I can remember that now. Julianne got me that far and then..." He closed his eyes. "Is she safe?"

"She's alive," Mark said. "She's fine."

Ridley opened his eyes slowly. "You're sure?" he asked. Certainty seemed to be Ridley's focus today. He wanted reassurance on every answer.

"I brought her out. I spoke to her. She's alive."

This seemed to mean something to him. There was no spoken response, but it was like a coil that had been wound tight inside of him loosened just a bit.

He pointed at the blanket and the tin cans. "If I'd had light left, I would have made it. No trouble. She was so damn close. It's a simple turn. But in the dark..." He shook his head. "When I ran out of light, I ran out of time."

"Nobody will blame you for it."

Ridley didn't answer that. He was shaking hard.

"We need to get you out of here," Mark said.

"Julianne's all right?" Ridley said. "She'll make it? You're not lying? I cannot hear any more lies. Whatever I hear has to be true now."

"It's the truth, damn it. Let's get you the hell out of here so you can see her for yourself."

"I wish it hadn't gone the way it did," Ridley said. "With her, I mean. Cecil Buckner, he earned what he got. But Julianne? She was good to me. She was scared of me, sure, but she was good to me even when she worked against me. You know why? Because she wanted to hear the truth, and she understood that I couldn't say it yet. Not without her."

"You just need to explain it. You can finally do that now."

"What I want explained," Ridley said, "is how hard it was. I want people to know that, but they can't. They can't ever know, because even if they believe it, they won't have *felt* it. When I got her out of here alone in the dark? Not many men could have done that. Not many."

He wiped tears from his eyes.

"That was a long trip," he said in a whisper.

"I know it was. We'll make sure everyone else knows too. Now you've got to—"

"There aren't many who will understand," Ridley said as if Mark hadn't spoken. "You will now. That's funny, when you think about it. You'd never even been underground. But now you get it, don't you?" He looked up, and Mark squinted against the headlamp glare. "You know how she is in the dark."

She was Trapdoor. Mark said, "I get it, Ridley. Yeah."

"You understand how a man's memory could go. Alone in the dark, down here? You understand what nobody else could. Things happen in the dark that you can't make any sense of. So then you try to. You do that by telling yourself a story. Maybe the story is wrong, but it's the only one you have, and so it becomes the truth. You *need* it to be the truth."

"People will understand," Mark said. "I'll help you with that. Julianne will. Hell, I think at this point, the sheriff will."

Ridley seemed uninterested in that. He looked around the cave with an appreciative gaze.

"She works on you. People will tell you that any cave will, but people are wrong. She's special. Trapdoor really is special."

"Can you get up here somehow, or do I need to go find help? There's a ladder to the top if you can just make it this far. You're very close to the surface now." Mark was studying the wall beneath the ledge. It was too smooth to allow free-climbing. They'd need ropes or another ladder.

"I'm going to get help, Ridley. I don't think you can make it up this wall. We need the right gear. You need to get out of the cold."

"Cold's not so bad." Ridley got to his feet. It took some

effort. "Thank you, by the way. What I wanted from you, from both of you, was just to know. It didn't go as planned, did it? But I know now. I don't need my name cleared, don't need to explain myself to anyone, never did. I just needed to know."

"I think more people will understand than you expect."

"I've never been much for talk," Ridley Barnes said. His teeth were chattering violently. "I'm supposed to go up there, sit with police, have cameras in my face, and then what do I tell them, exactly? I killed one man, and a girl died because of it."

"You just say what happened. Self-defense with Carson, and with Sarah Martin, good Lord, that wasn't your *fault.* You were the only person who even came close to saving her."

"I was never good up there," Ridley said. "I was better down here, always."

He stepped into the water, and for an instant Mark thought he was going to cross the stream and try to make it up the wall. Instead, he waded away, moving unsteadily through waist-deep water. On the far wall, his silhouette was an enlarged version of his staggering form.

"Damn you, Ridley, get out of the water!"

"Head on back to the surface and tell them all what happened down here," Ridley said. "That was the job, and you did it. You've almost done it, at least. The last part is in the telling. It will mean a lot to people. More people than either of us have met."

"Then we'll tell it. Get out of there. I'm going for help."

Ridley swiveled his head, and the beam of his headlamp threw a glare into Mark's eyes, forcing him to lift a hand against it.

"I was wrong about you," Ridley said. "And about myself. I thought I'd have to come back up, but I don't. You're the one who has the job on the surface. When things go dark, you're the one who will have to bring the light back."

"I understand. Now if you—"

"No!" Ridley's voice boomed with a near desperate sound. "You don't understand yet. There's a lot of responsibility ahead of you. A lot of pressure, Markus."

Ridley had never called him that. Never called him anything but Novak. *The new man, the stranger,* he'd said with such delight during their first meeting.

"Okay," Mark said. "I'll handle the pressure. Right now, I'm going for help."

Ridley turned away, the light traveling with him, and began to wade again.

"Get out of the water!" Mark looked at the wall, searching for any way down that wouldn't end with a broken spine. There wasn't one.

"It's beautiful up ahead," Ridley said, and then he turned his headlamp off, plunging the passage into darkness. He was out of the range of Mark's flashlight.

"Travel safe," he called from the blackness. "She doesn't want you yet."

Those were the last words Mark heard from Ridley Barnes. Mark called for him again and again, shouting for him to come back, but the only voice that answered was his own.

67

Searchers worked for four days straight without finding Ridley or his body, but then Sheriff Blankenship called it off, partly, he confessed to Mark, because they seemed to be growing more interested in the cave than in the search. There was a lot of it. Nobody could agree on the total size, but early estimates were high. Maybe top ten in the country. Maybe top five. Maybe better.

It was a remarkable find, they all agreed. Endless potential. Endless.

Evan Borders was arrested in Nashville, Tennessee, when a state trooper pulled him over for speeding and discovered the active warrant. Borders didn't resist arrest, which was a career first. He was due to be transported back to Garrison County on the same day that Mark left. The same prosecutor who charged Cecil Buckner with the murder of Danielle MacAlister said he was weighing allegations and evidence concerning Pershing MacAlister.

The first lawsuit over the Trapdoor Caverns Land Trust was filed before the search for Ridley Barnes had stopped. The news was filled with opinions on who should have the right to the cave, and legal experts weighed in on who already did and what could be done about it. Mark avoided those stories.

He went to see Julianne Grossman before heading out of town. She was still in the hospital but had been moved out of intensive care, and the doctors were pleased with her progress. She'd sustained a fracture in her skull but there had been no bleeding in the brain. He sat beside her bed and they talked in low voices for more than an hour and several times they paused so that she could weep.

"At first I wanted him to pay," she said.

"You weren't alone."

"But that's my job," she said, "to be open to the subconscious, to help others learn how to be. When I had to open, I closed down. I heard what he said, and I closed down. I stopped wanting to help Ridley Barnes when he said those things. I wanted to help Sarah Martin then."

Mark assured her that everyone had. That was the worst of it, really. Everyone had been willing to help and join the cause. It took a village to kill a monster, after all.

"I could have just walked away from him in the end," she said.

"What do you mean?"

"Once he was underground, once he was in trance, he was content. Maybe even *before* trance. It sounds strange, but it took a lot out of him to get back down there. I saw it. He was pushing himself toward the thing everyone claimed they wanted from him. By the end, I wanted to help him get there. Maybe I shouldn't have, though. Maybe I should have tried to convince him to just leave."

"He'd have gone back down soon enough," Mark said. "Or he wouldn't have, and things would have gone worse for him up here."

She nodded. They fell silent but he did not leave. For a long while he just sat there at her side and then she reached out and took his hand.

"Your mind has enormous potential," she said. "You might not want to hear that from me. Not after this. But...there are special things ahead for you if you want them, I'm sure of it."

He didn't know what to say to that, so he didn't say anything at all.

"You're going home now," she said. "Florida." She enunciated each syllable so that the word sounded like a song.

"Yes."

"Your firm understands what happened here?"

"They know."

"If there's any problem, I'll tell them what they have to hear. I'll tell them whatever you need me to so that you can return to work."

He thanked her and did not tell her that he'd written his resignation letter the previous night in his hotel room. His resignation letter, and a proposal. He wasn't sure how either would go over, but it was time to deliver them.

"Be in touch," he said. "And I mean that. I'd like to hear from you again."

"Likewise. Stay open, Mark. Stay open."

He nodded at that and then he squeezed her hand and left the hospital and drove out of Garrison for what he believed was the last time. He was headed north to the airport, and from there he would go south by plane. Jeff London was waiting to meet him in Tampa. There he would tell Jeff what he had to say, tell him the truth about how he felt about his wife's unknown killer, and about the possibilities that he'd seen in this rural place where good but overstretched police could have benefited from outside help from the start. That the questions *Did he do it?* and *Who did it?* had always been intertwined, and it was time for Innocence Incorporated to embrace that. He had a sense of how that pitch would go over, and that was why the resignation letter had already been written. But he would do things right, and he would not hide behind Jeff or anyone else. Whether he remained on payroll or not, he had his next case. It had begun on a lonesome bend where the cypress leaves hung low and cast long shadows over the road to Cassadaga.

The airport was far from the town, and Trapdoor was not on the way, but he stopped there all the same. He didn't get out of the car, just parked where he could sit and look down at the place where Maiden Creek became the Greenglass River.

She doesn't want you yet.

"It's just a hole in the earth," Mark said. "It's nothing but stone and water."

But he couldn't stare too long into the yawning blackness beyond the iron gate before turning away.

He rolled the windows down and let the cold air in and he took out his phone and pulled up the recording of his only willingly entered trance with Julianne Grossman. By now he'd listened to it several times and knew it well, and he knew the precise part he needed to hear before he left this place. Her voice filled the car, stronger than the sounds of the winter wind and the thawing ice fracturing across the surface of Maiden Creek. He listened to her ask him if he had feared death in Trapdoor and then to his own answer, a firm and swift response.

No, he said of the night that he'd nearly frozen to death beneath the earth, the night they'd had to use extracorporeal circulation to bring him back among the living.

And why were you not afraid of death?

Because there are places I still need to go.
Where are those places?
I'll have to go back to where she died. I have to do that.
To where Sarah Martin died? To the cave?
No. Back to Florida. Back to my wife. And then I'll have to go to the mountains.
Why the mountains?

Here he had paused for several seconds, and even on the recording you could hear that his breathing was labored, the sounds of a man in the midst of a struggle. Finally he had answered: *I'm not sure. But I've always known it.*

ACKNOWLEDGMENTS

As always, foremost thanks to those who make me look better than I deserve: My editor, Joshua Kendall, and my agent, Richard Pine, both kept the lights on in the dark for me throughout, and kept the batteries charged. Tracy Roe is a copyeditor without equal. And much gratitude to the readers who suffered through the messy drafts: Christine Koryta, Tom Bernardo, and Stewart O'Nan all put their unique and tremendous talents to work on this book. The team at Little, Brown continues to be the best in the business; thanks to Michael Pietsch, Reagan Arthur, Heather Fain, Nicole Dewey, Sabrina Callahan, Miriam Parker, Garrett McGrath, and everyone else at Hachette Book Group. It is an honor to be published by such an incredible company.

I'm grateful to the people who took me into caves and did their best to explain them to me, particularly Anmar Mirza and Ty Spatta, and to the people who attempted to explain the realities of hypnotism versus the mythology to me and helped me capitalize on both. In this regard, Rima Montoya was truly exceptional, and for her insight and patience I'm most indebted.

And to the readers, the greatest thanks of all.

ABOUT THE AUTHOR

Michael Koryta is the author of twelve novels, most recently *Rise the Dark*. His books—among them *Those Who Wish Me Dead, The Prophet, The Ridge, The Cypress House,* and *So Cold the River*—have included *New York Times* Notable Books of the Year and national bestsellers and have been nominated for numerous awards. He is a former private investigator and newspaper reporter, and he graduated from Indiana University with a degree in criminal justice. Koryta lives in Bloomington, Indiana.

. . . AND HIS NEXT BOOK,
RISE THE DARK

For an excerpt, turn the page.

I

The snow had been falling for three days above six thousand feet, but it had been gentle and the lines stayed up. At this point in the season, after a long Montana winter that showed no signs of breaking, Sabrina Baldwin considered that a gift.

Then, on the fourth day, the wind rose.

And the lights blinked.

They were both awake, listening to that howling, shrieking wind. When the omnipresent hum of electrical appliances in the house vanished and the glow of the alarm clock went with it only to return a few seconds later, they both said, "One," in unison, and laughed.

It was a lesson she'd learned in their first home in Billings, watching the lights take two hard blinks during a storm, Jay explaining that the system would respond to trouble by opening and closing circuits, automatically testing the significance of the fault before shutting things down altogether. You'd get maybe one blink, maybe two, but never three. Not on that system, at least.

In their new home in Red Lodge, the glow and hum of an electrified existence went off once more, then came back on.

"Two," they said.

Everything was as it should be—the alarm clock blinked,

waiting to be reset, but the power stayed on and the furnace came back to life. Sabrina slid her hands over Jay's chest and arms. For five fleeting seconds, it seemed the system had healed itself, that all would be well, and no one would need to travel out into the storm.

Then the electricity went out again, and they both groaned. The problems of the world outside had just moved inside, announcing themselves through the staggered blinks like knocks on the door.

"The phone will ring now," Jay said. "Damn it."

Sabrina shifted her chest onto his and kissed his throat. "Then let's not waste time."

They didn't. The phone rang before they were finished, but they ignored it. She would remember that moment with odd clarity for the rest of her life—the unique silence of the house in the power outage, the cold howling wind working outside, the warmth of her husband's neck as she pressed her face against it, each of them so lost in the other that even the shrill sound of the phone caused no interruption.

The phone rang again when they were done, and he swore under his breath, kissed her, and then slipped out from under the covers, leaving her alone and still breathless in their bed.

A new bed, new sheets, new everything. She was grateful for the simplicity of Jay's scent, the only thing that was not new, not different. They'd moved to Red Lodge only two months ago, and while everyone told her she'd appreciate its beauty, she still found the mountains menacing rather than enticing.

When winter finally yielded to spring, her view of the place would improve. She had to believe that. Right now, all she knew was that they'd managed to move somewhere that made Billings seem like a big city, and that wasn't an easy feat.

She could hear his side of the conversation, providing a strange blend of breaking news and the customary— storms, lines down, substations, circuits. Even the bad pun was familiar: *We sure don't want the hospital to lose patience.*

A joke that he'd told, and his father had told, and his grandfather. It gave her a sense of the situation, though. The outages were bad enough that the hospital was running on backup generators. This meant he'd be gone for a while. In weather like this, the repairs were rarely quick fixes. Not in Montana.

She followed him downstairs and brewed coffee while he explained what was going on, his eyes far away. She knew he was thinking of the map and the grid, trying to orient the issues before he rolled out. One of his greatest concerns lately was that he wasn't familiar enough with the regional grid. In Billings, he'd known every substation, every step-down transformer, probably every insulator.

"It'll be a long day," he said. He pulled on his insulated boots while sitting in the kitchen that still felt foreign enough to Sabrina that she often reached for the wrong drawer or opened the wrong cupboard. It was a lovely home, though, with a gorgeous view of the mountains. Or at least, it would be gorgeous in the summer. The windows that Jay loved so much because they looked out at the breathtaking Beartooth Mountains were facing the wrong direction as far as Sabrina was concerned. The worst of the storms blew down out of those mountains, and here they could see them coming. She wished the kitchen windows faced east, catching the sunrise instead of the oncoming storms.

She was so sick of the storms.

Jay, meanwhile, was looking out the windows right now, and damned if he wasn't smiling. The peaks were invisible, cloaked with low-lying clouds, and the wind rattled a snow-and-ice mixture off the glass.

"Enjoy that snow while you've got it," she said. "This may be the last one of the season."

"Brett told me that last year they closed the pass in mid-June for fourteen inches."

"Tremendous."

She struggled to keep her tone light, to use the good-natured kind of sarcasm, not the biting kind. They'd moved here for her, after all. Had left Billings because Jay was willing to give up the job he loved for her peace of mind. Out there, he'd been a member of a barehanding crew, an elite high-voltage repair team that worked on live lines up in the flash zone, perching like birds on wires pulsing with deadly current. In November, they'd learned just how deadly.

Sabrina had met Jay through her brother, Tim. They'd been coworkers, although that term wasn't strong enough. They were more like Special Ops team members than colleagues. Every call-out was a mission where death waited. The bonds were different in that kind of work, ran deeper, and her always-protective older brother voiced nothing but approval of Jay. She'd met Jay at a barbecue, had their first date a week later, and were married a year after that. Someone put tiny high-voltage poles next to the bride and groom on their wedding cake, and they assumed that was the extent of the prank. It wasn't. The miniature lines actually carried a low-voltage current that Tim energized just as Jay went to cut the cake. Jay had jumped nearly a foot in the air, and the rest of the crew fell to the floor laughing.

For several years, that was how it went. Tim and Jay were closer than most brothers. Then came November. A routine call-out. Tim on the line making a simple repair, confident that it wasn't energized. What he didn't know was that less than a mile away, someone was firing up a massive gas generator, unwilling to wait on the repairs. The generator, improperly installed, a home-wired job, created a back feed. For an instant, as Tim held the wire in his hands, the harmless line went live again.

He'd died at the top of the pole. Jay had climbed up to bring his body down.

Three weeks after the funeral, Jay told Sabrina he was done with the barehanding work. There was a foreman's job open in Red Lodge, and taking it meant he'd stay on the ground, always, and she would never have to think of him climbing a pole again, never have to worry about the job claiming her husband as well as her brother.

"Love you," he said, rising from the table.

She kissed him one last time. "Love you too."

He went into the garage and she heard his truck start and then she pulled open the front door and stood in the howling wind so she could wave good-bye. He tapped the horn twice, the Road Runner good-bye—*beep-beep*—and was gone. She shut the door feeling both annoyed and guilty, as she always did when he went out in weather like this, torn between the fear of what waited out there for him and the knowledge that she should be proud of the work he did.

She *was* proud too. She really was. This winter had been worse than most, that was all. The pain of losing Tim compounded by the tumult of moving—those things were to blame for her discontent, not Red Lodge. The snow would melt and summer would come. The coffee shop she'd owned in Billings wouldn't have lasted anyhow. The landlord had been ready to sell, Sabrina hadn't found a good replacement location, and so summer in Billings had loomed ominously.

Now summer was promising; she'd already found good real estate for a new location, and she had the peace of knowing that, whatever happened out there today, her husband would stay on the ground.

Red Lodge was a fresh start.

He called the first time at noon. She was outside shoveling the walk, out of breath when she answered.

"We lost a sixty-nine kV line just off the highway," he reported.

That translated to 69 kilovolts, which meant 69,000 volts. A standard home ran on 110 or 220 volts.

"The work is going fast so far, though, and the forecasts are good," Jay said.

She'd seen that. An Alberta clipper was blowing down out of Canada, drying out the air. The snow had tapered off and the roads were passable. At least up to Red Lodge, they were passable. Beyond, as the highway snaked toward eleven thousand feet, the pass had been closed for six months and would be for another two.

"Maybe there's a chance of a normal dinner," she said.

"Maybe." His voice held optimism.

A few hours later, it didn't.

The call at five was shorter than the first, and he was distressed.

"Definitely going to be a late one."

"Really?" She was surprised, because the storm had died off around one, and their power was back on.

"Never seen anything like it. Somebody's cutting trees so they fall into the lines. We're getting faults farther and farther up into the mountains, and they're *cut* trees, every time. Chain saws and some asshole on a snowmobile having himself a hell of a time, dropping trees onto the lines, keeping just out in front of us like some kid playing tag. We put one up, he cuts one down."

"Are the police there?"

"Haven't seen them yet. I'd tell you I'm almost done, but right now, I don't have any idea. They're fresh cuts; I could still see the sawdust in the snow on the last one. It's the damnedest thing…they've got a pattern, pulling us farther out of town. Whoever's doing it is probably watching me send my crew up on the poles and having a laugh."

Fatigue was often a factor in deaths on the lines, and the idea of Jay's team, men like her brother, climbing pole after pole in a snowstorm, gradually wearing down, all because of someone's vandalism was infuriating.

"I've got to go," he said. "Hopefully this asshole's chain saw is about out of gas. Actually, I hope his snowmobile is. I'd like to meet this guy."

She wished him luck, hung up, and, sweaty and tired, went upstairs to take a shower. At the top of the steps, she turned and looked back at the mountains, wondering where in them he was. They were already dark.

What's the point? she thought. Mindless behavior, drunk boys with powerful toys. But dangerous.

She wanted it to be mindless, at least. But as the water heated up and the room filled with steam and she stepped into the shower, she found that Jay's words were unsettling her more than the actual facts. It was how he'd described the fallen trees as *pulling us farther out of town.*

When she came out of the bathroom wearing nothing but a nightgown, a cloud of steam traveling through the door with her, she understood in an immediate, primal way exactly why it had disturbed her.

There was a man sitting on her bed wearing snowmobile

clothes, goggles hanging around his neck and a pistol in his hand.

Sabrina didn't scream, just reacted without thinking, recognition at warp speed—*Threat is in the bedroom, phone is in the bedroom, escape is through the bedroom, so retreat is the only option*—and she stumbled backward and slid the door shut. It was a pocket door, most of the interior doors in their new home were, and when they'd viewed the house she'd told the real estate agent how much she liked them. Now she hated them, because the pocket door had no real lock, just a flimsy latch that her frantic hands couldn't maneuver, and she could hear the sound of the man leaving the bed and approaching. She barely got her hands out of the way before he kicked the door, and the lock turned into a twisted shard of metal as the door blew off its track and the frame splintered. A large, gloved hand reached in and grasped the edge of the door and shoved it backward and now Sabrina was out of options. Everything that could save her was beyond him, and she wouldn't get beyond him. He was so large that he filled the door frame, and even though his clothing was unusually bulky, she could tell that he was massive beneath it. He had dark, emotionless eyes and his hair was shaved down to stubble against his thick skull.

"Who are you?" she said. It was the only question that mattered to her in that moment. His identity, not his intention, because the gun announced his intention.

"My name is Garland Webb." His voice was deep, and the words came slow and echoed in the tiled room. "I am very tired. I had to make a long journey in a short time for you."

"What do you want?"

"We harnessed air for this," he said, as if that answered her question. "That's all we need. People think they need so much more. People are wrong."

Then he lifted the pistol and shot her.

There was a soft pop and hiss and then a stab of pain in her stomach. She screamed, finally, screamed high and loud and long and he let her do it, never moving from the doorway. He just lowered the pistol and watched with a half smile as she fell back against the wall, and her hands moved to her stomach, searching for the wound, the source of the pain. Her fingers brushed something strange, soft and almost friendly to the touch, and she looked down and saw the arrow sticking out of her belly just below her ribs. No, not an arrow. Too small. It had a metal shaft and a plastic tube that faded to small, angled pieces of soft, plastic-like feathers. A dart.

She felt warmth unfolding through her body and thought, *Something was in that and now it's in me, oh my God, what was in there?* and she tried to pull it free from her stomach. It didn't come loose, just stretched her skin and increased the pain and drew the first visible blood. The thin blue fabric of her nightgown kept her from seeing the point of the dart clearly, but she could feel what it was—there was a barb on the end, just like a fishhook, something to anchor it in her flesh.

"Air," the big man with the dead eyes said again, sounding immensely pleased, and the unfolding warmth within Sabrina reached her brain, and her vision swam and there was a buzzing crescendo in her ears like the inside of a hornet's nest. She looked up from the dart, trying to find the man, trying to ask why.

She slid down the wall and fell against the toilet, unconscious, with the question still on her lips.

2

The man who'd been accused of murdering Markus Novak's wife was in prison for the sexual assault of another woman when a talented young public defender won his freedom by pointing out a series of legal errors that had robbed Garland Webb of his right to a fair trial.

Mark wasn't present for the judge's ruling. He was on a fishing charter out of Key West with his mentor and former employer, Jeff London. The fishing trip was London's idea. Whatever happened in the appeal, he said, did not affect the case Mark was trying to build. Whether Garland Webb was in prison or out of prison, he still hadn't been convicted of Lauren's murder. That was the next step.

It all made good sense, but Mark knew the real reason that he'd been invited out on a boat in the Gulf of Mexico while Garland Webb learned his fate: He'd had a few too many conversations with Jeff on the topic and made a few too many promises. The promises involved bullets in Garland's head, and Jeff believed them.

Upon winning appeal and earning his release, Garland Webb met one last time with his attorney, a young gun named John Graham who considered the case his most significant victory to date. The prosecutor had made a series of egregious errors en route to conviction, so Graham had always felt good about his legal argument, but you never could be sure of a win when the original conviction involved a heinous crime. At that point you needed more than the law on your side, you needed to be able to *sell* it, and John Graham had put all of his considerable powers of persuasion into the case. He also felt good about the appellate victory for the simple reason that it was *right*. His client had not been granted a fair trial, and John Graham believed deeply in the purity of the process.

All the same...

He was troubled by Garland Webb.

In their final meeting, John offered his best attempt at a warm smile and extended his hand to his client. "Sometimes, the system works," he said. "How does it feel to be a free man, Garland?"

Webb regarded him with eyes so expressionless they seemed opaque. He was six four and weighed 230 pounds, and when he accepted the handshake, John felt a sick chill at the power in his grip.

"I guess you're not the celebrating sort," he said, because Garland still hadn't uttered a word. "Do you have everything you need? There's a release-assistance program that will—"

"I have everything I need."

"All right. I'm sure it will be a relief to walk out of here."

"Just back to business," Garland Webb said.

"What's that?"

"It's time for me to get back to business. No more diversions."

"Right," John said, though he had no idea what Webb meant, and he was uncomfortable with what he *might* mean.

Webb fixed the flat-eyed stare on him and said, "I have a

purpose, understand? This detour was unfortunate, but it did not remove my purpose."

"Right," John repeated. "I'm just supposed to let you know that if you need assistance finding a job or locating a—"

"I'm going back to the same job," Webb said.

John fell silent. He'd spent several months on this case and he knew damn well that Garland Webb had been unemployed at the time of his arrest.

"Where will you be working?" he asked, and Garland Webb smiled. It was little more than a twitch of the lip, but it was more emotion than he'd displayed when the judge had announced the verdict in his favor.

"I've got opportunities," he said. "Don't you worry about that."

"Great," John said, and suddenly he was eager to get out of the room and away from this man. "Stay out of trouble, Garland."

"You too, John."

John Graham left before Garland did, although he'd initially intended to stay with him through the process all the way up to the point of escorting him out of the prison. That no longer felt right. In fact, winning the freedom of Garland Webb suddenly didn't feel like much of a victory at all.

On the day Webb collected his belongings and walked to a bus station, before he left, he bribed a guard to send a message to another inmate at Coleman. The message got through, and the inmate requested a phone call. Seven miles off the southernmost shore of the United States, Markus Novak's cell rang.

They'd been having a good day of it, but in the afternoon the fishing had slowed; the Gulf of Mexico began churning with high swells, and Jeff London turned a shade of green that matched the water.

"Bad sandwich," he said, and Mark smiled and nodded.

"Bad sandwich, eh?"

"I don't get seasick."

"Of course not."

When Jeff put his head in his hands, Mark laughed and set his rod down and moved to the bow, where he stood and stared at the horizon line, the endless expanse of water broken only by whitecapped waves. All of his memories of the sea were good, because all of them involved Lauren. Sometimes, though, when the light and the wind were right, the sea reminded him of other endless places. Expansive plains of the West; windblown wheat instead of water; storm-blasted buttes.

Not so many of those memories were good.

He'd been watching the water for a while when he heard the ring, a soft chime, and the charter captain, who was lounging with his feet up and a cigar in his mouth, said, "That's yours, bud."

Mark found the phone in his jacket pocket, and he remained relaxed, warm and comfortable and with his mind on this boat and this day, until he saw the caller ID: COLEMAN CORRECTIONAL.

For an instant he just stared, but then he realized he was about to lose the call to voice mail, so he hit Accept and put the phone to his ear.

He knew the voice on the other end. It was a man he'd spoken to many times, a snitch who'd contacted Mark for legal help, which Mark provided in exchange for a tip on who killed his wife. The police didn't believe the story; the snitch held to it.

"He sent me a note, Novak. For you. For both of us.

Here's what it says: 'Please tell Mr. Novak that his efforts were a disappointment, and every threat was only so much wasted breath. I'd hoped for more. Let him know that I'll think of him outside this prison just as I thought of him inside it, and, more important, that I'll think of her. The way she felt at the end. I'll treasure that moment. It's a shame he wasn't there for it. She was so beautiful at the end.'"

The man on the phone had once beaten someone to death with an aluminum baseball bat, but his voice wavered as he read the last words. When he was done, he waited, and Mark didn't speak. The silence built as the boat rose and fell on the waves, and finally the other man said, "I thought you'd want to know."

"Yes," Mark said. "I want to know. It is important that I know." His voice was hollow, and Jeff London lifted his head with a concerned expression. "Is that all he had to say?"

"That's all. He's made some threats to me, you know that, but ain't shit happened, so maybe he's all talk. Maybe about...about this too, you know? Just one of them that likes to claim shit to make themselves feel hard. I've known them before."

"You told me you didn't think he was that kind," Mark said. "You said you knew better. You said he was telling the truth."

A pause; then: "I remember what I said."

"Anything changed your opinion?"

"No."

"All right. Thanks for the call. I'll send money to your commissary account."

"Don't need to, not for this. I just thought...well, you needed to hear it."

"I'll send money," Mark repeated, and then he hung up. Jeff was staring at him, and the charter captain was making a show of working with his tackle, his back to them.

"That was about Webb?" Jeff said.

Mark nodded. He found the horizon line again but couldn't focus on it.

"He's taunting me. He killed her, he knows that I know it, and he's a free man. He wanted to let me know that he'll be thinking of me, and her. From outside of a cell now."

"It's a dumb play. He'll go back to prison."

"Yeah?" Mark turned to him. "Where is he?"

"Don't let this take you back to the dark side, brother. You've got to build a case, and you've got to—"

"Someone has to settle the score for her."

Jeff's face darkened. "There are lots of tombstones standing over men who made proclamations like that."

"I don't want a tombstone. When I'm gone, you take the ashes wherever you'd like. Just make sure there's a strong wind blowing. I want to have a chance to travel."

"That's a bad joke."

"It's not a joke at all," Mark said. "I hope you remember the request should the need ever arise." He looked at the charter captain. "You mind bringing us in a couple hours early?"

The captain looked from Mark to Jeff and shook his head when no objection was raised. "It's your nickel, bud."

"Thanks," Mark said. "We had a good run this morning. Sorry to cut it short. That's just how it goes sometimes."

Jeff's voice was soft and sad when he said, "He won't be in Cassadaga, Markus. You know that. He won't go back there."

"He could."

Jeff shook his head. "You're just feeding the darkness if

you do that. Think about Lauren. What she believed, what she worked for! What she would want."

"You're asking me to consider what she would have wanted in her life. She's dead, Jeff. Who's to say what she wants now? In those last seconds of her life, maybe she formed some different opinions."